INCIDENTAL CONTACT

JIM WHITE

A Stuffed Monkey Publications Book

Stuffed Monkey Publications, 349 S. Main Street, Winterville, Georgia 30683.

Copyright © 2022 by Jim White. All rights reserved.

No part of this book may be used or reproduced in any manner whatsoever without written permission, except in the case of brief quotations embodied in critical articles and reviews.

For further information, queries, contact author at Jimwhitemusic.net.

Though this is a work of nonfiction, the author has at times employed elements of fiction within the narrative. While he has endeavored to recreate events, locales, and conversations from his memories as accurately as possible, there are instances where the storyline and characterizations may deviate slightly from actual events.

Cover Illustration by Charles Laster

Cover Design by Gail Marowitz/The Visual Strategist

Copy Edit by Jim Beckman

Distributed in the United Kingdom by AB.C

ISBN:979-8-9856288-0-7

First Edition

Printed in the UK by Severn, Gloucester, a carbon neutral printer
on responsibly sourced paper

FOREWORD

The structure of this Magical Realism memoir was influenced by concepts set forth in the physics paradigm known as Spacetime Theory, which basically states that time as we know it is illusory, and therefore all history—personal and universal—exists simultaneously, not in the linear fashion we humans tend to perceive it in.

Subsequently, the sequence of events recounted in this tale are presented according to their relevance to the narrative, not their location on any chronological timeline. The period detailed herein covers a personal synchronistic epoch originating in the year 1980 and concluding in 2009.

For those readers who require a more linear orientation, the final page of Incidental Contact includes a conventional timeline account of the events described herein.

Jim White, February 14, 2021

BROWNSVILLE, FLORIDA, SEPTEMBER 2004

3am I'm awakened by a sweet summer rain…
the distant howling of a passing southbound coal train.
Was I dreaming, or was there someone
just lying here beside me in this bed?
Am I hearing things, or in the next room,
did a long forgotten music box just start playing?

The pig studies me from a nook in the brambles. It knows—there ain't a prayer in hell I'll prevail against its combination of superior intellect and low slung, primal speed. Not in this thicket. Wait—did I just see a smirk cross that diabolical creature's face? Goddamn it!

Pig feints a step my way then backs up into the thorny vines, a baiting move which pisses me off. "I'll rush you, pig! By god, I'll rush you straight on!", I think loudly for about the umpteenth time, then stupidly do so. Off pig gleefully charges, plunging back into the brambles where no human dare give chase.

Pigs—people say they're so goddamn smart, right? Well, hey, guess what? I'm smart too… it's just that presently I got zero patience for dealing with this trifling shit—what with that Cat 4 hurricane churning a slim hundred miles off the coast and my domicile sitting square in its crosshairs with but half the windows boarded up.

Way up high in the foliage canopy overhead the array of massive ancient live oak limbs pitch and buck, scatterings of smaller branches crashing down randomly, hither and yon, making my presence here a bona fide dicey proposition. It's not been but an hour since I came easing down that potholed, serpentine dirt driveway in search of said diabolical pig and already the wind's doubled, that limb snapping pattern growing in regularity, rendering me increasingly in fear for my mortal coil.

Where should I be at this moment in the time-space continuum? On the other side of town, hunkered down with provisions; flashlights and power bars and gallon jugs of fresh water and comforting shit like that, my mattress pulled into the safe, secure center hallway of my sturdy, boring little suburban bungalow. But instead, where do I find myself? Why, out here in the elements, bound to this place until I outsmart this four-legged Einstein and deliver it to safe haven.

I aim my good ear at the undergrowth, listening for signs of movement in the brush, the aeolian tree top symphony making this task a considerable chore. I guess to further vex my patience into my mind leaps that damn song again, the one I wrote some years back when things were so hopelessly fucked up, the one about the ghost lady, the music box and the train. It slips into loop playback mode on that OCD jukebox in my brain—my own personal pig-chasing soundtrack. Goddamn again.

> *3am I'm awakened by a sweet summer rain,*
> *the distant howling of a passing southbound coal train…*

Something about this bifurcated listening dislodges a goodly chunk of unrelated thought flotsam from deep within my memory banks. I watch said chunk break loose, a massive neon purple iceberg of remembrance, tumbling, shattering into a thousand prismatic pieces as it plunges into the tangerine sea of consciousness.

Such things you see while chasing pigs in hurricanes!

A stormy vision of this last decade washes over me, fitful snippets come fluttering by willy-nilly, fleeting images of the myriad trials and tribulations I've rode out since I first set my sights on chronicling the real life events conveyed in the melancholy lyrics of that song. A weariness settles over me as I revisit the rocky path traversed since that sorry epoch. And though that period is but six or so years in the big rear view of Life, my time forging that musical Sword of Damocles feels lost in the haze of eternity, as if born a dozen forevers ago.

> *And I know…it's a sin putting words in the mouths of the dead…*
> *and I know…it's a crime to weave your wishes into what they said…*
> *and I know…only fools venture where them spirits tread…*

Look at those words, how they come tumbling out all easy-breezy-like, belying the breech birth nature of the song. I swear to God on a stack of flaming bibles that wrangling those verses into a coherent shape nigh unto did me in. But I guess that's what a person gets for aiming high and weird, reporting on esoteric skirmishes with quixotic forces and sundry agents of the Unknown. Such ephemeral entities (call them Trickster Gods or haints or spirits or whatever) seldom hold still long enough to be properly assayed. You might catch fleeting glimpses of them from time to time, but cast your gaze fully in their direction and—poof—like this pig shooting off into the brambles, they're gone.

Months passed working on that song, me staring at various jumbles of highly charged words and phrases, knowing the content was there but the sequencing was wrong, wrong, wrong, not a clue how to properly order them, how to tell the story straight. I'd pass days moving a word here, a sentence there, then back again, over and over this went for weeks, months on end. Only after five years of such toil did I finally manage to wrench that song—called Static on the Radio—into passable enough form to lay down on a record. But even then it still wasn't quite right.

I ain't praying for no miracles, I'm just down on my knees…
listening for the song behind, everything I think I know…
'Cause everything I think I know, it's all just static on the radio…

But hey, don't get me wrong—why I'm presently hearing that tune on the jukebox in my brain is no mystery whatsoever. It's a straight A to B proposition—see, the woman in the song, the one whose ghostly presence I felt sleeping beside me, the one who haunted me with chiming music boxes, it's her pig.

She's long gone now—not dead or anything tragic like that, just absent from this locality where I presently find myself dithering about. She evacuated this morning due to her mortal fear of hurricanes, a fairly innocuous mania compared to the bevy of less rational terrors she compulsively entertains. From flesh eating bacteria to bridge collapses, shark attacks to F-5 tornados, jail-breaking thrill-killers, clear-air lightening strikes, terrorists, mega-tsunamis—you name it—if it's random, exotic and sensationally lethal, then in her mental framework it exists solely to track her down and gruesomely exterminate her.

And then once deceased, her destiny scenario only worsens, as somehow from that grim starting point her dead body thereupon invariably gets diced up into small pieces and crammed into mayonnaise jars. Buddy, the first time I heard that exotic narrative come sailing out of her pretty southern belle mouth, I regarded it as fiction and must admit I flinched in grotesque delight, but see, it wasn't fiction to her—she believed it. That's just the day to day ground zero reality in her mind.

So far as this evacuation deal goes, in this instance her actions could pass for nigh unto judicious, seeing how a bona fide hurricane is pending and it's a noteworthy agent of mayhem. But barring interdiction by Cruel Fortuna, Mother Nature, the Grim Reaper, Ted Bundy types or even Old Scratch himself, with a bit of luck right about now, her and our five year old daughter are chugging along somewhere up past Auburn, headed for safe haven at kinfolk's place on the north side of Atlanta—well, relatively safe haven (i.e. the relative's a dope fiend) but let's us just skip over that complication for the time being, shall we?

Of my ex I am not fond, nor is she fond of me. And yet here we are, raising a beautiful little human being together. I close my eyes and see my scrawny girl child, scared, crammed in the back seat of that ratty old Mitsubishi Montero, a big chow dog by her side, two ferrets and a fuzzy rabbit huddled in that ridiculously baroque antique wire birdcage strapped in the seat next to my daughter, eight or so miserable mewling cats imprisoned in sundry conveyances, plastic cat carriers, oversized purses, repurposed laundry baskets and more.

Scattered willy-nilly amidst them sits the jumble of evacuation supplies: feed sacks and shopping bags and Tupperware containers half to a quarter filled with Dollar Store cat food, Walmart dog food, Pet Zone ferret food, sale rack fish food, moldy bird seed of unknown and specious origins. The car interior is a study in tetras dementia: bundles piled, stacked and strewn across any and all available surfaces, all topped off with two duffel bags overflowing with boxes of Trix, Count Chocula, liter bottles of Diet Sprite and Diet Coke, and random packets of instant mac-n-cheese and ramen noodle packets.

No small wonder the pig got left behind.

So how did I get conscripted into rescuing said diabolical creature? Well, as usual I was just minding my own business, trying to make use of the relative calm in the wake of her departure early this morning. No mention of the pig then. But a couple hours on, me teetering up there on the extension ladder, halfway done boarding up the windows on my own house—that's when the phone rang.

Shit.

You can't just ignore it—not co-parenting with a Crazy Maker (yes, a proper noun). With a Crazy Maker, you tend to live in a perpetual state of terror for your child's safety—the year prior my daughter had her arm crushed after tumbling out the window of the Montero then being run over by it, the Crazy Maker behind the wheel, them running at thirty-plus mph down a rutted dirt road in hot pursuit of one of her errant pets. What with the steady stream of mysterious mishaps, midnight hospital runs and near fatalities over these first few years of co-parenting, it's a given that all phone calls must be answered, so down the ladder I scrambled, arrowing toward the back door.

Fearing the worst, up to my ear the receiver slowly rose, breath held, body clinched all over. But when no cop came on the line to inform me of some nightmarish scenario, when nobody had died, when it was just her at a roadside phone booth south of Montgomery pausing her evacuation long enough to dial my number and screech a few categorical imperatives at me, when said demands simply invoked yet another of her loony toons, same-old same-olds involving "rescuing" animals in distress, I was so wildly relieved that I almost broke into a giddy dance.

And therein lies the blueprint for the Crazy Maker's primary means of self propulsion; throw a nonstop, massive vortex of batshit crazy chaos at everyone in your gravitational field, then when instead of a nuclear bomb going off under their chair, it's something comparatively small like a pig rescue in a hurricane, an impending house foreclosure or a medicaid fraud investigation (yes, all those occurred) the support team is palpably relieved. Meanwhile, the Crazy Maker goes blissfully sailing along in the wake of lessened expectations, playing everyone's relief like a goddamn Stradivarius. And that's exactly how this deal went down. I was directed to drop everything, proceed to her house and rescue her soulmate, Jezebel the pig, so I did.

Of course, no sooner did I hang up than the life-math made itself abundantly evident: pig rescue mission + impending Cat 4 hurricane = top shelf lunacy. But I'd already committed, so no turning back. Besides, strategically speaking, how much wiggle room did I have in that telephonic exchange? None. Zero. Zip. If I stood my ground and refused the assignment, even with an ironclad excuse, she would have just hurled the usual string of invectives my way then hung up on me just like she always does when I dare say no to any of her whackadoodle demands. Then as payback, I'd be refused access to my child for some great stretch of time… weeks, possibly months.

Vindictive visitation extortion is my ex's primary weapon of choice in our dismal parental power configuration and she wields it with impunity. And I love my kid, so out into the maelstrom I drove, headed for Crazy Maker Acres (as I call it), where an hour or so later I find myself staggering though round seventeen of this pig trapping heavyweight bout. And all the while, as if impelled by the plunging barometer and rising winds, that jukebox in the back room in my brain keeps tormenting me with more and more lines from my very own goddamn song.

> *Midnight rendezvous with a pretty girl,*
> *wearing a torn and tear-stained wedding gown.*
> *Like a ghost ship she appeared from nowhere*
> *on a lonely highway and flagged me down.*
> *I gave her a lift downtown to the Greyhound station*
> *where, in the flickering of the neon lights…*
> *in the mirror of her eyes, as she kissed me goodbye,*
> *I saw my own reflection…*

As for Jezebel, she's no cutesy little plaything, not by any stretch—nothing sanguine or mystical about Jezebel. She's a hundred and twenty pounds of free range, low slung, high IQ contrariness. To complicate matters, the playing field where I've been tasked to apprehend her is neither small nor level nor safe. Falling limbs aside, Crazy Maker Acres covers a shambling, overgrown city block sized plot dotted with treacherous debris of all manner in the roughest section of this dirt-poor southern town.

The main house is a shabby two story affair that sits adjacent a tin-roofed cinderblock shed that in some long forgotten epoch likely served as a three bay shade-tree auto repair shop. The back end of said shed's engulfed by swaths and swarms of thorny, pestilent vines and hellish undergrowth, the furthest most thickets where Jezebel now lurks, smirking away.

It's that selfsame damn shed that I've been endeavoring to lure Jezebel inside of all this time. Buttressed by chunky wisteria vines and live oaks on three sides, with stout cinderblock walls, sturdy tin roof and ample nooks where a pig could shelter should said roof get carried off in an eye wall gust, it's as safe a place as any to ride out a storm hereabouts. There's only one catch—I apparently suck at pig wrangling.

For the better part of a sweaty, frantic windswept hour now, I've been chasing Jezebel this way and that, vectoring, triangulating, cajoling with sweet talk and threats, bribes and brute force. But every damn time I manage to herd that infernal pig anywhere remotely near the shed door, Jezebel gets wise and off she rockets, into the wall of briars. I hear her rustling around out there—she never strays too far, as the property's ringed on all sides by a flimsy fence separating it from the surrounding crack neighborhood. Yes, crack as in crack cocaine.

Said tumbledown field fence surrounding her property has been compromised in several locations, but Jezebel's smart enough to shun those areas, as there's regular foot traffic thereabouts in the form of local crackheads who often appear from the underbrush, zombie-like, shortcutting across the Crazy Maker Acres grounds, and with pulled pork barbecue being the delicacy of choice in this area, the pig wisely steers clear of such zones of imminent peril.

I must admit though, with this hurricane bearing down, it's just a crying shame how there's nary a zombie crackhead wandering about today, as I would gladly pay some passing doper good money to stop a minute and film the pig chasing hilarity.

I hear pig rustling and jump to it. There follows yet another failed herding scramble, then winded, hands on my knees, my super intellect finally kicks in and, lo and behold, there it is—a foolproof capture plan. We'll see who's the smart one here, pig. Into the kitchen I scramble, hunting up that box of Honey Nut Cheerios that I bought for my daughter a while back, the one that was scoffed at by the Crazy Maker for being "too healthy".

I start by dumping out a small pile of cereal near that spot in the underbrush where I last saw snout activity, then pour another cluster a few feet away. The sugary cereal bait trail purposefully goes curving this way and that, away from the big shed so as to not activate Jezebel's highly attenuated, paranoid pig pattern-recognition sensibilities. It culminates with a heaping mound of O's dumped in the back-most recesses of an oversized dog house belonging to the aforementioned Chow dog—a sturdy 3/4 inch plywood affair with a properly pitched, shingled roof and arched doorway standing four feet tall. Eyeballing it, I'd venture to wager it's spacious enough to accommodate a good sized pig. Let's hope that's the case.

Trap set, I hustle back to my truck, pluck a couple of shortish planks from the bed, grab my drill gun and a handful of drywall screws from the tool box behind the bench seat, then lay low behind that wall of azalea bushes opposite the doghouse. And then...I...just...wait.

Time stands still for a good long while, the whoosh and shush of tree limbs swaying madly in the growing maelstrom pleasing to the ear, at times hypnotically symphonic, so much so that I go kinda dreamy and almost miss the appearance of the snout near that first Cheerio pile in the bait trail.

Out from the brambles eases Jezebel, hesitant, snuffling the air, wary, skeptical of her good fortune. Pigs are smart, right? We'll see about that. Psychically I urge her onward, the storm around us growing in intensity with each passing nanosecond. Up one Cheerio pile gets gobbled, then the next. She studies the open door of the shed for a while, suspicious, eyeing the shadows therein for telltale signs of my presence. Nope, pig—he's not in there…

I hold my breath, watching as Jezebel edges forward, working her way from this little cluster to that. Minutes pass, sandy clumps of Cheerios getting champed up along the way. About twenty feet out from the doghouse door, she spies the big payday of Cheerios secreted inside it and gleefully beelines straight for it. My last glimpse of Jezebel proper is that happy pig posterior, half in and half out the doghouse door, tail wagging ninety to nothing.

Well buddy, that's it—game-set-match. Out from those bushes I spring like the original Hound of Hell himself, latching hard onto that two-by-four frame under the threshold. Then, with pig butt squarely situated in my face, in one fell swoop, I heave upwards, verticalizing that damn dog house on its backside, the doorway now aimed skyward. The pig disappears as the startled creature slides headfirst into the rear wall, raising high holy hell, squalling, squirming wildly thrashing, struggling to right herself. Sorry, Miss Jezebel, you been punked.

And to put a fine point on this brag, quick as lightening I slap that first board across the arched doorway and whrrrrr tack it down with that drill gun so as to forestall any potential dramatic leaping pig escape attempts. Super genius Jezebel still hasn't quite worked out the math here as I throw that second board across the top of the doorway and whrrrrr lock it into place, effectively blocking her only exit. Seeing all routes of egress barred, rounds of anguished, thrashing snorts commence to emanate from within.

"Tough titty, said the kitty…" I mutter through a crack in the boards, "You lost, pig."

Jezebel smirks no more.

Hard part's done, right? Now all I gotta do is ferry one imprisoned pig and dog house over to yonder stout shed. Sounds simple enough, but for that fifty or so yards of intervening terrain which consists exclusively of loamy, sandy turf. The math of this proposition looks daunting; you take a goodly sized homemade doghouse weighing in at a roughly eighty pounds, throw in a pig that goes another one-twenty, and what do you end up with? Yep, two hundred pounds of dead weight. Combine that with the coefficient of that soft, soggy soil and it translates to one major shitload of ergs required to convey this damn millstone across that damn expanse. I scan my surroundings, hunting up alternative solutions. Damn, my truck's too wide to fit on the narrow path here, otherwise I'd just throw a chain around this fucker and drag it to the shed.

The wind howls an uptick, bringing down some limbs nearby just as it starts spitting sideways drops of rain, adding a modicum of urgency to the problem solving. Fuck it—I fetch the rusty appliance dolly from the back porch, figuring this doghouse can't weigh much more than that pricey designer refrigerator I hauled across this selfsame stretch a few months back when the Crazy Maker was first moving in and I was similarly summoned.

No time for waffling here, not with that storm so close. The improvised pig containment unit gets strapped into place on the dolly, then, amidst recurring intervals of windswept drizzle, cornered animal hysteria and random plummeting oak limbs, I begin to heft that sucker through the loose dirt, scooting dolly, squealing pig and doghouse along inch by inch toward our final destination. And as I rhythmically lug and tug and grunt and yank this squealing heaving mess along, that jukebox in my head kicks back in as more lines from that spooky song of mine come looping into rotation.

And I know, the blind will sometimes lead the blind…
as we roll through shadow-lands and troubled times.
And I know, forsaking love we seek the signs…
as we go…toward truths forever hid behind,
the static on the radio…

Between the gale force gusts, the scattered bands of sideways precipitation, the late summer heat and this unwieldy, rusty dolly the present phase of Operation Save Jezebel devolves into a grueling, sweaty death-slog. On and on, this tedious incremental traversing goes. About twenty minutes into our sojourn to the shed, lost in that work trance, mid-heft, ruing the surreal mess of my existence, I hear myself absently mutter, "Fuck a goddamn duck. You can not make this shit up…"

I stop dead in my tracks, realizing that, by god, in this particular case that's not just some figure of speech—it's true. You CAN'T make this shit up. It IS surreal. Faulkner, they called him genius for dreaming up some sad sack character who fell in love with a cow, right? Gimme a break—I got a pig named Jezebel in a doghouse on a dolly in a freaking hurricane. That's got Faulkner beat by a mile. And besides, between me and the Crazy Maker, we're every bit as weird and literary and Southern as any Faulkner character…but see, the only difference is this—with us it's real.

Ping! Suddenly deep ruminatory engines kick on, thought cogs commence to slowly, incrementally spin, whereupon a quantum extrapolation arrives fully formed in my mind: if truth IS stranger than fiction, then axiomatically speaking that means stranger truth is therefore stranger than stranger fiction….right? That would go a long way toward explaining not just my present predicament, but pretty much the whole she-bang of my existence.

And—by god, yes, of course! That's why that song Static on the Radio was such a damnable chore to write—not only is it true, it's strangely true. Jesus, with that intuitive leap, huge swaths of my past history suddenly come swinging into focus. That's what my life's been, a relentless parade of stranger truths.

NEW YORK CITY, JANUARY 1992

Coldest goddamn day of the year, all of eight degrees in this waning afternoon sunlight. Bitter gusts of bone chilling wind come rampaging up and down the avenues like marauding armies, whomping the high holy hell out of the few poor souls forced out into the elements. Me, I'm slumped behind the wheel of this yellow cab, alone, heater blasting, stuck in the usual tangle of traffic just north of Rockefeller Center.

For the last ten or so minutes, I've been inch by inching my way past the corner of Fifty-Sixth and Fifth. I'm trapped in my existence like Sisyphus, only instead of a stone I got a battered yellow Chevy Impala. The traffic light pops green whereupon I commence this insidious inching forward, riding the bumper of the city bus in front of me, creeping all of two, maybe three whole feet in the forty-five second interval the light's in my favor. Then the light pops yellow, then red again, and I wait. The light pops green and I inch, then yellow and red again and I wait. This patten repeats itself ad nauseam.

All the while, harried pedestrians, hunkered down in their puffy parkas, their wooly caps, their colorful novelty scarfs, go scurrying this way and that, passing the gridlocked cars, their movements creating a tidy visual inversion in the process.

I'm burning daylight here and need to get shut of this traffic jam pronto so I can locate myself a fare or two. Time is money! I glance at my watch: it's five-fifteen. The odometer reads fifty-seven thousand five hundred and fifty-five miles. I'm driving cab number fifty-five and am approaching the corner of 5th Avenue and 55th street. Hmmm…buddy, that's a shitload of fives, is it not? Just as the confluence of fives fully align in my psyche, that odd tingling sensation hits, the one that visits me from time to time and feels like I'm about to get electrocuted or struck by magical lightening or something.

Oh shit…not now….

Boom, the cab's buffeted by another furious gust. Opposite me in the crosswalk this high brow pedestrian lady's designer hat gets blasted right off her finely coiffed head. Whoosh! Away it goes, tumbling madly back toward that curb she just so genteelly tiptoed off of in her million dollar Manolo Blahnik spikey heels. She strikes an elegant whiplash type pose, glaring momentarily, then regathers her inscrutable poise. In that fancy upscale mind of hers, she's triangulating a dignified hat retrieval narrative. She smiles knowingly, then goes stylishly skittering after said wayward apparel.

Sorry, lady, that devil wind, it's got other stories to tell.

Just before she reaches the hat another gust whips past her and off the hat goes, sailing, dancing in a whirlwind of styrofoam cups, cigarette butts, hot dog wrappers, filthy newspaper pages, discount store fliers, used tampons—you name it. High brow lady squints and glowers, does some hasty urban trigonometry (value of hat divided by the indignity of desperately pursuing it, compounded by the prospect of frostbitten, aristocratic ears) then, abandoning any pretense of sophistication, she breaks into a primal sprint in hot pursuit of that errant headgear. Good luck, rich lady! We've all got our hats to chase, now don't we?

As I watch her disappear around the corner of the Tiffany building that almost electrocuted feeling comes surging into my bones again as an odd sense of stillness suddenly permeates the air inside the cab. Hemmed in as I am, the mirrored windows of the skyscrapers towering overhead reflect a narrow meridian of late day winter sky above, all luminous and translucent, now turning that fugitive blue that descends just before true darkness sets in—the magic hour, they call it in the movie business.

Stranded in this tideline of crawling vehicles, no passenger in the back, no hat dramas to distract me, that electrocuted sensation pulses, kicking in harder, now humming foundationally, down to my very chromosomes. I hold my breath as the stillness further mutates; sounds become obscured and muffled while the visual world momentarily takes on a finely jeweled appearance. Time yawns, stretches, warps, like I just dropped a couple hits of top-notch LSD and it's kicking in pretty good.

Hey, what's up with my hands? They suddenly feel…well, just kinda wrong…like…well, like they're not exactly my hands. Like they're some stranger's hands stuck on the end of my arms…only backwards; thumbs positioned on the bottom instead of the top, left hand on the right side and vice versa. Of course my eyeballs register two perfectly normal human hands perched there at the customary ten and two positions on the steering wheel. This visual confirmation should settle my little mental wobble, right? But try as I might, I just can't shake this wrong-handed feeling. My rational brain identifies it as an errant impression then chides me, instructing me to pay this bogus notion no mind. But, hey, what can you do? A feeling's a feeling and has to be accepted for what it is, right?

"Okay hands, you're on wrong," I tell them. It seems important to let these alien hands know I'm not overtly hostile to their sudden expropriation of my terrestrial body.

The light changes. Ever so slowly, traffic starts inching forward again. "Hands," I say aloud, as if speaking to a truant child, "…you behave now and let me drive this taxi cab…got it?" But as I ease forward the wheel resists slightly, a foreign object to these backward appendages. For now, it's not especially disconcerting—I'm just creeping along in a nice straight line—but once I get shut of this Rockefeller Center snarl two blocks ahead I'll have to jump back into my usual hyper-manic weaving, dodging, lunge & parrying manner of navigating the juggernaut of city streets.

I figure I'd better nip this perceptual aberration in the bud—so I bark out orders to my rational mind, telling it to immediately expunge this insurgent wrong-handed impression and reassert the baseline truth that these hands are in fact both mine and correctly attached.

But no dice. Shit. Will the big tugboat of consciousness feature a batshit crazy pilot at the helm today? Apparently so—which could get tricky. Between the backward hands deal and that nearly electrocuted feeling my current psychological status rates a low-to-moderate "iffy". And the fact that I can't will back normalcy here is what's especially worrisome.

Now here comes my old nemesis Freaked-Out Me, rapping on my psyche's back door, pleading to be let in so he can commence to knocking over some mental furniture. My rational mind promptly throws itself against said psyche door, dead-bolting it hastily while chiding its irrational counterpart, shouting "Okay, wild man, go ahead and keep this up! Keep it up, and this time next week we'll end up homeless, standing on some street corner, filthy, half-naked, spouting frothy-mouthed epithets at innocent pedestrians; rich ladies with lost hats who we'll mistake for famous historical figures, or long dead childhood enemies!"

Jesus, I need to lay hands on some kind of anchor here. Like, quick! I scan my surroundings, hoping to locate some manner of foothold. Foothold, foothold, who's got the foothold?

There! Reflected high, high up and far, far off away in the glass windows of yet another china blue skyscraper towering over me, utterly removed from this incoming surge of mental chaos, way off in the upper stratosphere I spy several criss-crossing contrails from passing airliners. Ahhh, contrails and their serene arcs of basic purposefulness; the plane came from here, the plane is going there.

I follow the freshest contrail and locate the jetliner spitting it out, the cause and effect of this proposition immediately calming my frantic, racing mind. Ah, these elegant silkworms of the sky! I visualize the cabin of the plane—neat, orderly rows of travelers chatting, reading, listening to music, staring blissfully out the window at the majestic city below. Oh, to be one of these average Joe types with their bewilderingly normal affairs to see to; meetings to attend, contracts to sign, loved ones to reunite with, rental cars to examine for various minute dents and scratches—such pleasant, ordinary lives they lead! And down below in the hold of the plane, rows of neatly packed suitcases sit in orderly stacks, each filled with personal items: soap, spare socks, slippers, shaving kits, gifts for grandchildren, souvenirs, mementos.

I follow the calming progress of the plane until, like the desperate hat-losing lady, it disappears behind the horizon of yet another towering skyscraper. The light at 53rd pops red, the inching halts, whereupon that electrocuted feeling kicks back in, pulling even harder this time. It's like some weird psychic undertow.

Wait—did I just say "psychic undertow"? Yes! Behold, a resonant describer! I grab my ballpoint pen and jot down p-s-y-c-h-i-c u-n-d-e-r-t-o-w on my clipboard, so as to not forget it. By naming some previously unidentified threat doesn't that allow the namer some measure of commensurate power over it? It has to—think of it; when Adam and

Eve were in the Garden of Eden, before they named the animals, imagine the fear and confusion they experienced when faced with some menacing, unnamed predator. What would Eve shout out at Adam in times of mortal danger? "Look out for that huge, leaping, yellow and black striped carnivorous mammal with the enormous fangs and razor sharp claws!" Hell, if she goes that route, Adam's so busy processing the laundry list of describers he's a goner. But if Eve shouts, "Tiger!" then, see? How Adam's got a fighting chance? And just as Adam's nemesis is named "tiger", mine is named "psychic undertow".

Naming what you fear helps—it helps, it helps, it helps, it helps, it helps, it helps. It must help, right?

A workable chant leaps out from the shadows in my mind. "Psychic undertow, psychic undertow, go-go-go! Go-go-go! Psychic undertow, psychic undertow, go-go-go! Go-go-go!" Hell yes! Not only have I successfully named this terrifying existential abstraction, but I've incorporated it into a catchy little pep-rally style mantra. That's top shelf mental multi-tasking, especially for some guy driving a taxi with his hands attached backwards!

As I inch forward, I bark out a couple of rounds of punchy chants. The distraction provides a temporary respite, but soon enough it loses potency, the psychic undertow tugging's coming on even stronger.

Grounding thoughts of planes and travelers, bus bumpers and hatless pedestrians skitter off as my eyes go blankly fixed on the blue, blue, bluest north-facing side of one huge glass skyscraper, whereupon some truly whacko weirdness commences. In the past when such flashes hit me, I'd "see" them in a manageable way, floating in the shadows in the back of my mind, but not today. Nope. On the wall of the skyscraper towering over me a scene from a movie I once saw materializes. The actors are five stories tall.

Okay….

Realistically speaking, it's a juggling act here. On one hand, I'm none too thrilled about the possibility that I'm having some manner of psychotic break while driving this stinky yellow taxi—films have been made documenting the downside of cab drivers suffering mental health spirals. Things tend to end badly. But on the other hand, this latest development sure beats the hell out of murmuring hapless nonsense chants while blankly staring the curly black hairs on my backwards knuckles, located just there before me on this godforsaken steering wheel, so I give the side of the building my full attention.

It's that Woody Allen movie Crimes and Misdemeanors. I caught a matinee screening of it a couple years back at a discount theater down on 8th Street. Now it's playing on a skyscraper near me! I sit there mesmerized, watching that scene late in the film when, at this stuffy dinner party, Judah Rosenthal, the genteel Manhattan dentist played by

Martin Landau, gets that fateful phone call. The cool, metered voice on the line calmly informs Judah that his loose-cannon mistress will devil him no more. She's been brutally murdered.

The news should come as no surprise to Judah; after all it was he himself who orchestrated this killing. And yet, when notified of the heinous deed the dignified New York socialite seems to be caught flatfooted by the revelation. Staggered by the gravitas of his crime, he hangs up the phone then attempts to rejoin the banal dinner party gathering. He's got his alibi established, so all he has to do is act normal…but he can't—he's caught in his own psychic undertow (see, already it's coming in handy!). Written across Judah's face is this palpable sense of the true horror at crossing one of life's profound moral rubicons—murder!

It's a pivotal plot point in the film as we watch the patrician dentist struggling to portray himself as himself to the others in the room. He falters badly, and no small wonder, as he no longer has any idea whom to portray. Wow! Such a searing portrait of existential free fall, spectacularly rendered by Martin Landau, a performance so gripping that it actually earned him an Academy Award nomination.

It's a spellbinding, darkly transcendent moment perfectly rendered by both actor and director. For a moment there, as the protagonist struggled with his conscience, so at one with the character did I feel that I actually forgot I was a spectator in a movie theater…I disappeared beneath the surface of Woody Allen's fictional river, simultaneously becoming both Judah Rosenthal and some dark, heavy object—a paving stone or hunk of twisted metal—plummeting downward into the shadowy abyss of a vast, wayward human soul…

BEEEEP!! Beep beep beep beep!—a chorus of impatient horns howling out from directly behind me snap me back to reality. As quickly as Martin Landau appeared on the side of the building, he's gone and I see the red light I'd stopped for at 53rd Street and 5th Avenue is now solid green, the bus long gone, a crease in the traffic jam having opened up directly ahead!

What??

How long have I been sitting here daydreaming? Jesus, no telling. One thing's crystal clear; it was long enough to get the drivers behind me righteously pissed. Good old gritty New York City causality! Shit or get off the pot! No room for hallucinations here. As I hit the gas, I notice my hands feel normally affixed once again.

Yes!

Breaking free of the Rockefeller Center snarl, a block ahead I spy an older guy in a pricey lavender houndstooth overcoat stepping out the front door of Saks Fifth Avenue. He gestures to the doorman, who then hails me. A fare! Hell yes, things are looking up! I greet him with my customary, "Hi, what's your destination?" He blandly offers an address over in the West Village on Christopher Street, the gay mecca of the city.

My mind's still spinning from the weird mental projection I've just witnessed. I'm groping around for an anchor and desperately want to talk over what's just happened with someone. But who…? Maybe him?

We break free of the gridlock and as I pick up speed, I study my passenger in the rearview mirror, assessing him as a possible confessional candidate. He's definitely gay, which may be a plus, as gay people tend to be more open-minded when it comes to freaky shit like this. But then again, he doesn't look especially streetwise or spiritual or artsy. He's clearly a well-to-do plutocrat gay man in his late sixties, a portrait of aloof disinterest. Strangely, his grey hair is tinted a faint, putrid lavender color, I guess to match his overcoat and scarf? He's distant, impeccably attired and seems to be deeply invested in appearances, so I figure it's probably best to not broach the subject of the psychic event his cab driver's just experienced. He might get spooked, cook up some lame excuse, then leap out of my cab like those other times when I got on some esoteric talking jag with my passengers and they suddenly exited my cab as if afire. On a day like today with fares so hard to come by, probably the best thing I can do is keep my mouth shut, so I do. We ride in silence for a while.

When I was a kid these visionary episodes came and went uneventfully. Truth be told, I sorta enjoyed them—I'd be riding my bike past the filling station and notice that scraggly red-haired man with the coke bottle glasses leaning against the fender of his white Ford Falcon. I'd observe the dent in the hood and then recognize the whole scene as something I'd already viewed. Studying his face, that nearly electrocuted feeling would come washing over me. The flashes would hit and, like a movie was playing inside my head, I'd "remember" a flood of details about that man, including what he was gonna do next; reaching for the woven billfold in his back pocket, him tapping on his cheap Timex wristwatch then raking his left hand through his hair. I'd "remember" the denomination of the bill he'd pay for the gas with and the exact words he'd speak to the attendant. I'd see the entire scene play out in my mind just plain as day the instant before it unfolded in real time. As a shy, outsider kid such fits of knowing felt generally empowering…but suspecting this type of skill was abnormal, I kept it as my little secret.

As quickly as they'd come, these buckles in time would smooth out and life would snap back to normal. So far as I could tell, their advent heralded nothing—no asteroids would come crashing into the earth or flocks of flying monkeys would populate the horizon shortly thereafter. And since these previsionings appeared of their own volition, like so many brightly colored leaves tumbling willy nilly past some lonely window on a blustery day, I never gave any thought to trying to tap into them or exploit my secret gift. Once they ran their course, I'd slip right back into processing my typical kid thoughts; Johnny Quest! Weird bugs in the pine needles! Collapsing dirt wall at our fort! That knock-knock joke is for BABIES! Oh, you little honey, Dixie French! (new girl in my 4th Grade class). Normal kid shit like that.

In my teens, from time to time at those hardcore Pentecostal churches I attended, I'd cross paths with this or that tortured soul who claimed similar second sight abilities, but in them it mostly manifested in demon possession battles. It was all fairly dramatic—they'd get hit by similar fits and then have to fight off demons or ghosts, sometimes even aliens in UFOs or Satan himself. But I tended to steer clear of those demon-magnet types as they mostly seemed either flat out crazy or drunk on the notion of engaging in some heightened supernatural activity. Neither approach felt especially wholesome, so I avoided showing my hand to the spooky born-agains, never mentioning my own modest secret powers to fellow church folk.

I hit a little paranormal lull during my early-teens and at times wondered if maybe that phase of my life was gone for good. It wasn't until my late twenties when I moved up here to New York City and officially severed ties with all that Pentecostal nonsense that the synchronistic episodes started kicking back in again, this go-round materializing in more dramatic forms. I guess unfettered by the constraints all those previous religious strictures—the church and bible rules and Jesus and all—it freed up previously repressed energy, making the experiences a whole lot more vivid, occasionally veering off into scary territory.

Usually when those electrocuted feeling moments started coming on, I'd try to deflect the brunt of it by filling my dance card with manic activity. I'd walk the streets of New York, no matter the hour, taking photographs, talking to homeless types, documenting interactions in my notebooks, digging in garbage piles, really just anything to keep my mind otherwise occupied. As my former pastor Thurman Strange used to say, "Idle hands are the Devils's workshop!".

It's been a while since I got hit with a bonafide episode like this one today—especially considering the movie on the side of the skyscraper, but I guess it's just one of those magic kinda days. On the brighter side, when did the psychic undertow ever include me getting to watch part of a free movie?? And on the side of a building no less! So, who knows, maybe my luck is changing.

As we go crashing across 14th Street, I notice the old guy in the back seat's now studying me in the rear view. He meets my eye and attempts to strike up a conversation, asking do I enjoy my work. I offer an evasive answer, fearing that I might get sidetracked and launch into a harangue about my recent possible hallucination. I change the subject and ask about his work. He offers up a reptilian smile and tells me he's a proctologist on staff at the Socially Transmitted Disease Clinic over on 10th Avenue and 28th Street.

Well, okay. What, pray tell, do you say in reply to such a comment…? Certainly not "Do you enjoy your work?" Oh hell no—that could lead to all manner of conversational complications. So I change the subject and focus on current events and the weather. We make small talk for few minutes until I drop him at his destination, which turns out to be this hardcore gay joint called One Potato Two Potato. He throws me a big tip then, just as he's exiting the cab, mentions that he knows of a fabulous shop nearby that specializes in men's silk underwear. Might I be interested in him purchasing me a pair or two?

Jesus Christ, one minute you're navigating bizarre paranormal landscapes, the next you're fending off whacked out sexual advances from aging proctologists with purple hair. "No thanks, buddy!" I bark out at him as I go screeching off into the wilds of Greenwich Village.

That little psychological monkey wrench of his come-on puts me out of synch for a while. I circle block after block fruitlessly hunting up a fare, weaving my way first north then east. It's gone dark now and that bitter cold is setting in harder by the minute as everyone retreats to the safety of their warm, cozy apartments. By all indications, it's looking to be a murderously slow night for fares. Passengers will be scarce, competition for the few who do throw their hands in the air will be even more ferocious than normal. On nights like this, you can literally run empty, turning corners willy nilly this way and that, for hours on end without scaring up one single fare. And zero riders means zero revenue, which means your take-home pay dips lower and lower, until you're far below minimum wage territory. It's like some fiduciary corollary to the diving mercury outside.

Finally, whipping around the corner on Broadway and Thirteenth Street, I spy a woman emerging from the legendary Strand Bookstore with some bags in her hands. Her purposeful stride radiates that "I need a cab" look, so I floor it straight at her, slam on the brakes and give a little toot on the horn. She nods, smiles, then after the fact hails me and hops in. "You're psychic!", she chirps out, real friendly like "How did you know I needed a taxi?"

I greet her with my customary, "Hi, what's your destination?"

She's headed to some experimental theater deal down in Soho—probably hipster actor types taking their clothes off and throwing soggy graham crackers at each other's genitals or something like that.

She's toting a bag from the Strand. I went in there once when I first got to New York, stayed a few minutes then fled, overwhelmed by the tsunami of data surrounding me. Their inventory is vast, running the gamut from dry as dust technical manuals to whackadoodle esoterica. It's your basic musty haven for urban scholars, literary types and inbred brainiac oddballs.

This lady, she's an educated looking downtown type, exactly the kind of passenger who'd have no problem diving into a discussion about my prior hallucination. I strike up a conversation, asking her what book she picked up. She reports she works as a handwriting expert, like you see on those court TV shows. She's been hunting for this particularly rare book in her field of study and got a call from the experts at the special books desk saying they'd dug her up a used copy. Interesting! She's a firecracker, funny and smart and seems like an open-minded human being, so I take a chance and mention my recent cinematic vision.

"In midtown??" She scoffs. "It was probably just a PR stunt. Were other people watching too, or was it just you?"

"Just me…" I sigh, adding how these flashes have come to me all my life but this is the first time I've actually seen one on the side of a building.

"God, that must be weird! You must have been freaking out. Giant actors! What do you think," she adds, laughing mirthfully, "is it like some kind of sign? Is the earth going to be invaded by giant actors?"

When I respond with pensive silence not witty urban banter, she quickly drops the whimsical approach and thankfully follows up with some good solid logical questions; do I know anyone like the characters in the movie—someone with a mistress who's acting up? Have I picked up any dentists in the cab recently? (No, just horny proctologists) Have I ever been or am I thinking about becoming an actor? Do I have some special interest in Martin Landau? Am I a stalker type?

This line of eminently sane questioning is helpful and grounding—after her brief teasing she's accepted the fact that something real's happened to me. Thank you, hip urban lady, for not overtly rejecting my loony tunes proposition! Sadly, none of her questions resonate. Her approach is too rational and tonight it's looking more and more like rational just don't fly in the screwy yellow birdcage of my taxi.

It's a short ride. We arrive at the theater down on Wooster Street. As she's paying me, she points at my trip-sheet[1], which is attached to my clipboard, and off-handedly remarks, "Hey, can I see your taxi chart there?"

Puzzled by her request, I pass her the clipboard. "Normally I get paid a lot of money to do this, but you're cool so I'm gonna give you a free handwriting analysis." she says.

She studies my trip sheet for a moment, evaluating my scribbled fare data and peripheral notes in the margin, like, "p-s-y-c-h-i-c u-n-d-e-r-t-o-w". Her face clouds. She sucks in a breath, like a fortune teller who's just turned over the death card. "Oh wow. You're in trouble…" she says, face blanching as she hands the clipboard back to me. "Wow... okay, well, um, good luck…" she half-heartedly adds before diving into the freezing night air. And with that, she's gone. No explanation, just, "You're in trouble." What a day. And still there's nine hours of driving to go!

It's ninety minutes later. I've located exactly two short non-paranormal fares in that time period and that's it. This sucks. Back seat empty again, I go circling this way and that, that way and this, on and on. Presently I'm running up First Avenue in the teens surrounded by dozens of other similarly empty cabs driven by equally pissed off, desperate drivers: Pakistanis, Koreans, Jordanians, Poles, Haitians, all of them lending their own chaotic Third World twist to the traffic pattern. Tonight we're all brothers in misery, testy combative inmates trapped behind the wheel of our own personalized

---

1. The trip sheet is a log of details related to each fare; pick up and drop off locations and times, number of passengers, amount of fare, etc. Each driver is required to keep accurate handwritten records of all transactions.

yellow prison cells.[2]

Me, I've got plenty of fare wrangling tricks up my sleeve, but even employing my superior street and passenger flow knowledge I'll be lucky to break fifty bucks tonight—this for a full twelve hour shift of white knuckle driving; no mid-shift breaks, no stops for meals, just half a chronological day of racing madly around praying that some complete and utter stranger will randomly wander into the street at the exact moment I'm approaching, heave their hand in the air and command me to deliver them to a destination.

Jesus, talk about a cockamamie profession.

Further ahead of me on 1st Avenue, up in the mid-twenties there's a swarm of empty cabs charging the red lights as they pop green, vying for pole position at the head of the pack. They're likely rookies running up to where the theoretical fares are to be had—the Upper East Side restaurant/bar/cafe strip. Checking the side streets, I see they're likewise overrun with unoccupied taxis—these crosstown crawlers are typically cagey veteran drivers, ones who know that by creeping along east/west, trolling for fares fresh out of their buildings on side streets before the fare hoofs it down to the major avenues where cabs are normally hailed, they'll have a better chance of landing a warm body in the back seat, particularly when business is as dead as it presently is. On nights like tonight, you have to locate the passenger even before they raise their arm to hail you, like I did with that handwriting expert, you know, the one who thinks I'm in trouble.

Seeing there's too much competition up ahead, I bank west on 25th and gun it, knowing the lights at 2nd, 3rd and Lexington will line up in my favor, at least if no one gets in my way. Disposition-wise, I'm way too high strung to be a side street crawler, so for me hot-dogging it around corners and zig zagging crosstown, particularly if I can maintain a high speed, is a much more tactically efficient way to land fares.

I go booming across 2nd Avenue, peeking southbound to see it packed with empty cabs so I floor it straight ahead. There's empty crawlers ahead of me inching west on 25th between 3rd and Lexington so I bank north onto 3rd Avenue when—boom!—up at 26th Street I'm hailed by…what? I figure it must be a dwarf, but no, it's a little boy, maybe ten years of age, wearing a full-length sheepskin jacket and a Mets baseball cap. He looks like a tiny pimp.

In he climbs, unaccompanied by any adult. Before I have time to offer up my usual "Hi, What's your destination?" he immediately takes charge of the conversation. Although he's just a kid, there's this dazzling confidence to his delivery. With a slight Eastern European inflection, he says, "Hello sir, my name is Milosh. I am traveling today to

---

2. *In case you don't understand the stakes here, we're mostly all fleet drivers saddled with a hefty hundred dollar lease fee to pay at the end of our shift, a fee we have to cough up regardless of whether we actually clear a hundred bucks or not. Sometimes you can work the entire twelve-hour shift and, after you pay the lease fee, union dues (don't get me started) and gas, I shit you not, you can finish your shift not only not making a single penny for yourself, but actually OWING the fleet money! It's mind boggling.*

the northeast corner of 58th Street and 3rd Avenue but, I regret to say, I have spent my entire allowance for the week this very afternoon, and sadly I have no cash left to offer you for your services. Would you be so kind as to drive me there free of charges? I cannot pay you, but you are a good man I can see, and you understand it's not safe for a child my age to walk the streets at this time of night...especially with this cold..."

There's something simultaneously charming yet repellent in this kid's delivery. If it was an adult I'd point them to the curb, throw in some salty language to make my meaning clear, and tell them to take a hike. But Milosh is right, he's too little to be walking the mean streets of New York at this time of night. It's just thirty blocks straight ahead, traffic's light and with the synchronized lights going green in our favor there are no resistance or obstructions, so it's a three minute ride max, so what do I have to lose? I tell him he can ride for free, but only on the condition that he truthfully answers any questions I might ask. He calmly agrees.

My first question is what happened to his allowance. "Sadly, I spent it at the video arcade. Games and things. I assure you, sir, I have no money. Would you like me to turn out my pockets so you can see I have nothing to pay you with?" Jesus, a pro. I should ask him to take off his shoes and see what he's got stashed there.

My second question is how much cash he started the day with. "Over twelve dollars, but it's all gone now. I'm penniless and far from my home. This fact alone is why it's especially kind of you to drive me there without asking for compensation."

What a piece of work this kid is. In no way am I buying his routine, not because the spent allowance alibi doesn't sound plausible, but because his answers sound so fully rehearsed. They come too easily, like lines delivered by a bored actor. Clearly this is a standard routine with him—he never pays. That said, trading licks with this kid and his quirky con game beats the hell out of riding around alone muttering to myself about the psychic undertow.

On my third and final question I take a wild stab and ask if he's a gypsy. He's dark-eyed and haired, olive-skinned, has that touch of an accent and lyrical confidence that a few of my gypsy friends have. He nods, smiles discretely adding, "You, sir, would make a fine detective."

He tells me his mother's a storefront fortune teller on 58th Street between 2nd and 3rd, and that she'll be furious with him when he comes home late and broke. "I'm really in for it." he confesses. "But, what can you do? To live is to suffer."

We're there. I stop at his corner. Before he climbs out of the cab, he offers me his hand. As we shake like proper gentlemen, he solemnly intones, "May God bless you and keep you sir." He shuffles off, half little kid in the doghouse, half con man working his game to perfection. Somehow I think he'll be fine. His mother will lay furious eyes on him, but as the belt comes off to whip him savagely he'll open his mouth and magic vapors will commence to pour out, filling the room, anesthetizing her. By the time he's done with his spiel, she'll be feeding him cherry pie and ice cream. I watch him amble down the block. He turns and waves to me just before he ducks into the street level doorway of a gypsy fortuneteller.

Home.

Back to work. I gun it, aiming to shoot up 3rd Avenue, but no, I'm a fraction of a second late and catch the red light at 59th. It's no big deal; ahead the uptown streets are awash in yet another sea of empty cabs. While I'm waiting out the light, further ruminations regarding the afternoon's psychic undertow event bubble up in my mind.

It's that Martin Landau, his face during that scene keeps coming back to me. When I was a kid, I loved that TV show he was on, that Mission Impossible. It was his first big role. He played Rollin Hand, this brilliant thespian/magician spy. Each week his character would utilize his dazzling acting skills to dupe the bad guys: Communists, evil dictators, crooked mafiosos, other useless scum of the earth. Most episodes would culminate with some fantastic moment of denouement when Landau's character would remove whatever fake face or ingenuous costume he'd donned and reveal who he actually was. Oh, how the villain would recoil in horror!

I guess that sounds sorta hokey now but as a kid I was just flat out mesmerized by his sleight of hand with all those baffling disguises he wore and foreign accents he adopted. Mission Impossible ran maybe five or six seasons, then after that, so far as I know, Martin Landau dropped off the face of the earth. I never saw him on any of the syndicated network shows like Hawaii 5-0 or Barney Miller or in some cheesy film by Mel Brooks or even B-movie flicks. In fact, I didn't see him anywhere until thirty years later when he resurfaced with the starring role in Woody Allen's art house masterpiece, Crimes and Misdemeanors. What's notable, and slightly weird, is that in some ways he played exactly the same character those three decades later; a man who masqueraded as someone he wasn't.

Actors…they make their living pretending to be someone they aren't, right? So what's their goal? Just to make a buck? To slake some insatiable hunger to be seen? Fame? Power? Maybe to pretend to not be themselves so often that eventually they forget who they actually are, slipping the surly bonds of self and morphing into some sort of idealized collage of their adopted roles? Or is it the reverse? By habitually absenting themselves from their given identity, are they intent on stripping away the layers of unwanted artifice until they become truly who they are? I guess it all depends on the actor.

The light goes green, but instead of flooring it, I hang back, letting the inevitable first wave of madly stampeding rookie cab drivers whoosh by. I bide my time, trailing far behind them at the back of the green light interval, catching the yellow lights just as they go red, hoping to pick off a fare that way.

But what about this actor Martin Landau? What's his motivation? Was he cast in these two roles decades apart because he's especially adept at not being himself? Is his real-life disposition similar to these clever, disingenuous characters he plays, and if so is that common knowledge among casting agents in the movie business?

Judging from his accent, he's a New Yorker. He has to live somewhere, so if he lives in Manhattan then sooner or later he'll have to walk down to the corner, lift his famous arm in the air and hail a cab. Everyone does. Over the years, I've had plenty of celebrities raise their famous hands and hail me: Kevin Kline and his pleasant young wife Phoebe Cates, Allan Ginsberg, John Sayles, John Malkovich, Nipsey Russell, Howard Cosell, Jesse Norman, James Remar, even Kathy Ireland the bubbly supermodel turned "serious" actress.

So who knows, maybe the flash I saw on the side of the skyscraper was hinting at some possible future incident where Martin Landau and I intersect right here in my cab. That'd be wild. He'd throw his academy award nominated arm in the air, I'd yank the cab over to the curb, the door would open, into the back seat he'd settle. I'd say, "Hi, what's your destination". He'd name the Stage Deli or some such famous joint in the theater district or CBS studios on the West Side Highway and off we'd go. Along the way what would I say to him? How would I broach the subject of my hallucination/vision? "Excuse me, Mr. Landau, let me relay this hilarious incident that happened a few weeks back…see there was this rich lady whose hat blew away…"

Wait! To the left under that canopy, a hand rising in the air! I bank hard, narrowly edging out two other vectoring cabs to pick off a couple emerging from a ritzy bistro called Sign of The Dove on 63rd and 3rd. Sadly, it's not Martin Landau. It's a couple of mainstreamers, a man and woman, high rollers, by all appearances. I greet them with my usual "Hi, what's your destination?" The man politely informs me it's an odd address in Queens so he'll direct me and with that he recommends I make a right at 64th Street.

Despite his genial tone, this is a no-no. I got serious issues when it comes to being blindly directed.

"Sir," I tell him in my best non-Southern dialect voice (to avoid explaining for the millionth time how a southerner like me ended up driving a cab in the Big Apple), "I've been driving a cab for many years now and pride myself on my extensive knowledge of the streets. If you tell me where you're going, I'll probably be able to tell you the best route." He's game and relays a fairly exotic address out in Flushing, Queens. I come back with the route—this bridge to that boulevard to that expressway to that exit, etc.

He laughs, then cordially compliments me on my street knowledge. This is all starting out so well. Normally a fare to Queens is a shitty proposition—most times you end up deadheading all the way back to Manhattan empty, but since there's no business in Manhattan tonight this'll do just fine, and then some. Thanks to my good deed with Milosh the gypsy kid, I now have a substantial fare! Taxi cab Karma!

I double back down to 2nd Avenue then go bombing across the upper level of the bridge immortalized by Simon and Garfunkel. In the back seat, the man and woman are conversing in hushed, intimate tones as we hit the Brooklyn-Queens Expressway. Her laughter is magical tinkling bells, his a giddy bull-moose clearing his throat, hers stardust cascading from some wondrous chandelier, his a timber wolf baying at a beguiling moon.

Clearly they're having a top shelf romantic evening out—and a pricey one at that. The guy probably dropped a couple hundred bucks just on their dinner alone, plus the cab ride will run another twenty to thirty. They're having such a fine old time I don't pester them with small talk or disconcerting remarks concerning my recent psychic event. I let the love flow and just settle in and do my job, connecting the geographic dots efficiently, hitting my turns crisply, making lights, jogging left, then right. This purposefulness has my mind feeling calmer by the moment.

I drop them on a tidy upper middle class block near Kew Gardens and start working my way back toward Manhattan. Since business in the city's dead, I figure I might as well troll through some of the Queens neighborhoods that lead back to the 59th Street Bridge, hoping to maybe pick up a stray passenger along the way. It's a long long shot, as typically nobody hails yellow cabs in Queens, instead using phone-in car services, but stranger things have happened, right?

I consider swinging through Laguardia Airport to check for possible inbound flights, but, Jesus, even from the highway I can see swarms of empty taxis circling everywhere. At every single terminal the sub-Hades-level taxi holding lots are overflowing with empty cabs. Hundreds and hundreds of fellow yellows sit trapped in dismal cab queues that reek of body odor, stale piss and cigarettes. And sit they will, waiting, hoping, praying for a succession of magnificent jet planes full of filthy rich tourists to come swooping in out of thin air. And if no planes arrive? You're fucked, gridlocked, stranded in that putrid, stinking lot until fate intervenes—sometimes hours and hours later, sometimes never. No thanks.

I arrow on ahead, hitting the BQE then hopping off on Northern Boulevard, riding Northern into Long Island City. It's a ghost town all the way into Queensborough Plaza—no fares, no pedestrians. Too cold! I'm sitting at a red light under the elevated train platform when a raggedy gypsy cab screeches up next to me. The driver honks his horn and makes some kind of excited, indecipherable hand gesture my way. On his passenger side the rear back door flings open and I catch a fleeting glimpse of woman racing around the rear of his car, tearing open the back door of my cab and leaping in. Only it's not a woman. It's a man dressed as a woman—a trashed-up, vixenish woman. The gypsy cab speeds away.

Like with Milosh the hustler kid, the woman/man doesn't give me a chance to speak. "That motherfucker try to murder me! Had his hands around my goddamn throat!"

Unexpected development. Startled, I say, "Who?? That driver??"

"HIM? No, he my guardian angel! He save me!"

"From the man who was trying to murder you??"

"No! From them Bronx hoodlums that was chasing me!"

Hmmm. The light changes to green. The majestic 59th Street Bridge lies just ahead of us, the shimmering jewel of Manhattan radiating on the other side. "Um, what's your destination?" I ask the hysterical transvestite.

"30th and the West Side Highway. Lord, lord, lord..."

Oh, great. Any cab driver knows that dismal stretch of abandoned warehouses where she/he is headed. A high crime area with a turbo charged incidental mayhem coefficient, it's a cruising zone for low level hookers, both straight and transvestite. Even in bitterly inclement conditions like tonight, these scantily clad streetwalkers stroll up and down forlorn, blighted side streets, climbing into random cars, performing sex acts on complete strangers, usually right there in the vehicle. They smoke crack incessantly to numb their ravaged minds and bodies. Most of these poor souls are so high it's a miracle they can walk, much less successfully perform fellatio in the cramped back seat of a late model Toyota Corolla.

So, 30th and West Side Highway. The bottom line here's simple; if I agree to take this hysterical crime victim to that particular destination, I run the very real risk of being drawn into some senseless criminal activity, as there's no shortage of ways a simple passenger drop on one of those depraved side streets can go terribly, terribly wrong in the blink of an eye: stray bullets from drug deals gone bad, street fights between hookers and pimps, hookers and johns, johns and johns, pimps and johns, pimps and pimps are the rule of the day, and more so the night. Even if the side street drop of my passenger goes uneventfully, you can roll ten feet and some knucklehead steps out in front of your cab with an Uzi leveled at your forehead. And don't bother trying to escape via backing up—his partner in crime, similarly armed, blocks the rear.

So, your average yellow cab driver would just blow this person off—"Sorry, I'm off duty, catch another cab." That's the go-to tactic with sketchy passengers headed to dangerous destinations. And if the troublesome fare refuses to exit the cab? You covertly engage the parking brake, then ease down the gas until the engine conks out, faking engine trouble.

There's a million tricks for weaseling out of this variety of high risk fare, but that's not really my style. Why? Because just like anyone else, nearly murdered transvestites should have the opportunity to be transported. I mean, if not me, what yellow cab's gonna pick her/him up looking the way she/he looks—all beat up and hysterical, campy-vampy and half-strangled like that?

Besides, it's deadly cold outside, unfit for even an appropriately attired soul to be out walking around, much less someone decked out in vinyl hot pants, torn fishnet stockings, platform heels and a flimsy fake rabbit fur jacket. She/he deserves a break, not more grief. Besides, this is shaping up to be a compelling mystery and I'm a sucker for mysteries, so I hit the gas and off we go, rocketing up the on-ramp to the lower roadway of the bridge. Once rolling I ask, "Hey, are you okay? You need a doctor? The Bellevue ER's just a couple of minutes away."[3]

The transvestite recoils, "No, no, no! No doctors! No hospital. No po-lice." Typical street person response—no big surprise there.

As we hit Manhattan proper and bank south on 2nd Avenue, I muster up the courage to ask what went down in the Bronx. She/he leans through the open partition and begins to cry. "Look at my throat! Can you see? Them finger marks where that man was strangling on me?! I was good as dead! Why would anybody want to do that? Why? I should have knowed when he took me there, to that filthy hotel all that way up to the Bronx! All I did was ask him what do he want, you know, how he like his pleasure to come and what he go for. And what he do? Start whooping down on me! Knock me to the floor and go to choking on this very neck! Saying I was trash and after he kill me he gonna throw this little black body right here—my body—in a mother fucking dumpster! I hear that, and I say, "Uh-uh! No sir you won't!" That when the man in me come out! The man in me hit that mother fucker square between the eyes, hard! Heard his nose bone go crack! Two sounds, kee and rack, like that! And let me tell you, when mister man went down I didn't wait to see was he gonna get up again. No sir! I ran! Like the wind! I flew out that damn door! I look around and where the fuck was I? Hell if I know! Some damn street in the mother fucking South Bronx! I ran and I ran, just looking for something, lights and peoples, but that's when these boys, these hoodlums, they be calling out at me, teasing me for running and I told them to not to fuss with me, but they all bad up there. They set out after me and I ran and ran some more and they would have got me but for that man there in that black car. He stopped, bless him, and told me get in and brung me all the way down there to where you got me. He just come flying in out of nowhere and saved this little girl's black ass."

So many possible conversational vectors for a response! But where do you even start? Like with the lavender haired proctologist, I figure it's best to just sidestep the obvious dialectic angles and so dive into some small talk as we weave our way south. The transvestite hooker calms down and we begin to swap stories. I tell her/him about the slow night, the gypsy kid, eventually even the hallucination, while she/he shares with me the many complications of street life, her/his heartbreaking childhood, dropping out of cosmetology school and more. Eventually somehow we settle on the topic of her/his upcoming breast implant surgery.

Since this fare traverses the entire island of Manhattan east to west, we're afforded extra time to trade stories. Why? Because, as Jimi Hendrix so accurately noted, crosstown traffic is in fact hard to get through. The causality's pretty simple; to facilitate smooth

---

3. Bellevue, for the uninitiated, is a public hospital that boasts as grim an inner city Emergency Room as any you might find in the civilized world.

passage on the main uptown/downtown, north/south avenues the city traffic engineers employ a synchronized sequential pattern for uptown/downtown traffic lights. Barring congestion, delays, construction, etc, if you roll at around 30 mph on any of the major one-way north/south conduits in Manhattan you can drive from 1st Street to 125th Street non-stop. But this north/south synchronization comes with a cost, as it plays utter havoc with the east/west crosstown light sequencing.

That said, here's the twist; by coincidence, not design, a handful of east/west crosstown streets do allow something akin to constant forward movement, just like on the synchronized north/south avenues—but it's not widely known, even among cab drivers. A few crosstown streets, like 17th Street going west and 22nd going east for example, allow you to run the full width of Manhattan non-stop, but only under ideal conditions—zero traffic, no malfunctioning lights, no street repairs going on, no garbage trucks or double parkers.

So, say it's 9pm on a Wednesday night and you pick up a fare at 4th Street and 1st Avenue and they're going to Madison and 90th. The average driver might catch upwards of five to seven red lights along the conventional route. But see, they don't have to—if they run with the green lights up 1st Avenue to 27th Street, then bank west they can get from 1st Avenue to 3rd Avenue moving nonstop without hitting a red light. So, say you get to 3rd Avenue and there's congestion moving west ahead on 27th, then you simply bank north and go flying up 3rd Avenue until you intersect with another westbound street that features semi-synchronized lights, anywhere from 33rd to 77th Street, using whatever route suits you and the time of day. Once you intersect with Madison and turn north, you lock back into that remedial light synchronization pattern and it's easy-breezy from there.

Play the light game right and you won't catch one single light going the entire distance. It's fun, especially when your passengers take note how you've delivered them to their destination in half the time it normally takes, often saving significant coinage for them in the process. Bigger tips tend to come your way and since you get paid by the distance rather than the time, you make your money faster which allows you to get back into the hunt and grab more fares.

For the novice, uninformed or indifferent driver who's booking thirty fares a night, they'll spend a good ninety minutes per night needlessly sitting still at traffic lights making nothing. By implementing my system continuously, if I average even two minutes less per fare because I'm employing that knowledge of the crosstown light intervals in Manhattan, then over the course of a twelve hour shift I gain an extra sixty to ninety minutes per night of potential earnings. That translates to another ten to fifteen fares and twenty to fifty dollars profit per shift, depending on how busy the city is.

Interestingly, the best crosstown routes aren't the wide, storied streets like 14th or 34th, 42nd or 57th. No, it's side streets like 13th, 17th, 22nd, 27th, 33rd, 40th, 50th and 77th that line up best. After studying the sequencing patterns for years now my hypothesis is that you'll find a relatively synchronized crosstown street roughly every seven blocks. Why? Got me. It probably involves some mathematical schematic dealing with linear intervals occurring within a grid pattern.

In our case, me and the transvestite run south down 2nd Avenue to 39th Street then start charging west across the city. On 39th, the lights heading westbound run fairly synchronized, but you have to know when to hit it hard and when to lay back. If the traffic flow is light and the bitter cold hasn't frozen traffic lights red in one direction (it happens!) I should be able to run all the way from 2nd to 9th Avenue only catching one or two red lights. I'll bank south there, head down to 33rd Street, then modulate the rest of the way over to the West Side Highway. For me this fare will involve sitting at three, possibly four full red lights for a total of less than three minutes standing time.

As we're sitting at one of said red lights, my new favorite transvestite starts elaborating about her/his upcoming operation. She/he explains how having boobs will pay for themselves in no time, as men go for that kind of shit crazy-like and are willing to cough up more to the transvestites who offer that extra added package. She/he has been saving up for the operation for months now and is smoking much less crack in order to stash away enough dough to cover pricey surgery bills.

Since we're kinda on the subject, I ask if she/he ever considered going all the way and fully transitioning. I get a big "Oh hell no!" to that. She/he would like to, truly, but she/he has a bad heart and is way too scared to go under any of that full anesthesia nonsense for fear her/his heart will fail. "I'm too young to die honey…just yet anyhow." she/he tragically remarks. I remind her/him that streetwalking is a fairly whacked out choice for someone with a bad heart who's afraid to die.

"I know, I know." she/he woefully admits. "It all messed up, ain't it?"

We arrive at her/his destination. The fare's nine bucks and change. She/he digs around the crotch of her/his hot pants and extracts a horrifically moist, crumpled and, yes, stained ten dollar bill, then offers it to me. Hmmm. I politely instruct my new favorite transvestite to keep the ten, consider it my contribution to her/his upcoming operation. Simultaneously I make a mental note to vigorously wash my hands with powerful industrial disinfectant after each and every cash transaction I ever conduct for the rest of my days on this earth.

She/he is touched by my gesture and tells me I'm her/his guardian angel, just like that other driver. "So much good in the world…and so much baaad" she/he adds, playfully slapping her/his rump as she/he exits the cab, obviously not too traumatized by that murder attempt she/he narrowly survived a mere hour or so ago.

Sitting there at the corner of 30th and the West Side Highway I watch her/him sashay down the shadowed street, wobbling toward the yellow pools thrown out by the line of sodium vapor streetlights. By now the temperature's dropped to low single digits. Further down 30th street, I see a parade of silhouettes similarly dressed, some women, some men—someone's sister, someone's brother, someone's child, someone's friend. A line of sinister cars ease past them, windows roll down, deals are made, desperate human beings disappear into the shadowy recesses of dark, unknown vehicles.

The night drags on. A few paltry fares come and go, meaning I'm saddled with extended stretches of naval gazing time in between. That movie scene keeps drifting back into my mind…so, haunting, so rife with pathos.

What's most confusing, though, is who's the director. Woody Allen? I mean, seriously? He's an unlikely candidate to deliver such a searing examination of the shadows of the human soul. In most of his films, like say Sleeper or Broadway Danny Rose, he's always playing the pathetic funny guy, right? Mr. class clown. So how did he give his goof-ball identity the slip and conjure up such a top shelf cinematic moment? But wait, didn't I read somewhere how he'd briefly studied philosophy? A wise cracking comedian who studies philosophy…hmmm…that's a weird juxtaposition. Maybe, akin to the Martin Landau dynamic, Woody Allen also wears a mask, the mask of a clown, and hidden under that mask is what? Some other-creature awash with shadowy secrets and inexplicable contradictions?

But unlike on Mission Impossible where Martin Landau would eventually just peel off his ingenious disguise, what a chore it must be for Woody Allen to scrape away his! And why even bother? Why forsake the loony, neurotic funny-guy facade to reveal some melancholy poet hidden beneath? Nobody wants to see that—not normal people anyway. Who wants to cry when they can laugh?

But wait, if this split personality deal applies, then god, what a life Woody Allen must lead! Every single new goddamn person he meets must be agog with giddy anticipation, waiting for him to deliver some hilarious, rib-cracking zinger, you know, like the dialogue in his movies. Just enduring the average sophisticated dinner party must be excruciating for him—ie: "Woody passed me the salt and it wasn't even funny!" The relentless burden of so many yuk-yuk-yuk expectations! Every time he meets someone new, he has two possible options; throw the funny switch to the on position and keep them rolling in the aisles or dig in your heels and be true to yourself as a brooding soul nobody can love.

But, hey, you know what? If making people laugh is the easy, lazy disingenuous way for Woody Allen to fit in and he chooses to abandon it for a more challenging, resonant lifestyle, well then more power to him. Think about the genesis of that Martin Landau scene; the writing of it, the casting, then finally the staging. How liberating it must have been for Woody Allen to witness that moment where he finally gives his inner clown the slip and reveals the nuanced, shadowy depths of his psyche.

And Woody Allen, like Martin Landau, is also a New Yorker. So, if it's Woody Allen instead of Martin Landau who one day raises his famous arm and hails my cab, after I ask him his destination and we're just tooling along down various synchronized avenues and such, I'm going to make a big deal out of congratulating him for escaping his jester persona and creating that searing portrait of humanity in Crimes and Misdemeanors.

"Good work, Woody!", I'll tell him, "...Keep it up and one day you'll be free of that clown within for good!"

He'll look momentarily bewildered, then he'll reply, "Wow! You get it! You...you... you understand! Thank you! I'll keep working on it. The clown within—I like that! That's a good phrase! Hey, uh, do you have a pen? I better write that down..."

Peeling false faces away. Yeah boy, ain't that a universal chore? For transvestites and cab drivers, deviant proctologists, movie stars and auteurs alike, we're all in the same face-peeling boat. It's taken me a good twenty years to work out the life-math that landed me where I presently am, finally admitting I can't honestly live with myself as the person circumstance has shaped me to be; the dutiful son, the Pentecostal hymn singer, the straight-laced goody-two shoes type. No, I moved to the Big Apple expressly to roll up my sleeves and start peeling away this paralyzing false face that fate pasted on me, a pseudo-visage affixed with the superglue of time, religious indoctrination, self-deception, misplaced faith, on and on.

But hell, things could be worse couldn't they? At least I'm not that transvestite, or Woody Allen or Martin Landau for that matter. I may have one hellacious road of self-realization ahead of me, but at least I can claw my false face away in the privacy of my own relative obscurity.

That hard core fundamentalist Christian phase of mine came to an end after a run of unsuccessful grasps at magical needles in the big haystack of Life; I left the church and abandoned any hope that Jesus, America's favorite interventionist puppet-master, would rescue me from much of anything, especially self-inflicted mental duress. My twelve years spent in the Pentecostal church proved beyond a shadow of a doubt that no divine rescue was coming. Endlessly begging Jesus for inner peace only seemed to magnify and exacerbate the chaos in my mind. Once I accepted this baseline reality, that was when the first bouts of serious depression—the psychic undertow or whatever you want to call it— hit me and those childhood previsionings returned, this time kicking in harder...allowing fleeting glances of transcendence and beauty, violence and horror, all begging to be somehow actualized in a real world context.

The initial action I took in peeling the mask away involved nothing especially sensational. No creepy orgies, or wildly addictive mind altering drugs, no crime sprees, shock therapy or weird voodoo rituals or anything like that. I just relocated my lost self to New York City, figuring in the midst of all that urban duress and mayhem the wheat would automatically separate itself from the chaff.

Sometimes I'd walk the streets late at night in sketchy neighborhoods, waiting for a sign, a word, a clue, for something meta to happen. An hour would pass, then two, but nothing much cathartic ever went down. I didn't even get mugged. Bottom line, this tactic of throwing myself into peril to provoke catharsis proved to be mostly ego based, and thus just more unhealthy shit to contend with—an experiment that I'd hoped would provide me with certain enlightenment basics I couldn't lay hands on by behaving sensibly.

Essentially I was a reluctant lamb ill at ease with my weakness and vulnerability. I figured my only escape route involved trespassing through the realm of lions. In my hubris, I banked on the vain notion that my heart was so good, so pure, so brave, so sincere that no lion could in good faith devour me. But lions will be lions. It's bullshit to expect them to behave otherwise.

But after my initial grace period, later the lions came. Sometimes in the heat of those moments of extremis I did actually learn something, but it was seldom anything profound, like about general universal notions of enlightenment. Mostly I'd catch fleeting glimpses of what an utter chickenshit I was—a confused, naive child refusing to accept the role of manhood, an insecure seeker scrambling to avoid any real enlightenment, a tap-dancing big mouth desperately trying to sidestep getting his ass royally kicked by Life.

Most often these lessons came when I was driving the taxi via encounters with hard core thugs, gang bangers, criminals I should have never picked up in the first place, the ones who settled into the back seat, smelled weakness and pounced. It became clearer and clearer that if I kept up that risky line of behavior, I'd be dead within the year.

So I undertook a strategic retreat and willed the darkness away. My death wish ebbed. Off it scuttled, retreating back into the shadows. I imagined myself a house on a low-lying island. As each deluge of worrisome events beset me, I'd sandbag the gaps surrounding my little mental compound in an effort to keep the rising floodwaters from sweeping all my mental furniture away. It was a full-time engagement. I endured as best I could with aching muscles and soggy feet for a year or two but eventually the flood tide of strange visitations and death wishes receded.

That said, even to this day I have to remind myself that I still live by that river, that it will rise and fall as it pleases. It's always there, waiting to reassert itself in my mind like it did this afternoon. At least today nothing bad happened. In fact, other than the weird, unprofitable night I'm having, all that nonsense earlier in the day amounted to virtually nothing.

Twenty more navel gazing minutes pass thusly. I'm empty, running down 9th Avenue and, seeing a swarm of empty cabs jockeying for pole position ahead of me, I bank left onto 22nd, which is one of the nearly synchronized crosstown streets heading east. I come charging down past 8th Avenue, then hurtling past 7th, then just north of the intersection of 6th Avenue I spot a middle aged white woman striding from the sidewalk into the parking lane, headed toward the corner of 23rd Street. She throws her arm in the air. I slam on the brakes and bank hard left.

"Hi, what's your destination?" I ask as she jumps in the cab. She's prim and proper, an energetic, waspy type decked out in high end conservative business attire. She's headed up to Park Avenue in the 90's, where the wealthiest New Yorkers live. It's roughly a seventy block ride with mostly synchronized lights and easy transitions along the way. Not a bad fare at all, provided I don't end up stranded on the Upper East Side after I drop her, endlessly circling, searching for a passenger to bring me back downtown.[4]

We head east on 23rd then bank left at Madison and now are picking our way up the potholed mine field that extends from 23rd to 34th Street. As we hit smoother pavement and accelerate, I'm already working out a general stratagem for after I drop the proper socialite lady. Stay on the East Side? Go bombing across Central Park to the West Side? Just dead head back downtown empty? As we pass 57th Street my passenger leans forward and in a clear clipped tone says, "Driver, I'd like to make an on-course adjustment. Take me to 69th and Madison instead."

Wow! What a term. "An on-course adjustment???" I say.

"Yes, an on-course adjustment. Do you understand what I mean by that?" Her question's reasonable enough, seeing how the majority of cabbies in New York speak English as a second or often third language and that variety of formal, clinical sounding English might utterly baffle some of them.

"Not only do I understand it, I appreciate the full value of it." I tell her, "On-course adjustments are an integral aspect for cab drivers such as myself when we're hunting for fares. When I'm running empty, every corner I choose to turn, every red light I catch, every minute decision I make while trying to connect with folks like you completely changes the entire disposition of my night. For example, because I made an on-course adjustment and modulated east on 22nd Street at 9th Avenue just a moment before I picked you up, now the remainder of my night will play out completely differently than if I'd continued rolling downtown instead. Because of that choice I'm now here, instead of now there, which lands me in a succession of now-heres that I likewise wouldn't have arrived at. It's like the butterfly effect in physics, except with taxi cabs and passengers. And now, thanks to you, each time I make one those strategic choices,

---

4. Traditionally at this time on a weeknight, around 9:30 or so, the flow of passengers starts to reverse, with the cab riding crowd returning to their deluxe apartments in the more affluent northern sections of the city from downtown social engagements. With so many passengers getting dropped off in such a narrow corridor (Upper East and West sides) this creates a glut of freshly empty cabs in those neighborhoods. With very few options to fan out in search of new passengers to the north (starting at 96th Street, Spanish Harlem and beyond is an unofficial no cruise zone for yellow cabs due to the rampant drugs and violence up there), and very little business heading toward Midtown from there, at that hour often there's nothing to do but deadhead all the way back down to Greenwich Village or Times Square, then jump into the hunt down there. This can lead to running empty for upwards of an hour, resulting in a large loss of income. Some drivers try to get lucky, remaining in the cab saturated area, circling, turning corners, crawling side streets, hoping to pick off the stray passenger going against the grain. In the best of times this makes for fierce competition at this time of night in posh uptown neighborhoods. Throw in the bitter, street-clearing cold tonight and there's a real likelihood that after dropping this lady I might circle these streets for hours without finding another fare, like a few nights back when I drove a full ninety minutes empty in a similar context.

I'll have a name for it; the 'on-course adjustment'. Having accurate names and descriptions for abstractions is very helpful, wouldn't you agree?"

"Oh definitely." she says smiling, yet without any real warmth.

"So from now on when I say to myself, 'Hey this tactic for finding a fare isn't working, I'd better make an on-course adjustment!' I'll think of you."

"Excellent. Feel free to use it whenever you wish…" she adds, a slight brittle tone slipping into her delivery. Maybe she thinks I'm trying to hit on her. I decide I'd better make an on-course adjustment with our conversation.

"I will, thanks. Now, which corner would you like at 69th and Madison?"

"Southeast, thanks."

A few mere seconds pass in silence and we're here. I drop her, then sit a moment while I correct the information I wrote on my trip sheet when she entered the cab. I scratch out 93rd and Park Avenue and in the margin above correctly note 69th and Madison.

Looking at my trip sheet, I see how cramped and anguished my handwriting is and wonder what the hell that handwriting lady was getting at earlier in the night when she said, "You're in trouble." How am I in trouble? Will the psychic undertow return in some less than wholesome long term way? Will I end up homeless and crazy?

Shit! In the brief time that I've paused to consider this notion twenty or so empty cabs appear, running with the fresh green light cycle and come whizzing by me. I realize that, by allowing my mind to drift I've inadvertently just made an on-course adjustment to the trajectory of my night. I drop the clipboard and gun it, trying not to get caught by the red light at 72nd, which typically changes five to seven seconds ahead of synch and, whew, I just make it.

There's no point in heading further north, as there's a glut of empty cabs up ahead already. I consider banging a left at 77th Street, as turning there will afford me a connecting green light at 5th Avenue but decide against it, as I see there's already an empty cab doing that. My next logical turn west (no sense turning east where there are even more empty cabs) is 85th Street, which leads to one of the Central Park Transverses.

Hmmmm. I work over my options.

If I deadhead across the transverse to Central Park West I can make three possible on-course adjustments once on the other side. I can do the logical thing and turn south onto Central Park West, hoping to pick up someone departing one of the numerous swanky doorman buildings in the 70's. I can go straight west toward Columbus, where I will most certainly intersect with a veritable tsunami of other empty cabs all washing back downtown, or I can behave illogically and go against the grain, turning north and running for ten or so blocks back up towards Harlem, if need be doubling back at 96th Street, the end of the theoretical safe cruising zone for yellow cabs. Since logic is of little use in conditions as adverse as this, I decide that once across the park I should opt for illogic. Either way, it's time for that modulation westward on 85th Street.

I bang a hard left off Madison Avenue and to my surprise see no empty cabs crawling the block westward toward 5th Avenue. Good! Although the light's presently red at 5th Avenue I gun it because I know the green will come in the three to five seconds it'll take for me to cover the long city block spanning Madison to 5th. If I hit the freshly green light at 5th and 85th at full speed that'll give me a shot at catching another green light on the far side of the park at 86th and Central Park West, which typically is a tough connection to make moving at normal speeds. If I make that light and I can zip unimpeded all the way up to 96th street without catching a red light. Such a string of successful maneuvers would greatly enhance my chances of actually locating a fare.

Pop! The light at 85th and 5th Avenue goes green right on schedule just as I reach it going full throttle—86th Street Central Park Transverse here I come! But as I hit the middle of the intersection doing a good fifty miles per hour, out of the corner of my eye I spy something to my left moving further down 5th Avenue.

I whip my head, and lo and behold, what do I see? Between 84th and 83rd, a doorman from some mega swanky building directly across from the legendary Metropolitan Museum of Art is stepping into the frozen roadway…to do what? WOAH NELLY! His hand flies into the air! He whistles! He's hailing a cab for one of his zillionaire clients—A FARE! And it's heading downtown! The trouble is I've already committed to the park transverse and can't slow down enough to bank the cab southward and make that on-course adjustment! Damn! I go barreling into the park, grudgingly eyeing that doorman standing in the road.

Hmmm. But see, here's the layout: true, there's a waist high stone wall median as you enter the park, but soon enough said wall ends, giving way to a tall steep curb that's roughly six inches high. From thirty feet in said curb is the only barrier between oncoming traffic. It runs another forty or so feet.

Hmmmmm again.

I do the urban trigonometry in my head (like that elegant lady who lost her hat) calculating the possible damage to the suspension of the cab should I hit that curb at full speed, the amount of green time left on the traffic light at 84th and 5th, which I estimate at around twenty more seconds, the lack of oncoming traffic (particularly other empty cabs or, worse, cops) the likelihood that I won't find a fare on the other side of the park and most importantly how long it will take me to redirect this hurtling ton of vehicular mayhem should I attempt what in avionics parlance is known as a bat-wing turn. All this information goes surging into the terribly flawed computer that is my brain and without another thought I lock the brakes up, yank the wheel hard left and hit the vertical curb going a full forty miles per hour.[5]

There's a terrible scraping, crashing, whirring sound. The frame hits the curb and sparks fly as the cab leaps into the air, fishtails then lands, the back wheels catching on the pavement with an ear-splitting screech. Smoke pours from the spinning tires for an instant, then suddenly I'm building speed in the opposite direction, hurtling east now toward the fare. Yes! Bat-wing turn successfully executed!

Two empty cabs, ones who apparently were behind me on 85th Street, have turned the corner heading downtown on 5th Avenue, but are blocked by the red light at 84th Street. Salivating at the sight of that doorman with his hand in the air just the other side of the intersection, they sit side by side in pole position, primed for action, agonizingly separated from the manna of a paying customer by a single abstraction known as a "red light". Their revving engines suggest impatience, like drag racers chomping on the bit at the staging gate, ready to do battle.

There stands the doorman in the bitter cold, hand in the air, tooting on his ridiculous little doorman whistle. There lies my fare, my trip downtown to where other fares and theoretical subsequent redemption for this terrible night of entrepreneurship awaits. Nobody's seen me yet, not the doorman, not the two impatient empty cabs.

I'm building speed, counting the blinks of the flashing crosswalk lights, said indicators signaling my green light interval is all but done. Most crosstown crosswalk lights blink eleven times, whereupon the light modulates yellow, then three seconds later goes red. These particular crosswalk lights were already blinking when my eyes landed on them after the bat wing turn so there's no telling where in the sequence I am. As I hurtle towards them, I count...five, six, seven, eight...Jesus! At nine the traffic light pops yellow but, hey, no problem, because I'm now in prime striking position. I come power sliding around the corner and screech to a halt, sending the doorman scurrying for the relative safety of the curb.

"Jesus fucking Christ! Are you mad?" he shouts. In my heightened state of awareness, I detect some distant remnant of an Irish accent in his brief outburst. Galway?

He grudgingly shakes his head at me, then waves to the high roller waiting in the nice warm lobby, signaling that his cab is here. Out a smallish figure bolts, scurrying along, his coat yanked up over his head, ostensibly to protect his plutocratic ears from the bitter cold? The doorman invokes his namesake and fulfills his sad, narrow destiny by throwing open the cab door. In my next passenger leaps. I pick up my trip sheet clip-

---

5.This is not my cab. I lease this vehicle by the night. It belongs to a multi-millionaire who lives in one of these opulent Upper East Side mansions. He owns a taxi fleet comprised of one hundred cabs and his lavish lifestyle is funded exclusively by three hundred poor saps like me who pay him a hundred bucks a shift (twice a day!) for the privilege of enduring twelve hours of life threatening, soul sucking minimum wage-employment. He rakes in a cool ten grand per night shift and does little other than collect our blood money, so I have no qualms about damaging, even destroying his property. I've paid for this cab ten times over and don't give a shit about it.

board and greet him with my customary, "Hi, what's your destination?" In response he aggressively shouts, "Go!"

So I say, "Yes, go where?"

"Drive! Just drive!" he snaps back.

Wow, that's uncalled for. Maybe his thin millionaire blood is just terribly chilled from the fifty-foot sprint from the toasty lobby to my lukewarm, stinky cab?

"Sir," I tell him, just as I did the friendly rich guy going to Queens, "I've been driving a taxi for many years now and pride myself on my knowledge of the streets. If you tell me your destination, I'll be able to get you there via the fastest, most efficient route. I just need a street address from you."

That's reasonable enough, right?

But the fancy millionaire guy isn't having any of it. In response to my reasonable request for pertinent information he barks, "Straight ahead! Just drive! Go, would you!"

In my taxi, my sad, smelly little yellow fiefdom, I have few rules, but first and foremost is the destination rule; I refuse to go anywhere until I know where I'm going. This is not out of obstinance or some perverse hunger for control, it's a straight-up matter of expediency. I need to know the destination simply so I can, by using my superior knowledge of the intricate mathematics of traffic patterns and lights in the city, pick the best, fastest route.

This fact alone deters me from obeying my pissy passenger's demand. But aside from that glaring issue, there's something else that keeps my foot from crushing the gas pedal; my passenger's voice sounds strangely familiar. I check the rear view, much the way I did with the lavender haired proctologist, to see if I can size this bossy character up. Maybe he's drunk. Maybe he's just an idiot. Maybe he's my ninth grade geometry teacher. I see he's dropped his coat from over his head, but is shrouded in silhouette as a wave of cabs (all empty) on 5th Avenue approach us from behind, so I can't see him clearly. Then a strafing headlight from a passing cab momentarily illuminates his face and I recognize him.

Who is it? Is it my ninth grade geometry teacher? No, it's Woody Allen.

You've probably deciphered by now that it'd take one walloping dollop of strange for me to be left at a loss for words. But here I am, reduced to an utterly stunned, flabbergasted silence. A million variables flash through my mind. First and foremost, it occurs to me that that vision I beheld on the side of the skyscraper was definitely neither a mere hallucination, nor some such physiological anomaly, perhaps explained away by neurological jargon involving the double processing of optic information. It was no movie PR stunt. It was in fact some kind of bewildering prescient event…involving Woody Allen… INTERESTING!

And through a series of intricate "on-course adjustments" that involved interacting with the proctologist, the handwriting expert, the gypsy kid, the rich couple from Queens, the nearly-strangled transvestite, the prim articulate white woman who CHANGED her destination, the harrowing bat wing turn over the median in the Central Park Transverse, plus a million other lesser variables, I apparently am now exactly where I need to be in the intricate clockworks of The Universe... AMAZING! WOW!

And now here sits Woody Allen in my back seat, (the same exact patched square of vinyl that the transvestite sat on!) and all I have to do to fulfill the purpose of this elegant equation is to deliver my uplifting message to him. I'll congratulate him for giving his inner clown the slip, for his brave efforts to become a person of substance, a creature of deeper meaning. But wait, what effect might these words have on him? Is this a low moment in his day? Will my exhortation cause him to make some decisive choice on an upcoming project? Will he nix the big Miramax comedy he'd agreed to do and take on staging that experimental Ibsen play in rural Romania? With an all lesbian cast? Who knows?

"Hey! Driver, what are you waiting for here? Go!" My passenger mincingly barks at me. Woody's certainly not in a very civil mood. Of course he's unaware of the magnitude of meaning attached to our meeting. It's my job to make him aware of that. But first he needs to tell me where he's going.

"I'd be happy to go sir, once you tell me your destination."

"What??? Just go!"

"I can't…not until I know where we're going."

Even as I'm saying the words, I feel an unhealthy sensation washing over me. No, it's not the psychic undertow, it's worse…one that I'm sure poor Woody Allen is all too familiar with. See, by speaking to him, by hearing him respond to me, I'm suddenly struck by the uncanny impression that I'm not just acting in a Woody Allen movie, I'm actually writing and directing it.

"What's the hold up here! Just...put your foot on the gas pedal and…you know, go!" He complains in his trademark whiny voice. I find myself restraining the urge to say to him, "...And cut! That's a take! Now, Woody, once more, but this time really...you know...with feeling!"

Now, for the record, yes, I'm mindful that I'm a messenger from the Universe here. I am. And I desperately want to convey to Woody Allen that kernel of crucial information that the Universe seems intent on him hearing, but how to convey it? By what angle of approach? Where do I start? Tell Woody about my childhood skirmishes with all that paranormal shit? The vision on the side of the skyscraper? The whole butterfly effect night of weird coincidences that've led me to his doorstep? Where do I start?

Considering his feisty tone, the answer might just be nowhere. His intransigence and overt hostility with such a simple request as providing his destination suggests it's likely that he may just be incapable of accepting a magical message from the Universe by way of a random cab driver tonight. What a shame! What a waste of serendipity!

So, if there's no graceful, organic conduit to deliver that message, and it sure looks that way, what do I do now? Well, frankly, I opt for crass entertainment. I do. I'm not proud of it but that's what makes the most sense right here, right now. So what I do, just for laughs I decide I'm going to make Woody Allen talk some more. Whether he likes it or not. Why? Because, I'm ashamed to admit, it's fun. In arguing with him, for moment at least, my tawdry cab driving life feels magically lifted to a form of fine art. "Sir," I tell him, feigning anger, "We're not going anywhere until you tell me your destination."

Well, this gets him really steamed. After all, he's the director, not me. "What? What… do you mean? Destination….? Just drive! What's so hard about that?" With each syllable he spits out I feel more and more like I'm running a scene with him. Where are the cameras, the lights, my hairdresser, my trailer?

"Without a destination, sir, we really can't proceed." I patiently inform him, as if speaking to a small, confused child.

Then it hits me; this is the comedian who studied philosophy, right? I'm no scholar, but isn't one of the primary goals of all philosophical inquiry to deeply consider man's destination, and by that I mean the ultimate destination of the soul? Where are we going, why and how? That's philosophy in a nutshell, right? It's all oriented around destinations, and here I am asking Woody Allen about his destination, so that term should carry some extra weight, some serious resonance for the guy who wrote that riveting scene in Crimes & Misdemeanors, right?

There's this awkward pause, then finally I sigh and deliberately, with overdone theatricality say, "Sir, where are you going? Do you know? Do you really know? What your destination is? Can you name it?"

Woody's slightly taken aback, then says, "What…what are you talking about?"

"I'm simply asking you this, sir; what is your ultimate destination?"

And my delivery is so stilted! So obviously theatrical! How!?! How!?! How he can miss the all-important ironic-mystical subtext? It's just hanging out there like some massive banner flapping in a gale force wind. It's all about the destination, Woody! Come on, shape up here buddy! This is what educators call "the teachable moment" where real breakthroughs can occur, when deeper meaning eclipses the inertial forces of life's innumerable mind-numbing ruts.

I wait for a revelational reply, but nope—Woody's not listening. He huffs in frustration, grabs the door handle with his famous hand (attached to the famous arm that didn't hail me) pops the door halfway open, and in a threatening tone mewls out, "Drive! Straight ahead right now or I'm getting another taxi. Got it?"

The subtle magic of our enigmatic encounter is resolutely shattered into a million worthless shards. With no transcendent juice to propel our physical union I now have two options: I can break my own rule and drive straight ahead without knowing my destination, or I can let Woody Allen exit my taxi.

But if he exits, how will he ever learn that the Universe has a REALLY IMPORTANT message for him? Legions of empty cabs are sailing by. In the microsecond that it takes him to raise his famous arm in the air three or four cabs will descend upon him like hyenas converging on a sickly wildebeest and poof, he'll be gone from my life forever. And what profound message would those drivers have to deliver to him?

So, what do I do…? I sigh, then cave, grudgingly ease down on the gas and, in a state of utter defeat, start to drive. His door closes, and let me tell you, I feel every bit as miserable about knuckling under to his threat as I do about not being allowed to deliver my good word of supernatural exhortation.

He's fuming in the back seat as we pick up speed, heading downtown. We cover maybe ten, twelve blocks, then around 70th Street on 5th Avenue he mutters something to himself, then sighs heavily, calling out, "Turn at the next corner. There's a canopy on the left. First one. Stop there."

So now it's clear why he was instructing me to drive straight, as it's a straight line these twelve short blocks from 84th and 5th to here. But still, an on-course adjustment was necessary before the fare could be completed—I had to turn left to access the swanky Co-op canopy, which is on 70th Street, not 5th Avenue. Either way it doesn't matter. I've given up trying to deliver the Universe's message. I'll say nothing more to Mr. Woody Allen. I'm now just the mindless hunk of human meat aiming a yellow conveyance unit at some random, opulent doorway.

Before we've even fully stopped, Woody Allen thrusts his arm forward through the same partition that the gypsy kid shook my hand through and the transvestite showed me her/his strangulation marks, and shoves three one dollar bills at me. The fare is exactly two dollars. Without a word he manically leaps out of the cab, the coat once again bizarrely pulled up over his head as if a swarm of bees were attacking him. What is he doing??? Fleeing some invisible paparazzi or something? Despite the fact that I defied and infuriated him, he's tipped me a handsome fifty percent. Thanks Woody. The entire episode takes exactly four minutes. I drive away, thinking what a truly unfulfilling end to the story this is.

It's now the following morning. I wake up around eleven after turning the cab in at three thirty am. At shift change, I counted my take and after paying the hundred dollar lease fee and gas tab, for twelve hours of motorized anguish I pocketed a whopping forty-eight dollars, three of which were contributed by Mr. Woody Allen. High living. I could make more working at McDonalds. I slump on the edge of my bed, rueing the fact that in an hour I have to head back out for another grueling twelve hour shift.

I mosey over to Leshko's Restaurant, a nearby Ukrainian greasy spoon diner, intending to load up on cheap eggs and home fries before I head back to the fleet for another long day of mixing it up with humanity and the cockeyed universe that engulfs it. I take a stool at the counter and order my breakfast. The guy next to me's reading the New York Post, which is par for the course at working class Lesko's. What's not par for the course is what's on the cover of the Post. It's a full-page photograph of...who? The transvestite? The gypsy kid? Martin Landau? No, it's Woody Allen.

Tingles run up and down my spine as the nearly electrocuted feeling returns. I survey Leshkos dining area. Everywhere patrons are reading newspapers with Woody Allen's photograph plastered all over the cover: The Post, the Daily News, The Times.

Is he dead? Did I kill him somehow?

I walk next door to the news stand which likewise is swamped with images of Woody Allen. Is this a hallucination? Is the psychic undertow back, this time with a vengeance? If so this hallucinatory episode makes yesterday's look feeble in comparison. Yesterday I was merely seeing giant actors on the side of the skyscrapers…

So what will today's flashes reveal? I feel, well, kinda jumpy, and sorta like don't even want to know. I stand paralyzed there for a while quietly invoking my catchy new mantra "Psychic undertow, psychic undertow, go-go-go", then open my eyes but the Woody Allen newspaper covers remain. Finally, I have to accept the fact that this isn't some kind of vision. There's just too much peripheral information to confirm this as real. I buy a copy of The Post.

The newspaper reports that Woody Allen has been accused by Mia Farrow of improper sexual conduct with their underage adopted daughter Soon Yi. A timeline instantly presents itself to me: countless variations of this ruinous story were likely being written, vetted by lawyers, then approved late yesterday afternoon in newsrooms all over the city, newsrooms not far from where I sat in that traffic jam. Woody Allen probably received word that the story was breaking and that he was up shit creek without a paddle sometime between then and eight pm, give or take an hour. This would put my episode of the psychic undertow dead center in the midst of Woody's personal Waterloo.

Interesting.

So what's the actual causality here? Did Woody's mind, upon hearing the news that he was massively busted and would face catastrophic shame and scandal, send out a powerful frantic psychic SOS into the airwaves of New York City? Is that what I saw on the side of that building? Some mental projection from Woody Allen's panicked mind? Wow. Who knows… maybe so.

That does clear up several mysteries; now I see why my famous passenger was in such a foul mood. And why he was running with that coat up over his head—obviously he was practicing for a moment in his near future when he would be escorted to a police cruiser, the slavering packs of paparazzi hyenas swarming all around him.

I read the article as I wolf down my eggs then hop on my bike and head over to 21st Street between 6th and 7th, where the taxi fleet I work for, Ann's Taxi Service, is based. It's now one thirty in the afternoon. I walk in the door to find twelve night shift drivers already seated around the main table waiting to be dispatched, or as it's known in the taxi trade, doing the "shape up." [6]

Sitting in a corner of the shape up room is my counterculture genius friend Richard Osterweil, a cab driver buddy who's both a visual artist of some note and an infamous New York social scene party crasher. His unique and slightly seditious hobby is sneaking into the high society weddings, gala balls, bar mitzvahs, funerals, etc. of famous people here in New York City. He dons disguises and incorporates props much the way Martin Landau did on Mission Impossible, although his goal is not to protect freedom and the American Way, but rather to have his photo taken standing near A-list celebrities and New York society aristocracy like the Vanderbilts and Peabodys and such, this while gobbling down the sundry free catered delicacies available at these events. In some ways, he's the perfect person to talk this bewildering incident over with.

I inform him of the previous day's events. He listens carefully, politely ignoring my glaringly esoteric references to the supernatural, then deftly deciphers some of the simpler X factors in my story. It turns out that the location I picked Woody Allen up from on 5th Avenue was Woody's therapist's office. He must have been talking over the impending scandal with his shrink—just like in a Woody Allen movie! The location I dropped him at was Mia Farrow's apartment. Woah! Ouch! No matter how chilly it was outside, I bet an infinitely chillier reception awaited him inside that sumptuous celebrity penthouse!

It's all so interesting! There are so many questions swirling around my brain! I tell Richard that it's crucial that I somehow speak with Woody Allen, to let him know that everything's going to be okay, that this scandal will probably only serve to hasten his severing those paralyzing ties with his inner clown. Richard shakes his head ruefully, informing me that I won't be able to get within fifty yards of the famous director at this point, as he's presently America's most besieged human being, lying at the epicenter of an unprecedented media blitz.

But this seems so unfair! In Woody's hour of tribulation, it seems crucial that he know the Universe is listening, perhaps even sympathizing. I tell Richard that one way or another I'm going to find a way to contact Woody. Richard knows me well enough to

---

6. "Shape up" is a catchy term for the agonizing period that night shift drivers endure each day as they wait in a remarkably drab, indescribably inhospitable room, seated on long, uncomfortable, crudely hewn benches and broken office chairs. It's a sort of queue, as British people say. Why do the night shift drivers arrive hours early? They're waiting for the first of the day shift drivers to come trickling back in. The official shift change is listed as 3:30, but some come in earlier, and if you show up at the exact shift change time you'll find roughly a hundred divers waiting in line ahead of you. The average "shape up" wait runs around two hours. Add that to the twelve hours that you spend driving nightly and the actual work day ends up running a minimum of fourteen hours. And that's without the commute.

fully grasp the ramifications of my pledge and promptly warns me that if I physically wait outside either Woody's place on Central Park West or Mia Farrow's apartment on 5th Avenue and try to relay my message, long before I get within earshot, some burly Samoan bodyguard type will likely attack me, put me in a full Nelson and break my jaw for good measure. Richard is the mountaintop on this subject, so I have no choice but to heed his warning. Thankfully, since this is his bailiwick, he effortlessly suggests another solution.

"Are you familiar with the Princeton Club?" He asks knowingly, "Between 5th and 6th on 43rd? The day shift lobby guard there is very lax and so it's a breeze to sneak in. I do it all the time. Lovely sauna there. Take the center staircase and go to the second floor. There you'll find a reading room. There are several desks in the reading room that are stocked with official Princeton Club stationary. Fancy stuff! You should see the letterhead! Steal some of the stationary and write Woody Allen a letter. But make sure you also steal an envelope with the Princeton Club letterhead as the return address. That's the most important part. Now, are you right-handed or left-handed?"

"Right"

"So, use your left hand and address it as if you were a very old, very venerable member of the Princeton Club. Hopefully that'll get Woody's attention. Place whatever message you feel is necessary inside. This way you've at least got a fighting a chance of it reaching him. Mail it to Mia's address, which by now you're familiar with, and worst case scenario it will be forwarded to him, as it's a felony to tamper with the delivery of US mail."

Richard's calming assurance is both encouraging and infectious. I now know that somehow, employing Richard's brilliantly devised strategy, I will contact Woody and comfort, perhaps even guide him. Since it's shape-up time and I have two hours to kill before I'm dispatched, I hop on my bike and dash uptown to the Princeton Club. I lurk in the foyer for a few minutes until, as promised, the lobby guard steps away from his post. I slip upstairs and purloin quite a pile of their deluxe stationary. What's that I hear in the back of my mind? Is that the theme song to Mission Impossible?

The night sails by, my mind fully engaged with considerations regarding the composition of my message to Woody. After my shift is done, I hurry home and frantically draft my letter, finishing just after dawn. I make sure to compose the missive in a manner that absents any suggestion that this is some creepy attempt to insinuate myself into Woody's world, to become his sidekick or land a role in one of his films. I make no mention of my name, include no contact information or clue to my identity and simply stick to the facts—the lost hat, the nearly electrocuted feeling, the psychic undertow, the movie on the side of the skyscraper, the transvestite and the gypsy kid, the butterfly effect sequence of events. It's a masterpiece. Woody will surely be riveted by the tale, both enlightened and encouraged! And who knows, maybe even entertained! Solace in his time of great need!

Now for the envelope. It's harder than you might think to create an authentic looking forgery of a wealthy old plutocrat's handwriting—they teach penmanship at those stuffy Ivy League prep schools after all. That's your starting point, but then you have to deconstruct that baseline aesthetic to account for atrophied motor skills. I make a few practice forgeries on scratch paper, ultimately realizing that if I lift my elbow free of the table so that my hand wobbles with less deliberation it lends a certain erratic realism to the end product. I think of the handwriting expert and what she would make of THIS handwriting.

The letter's addressed and I'm now trying to envision what Woody will think when he sees he's received correspondence from the prestigious Princeton Club? Maybe they're inviting him to be a member? Richard is a genius. Woody'll be eaten up with curiosity! He'll have to open it. And once he reads the message, what will he think? I'll never find out—that much I know—but it's okay. I understand that the Universe doesn't work that way. I'm content knowing that I'm a tool of some unseen forces and happy to be of service to any and all.

I head to the post office and buy a stamp, then place the envelope halfway in the slot, but don't release my grip on it just yet. I study that letter to Woody Allen hanging there, teetering on a pivot between ignominy and greatness. I smile, happily regarding the slim white rectangle with the forged handwriting and Princeton Club letterhead, envisioning the path it will take; into the belly of the mail box, shortly thereafter transferred to the cramped confines of a grimy canvas mail bag, then dumped into a wheeled sorting bin, then on through the labyrinth of conveyor belts, jogging this way and that, shuttling along at wondrous speeds, finding its way, following its path, eventually landing in a block-specific box which is then plucked up by a postman, bundled and loaded in a mail truck to be ferried past the very same traffic lights that Woody and I passed on our short but momentous journey last night, that ride to the first canopy on the left just off of 5th Avenue and 70th Street. Tomorrow it will be deposited in the mail slot marked Farrow/Allen and my obligation to the Universe will be satisfied.

Just before I release the letter, bubbling up from some mysterious shadow realm below I feel the strange urge to speak to it, to offer it my usual cab greeting of, "Hi, what's your destination?". But of course I don't, as there's no need. This letter knows exactly where it's going.

BROWNSVILLE, FLORIDA, SEPTEMBER 2004

Down a big live oak limb comes crashing a mere twenty feet off. Jezebel protests, flexing the interior walls of the doghouse/pig containment unit as she thrashes that hefty body around, reminding me of the imminent task at hand, this latest chapter in my life of stranger truths.

But ain't it uncanny how the sweat of a brow greased just right can free up some inner thought mechanism or memory assembly otherwise frozen via acts of stale intellectual intentionality? It's as if some essential gears can only be engaged by accident—if so, I should be thusly challenged more often! Maybe everyone should.

Take Woody, for example. Had he been tasked with transporting a diabolical pig to a shed in a hurricane that day we crossed paths maybe he would've been more attuned and open to the message the Universe was sending his way. And maybe his life would be the better for it.

I close my eyes and try to envision scrawny little Woody Allen hefting Jezebel and the doghouse across the expanse of soft ground over to the shed, and there on the little movie screen in my head everything goes anachronistically slapstick, like a silent film from some bygone epoch: Woody takes a tumble. The doghouse topples over, the pig breaks loose and attacks him. Woody rises, sprints, stumbles again, pig in hot pursuit tugging on his pants leg—it's like Keystone Cops, but with livestock and celebrities. I feel a rueful grin spreading across my face, sufficient enough in intensity to generate a quiet, muffled laugh and rueful head shake, the momentary relief like a cool breeze on the back of the neck, a sense of weightlessness momentarily skimming over me.

But there's pigs to transport here, so I lean into the dolly and resume my hefting as the sojourn to the shed resumes. Then, as if on cue, that juke box in my head starts looping those opening lines to Static on the Radio again,

> *3am I'm awaked by this sweet summer rain…*
> *distant howling of a passing southbound coal train.*
> *Was I dreaming, or was there someone*
> *just lying here beside me in this bed?*
> *Am I hearing things, or in the next room*
> *did a long forgotten music box just start playing*

Come about thirty-five minutes into the slog of the century finally, here it is—the dolly wheels hit that concrete slab the shed sits on. Oh thank you, Jesus, Buddha, Allah, Zoroaster, Shen Dzu, Jimmy Dean and sundry other pig affiliated gods. I may be drenched in sweat and lightheaded from exhaustion but from here on out this pig rescue is a cake walk. I wheel the doghouse into the relative safety of the musty, crowded shed interior, weaving this way and that past chaotic, teetering piles of cardboard boxes overflowing with bric a brac, family heirlooms, irreplaceable photos, plastic Christmas trees, broken toys, defunct bicycles, all in various states of moldy, mildewing decomposition.

The centerpiece of the room, a Deep South automotive spin on Miss Haversham's wedding gown, takes the form of a broke-down convertible Triumph Spitfire that belongs to the Crazy Maker, a precious gift she received as a teenager. Mold being the dominant life form hereabouts, everything simmers in one state of decay or another—it's as if within the confines of this shed the force of entropy exists in some accelerated, supercharged state.

Jezebel, she's gone all quiet except for occasional exploratory snuffling. She's triangulating, no doubt plotting and scheming, biding her time until she can leap into diabolically vexing action. What's crystal clear here is that before I free Jezebel I'd best work out a top shelf exit plan.

I set to clearing a path back to the door, shuffling piles of moldy boxes around, eyeballing the straightest possible route, then—wrrrr, wrrrr, wrrrr—off comes one board covering the still-verticalized doghouse door. I peek down inside and spy Jezzy panting warily, cagey pig eyes assaying the open orifice. I set my feet, ready to run like hell as I pop that last board loose, but when I do and toss it aside nothing much happens. Finally, out peeks the snout, snuffling this way and that. There's some shifting around inside the doghouse, but the remaining pig body appears unable to surmount the sky facing doorway. What are the stats on pig vertical leap abilities?

Well, I guess I'll have to unverticalize this dang thing to let her out. That's a lot more dicey of a proposition, so I size up my exit route again and realize it's too risky to try to free her then run from doghouse to doorway so I grab a ten foot length of PVC pipe leaning in the corner, ease back over toward the doghouse and, edging as close to the door as I can, give it a hardy shove, tipping it over as I run like hell for the exit. Whomp, the doghouse comes crashing down on the floor, a cloud of moldy dust kicking up into the air. Out of said cloud, like some furious, stubbly pink bowling ball, comes Jezebel banking hard at full speed, barreling my way as we both aim for yon open doorway.

She's got daylight in her crosshairs but, no-no-not this time—slam goes the door in her face, her on the inside, me on the out and victory is mine. Jezebel squeals wildly as I throw the padlock through the hasp. Wham-bam, thank you ma'am. Now I can triumphantly report to the Crazy Maker that her soulmate Jezebel is safely ensconced in a place of refuge, and hopefully with that I'll be allowed visitation with my child upon her return from evacuation, whenever the hell that might be.

Into my truck I leap, hauling ass, weaving my way past the obstacle course of freshly fallen limbs scattered across the winding, rutted dirt driveway. For once, my timing is good. Sheets of the heavy rain from the hurricane's first big feeder bands start pummeling the truck even as I hit proper pavement. On go the wipers. No crackheads loitering around her gate today, the blighted streets of West Pensacola are deserted as I go crawling back toward my place, the meditative whop-whop tempo of the wipers setting my mind adrift, kicking on that OCD juke box in the back of my brain.

> *Now, there's a church-house about a stones throw down*
> *from this place where I been staying.*
> *It's Sunday morning and I'm sitting in my truck*
> *listening to my neighbors sing.*
> *Ten years ago I might have joined them*
> *but don't time change those inclined*
> *to think less of what is written,*
> *than what's wrote between the lines*

Over the years from reading sundry reviews and comments about that song (it's the second most popular in my catalog) it appears that fans, critics, culture vulture pundits and all, they tend to interpret the content of that song as being the product of some wild-eyed, mystical imagination that I possess. It's not. The lyrics to Static on the Radio are just my attempt to document the actual experiences of a person navigating a realm of stranger truths.

NEW YORK CITY, JANUARY 1985

Good lord, this Yankee desk cop is getting on my last nerve.

"Look, officer, it's a green and black striped 1964 Buick LeSabre…like with tiger stripes, you know…?" I repeat, this time mincingly, into the receiver. The precinct desk cop guffaws, then relays what I said to his cop buddy, apparently sitting nearby. I hear whoops, knee slaps.

"No! Listen! It's not a joke. It was my first grade teacher's sister car!" I bark into the phone, "And I just bought it off her a couple of months back…." The cop asks me to hold momentarily, then relays that spicy detail to the other cop, whereupon more hilarity ensues.

"I'm serious! And she bought it new the SAME EXACT YEAR I was in first grade, like twenty years ago! Think about that! All those years! Don't you see—this car's got, like, extreme sentimental value to me. Please, please, please let me report it stolen…"

The cop's in hysterics, dishing out more details to his jolly chum who I can hear repeating, "…wait, it's a tiger-striped LeSabre? And he says it was his first grade teachers car?" Then my cop adds, "No, her SISTER'S——Riiiight…" whereupon he collects himself, then says, "Get the fuck outta here wise guy! Go eat some grits! Ha-ha-ha!" And with that the cop hangs up on me.

Is that even allowed?

And who knew? That without some random piece of paper, a title or registration, a body can't report their own damn exotic green and black, tiger-striped vehicle stolen? I mean, aren't those the same papers that cops ask you for when they pull you over? Title and registration—right?

It's my first winter in wilds of New York City. I came limping up here from the Redneck Riviera in early fall and, after freeloading on a friend of a friend's couch until he kicked me out, grabbed the first place I could afford. It's a walk-in closet out in Long Island City, Queens. And when I say walk-in closet, I mean that literally—it's a walk-in closet…which I fork out a hefty $300 a month for. It's a 3rd floor walk-up in a dismal tenement over a roach-infested Chinese take-out restaurant on a side street near Queensboro Plaza. Welcome to the Big Apple, right?

I figured I could handle the tight quarters, but no, cabin fever started eating on my psyche harder and harder as the cold weather set in. It looked like I'd caught a major break when my mercurial new paralegal girlfriend set up this house-sitting gig for me over in the trendiest stretch of Greenwich Village—11th Street and Washington. Swanky doodle poodle type territory.

It's an upwardly mobile young corporate lawyer couple's place. New girlfriend paralegals at their legendary midtown law firm. They mentioned how they were terrified to leave their charming little West Village carriage house full of impressionist paintings and life-sized Fred & Ginger cut-outs unattended while they were off frolicking on some idyllic tropical paradise for three full weeks in January, and so paralegal girlfriend pitched me as a house sitter. They bit.

So, a West Village house-sitting gig! This was looking to be a major temporary upgrade, especially with that bouncy king-sized water bed they had—not that me and the paralegal girlfriend are gonna be doing any rolling around on it tonight. Nope. No sooner did we pick up the keys from the super and walk in the door than the fight commenced.

Paralegal girlfriend's a born and bred New Yorker. She's what you might call scrappy, and her scrappy premise went as such: these lawyers are almost the same age as I am and look at all the nice shit they have compared to me. This segued into her diving into a generalized appraisal of what an overall fuckup I was—minimum wage restaurant job, living in a closet in Queens. She made a few apoplectic circuits around apartment, Fred & Ginger cutouts mutely looking on, then promptly went storming out of said charming carriage house, stomping down 11th Street ten paces ahead of me, ripping me a new asshole for all the world to hear.

Such reckonings we encounter on trendy, narrow, dog-shit riddled sidewalks!

Since she's a native big city type, I figured maybe this was just New York style romance, so even in the face of her barrage of insults I kept aiming for conciliatory territory. After offering several times to drive her back to her apartment, which was way the fuck out in the boonies of Queens, she finally stopped yowling, turned back, looked at me like I was a lunatic, accepted the offer, took a deep breath, then promptly launched headlong back into her harangue.

And that's when ye olde shit truly hit ye olde fan. See, we hooked a right onto Perry street headed toward the West Side Highway, aiming for the space where that tiger-striped LeSabre was last seen parked. We stood there a minute, staring dumbly at the gaping eighteen-foot long gap at the curb where my giant car sat just twenty minutes earlier. Me, I was just foundationally unable to process what had apparently transpired. Gone??? Really? My first grade teachers' sister's car? The one I painted black tiger-stripes on?

Then, like a fully vexed infant winding up for a world class tantrum, girlfriend, she started sputtering and squawking, finally letting loose with a howl of, "WHERE IS YOUR CAR???" Over and over, like I was hard of hearing or something.

Of course, I made things worse by trying to smooth things over. I asked her to calm down. More howling ensued. Then I threw out the lame suggestion that maybe we were just on the wrong block. Whereupon she screamed, "You can't even find your own fucking car! I rest my case! You are a total fuck up!". With that she wheeled around, stepped out onto Washington Street and hailed a passing cab, and poof, off she went, disappearing into the night.

I moped back to the carriage house, licking my various wounds. Then I phoned the parking enforcement squad, figuring maybe the jig was up and they'd finally caught up with me. In my three months thus far in New York, I'd tallied maybe a couple of dozen unpaid parking tickets—not that I mentioned that to the impound guy. Real blasé-like, I inquired if anyone had noticed a big green and black tiger-striped '64 LeSabre in the city parking impound. Real blasé-like, he said nope, but when he asked for the tag number I hung up on him, figuring offering such specific information might complicate matters considerably. So then I phoned the nearby 6th Precinct to officially report it stolen, whereupon the telephone hi-jinx I just endured went down.

Feeling at loose ends, I slouch back out into the cold, thinking surely my car's parked nearby somewhere. As I fast-walk a grid pattern around the neighborhood, the peace and quiet feels good, but in my nagging girlfriend's absence soon enough my sanity anchor becomes slightly unmoored and I get to fantasizing a little too much about the manner in which I'll locate my errant vehicle.

First lap around the wilds of my imagination I find the LeSabre and it was just parked somewhere other than where I thought. From there I start discovering it in increasingly exotic theatrical contexts—a gaggle of stereotypical thugs, like with switchblades and tight-fitting jean jackets with the sleeves cut off, are hanging out in it. We have some words then I run them off with a lead pipe or some such improvised weapon— you know, take it back with force. Or I come around a corner and there's an apostate priest slumped down in the front seat reading this racy pulp fiction novel, like with illicit illustrations. He speaks only Italian, but no problem-o, because I speak a little Italian myself…

Jesus. I snap out of my car retrieval reverie. I might as well just go ahead and admit it, my fireball girlfriend's right; any person who can lose a two-ton, eighteen-foot long tiger-striped hunk of vintage steel, then fantasize about taking it back from an imaginary pervert priest is a fuck up. All hangdog like, I continue canvassing the surrounding blocks, fully expecting with each corner I turn to find my car magically sitting there.

It's after 3am now. I've been walking in nonsensical grids for hours. It's cold and the search has proved fruitless, so I just officially threw in the towel and decided to accept the fact that my first grade teachers' sister's 1964 Buick LeSabre is gone for good. Terrific. I trudge back to the townhouse then just for yuks phone a different precinct, hoping for a different outcome. I get the same story albeit sans the hilarity; if I can't prove legit ownership of my first grade teachers' sister's giant car, the city of New York will not permit me to report said vehicle stolen. Well, fuck a duck.

What's truly infuriating is how this particular crime would be so unbelievably easy to solve. Jesus, I mean, how many giant tiger-striped green and black 1964 Buick LeSabres could there be roaming the streets of New York City? A mile away you could see it and—boom—crime solved. And yet here some car thief is, tooling up and down the avenues without a care in the world.

It's past 5am. I tried sleeping—no dice. I take to relentlessly pacing these spaciously chic quarters trying to formulate my next step. Finally it hits me—hey wait, this is New York Fucking City—I'm being way too passive here: fuck it—if the cops won't get my car back for me then I'll just have to take it back myself.

I throw on some street clothes and schlep the eight blocks to the subway at 14th and Hudson, heading back to my cozy slum in Long Island City. So what's the plan?

1) Grab my shitty old bike and ride it into Manhattan,

2) In this vast, teeming, often lawless metropolis of eight million souls spanning five sprawling, disparate boroughs, I'll track down my car and take it back from the thief.

What could possibly go wrong?

It's two subway rides home and a long walk from the station to my shit hole digs. Along the way I go semi-zombified, slipping back into various daydreams of exciting car retrieval narratives in my mind. I'm peddling my bike down this busy city street or that when suddenly I spy my car! I pursue it, apprehend the sleeze-bag car thief, give him the old heave-ho out of the front seat. Out he goes tumbling onto the sidewalk as I leap into the front seat and speed away.

All this obsessive daydreaming, it's generating jittery knots of displaced psychic energy in my mind, so much so that by the time I hit the third floor landing where I keep my bike chained to the bannister I'm wound up tighter than a discount wristwatch. Surfeit of mental energy peaking, here I am primed to hop on said bike and make some magic car retrieval shit happen when—WHAT—WHERE IS MY BIKE??? I stare at the empty bannister where I left it chained a few days back in utter disbelief, then kind of lose it.

Tourettes style, I bark out "SHIT!" maybe ten, fifteen times in a row there in the hallway. I punch the wall a couple times too, which hurts, but helps as it discharges a portion of that bad juju welling up inside me. I try to calm myself down by looking for clues as to how my bike was stolen.

Okay, so there's no broken lock, no telltale severed chain link where the bolt cutters bit through, no damage to the banister, nothing indicating how the thieves made off with my crappy bike…or why they'd even want it. First my shitty old car gets jacked, now my fucking bike! And here comes the Tourettes kicking in again, whereupon I go off, shouting SHIT multiple times again, punching and clawing at the air.

I hear a sound behind me and whip around to see my neighbor's door crack slightly open. He blearily regards me, looking scared. "Oh. Hey…" he mumbles, still half asleep, "I heard someone shouting shit out here. Was that you?"

Oh yeah, it's only six-thirty in the morning. So I tell him about my car and subsequently my bike. He blinks, rubs the sleep from his eyes then says, "Oh. Wow. Sorry about your car. But don't you remember? You loaned me your bike. It's in here. But it's got a flat tire."

Hell's bells. My feisty girlfriend's sounding more and more on target with each passing minute here—what a colossal fuckup I am. Of course! Now I remember; I loaned my neighbor my crappy bike to use while I was staying at the fancy lawyer's townhouse. Despite the fact that I spaced on yet another important detail here, just knowing that my bike isn't also stolen helps me feel infinitely more grounded. There's no eerie coincidence to decipher, no obscure transportation-related message from the Universe intended just for me. My car got stolen is all. And my bike has a flat tire. That could happen to anyone.

Okay, so, back to Plan A, with the added twist of resolving this flat tire deal. I snatch the three speed from his living room, go clomping down the stairs then jog ten blocks to the nearest gas station, bike all the while slung over my shoulder. There's no time for a patch job, so for my new slightly altered car retrieval plan to succeed it's key that the inner tube only has a slow, slow leak, not a major puncture—my LeSabre needs me!

I air up the back tube and say a prayer, "This tire will hold air!" I solemnly assert to myself, then hop on the bike and barrel full speed toward Manhattan via the legendary 59th Street Bridge. Acts of interventionist destiny, they're in the air. They must be. They just must.

I hit the lengthy incline of that massive structure and hunker down, pedaling hard into a freezing headwind. The slow slog uphill gives me plenty of time to check out the mind-blowing expanse of cityscape stretching out as far as the eye can see in both directions.

Look at this goddamn teeming metropolis! It's vast, fathomless. How am I ever going to locate my car in all that asphalt, concrete and glass? From the lofty vantage point nearing the top of the bridge at this very moment, I behold legions of cars zipping hither and yon, passing below on the FDR Drive, navigating narrow roadways on Roosevelt Island, coursing up and down every Manhattan cross-street and avenue.

Faced with a city of wall-to-wall vehicles a sort of cockeyed spin on Coleridge's "Water, water everywhere but not a drop to drink" line comes winging into my mind and instantly morphs into a workable chant: "Cars, cars, everywhere, but where's my goddamn car?!?" I begin intoning, over and over, as I pedal ever upwards.

Hitting the apex of the bridge and leaning forward, I begin to build speed, arrowing downward, hitting speeds of thirty or more miles per hours before catching the green light and banking south onto 2nd Avenue. No sign of my stolen LeSabre ahead on the gentle downward slope of 2nd Avenue so randomly I bank a hard right onto 55th Street then go to manically pedaling west, hurtling through the teeming maze of early morning rush hour humanity.

My mind's buzzing like a thumped-up beehive, continually vectoring back off into sundry far-fetched narratives of me reclaiming my car. I'll see it and do this, I'll see it and do that, I'll see it then—WAIT! Suddenly here I am, nearing 5th Avenue—What? Damn! I'm getting so lost in my car-grabbing daydream that I'm not even looking for my damn car! Shit! I need to stop being a space cadet and get down to business here! Did I miss my chance? Did my car already pass by without me even noticing? Damn-damn-damn!

I pull over for a second and try to regroup. Instead of just randomly lashing out this way and that I figure maybe I should try to rationally consider the dynamics of this big sprawling city. So, where might a car thief be found? Hey, what about that skanky Times Square area, ground zero for porn theaters, live sex shows, nefarious throngs of hookers and thugs and dope dealers, grifters, cons, pimps and riff-raff of all shape and size? Of course—that's prime crime real estate! Home to all manner of low life and scruffy folk. And I'm in striking distance! Away I go!

I churn ahead westward, merging left into the center lanes as 7th and Broadway converge in the upper 40's, whipping my head left and right methodically, scanning the side streets for some telltale sign of that green and black tiger-striped LeSabre, my first grade teachers' sister's car.

"Cars cars everywhere, but where's my goddamn car?!?" The workable chant goes pin balling around in my mind, at times audibly escaping my lips.

As I hit the true convergence of 7th and Broadway at 45th I'm running out of pimp & crack head-riddled Times Square turf to search, so I whip my bike west on 42nd Street, sailing past the rows of sleazy porn theaters and abandoned buildings. Vast swaths of vehicles surround me in the densely packed morning rush hour traffic pattern, but there's nary a sign of mine. So what are my odds here? Just how needle in a haystack-y is this quest? One in a million? Ten million? At the corner of 8th and 42nd I stop again to regroup—I need to just calm down and breathe, try to think objectively; if my car's not with the sundry reprobates inhabiting Times Square then where else might it be?

Wait—a few weeks back on one of my walkabouts I saw what? The carcasses of countless vehicles stripped and abandoned over on the West Side Highway! It's a desolate, lawless no man's land over there—the perfect locality to ditch a stolen car! So to the West Side Highway I will ride! At a breakneck pace! Before myriad sleaze bag car strippers defile my first grade teachers' sister's LeSabre!

Crossing over 8th Avenue and passing the Port Authority I hit a nasty snarl of stalled, bumper-to-bumper Lincoln Tunnel traffic. But even with the swarm of vehicles around me frozen in utter gridlock, on I roll, breezing along down the narrow center corridor between the opposing lanes. I zip past idling taxis, Jersey drivers, shiny limos, battered delivery vans, etc. in my own personal bike lane and as I furiously pedal and build speed, at the top of my lungs I shout out that newfound chant, "Cars, cars, everywhere, but where's my goddamn car?!?"

I cross 9th Avenue, manically scanning the numberless sea of vehicles engulfing me: parked cars, moving cars, cars in driveways, cars on tow trucks, cars above in parking garages, below in sub-basements, cars ahead, cars behind, cars moving toward me, cars moving away. "Cars, cars everywhere, but where's my goddamn car?!?" This manic car-hunting energy surging through my being is almost too much to bear.

Mid head-jerk I glance up ahead at the intersection of 42nd Street and 10th Avenue. Maybe fifty yards off I spy an anachronistic green and black shape as it goes sailing through the intersection. Wait! HEY, THAT'S MY CAR!!—FUCK YES, IT'S MY CAR! There's no mistaking it! It's my first grade teachers' sister's green and black tiger-striped car! The LeSabre clears the tunnel traffic gridlock at the intersection of 10th Avenue and 42nd Street and grandly rumbles north toward Harlem, the Bronx, Canada, who knows where.

A redoubled jolt of supercharged adrenalin surges through my veins, hitting my eyeballs with such force that everything in my field of vision instantaneously goes blood red. Is "I was so mad I saw red" just a figure of speech? Apparently not.

Pumped on adrenaline, I'm suddenly rocketing along at an inconceivable speed, zipping madly between the gridlocked vehicles. I blow through the red light at the corner at 42nd and 10th, traveling at what must be upwards of thirty-five mph. Banking hard and low like a motocross rider power sliding through a big graded turn, I look northward, hoping to catch some glimpse of my car moving running with the green lights in the distance further up 10th Avenue, but, not, it's not moving up 10th Avenue. Why? Because this hapless fucking car thief caught the red light at 43rd Street! My first grade teachers' sister's car is sitting motionless RIGHT HERE!

But this fucking manic brain of mine! Even as I'm closing the distance between us, my brain is getting sidetracked, wondering why that particular stoplight happens to be red. It makes no sense. The uptown/downtown lights in Manhattan are synchronized, right? So that traffic light should be green. For him to have caught that light at 43rd and 10th means it's badly out of time, and as I close the distance between me and my car, my sidetrack prone mind takes a momentary excursion off into bizarre extrapolation territory: see, were the traffic light in synch, this piece-of-shit car thief would not be sitting at the red light, he'd be cruising up 10th Avenue blocks away and no matter how adrenalized I might be, with that uphill slope there ain't a snowball's chance in hell of me ever catching him. So what mysterious hand caused this traffic light to turn red prematurely? Hand of Trickster God? Baby Jesus? Random Chance? The Devil himself? Who organizes this type of shit?

Screeching up beside the driver's side door, for reasons totally unknown to me, I heave the bike upwards, like vertically into the air while shrieking in an ear-piercing wail. The bike arcs, gravity does its thing, whereupon said bike comes crashing dramatically down onto the hood of the LeSabre, surprising me almost as much as it does this fucking car thief.

Why did I do that???

The bike bounces in slow motion, settling on the hood. I need to focus on the formidable task at hand, but further extrapolations are dogging me. The temporospatial variables at play are dazzling. How did both this thief and I come to be in this exact place at this exact interval of time? The sequence of events that synchronized our union is beyond mind boggling, starting with the jaded cop, the girlfriend argument and subsequent pacing in the lawyer's swanky digs, the subway rides, the flat tire on the bike, the slog to the gas station, the traffic, the speed at which I pedaled, the moments I stopped to regroup, hell, omit any one of those variables, and this intersection doesn't happen.

But that's only half of the equation. What about him? If he'd done one simple act even slightly differently, we wouldn't meeting here at 43rd and 10th—him, me and my first grade teachers' sister's car. Do you see? There are limitless ways for us to fail to intersect and only one way for us to not fail, and yet here we are. The odds are mind boggling.

Before the bike's fully settled on the hood, like I did in my various daydreams, I lunge through the open driver's side window, violently seizing the shirt lapels of the small hispanic man at the wheel. I wrench my fingers into the fabric then yank wildly upwards, knowing that in one seamless motion this little man will come rocketing through the window of the car and commence to be rendered airborne. He'll go bouncing across the nearby sidewalk and wisely flee in terror of the psycho bike-flinging gringo.

Sadly, my storyline doesn't anticipate one all important detail: the thief unexpectedly is wearing his seat belt (well, technically my seat belt). So instead of being ejected from the car in one smooth economical movement, a tug of war ensues wherein the car thief, apparently thinking I'm some random bike-flinging passerby goofing on him, guffaws, blurting out, "Estop, Estop, okay, okay, Wait! No cosquillear me! Senior! No tickle!"

The traffic light goes green. Uptown traffic is starting to pile up behind the LeSabre. A symphony of horns arises, like some abstract jazz soundtrack—Miles Davis, help me get my car back!

Something about the thief's incongruous reply creates a rift in the real world proceedings. A roar is developing in my ears, like there's a jet plane or two taking off inside my brain. My surroundings are suddenly rendered in acute slow motion, like one of those movie scenes where the action is about to take an egregiously violent turn.

During this frozen microsecond of hyper-awareness my perceptive abilities expand exponentially as I methodically observe the following: a small master lock key is jammed in the ignition of the LeSabre. The serial number on the key reads 4736 which suggests a downward sequential pattern. There are minor scratches in the chrome around the ignition mechanism which leads me to surmise the car was not hot-wired, rather the ignition key mechanism possesses a design flaw which allows random keys inserted into it with enough force to engage it.

The man's apparel? Mexican cowboy oeuvre. Chiapas region? A ranch hand, definitely. Five-foot five, maybe a hundred-forty pounds. Tidy, but in need of a shave. That sickly sweet smell in the air? Aftershave? No. Ah, the drab stick of incense hanging out of the ash tray, still burning. Peaches? Peach incense? Stuck to the dashboard just above the ashtray is a yellow Post-It. Whatever's haphazardly scrawled on it in smudged pencil is obscured by the gear shift.

Via this series of non-sequiturs, the car reclamation narrative in my mind bifurcates, splitting into two simultaneous story lines. In Narrative One out the thief goes, in I climb, and I heroically retrieve my car. In Narrative Two, in horrifying slow motion, the compact, genial hispanic man, leans forward, reaches under the seat for that silver-plated snub nosed .38, levels it dead center at my chest, grins widely and pulls the trigger. I note the muzzle flash, the smell of sulfur and understand I'm hit, will possibly die, but as of yet feel no pain.

Why no pain? Where is the pain?

Thankfully, as disparate narrative threads pull tight, merging into "reality" I neither throw the car thief to the pavement nor get shot. Instead, the thief, who could simply press on the gas pedal and race away, inexplicably frees the latch on his seatbelt, swings his legs out, places his stylish gaucho boots on the pavement and graciously exits my first grade teachers' sister's car.

He's stout, muscular, weatherbeaten, standing a full head shorter than me. That goofy, beatific stillness in his gaze? Drugs? Supernatural forces? Sheer stupidity? A line from Sam Shepherd's Motel Chronicles leaps to the fore of my thoughts, "His eyes look like they've plowed a million acres."

I wait for him to flee, escape, do something but nothing happens. He smiles widely, calmly, then remarks, as if with genuine bonhomie. "Ees your car?"

"YES!!!! YES!!!" I spit out, "It's MY car!!!"

"Okay. Okay. Essa…a berry…berry nice car. Yes. This car. Berry nice." whereupon he pats the roof of the LeSabre lovingly. Then I watch in disbelief as he extends his hand to me. A handshake? Really? Okay. So I warily shake this man's hand as he repeats, "Ees a berry berry nice car."

The car horn crescendo is disrupted when some wiseguy in a passing delivery van shouts out the window, "It's Howdy fucking Doody time!" This is quickly followed by a good Samaritan calling, "Hey! Don't hit him!! Just call the cops!"

Cops? No-no. At this point, cops are the last thing I want. They're not part of this story, particularly since I got my car back and still am on the hook for all those unpaid parking tickets. So let's just leave the cops out of this if at all possible…

What I want is rapid event closure, but that can't happen until the little man disappears. I want my car back and I'm so close, but the little man, he's not cooperating. I lean forward and slowly, clearly, as if speaking to a small child, enunciate, "This is MY car! You stole it! You're in big trouble…." waiting for him to recoil and flee or fight me. But he does neither.

Vexed, I sputter out, "You should run away before the policemen come! Got it! Police? You understand? Policia?" But the words have zero effect on him. He doesn't run. He smiles serenely at me and that smile, I must admit, is slightly intoxicating.

Then our eyes truly meet. In deep into the foggy recesses of his uncrowded mind I detect an ancient clockworks, a massive assembly of huge, anachronistic cogs that sits motionless, frozen in time for epochs and ages. I understand that for this story to end well I must find some way to activate these cogs. So I loudly repeat the word "policia" to the man once, then twice more.

A moment passes, then I see it—a slight flicker of recognition in his dark, soulful eyes, and with that one massive ancient wheel moans, then creaks to life. Slowly…. tick…….tick……tick…..THUNK, the huge cognitive cog drops into place and the man clearly comprehends this thought; "policia".

His beatific smile wanes ever so slightly.

As I continue to repeat salient words to him a second ancient cog creaks to life, then lurches forward. Tick…….tick….. tick….THUNK, "Stolen car…" is registered, and his smile wanes ever so slightly more. We're building momentum here, so much so that now he's extrapolating on his own! Another cog engages, tick…tick….tick…THUNK, "That I am driving…" Tick….tick….tick…THUNK, "And this angry gringo, he says this fine car is his car…" Tick……tick……tick….THUNK, "..and he speaks of policia…"

His ancient internal reasoning machinery now fully engaged, the car thief's serene countenance slowly drifts in the direction of an expression of concern. Progress! In his own mysterious, obtuse way he's connecting dots: He's in a stolen car. The owner is here. The owner is angry. The police are being summoned. He must depart.

With that he bows slightly toward me, shakes my hand again, regards the LeSabre warmly once more and says, "Thanks you, muchacho. Yes. Ees…a berry berry nice car." With that he turns, waves genially to the crowd of passersby who've stopped to ogle the impending fight, slips his hands in his coat pockets, then casually strolls westward on 43rd, whistling a little mariachi tune as if he had not a care in the whole of the goddamn world.

I'm left momentarily hypnotized by his departure. Blaring car horns snap me out of the spell cast by the little man. We're firmly back to Narrative One here—the happy ending! I pinch myself just to make sure I'm not sloshing feverishly around in the lawyer's water bed, lost in yet another escapist dream. Ouch! Nope, this is actually happening;

my first grade teachers' sister's car sits idling before me. Drivers are honking, furious that this massive whale of a car is blocking traffic flow. I heft my crappy bike off the hood, heave it in the trunk, leap in the driver seat, slide that gearshift to D, hit the gas and away I rumble.

Two blocks north I catch a whiff of something sickly sweet burning, then remember the incense stick. I glance at it briefly then get a clear view of the writing on the Post-It. In crude scrawl it reads,

"The future sure looks peachy."

ENSLEY, FLORIDA, MAY 1998

Me and The Crazy Maker, we're what relationship experts refer to as "estranged". She's pregnant, working a grunt job at some insurance office over in Valdosta, wishing me dead no doubt after I dropped her off at her mother's house two months back and just kept rolling. I've quit cab driving for good and now am a destitute folk singer holed up in Ensley, Florida, a downtrodden outlier of the poorest urban area in the panhandle of Florida. Aside from meth and crack dealing, there ain't a goddamn thing going on in Ensley, Florida, so being a forty year-old unemployed, penniless failure with a kid on the way, my presence here sounds about right.

It's a childhood friend who took pity on me, offering shelter in the form of an abandoned house he owns a couple blocks east of Highway 29. Thankfully, the place had only been sitting empty a year or so, so there's still functional electricity, some furniture and indoor plumbing. But that's about it—no phone or TV or HVAC or laundry or cable or any such amenities. Some of the rooms are stripped down to bare studs, others are half sheet-rocked. I got no car presently so I might as well be living in a yert in Siberia.

Being nocturnal by disposition, most nights in Ensley I navigate that lonely, liminal zone between midnight and dawn sitting at the kitchen table typing out reams of song lyrics on an old Smith-Corona that I dug out of a dumpster up in New York right before I left, then wailing them out to the nowhere and nothing of the kitchen walls, the ceiling, the floor. The fare is grim, focusing mainly on romantic betrayals, murders, suicides and various forms of symbolic death. Some may call what I'm doing here folk music, but it's all just codified nihilist anthems wishing myself gone from this plane of existence.

But this particular evening there's no songwriting on the menu. On the kitchen table sits a letter from The Crazy Maker, delivered in the afternoon mail. As best as I can make out from her loopy, florid handwriting and elliptical logic she's lobbying for us to get back together, for the sake of this upcoming baby.

The only issue with that proposition is that she's bat-shit crazy, I'm bat-shit crazy and last time I checked bat-shit crazy squared does not equal a viable parenting configuration. The thought of a lifetime of psychic tussling with this woman over an innocent child sends my thoughts spiraling downward, plunging through zones of profound regret and self-hatred, triggering a bout of what health care professionals might rightly call implosive mania.

Letter read, down I sit at that typewriter, deciding it's high time I lay out in straight talk why two human beings as hopelessly fucked up as her and me got no business raising a child together. Fair is fair, right? So I start with myself. My appraisal goes as such: age forty, unemployed, history of serious depression, possible Narcissistic tendencies, hopelessly in debt, major issues with any and all authority figures. Basically, I'm an unstable, suicidal loner raging against my inevitably dismal fate.

It's a blunt unflattering appraisal but feels accurate enough. I figure showing candor about my own shortcomings entitles me free license to be equally frank on the flipside so I move on to detail her extensive list of crippling traits—such is the hapless, reductive nature of my thinking presently.

And so for hours now, I've been doggedly hammering away—typing draft after draft, ripping them to pieces, then starting over, ripping again, on and on. But just now some manner of word magic descended, delivering concise descriptors into place on these pages before me, and finally hard truths feel properly assayed.

Manic me reads and rereads the letter a dozen or more times, checking for typos and continuity lapses, grammar issues and other such what have yous. Finally I nod, deeming it an airtight masterpiece of positional lucidity and hard line statesmanship. With that the six-and-a-half-page single-spaced screed is folded, slipped into an envelope and laid on the kitchen table. First thing tomorrow this fucker goes in the mail.

With that psychic gauntlet run, it's coming up on two in the morning. After all that manic tip-tap-typing a deathly silence now settles over the already gloomy room. I'm just sitting here drumming my fingers, eyeing the envelope, as one might regard a nearby venomous snake or spider, or maybe some improvised explosive device that occasionally offers up a random tick.

Lately I've been way too wired to sleep, but that's to be expected, as sleep's a chore for me even under ideal conditions, which these clearly aren't. Younger me would seek refuge in a round of potent self-medication via pharmaceuticals/alcohol or some spicy cocktail of both, but thankfully those days are long gone, forever lost in the rearview of Life.

So here I am, resolutely trapped, both in this shabby, borrowed house in Ensley, Florida and, hell let's be honest, in Life in general. Overflowing with pent up psychic rage, when waves of implosive currents come surging forward into my consciousness, further into the shadows of Self I duck.

"It's bullshit like this that makes girls cut themselves," I hear myself say to the empty room, then agree with the sentiment, reckoning that when the split between physical and emotional realms grows too extreme a person just has to find a way to equalize the pressure somehow.

Typically when I'm troubled I don't cut myself, I walk—often for hours on end, mile after mile. But seeing how outside my door lies Ensley, Florida, at 2 am, walking's not an option. It's a high-risk proposition to stroll through the streets of Ensley, Florida in broad daylight much less at 2am. Take yourself a little ramble hereabouts and you'll see—if the dope fiend low-lifes don't waylay you, the roaming packs of stray pit bulls surely will. Since I got no transportation other than my feet, in this shabby domicile I am resolutely stranded.

Twenty, thirty minutes pass, cabin fever hitting harder and harder. I take to pacing around the kitchen like a caged animal, navigating a micro circuit from the stove to the side door and back again. Round and round I go, obsessive thoughts racing hither and yon, and every damn time I pass that kitchen table and lay eyes on that letter I just wrote I feel this growing sickness of mind and spirit overtaking me. That bible verse from Proverbs comes bopping into my head, "As a dog returns to his vomit, so a fool repeats his folly." I try to put it out of my head, but can't seem to shake that verse off so after another few laps, I go the way of the dog, snatching up the letter that I already know word for word, whereupon I commence rereading it over and over, again and again.

Round and round I go, pacing the kitchen circuit as I read. I know I should put these goddamn pages down and move on, know serious wires are getting crossed here and sparking in highly combustible cognitive processing centers, know that I'm only making things worse with every choice I make presently, but there's no brakes on this runaway train. A twenty-minute stretch passes, pacing and reading, reading and pacing, fuming all the while about this bullshit situation with The Crazy Maker, the reality of those dire descriptions sinking in further and further, searing a hole in my very soul. I'm striding past the stove when I pull up short—what was that? Is there something… or someone…?

Again, this is Ensley. One block east lies a row of crack houses, a block west a meth lab or two. Hell, my neighbor next door got busted for fucking his dog in the front yard in broad daylight. Bad things happen with great regularity hereabouts, so I go very hushed, listening, straining to isolate whatever snatches of information might avail themselves to my ears.

Though barely audible, I can tell what that faint sound is not: it's not voices, or the sound of rats gnawing inside the walls. Not the sound of a window being pried open with a crowbar. It's delicate yet steady. Melodic? What's big time worrisome is it appears to be emanating from somewhere inside the house, toward the back bedrooms.

Over on the counter lays a sizable butcher knife. I snatch that sucker up and take a few exploratory steps toward the rear hallway. Listening harder I make out rhythmic, almost…musical tones? Strains of some spooky melody? Shit. Did I unwittingly stumble into some cheap horror flick? Is it "cue the creepy clown figure to come leaping out of the shadows and decapitate the protagonist" time? A few more steps toward the darkened hallway the sound becomes more audible, until finally I identify it—it's a music box, playing somewhere there in the shadows. Damn. That stops me dead in my tracks, the hair on the back of my neck standing straight on end. Frankly, I'd have preferred the maniacal clown.

The Crazy Maker, she told me about this; how her long since deceased father speaks to her via randomly playing music boxes. She'll be alone in a room thinking of him when out of nowhere a music box somewhere nearby will kick on. I shrugged the story off when she first told me, figuring it was just more of her loony tunes rambling but no, here it is—the gentle notes of a music box wafting down the hallway. I stand frozen for a good long minute, figuring the best I can hope for here is that this is some form of hallucination.

But it isn't.

And bear in mind this place I'm staying, it's no crossroads type locale. This is an abandoned house out in the white trash sticks, one that's sat empty for the better part of a year prior to my arrival. The yard's overgrown with weeds, several blankets of decomposing oak and sycamore leaves covering the modest, untended flower beds. It's got that creepy, run-down look, the kind of house little kids fret about, steer wide of when they go walking past on the way to school.

I step forward, hesitantly picking my way down the low, narrow hallway past a series of pint-sized bedrooms following the daisy chain of musical chimes. The hall light's conveniently burned out and as I venture further into the shadows I feel what can best be described as stone-cold existential dread. Eventually in that last bedroom, I flip on the light and find it, tucked behind a baseball trophy on a dresser, one of those little heart-shaped, fake-gold ballerina deals.

Hell, all the weeks I've been staying here and not once did that thing chime or ping or in any way make its presence known, yet the moment I pick up that letter and start fretting about what's in it, there it goes, gently spinning as a herky-jerky version of Fur Elise leaks out of it. I stare slack jawed, the notes lifting, rising up into my ear canals, reverberating inward, straight to the very core of my being. Someone's trying to get my attention, but who? And to what end?

I pluck the music box up off the dresser top, studying it as the final halting notes filter out, the covering of dust confirming nobody's tinkered with this thing in a good long while. The room goes silent as the spring winds out. A life of stranger truths, indeed. This bad creeping physical paralysis starts overtaking me, my brain spins wildly, struggling to puzzle out what in the high holy hell just happened.

Time passes, maybe it's ten seconds, maybe ten minutes—I can't exactly say, as I've lost track. In the distance, even miles off I detect murmurings of life heretofore beyond the reach of my senses; crickets and tree frogs, distant dogs barking, big rigs downshifting out on Highway 29, the dull thud of moths throwing themselves at the kitchen windows, salutations called out between unknown passersby. Spooked, I beat a hasty retreat back to the lighted part of the house.

I've still got nowhere to go, so down I sit, back at that selfsame table where I've spent the last hours madly typing away. The dog returneth to his vomit, does he not? Suddenly every goddamn thing around me feels booby-trapped; the typewriter, the chair, the envelope, that pernicious letter, still clutched in my hand. One wrong move and—boom—some world or other goes up in flames.

It's no big mystery as to the locus of negativity here—it's this damn letter. It just hums with bad juju and since I'm the one who wrote it, well, that makes me the author of bad energy, right? Shit and shit again. I sit there a while, trying to conjure up enough humility to accept this revelation for what it is; the Universe has spoken, and it's none too pleased with me.

Okay, so I've been warned. Only a dumbass would send that masterpiece of solipsistic posturing now. So what do I do with it? I can't trust myself to just throw it in the garbage for fear out of vanity I'll just drag it out an hour later and mail it anyway. I do dumb shit like that all the time. No, it needs to be gone from the world of objects in time and space—and the sooner the better—so I grab a can of lighter fluid, step out on the driveway, douse it and all the previous drafts and set these talismans of wrongness ablaze. It takes all of a scant few seconds for the evidence of those anguished hours of configuring to vanish forever and feels like some parable of the physics of existence; destruction arrives hard and fast, whereas construction requires slow incremental time and abiding, abiding and time, on and on.

It's getting on past three in the morning. As the last flames nick and pop at the remnants of the pages, I hear a passing pulpwood train bound for that big paper mill some miles up the road. The horn wails in the distant night, timeless and forlorn, and, triggered by that archetypal nocturnal howl, my mind takes flight. Sounds mingle in alchemic ways as a trippy vision of transfiguration takes shape in my mind's eye.

I watch the remnant smoke trails of these combusted pages rise heavenward, drifting northbound, shedding along the way any vestige of woe my hands etched upon them. Once fully purged of my tainting hand, gently they'll go wafting back to earth, scattering over the pine logs stacked on those sundry lumber cars now come to rest on a side rail up in the mill yard miles to the north. Come morning said logs will be off-loaded then pulped and pressed, shaped and reshaped, refined, soaked and bleached over and over until no vestige of past form remains, until any and all disparate elements are merged into a seamless whole in the form of one those massive virginal rolls of blank paper. The thought sets my heart to aching, wishing some similar form of cathartic remaking for my tormented soul.

Lost in a half trance, eyes closed, ears wide open, I just stand there, a passive attendant, as diverse sonic atmospheres wash over me. Finally the airwaves clear, and when no further evidence of letter, fire or train remains I shuffle back into the house, slump down at the kitchen table, sigh, lay hands on the Smith Corona and, chastened by my communion with that ghostly music box, slip a blank sheet of paper in the roller and set to typing anew.

3am I'm awakened by a sweet summer rain
Distant howling of a passing, southbound coal trail…
Was I dreaming, or was there someone just lying here
Beside me in this bed…
Am I hearing things or in the next room
Did a long forgotten music box just start playing?

NEW YORK CITY, MARCH, 1987

Lord, I'm a ragged hem. Another grueling taxi shift behind me I'm skittishly biking home through the wilds of Alphabet City, down on the Lower East Side of Manhattan. It's the early hours of March 9th, which happens to be my thirtieth birthday.

The streets are desolate, spooky-empty, which makes me all the more a target for the ones lying in wait. Typically, there's no shortage of lurkers in the war zone known as Alphabet City. And here I come riding along, flush with a good night's pay in my pocket, maybe two hundred hard-fought bucks, which makes me a bright neon target to the legion of desperate souls hereabouts in dire straits, shy of drug drop money.

A block away lies the relative safety of the tenement where I've been staying these last few months. It's a cramped one-bedroom place, made all the smaller and more claustrophobic by the crappy sheet-rock partition I built to separate the former living room from the kitchen. I sleep on a foldout couch in said sheet-rocked space, paying four hundred bucks a month for the privilege.

My roommate, it's her place so she takes the spacious bedroom. A sweet-tempered college girl who dreams of becoming a film auteur, she hails from a wealthy Connecticut family. She's talented but the competition is pretty stiff over there at NYU, where we both study, and frankly she's not flying at that manic juggernaut level you gotta sail at to be successful in the movies racket.

NYU's how we met; a few months back I conned my way into that pricey institution of higher learning, wrangling a partial scholarship gleaned from a fairly extensive con I perpetrated on the Dean of the school. He bit on the bait I threw out which was both cool and surprising, but now I'm having to produce work that backs up my pie in the sky claims, and this while driving a yellow cab full time to cover rent and food and the hefty chunk of remaining tuition. So I'm worn fairly thin. It's like my buddy The Count says when the going gets tough, "This ain't no hill for stepping!" He'll cheerfully announce—although juggling work and school feels less like a hill and more like the backside of K2 I'm scaling…in a pair of recently greased roller skates.

I do a quick scan of the vicinity, circle once then come charging up onto the sidewalk adjacent the building doorway. This is the sitting duck portion of my transition, so I hastily secure my bike to the banister railing via a Kryptonite lock and scuttle through the double security doors into the building, safe at last. Up the staircase I charge, navigating the various dead bolts with a practiced hand and then I tiptoe into my little cubicle.

Ah, I will not be robbed tonight.

I can hear my roommate snoring softly in the next room. It occurs to me she may be pocketing the rent I'm paying her without telling her dad, who covers her exorbitant college expenses, but who cares? I damn sure don't. I got zero credit and couldn't land an apartment anywhere in New York, much less in Manhattan, so to me it's a win-win type of deal, at least for the time being.

It's not the Ritz or anything. We live in a tenement on the boundary between a recently gentrified area and a stretch of lawless turf overrun with gang activity and dope addict muggers. It's mostly Puerto Ricans here, with a scattering of anglos; a few artist/hipster/insurgent types—we're the front line gentrification force.

Opposite us on the third floor lives this sweet, frail little hermit man by the name of Smolynsky. He's damn near a hundred years old and it's said he's been in that same apartment since the mid-nineteen thirties, when the Ukrainians ruled this area—so, fifty plus years. Once or twice a week, he emerges into the darkened hallway, comes tap-tap-tapping on our door with his milk bottle glasses and bristly, skeletal, unshaved face, asking sweetly will I do this or that for him, which I do. Buttermilk from the corner bodega. Crutch tips from the drug store. That sort of thing.

I fold out the couch and set my night's take on the table then just sit there admiring it. Up until the last fare tonight was your typical bust-ass interval of white-knuckle vehicular mayhem, aptly tagged the "graveyard shift". With the stock market boom going hard and heavy, fares are plenteous but traffic has been pure hell—it's always something. I spent most of the night hauling cocky stockbrokers and insufferable plutocrats from offices in midtown and wall street up to the highbrow real estate zones; Park Avenue, Madison Avenue, York Avenue, Fifth Avenue, West and East End Avenue—all those avenues where the upper class scions exult in their wealth and power.

The well-to-dos constitute the majority of my fares, but Lord, them fuckers bore me to tears. I get to hungering for a change of pace in the grind of the people conveyance trade but then when it comes along sometimes it's more than I bargained for.

Case in point: that last fare tonight. It was just past one AM, a spitting rain coming down, so lots of hands in the air everywhere. I'd just dropped a fare on Columbus Avenue up in the seventies—a booming, upscale neighborhood—and rolled a few feet ahead when out from between two parked cars stepped a couple hundred pounds of blinged-out, ghetto-strutting, gold-toothed criminality. He flagged me down then casually lowered his big frame into the back seat and real matter-of-factly announced he was going to a housing project way the fuck out in the south end of Coney Island. Right away, major alarm bells went off. Shit. Even in broad daylight, that stretch of Coney Island is a no-go zone due to the high crime and homicide rate there. My instincts were screaming no, no, no—bad idea. You'll end up the recipient of an early birthday present in the form of a slug from a Mac 10 to the back of the head.

We sat there, quiet for a second as I worked over the proposition. A sketchy fare to a hell-hole neighborhood in the small rainy hours of the deep dark night. Proceeding would be a categorically wrong-headed thing to do, but here's the deal; for a year or so now I've been slowly edging my way toward this contrary philosophy of Life. It was prompted by the realization that all along in that wholesome, devoutly religious lifestyle I'd lead prior to coming up to New York, even while desperately aiming for what was right, I always made a complete fucking mess of everything I touched.

So, if trying to do right leads you to wrong, maybe try the opposite and see what happens? Like just right off the bat aiming for wrong. Like maybe by aiming for wrong somehow I'll backdoor my way to right. That's the crackpot theoretical model I've been eyeing, and so I figured this was as good a chance as any to test it out. Talk is cheap, right?

So I threw the meter and as we eased out into Columbus Avenue traffic headed south toward the wilds of Brooklyn gangster man, he chuckled, then, slightly puzzled, murmured, "So we going? No questions asked? No up front money?" I confirmed that, adding everybody's to get home somehow, to which he replied, "True. But for some home is further than others."

Hmmmm. Unexpected reply.

I needed to size him up before the end of the ride, parked on some shadowy side street in Coney Island, so I jumped into small talk mode. Turns out he'd hailed about ten cabs before me and they'd all refused to take him because his acutely wrong looking self was going to the most terrifying corner of Coney Island. And, by saying he looked wrong, I don't mean he looked black, I mean he looked like a criminal. He moved like a criminal. He emanated foundational criminality.

And why was that? Because he was a criminal.

This was confirmed when I asked him if he knew Coney Island well, because where he was going was gang territory. He chuckled softly, saying "Shit man. That my turf. I own Coney Island. Nobody mess with me there. He be a dead man he do." With that he matter of factly explained that he ran a major drug operation out of a project there. At twenty six years of age, he was a multi-millionaire fresh out of prison, this after his team of hi-octane lawyers got his recent murder conviction overturned. He'd been out celebrating.

Comforting, right? Strangely, I found his candor refreshing.

Even in light traffic it's a hellacious slog to Coney Island—maybe a forty-minute ride—so how often do you get to shoot the shit with a drug lord? I quizzed him about this and that; his time in Rikers and later up in Sing Sing, the disposition of God and notions of Grace, sorrows of the heart, family…shit like that. He kept circling disparate threads around to the subject of chess, talking up this philosophy he'd developed while playing chess with the Muslim lifers in prison.

His ideas resonated strangely, his language and delivery were intrinsically musical, like great jazz; elusive, seductive, nigh unto mesmerizing at times. Despite his worrisome appearance and downright deadly profession, it was indisputable that an eloquent poetry emanated from this man, in his every word, his every gesture. Clearly, he was tapping into something powerful and at a certain point I don't know what got into me, but I got mad at something he said about his work and commenced to scold him for being a drug dealer. I told him he'd been given a gift with his ability to think and speak so beautifully and that he needed to use that gift to make things better not worse.

He went quiet, then said, "That may be true. That may. I been thinking on that too." Then he put his big meaty hand through the open partition and told me his name; "Molock" he said, "Just Molock. You come to Coney Island, you tell anyone you know Molock, they leave you be." And with that we shook on his assertion.

Fucked up as his life was, Molock was definitely connected to some essential life force. I hated to admit it but drug dealing and murder aside, I found him to be a deeply compelling human being. The feeling seemed mutual too. So much so that at the end of the journey, after navigating the maze of blighted streets in that urban wasteland, as we came easing up to a grim project, the arched entranceway guarded by six or so menacing young hooded gangsta types who snapped to when they spied my passenger, we just sat there talking for a few minutes. Then Molock went so far as to invite me to park the cab, come up to his penthouse apartment, meet his posse and girlfriend and have a drink in honor of my birthday and his prison release. "You be safe here. Nobody mess with you. Come on up." Interesting proposition—if I say no, will Molock be offended and execute me there in front of his posse? Definitely in the realm of possibilities.

The offer felt authentic, you know, not like some set-up or something. I weighed the variables, and despite the threat of dissing Molock on his home turf, I politely passed. He nodded, saying that was cool, he understood. Then he thanked me for the ride and good conversation and tossed me a fifty on top of the twenty seven bucks for the fare. As he was leveraging his big frame out of the cab, I reminded him about that gift he had and how he needed to start using it right. He laughed and said, "Might just be I will." And away he lumbered, his crew nervously circling around him as he entered the building.

I hit the gas, rolling the red lights in that neighborhood, knowing a yellow cab thereabouts is a screaming advertisement for highwaymen toting Uzis and Glocks and Street-sweepers and such. I found my on-ramp and jetted onto the Belt Parkway arrowing back into the city then dropping the cab off at the 21st Street fleet garage. By then it was around two forty-five, just a few minutes shy of my due time. I hopped on my bike to ride home, pockets bulging with cash, a big chunk of it blood money courtesy of a dope dealer named Molock. Life gets complicated, does it not?

Safe inside my little slum, while brushing my teeth I get to wondering about Molock and what will become of him. What future does a human being thusly configured have? Sooner or later down he'll go down, be it via local cops, the feds, a rival drug lord or his own people and that gift will vanish forever. That's just how things play out.

Leaving the bathroom, I notice a faint, mysterious odor seeping from the air vent over the mirror. I puzzle over it for a second or two, that sour, musty smell, but I'm beat so into my rickety fold out couch bed I go crawling, hoping to see the sandman before the sun rises.

Mid-flight through my typical jumble of dreams I hear something wrong, something alarming. Bang-bang-bang-bang! What the fuck is that? I wrench my eyes open. Bang-bang-bang, shit, someone's at the door. It's light out. I check my bedside clock—Jesus! It's only a little after seven AM. Who the fuck is pounding on my door at this hour? I drag my ass out of bed, sling the door open and there stands Balzora, the creepy old Romanian super of the building, looking pissed as usual.

What a piece of shit Balzora is. Except for the freaky contradiction of his trademark workman's overalls, he's the spitting image of Count Dracula, generating all the warmth and charm of that legendary bloodsucker. He's Romanian or Bulgarian and with his heavy accent grunts something about needing to use my phone. He barges in without being asked, picks up the receiver before I can tell him to go fuck himself, use his own damn phone. He dials then asks for Jakobsen, the slumlord who owns the building. Okay, this peaks my interest. He wouldn't be calling Jacobsen at this hour unless something serious is going down. Balzora's cleaning dirt from under his fingernail a moment later when the big boss hops on the line.

"Mr. Jakobsen," Balzora mumbles. "Yeah. Okay, so Smolynsky, 3A. Dead." He goes silent for a moment, then puts on this bored, condescending tone adding, "What I mean? What I tell you—Smolynsky, dead…like kaput. Like, stink up the building. Yeah, Smolynsky. 3A. Three, maybe four days. So what I do, call cops? Or you come see…?"

Jakobsen barks something at Balzora. I'm guessing he's none too pleased about being bothered with incidentals like the death of a tenant at this inconvenient hour. Balzora shrugs at the phone and hangs up, shrugs at me again then departs.

A few moments later here comes the cops banging on the door downstairs, no doubt summoned by slumlord Jakobsen, who in the intervening seconds surely realized that the sooner Smolynsky's body is gone, the sooner he can jack up the rent on that one bedroom rent stabilized apartment and buy himself another slime covered million-dollar Armani suit.

Paramedics arrive. More cops too, then the morgue truck.

Poor old helpless Smolynsky; he apparently died alone some days ago, a natural death they're saying, as if death can be viewed as anything remotely natural. The stench in the hallway's bad enough, but inside his apartment it'll about knock you down. Posthaste they heft my elderly friend's body, light as a feather, into a black zippered bag, hustle him down the narrow stairway and plop him in the back of the waiting coroner's wagon.

And away they go. So long, Smolynsky.

It's maybe twenty minutes later when I hear a commotion outside. I crack open the door and see a puzzling contingent of supervisor types milling around, followed in short order by several agents in blue wind-breakers with the word REVENUE printed on their backs. A protocol develops wherein each arriving person wraps a handkerchief around his lower face, bandit style. Then, courtesy of one veteran cop who had the foresight to bring along a jar of Vicks Vapo-Rub, a dab is smeared on the bandana between the upper lip and nose to neutralize the death stench.

Lastly comes two bespectacled men in tweed suits, one sporting an actual bow tie. They gotta be professors or academics of some kind and might as well be a couple of little green Martians crashing a Pentecostal healing service. It takes me a second the shake off the mental image of ET at the altar getting prayed over by a gaggle of tongues-speaking deacons and elders, but then I get to wondering who the hell are all these bozos?

So I ask around. According to the one cop who'll actually talk to me, Smolynsky's left no will, has no heirs, and most likely will be buried in an unmarked paupers grave over on one of those spooky little islands in the East River. So why all the fuss with the suits and revenue agents?

It turns out that sweet, withered, run-down raggedy-ass old Smolynsky, a lifer in the violin repair trade, is the unlikely owner of some valuable property: Stradivarius violins. One's on loan to a museum, and they suspect he's got another one right here in his apartment.

After some preliminary digging the revenue team finds an old case stashed under the very bed where the old man died. Carefully they maneuver the ancient object out from under the sagging springs, handing it off to the two professor types, who it turns out are musical instrument experts from some highbrow auction house like Sothebys.

They reverently open the case then set to studying the fiddle with scholarly care and restraint. There's some whispered discussion, then, as they began grinning and slapping each other on the back I gather they've determined it's the real deal. Big score for the city, but I can't help but think about poor old Smolynsky living in poverty all those years then being dropped into that cold March earth in some unmarked pauper's grave. Such are the ironies of life, though—anyone can tell you that.

Seeing how they showed up so quick on the scene, I'm figuring those revenue boys must have had their eye on Smolynsky for some time now. Probably they were just waiting for him to keel over so they could turn his place inside out looking for more magical mystical musical instruments. One of the scholars depart, bearing the violin found under the bed.

The revenue agents and remaining scholar begin, piece by piece, to dismantle everything in that place, I guess looking for more pricelesss violins. It's no small task, let me tell you. That apartment may be small—it's a mirror image of the one bedroom deal like ours–but it's crammed, and I mean like hoarder style C-R-A-M-M-E-D, wall to wall, floor to ceiling with piles and piles of moldering junk.

Having never seen the inside of his place before, I'm saddened by what's revealed from my view through the open doorway. There's a narrow trail leading from the front door to the bathroom and kitchenette, there's the decrepit, sheetless cot he slept on in the equivalent of my living room space—where Balzora found him lying dead this morning. Aside from a few central pathways the remaining space is a nightmare of clutter, featuring stacks and stacks of boxes and suitcases and trunks all overflowing with a dazzling array of junk, the majority being damaged stringed instruments of every shape and form.

It's not just instruments either. The bandit-faced revenue buzzards unearth one oddity after another. Here's a steamer trunk stuffed full of theater costumes and another with twenty extravagant Baroque style wigs. There's a twelve-piece serving set of English stoneware, and, look, to everyone's surprise, it's an altimeter from a 50's era jet plane. These curiosities are quickly tossed aside though, for, like grim pearl hunters combing through a pile of oysters for their prize, these boys got one thing on their minds—high dollar fiddles.

To that end, they tump over this pile of moldy old newspapers and lo and behold, here's a violin. The remaining expert sets to examining it, then in another pile of cardboard boxes they find mandolins and balalaikas. Each instrument is carefully scrutinized first by the revenue guys then the expert, who shines his penlight into the sound-holes in the body to read the makers label. The discard pile grows and grows, like some cockamamie Auschwitz death pit for stringed instruments. In the end that one violin they found under his bed early on is the only manna to come floating down from the priceless artifact heavens.

I'm leaning in my doorway, watching the revenue team pack up their stuff when here comes the postman ambling up the stairs, looking puzzled by the spectacle. I sadly report on Smolynsky's death. The postman shrugs, probably relieved to have one less drop on his route. He hands me a yellow slip, one of those notifications you get in New York City when someone mails you something bigger than a can of cat food, and tells me I got a package waiting over at the main post office on 14th Street. I smile—it's my thirtieth birthday, and someone, somewhere has remembered. After the grueling graveyard shift, no sleep, then the death of my friend, it seems only fitting that some little blessing should come my way.

But wait. I check the zip code of the sender and right away I know that whatever it is, this damn sure ain't no blessing. See, it's from Tulsa, and I know but one sorry soul in Tulsa, and that's this distant cousin of mine. I met him face to face only once, when I was maybe thirteen and in my full-blown hoodlum phase. He was two years older than me and had come down to the Florida Panhandle for a visit one fall. It was a Friday night so we ended up attending a high school football game. We got bored, so my cousin drummed up the bright idea of getting us some drinking money by stealing a purse. He'd bragged on how easy it was, how they did it all the time at football games back home in Oklahoma.

He laid out the plan, which seemed viable enough, so after half-time, as the game tension ramped up, him and me snuck under the bleachers, spied some poor lady who'd laid her handbag at her feet, then waited for a big play. When everyone went to jumping up and down and cheering, he snatched the purse and off we sprinted, breakneck pace.

It would have played out fine for us but for the fact that my cousin is a natural-born-fuck-up. While jumping the chain link fence back behind the bleachers, his sweatshirt got hung and down he went, ass over elbow, landing hard and breaking his wrist. We still managed to get away, but he was hurting too bad for us to have any fun.

There was all of four dollars in the purse so we ditched it and schlepped back to my house, where I solemnly informed my mom and aunt that me and this cousin were out climbing apple trees or some such wholesome bullshit story. Off to the hospital they raced. I never let on to anyone about how his arm really got broke and as such I guess my cousin felt beholden to me.

Now grown, he's your basic loser (in fact, that's what I've taken to calling him in my mind, "Cousin Loser") doing a life sentence as a security guard out there in God's country, combing his wispy mustache with his fat fingers, riding around a mall at night in a golf cart, checking doors and windows and such. Every couple of years on my birthday, even though we got nothing in common but a poorly executed teenage crime, Cousin Loser sends me some deeply confused article of clothing, like a polyester sweater with a Leroy Neiman painting on the front of it, or a flimsy plastic jacket with tandem zippers in the elbows for some god-forsakenly unknown reason.

Cousin Loser is a bonafide bottom feeder in the fashion food chain and what's worse, invariably, at some truly inopportune moment, months down the line, he'll call on the phone, all creepy-voiced and breathing too hard into the receiver, asking did I like the gift he sent. I don't know why I lie and thank him for his kindness, but I do, which of course just sets the wheels in motion for the horror-garment cycle to begin anew.

The gifts puzzle the hell out of me—I mean, what's the bottom line here? Is he simply grateful for my complicity in what was possibly the highlight of his miserably dull teenage rebellion years? Is it a payoff for my continued silence? Is this just the milk of human kindness at play? Or is it something more overtly pathetic, like maybe he's wanting to play Fashion God with me and remake me in his own flawed image? Who knows. I've written Cousin Loser's gift cycle off as one of Life's unsolvable mysteries and so whenever one of these packages arrives I tend to regard it as such, like a hideous question mark.

But here's what galls me most about it; over the years I've opened package after package, winced, then hung whatever manifestation of bad taste that's caught his fancy in my closet, whereupon every damn time thereafter that I catch a glimpse of the offending article I wince again and then feel guilty for not wearing it. So what exactly is wrong with me? Why I don't just throw the damn things out soon as I get them I cannot say. But I don't. I keep them for years. It rankles me when I know I'm justified in doing something, know I have every right to do it, but still I don't. Why is that? Sometimes I get this feeling like unseen forces are twisting my arm to do their abstruse bidding.

So here lays Cousin Loser's zip code before my wincing eyes. Seeing it scrawled on the yellow slip makes me want to just cuss out loud because I thought I'd finally given that fucker the slip when I moved up here. I abandoned the bulk of my belongings when I fled north in the big LeSabre so for the first time in years my closet is free of the pox of his misguided good intentions.

"Jesus, first Smolynsky dies, now Cousin Loser finds me…" I think to myself." Is this a bullshit way to start your birthday or what?" I envision the whole ugly-fied fashion cycle starting up again in my minds eye; the closet filling up, the wincing and the recriminations, the guilt and wondering why I tolerate such incarnations of bullshit in the first place.

But you know what? Why not just say fuck it? Why not just leave the package at the post office until it gets sent back? Let the USPS deal with it. That's my knee jerk inclination. But it's only a fleeting impulse. I realize I'm alone in the world and it's my birthday, so this may be my only shot at a gift today. Jesus, that's depressing. I lay the yellow slip on the counter, muttering all the while, aiming to go back to sleep.

It's hours later, still no dice on the sleep front—with all the cops and commotion my brain's running full speed so I get back up and feed myself, wash the dishes, fold up the couch. A couple of times during my morning rituals I spy that damn yellow slip sitting there on the counter, like some dog turd stinking up the room.

Finally, I cave. Throwing on a coat, I go trudging west on 5th Street up to Avenue A, Cousin Loser's yellow slip in my pocket. Why I'm headed for the post office I have no idea. I know nothing good awaits me there. Twice I stop and stare at the yellow slip, pissed at myself for perpetuating this idiocy. I get mad and turn around, taking a few steps in the direction of home, but it's weird, both times it's like some physical force spins me back the other way and on I go. Again I'm hit with this weird sensation like I'm being guided by mysterious unseen forces.

Or is it Unseen Forces? Like official ones, like the ones who helped me get the LeSabre back?

Headed up Avenue A I remind myself why I've fled the South and come to New York City. It's all about trying to shake free of the suffocating inertia of hardcore Christianity that was slowly, incrementally strangling me to death back home. It's no small feat giving the Gordian Knot of Jesus Christ the slip, lemme tell you, especially if you're sensitive to the movements of Spirit, like I've always been.

Step one in the undoing process is to learn to eschew stale religious reflexes and consider the more enigmatic shapes that lay half hidden in Life's mysterious shadows. It's confusing though because, free of Christian causal thinking, it's a chore laying hands on a viable framework to process what those Unseen Forces are steering you toward. With no devil, no angels, no demons, no prayer, just abstract esoteric energy fields to consider, you simply wander forth, forever hoping you're on course, following whatever bread crumb trail of Grace is laid out so as to hopefully be in the right place at the right time.

To complicate matters, the rules of engagement for Life's trials and tribulations appear to be completely fluid. There's no static blueprint for doing things right, what works one time doesn't the next, so experience appears to be fairly superfluous. Successful navigation boils down to a case-by-case kind of approach, a feel-thing, like I did last night with Molock. I knew I shouldn't take him, but I did anyway, because on some molecular level it worked.

When I've broached this subject with select passengers in the cab, invariably they go off half-cocked saying I should just trust my instincts, like instincts are infallible, but what do they know? Not much in regards to weird metaphysical shit. They clearly don't know that working out which feelings are authentically connected to larger, more integral structures and which are just free-floating brain-generated holograms, that is the real chore in Life. At the end of the discussion, everything circles back around the notion of surrendering, and not just surrendering blindly—surrendering with eyes wide open. It's harder than it sounds, especially when a package from Cousin Loser sits dead center in the mix.

The main post office over on 14th Street is the usual juggernaut of efficiency. I endure the customary maze of battered velvet ropes for nigh unto forty minutes before handing the clerk my slip, all the while cussing myself for this fool's errand. He regards it obtusely, then shuffles off, disappearing for a long time, leaving me standing there alone at the window absently regarding row upon row of boxes waiting to be claimed.

So many lives, so many boxes, so many trajectories!

Finally he returns, sliding my package across the worn marble counter. I see Cousin Loser's return address on it and just kind of freeze up. The proportions of the package suggest one of those fancy department store shirt boxes. I guess I get kind of lost in my mind envisioning the horrors awaiting me within, because eventually the clerk clears his throat and says, "Hey…buddy. Wake up. Sign here." So sign I do, then off I go, package in hand.

Sitting just to the left of the main doors is your basic blue plastic rectangular garbage can. I stop, stepping out of the flow of foot traffic and stare at it for a moment. Coincidentally, the slot in the garbage can is exactly the same size and shape as the box in my hands. The similarity of form creates an impression of shared purpose, so reflexively I place the unopened box into the mouth of the garbage can. It's a perfect fit, so I slide it about halfway in before something stops me. Unseen Forces, is that you? Or is the impulse to not jettison the unopened box a product of my mind's resistance to said entities? And, really, what the hell do I really know about these Unseen Forces anyway; are they benevolent? Malevolent? Some combination of both? Neither?

I let Cousin Loser's box hang on the lip of the postal garbage can for a moment, frozen in time, half in my sphere of influence, half out. To drop the unopened package into the can seems like such a concise, perfectly logical solution. One carefully placed thrust of the arm and I'll be rid of this burden—I could just wash my hands of it, like Mister Pontius Pilate did with poor old doomed Jesus. But instead of pushing the unopened box all the way in, I find myself pulling it out.

Sigh.

Then, as if those pesky Unseen Forces are shoving me from behind, out I go, staggering into the blinding sunlight onto 14th Street, blinking like the village idiot, still in possession of Cousin Loser's unopened birthday package.

The sidewalk is a typical maelstrom of urban humanity. Confused, and pissed at myself, I take a few steps in the direction of home before just ahead spying a familiar form; orange wire mesh cylinder of a New York City garbage can. I aim for it, extending the package in my arms until it hangs precipitously over the mouth of this second garbage can, but when the critical moment arrives, once again my damn hand won't cooperate and drop the box.

Puzzled, I walk on, watching as a black cloud of curiosity begins to well up in the sky of my mind. What exactly is inside this box that the Unseen Forces want me to see so badly? Could it be something important, something other than what my prejudiced mind and experience is telling me? Maybe a hidden treasure akin to that priceless violin they'd found in Smolynsky's squalid apartment? Or something like Molock's fifty dollar tip last night? Maybe this whole sequence of apparently random events is part of some larger design? Is that the lesson here? That sometimes what initially appears to be a curse can in time be transformed into a blessing?

Sadly, there's only one way to find out—open the damn box. I sit myself down in a doorway stoop on Avenue A, take a big deep breath and, handling it gingerly as if were booby trapped, set to unwrapping the package. Peeling back the beige postal paper cover, not only does it not explode, but beneath the drab exterior lies a strangely luminous orange wrapping, all glittery and metallic with a pattern of little diamonds, like the scales on a snake. The bow's a bright sunflower yellow hue and looks to be made of some fine silk.

This is a paradigm shift. Cousin Loser's never before bothered to wrap any of the other gifts he's sent me. A sliver of hope worms its way into my mind, like a slender ray of sunshine penetrating some bleak, subterranean prison cell. Clawing away the last of the brown paper and beholding the package in full, I have to admit that this is, without question, the most beautifully wrapped package I've ever laid eyes on.

I hold it out at arm's length to admire the colors. When viewed all together, they seem to pulse and glow, as if generated by some internal light source. A couple of hipster girls strolling past take notice. "Oooooh, trippy!" says the one with the spray painted leather jacket. I get a big thumbs up from the other one with the close-cropped florescent pink hair. "Rad," she murmurs. The box apparently is generating some form of hipster gravitational field. Interesting!

Carefully peeling away the scotch tape bindings on the bottom so as to not damage the gorgeous paper, I slip loose the shiny outer wrapping. Beneath it lies not the flimsy white cardboard box that most dress shirts come in, but rather a faux antique-looking box of a brilliant aquamarine color embossed with a border of golden filagrees around the edges. Lovely!

I gently tug loose the lid, setting it carefully on the stoop beside me. Inside the box, the mysterious gift still lays hidden, concealed beneath layers upon layers of diaphanous tissue paper, sheets of pale yellow sandwiched between blues and dreamy pastel greens.

By now I'm so taken by the neon beauty of the wrappings that I half expect whatever's hidden there beneath that paper to levitate out and fly around my head like some goddamn magical bird of paradise. I hold my breath, digging down through the tissue, ferreting out the garment within. Lifting it, I behold in full the gift Cousin Loser has sent. Clearly, he's outdone himself this time, for in my two trembling hands I hold what has to be the world's ugliest shirt.

To set the record straight, to call this shirt ugly is a criminal injustice to the word ugly. This is a graphic design train wreck of colossal proportions; pink and purple and green and brown checks, cross-hatched in a bold irregular patten grid with a right little, tight little button-down collar that screams out a banal conservative middle-class American conformist mindset. Even worse, stenciled on the pocket is that idiotic symbol of half-assed romanticism, a unicorn (baby blue!) which pretty much seals the deal—this is the world's ugliest shirt.

I stare in disbelief, wondering how something so utterly wrong could have emerged from such a dazzlingly beautiful box. But that's life, isn't it? Lots of pretty packages, and yet all too often the prettier the wrapping, the uglier the gift (see my file on certain ex-girlfriends). Maybe this is what the Unseen Forces are trying to teach me? It's becoming quite the chore keeping up with all the possibilities!

Despite the utterly repellant appearance of this object, I can't take my eyes off it. It has a sort of mesmerizing quality, so much so that I get lost in a sort of trance, like I do sometimes. Next thing I know, I'm zombie-walking south on Avenue A, holding that damn box at an arm's length from my body, like it's a dead cat or something.

"If thine eye offendeth thee, pluck it out."

I hear that bizarro biblical edict suddenly echo through my mind, a visceral imprecation from King James himself. No doubt this is equally true with shirts and, buddy, this shirt doth offendeth mine eye. Big time. Something is intrinsically evil with this alluring package, therefore I must rid myself of it. Up ahead I spy another standard orange city garbage can and determine to clear my mind of all thought and simply function as a machine. I—will—drop—this—box—in—that—garbage—can. It's a mechanical fact.

But I don't.

The machine fails as I go sailing by the waste receptacle. Why can't I just throw this damn thing away??? Is it because it still has the tags on it? Because it's a brand new shirt and years of abject poverty have left some stain of desperation on me? Unseen Forces, can I not just this once be wasteful? What manner of spell has Cousin Loser cast over this repulsive garment?

"Dude! Watch where the fuck you're going! "

An angry voice snaps me out of my trance. I've almost bumped into some punk rocker, nearly knocking his sparkly nose ring askew. Thankfully, hearing the screech of his rebuke happily disrupts my spiral of thoughts at a propitious moment.

Gathering my bearings, I realize that I'm standing on the corner of Avenue A at 10th Street, the north end of Tompkins Square Park, an infamous inner city ground zero for homeless dopers and winos, scores of urban marginalites, mentally ill, possessed and dispossessed. It's a sad tract of dog shit, long-suffering trees and shrubs set along a maze of winding wrought iron fences featuring endless serpentine rows of weathered benches packed to the brim with supine homeless lost souls who, I now realize, bear one unifying characteristic— tattered, torn old stinking clothing.

Hmmm.

While to me this is the world's ugliest shirt, perhaps to someone else, someone not as fortunate as me, who knows, might it be a thing of beauty?

I suspect Tompkins Square Park is where the Unseen Forces are steering me, so into Tompkins Square Park I march, striding along, searching the faces of the myriad suffering souls parading around in their dingy, soiled garments. I study each derelict visage, trying to decipher which one the Unseen Forces are guiding me towards; that special bum whose puzzle of experience lacks only a shirt-shaped piece to be set on the high road.

"Here you go, friend, a gift...compliments of the Unseen Forces," I'll say. His face will light up with gratitude, his beatific gap-toothed grin a birthday gift I can truly cherish. The curse of Cousin Loser's gift will be transformed into a blessing, and instead of eternally wincing every time I look in my closet, I will shine and glow each and every time I pass Tompkins Square Park as I recall this fine moment of redemption.

Up ahead asleep on a bench I spy this grizzled, spooky-eyed drunk that I vaguely know. We spoke a few weeks earlier when I was photographing the homeless characters in the park. I aimed the camera at him whereupon he noticed and objected. He came charging at me, got all up in my grill, barking out "I'M NOT YOUR MOTHERFUCKING SPECIMEN!"

And he was right, so I told him so.

We sat and talked a while. He's a PTSD Viet Nam vet turned drifter who claims to have once been a close confidant of Jack Kerouac, and like most Beats who bought into the movement whole hog, he's now nothing more than a ruined husk of a human being swaddled in a pile of rags sleeping on a bench.

As I study his torporous form there, I'm tempted to just set the box on the bench next to him, so that when he wakes up he'll wonder at the mystery of the gift. But no, the Unseen Forces resist, saying he's not the one. So on I wander, circling deeper and deeper into the park, searching for the perfect candidate, the one for whom the world's ugliest shirt is destined.

Twenty minutes of meandering past enclaves of low life punks, stumble drunks, schizophrenics and junkies, I find him, tucked way back in a shady corner toward Avenue B. He's a skinny old bum, like a slightly younger, crazier looking version of Smolynsky. Dressed wrong for the cool March air, wearing only a t-shirt, there he sits on the park bench sort of hugging himself, rocking gently as he moves a filterless cigarette in and out of his mouth.

There's a sly, lunatic look about him that's attractive and since he's about my size and it's much too cool for the skimpy t-shirt he's wearing, I see now that the pieces of the puzzle have fallen perfectly into place. Approaching him cautiously, he finally notices me nearing. With outstretched hands the beautiful box is offered and I say, "Here you go, sir, a gift...compliments of the Unseen Forces."

He looks away, takes a tug off his cigarette before he raises his gaze back up to meet mine. His eyes are a dazzling pale blue color, sharp as diamonds. As he studies me, I have the unsettling impression that he's seeing more of me than what I know to be here. A long moment passes, then finally he blinks, saying, "Repeat yourself." Not making any move to take the package from me.

"Uh…what??" I say.

"Repeat yourself. If you dare." Voice confident, and is that a hint of Irish brogue in the bum's voice?

"Oh, uh, okay…" puzzled. Maybe he's hard of hearing. Again offering the dazzling package, I say, "Here, this is a gift for you, from…um, the Universe." I scuttle the

"Unseen Forces" detail, thinking maybe it's a touch too esoteric an angle to approach an indigent stranger with.

He considers this, thinking it over, then nods. "I thought you couldn't."

"Couldn't what?"

"Repeat yourself."

"But I did…"

"No, you didn't. You first spoke of unseen forces."

"Oh yeah, I guess I did. But, really, basically it's the same idea. Basically I'm offering you a free shirt." Here I am on my birthday, standing in dog shit park holding the world's ugliest shirt, arguing semantics with a homeless bum.

"Basically?" He says, as if considering the weight of the word.

So this isn't exactly the fairy tale exchange of the world's ugliest shirt box I had in mind. I figured the whole transaction would be seamless, going down in the blink of an eye—you know; recipient happily clutches the package to his bosom, generous shirt giving stranger vanishes into the crowd like the Lone Ranger, the gift box a silver bullet left behind. Maybe a week later passing the park I see the recipient joyously wearing the shirt—something like that. But here we are, with this strange old man writing his own version of the story. Maybe the pump just needs a little priming. I hold out the box a little further.

"It's okay, really. It's a brand new shirt sir. Never been worn." Looking down at the box I smile falsely—a signal to him that it's time to transfer this object into his possession. But no, he doesn't take it. Instead he turns that perplexing gaze on me again, studies the box for a while, then looks away, sighing. He run his fingers through his hair, apparently still musing over my offer. He looks back at me as if to assay my general character, then regards the box a bit more as if debating what to do next. Finally he leans forward as if to get down to business and says, "Let's have a look."

"At what?"

"This shirt these unseen forces have sent me."

A rueful sigh escapes my lips, though I suspect not so audibly that he can hear. This is a microcosm of the story of my life, trying to do right and somehow ending up all wrong. I feel simultaneously like me and not me, weightless, like I'm here but I'm also floating twenty feet above the park bench, hovering, watching the scene from on high. Look, there I am, standing a few feet from the bench, from the bum, holding out the box as if it were some sad, withered penis.

I lay the package on the bench next to him, doing my best to flash the attractive wrapping and elegant tissue paper prominently while opening it. When I pull back the paper and reveal the shirt, he shows no response, just studies it long and hard as he takes a tug off his cigarette. Then he looks away and goes back to rocking. After a pause he rubs his scalp and says, "It's been seen. Now, take it away."

"Why?"

"Why? Because it's a pernicious abomination."

Okay. So this is my birthday gift from the Universe? Being insulted by a bum? Normally I'd at least have a few words with him, but in this case, how can I refute his assertion? He's right, the shirt is a pernicious abomination—it's the world's ugliest shirt. We both know it and therefore I have no right to rebuttal. Being that this situation is so cut and dried, I curtly nod to him, grab the package and commence to head back off into the park to continue my quest for a societal dreg so low down, so desperate as to be willing to take Cousin Loser's pernicious fashion abomination off my hands.

I'm a good twenty yards off when I hear, "Hey you. Shirt man. Come back."

It's the bum. I turn around and look at him. He discreetly waves me back, looking slightly conspiratorial and solemn. "Come back," he says. "I've got a question about that shirt."

So maybe I was wrong? Maybe he is the one intended to receive the shirt after all? Maybe that first part there, where I got snubbed by this fucking bum, that was just a test of my faith? Did I pass? Is there a God who organizes shit like this? I'm suddenly reminded of a story I read once that was called "God Hears Our Prayers And Remains Silent."

God, are you quietly amused?

Back to the bench I go. He ignores me for a while, making a big show of staring off in the distance, doing the rocking and smoking thing. I stand there with the box in my hands, finally saying, "So?"

"So indeed." he says, as if in agreement.

"So...I came back."

"You did. You're back." he says, addressing the thin air off to the left of my head.

"You said you had a question."

"I do. Many, in fact."

"Yeah…but, about the shirt…"

He nods toward the shirt. "Yes. This shirt…mind telling me what size would it be?"

I sigh, opening the box up and looking at the label. It's a large. I show him the label. He studies it with interest then nods knowingly, saying, "No. That won't do. Wrong size."

"It'll fit you." I say slightly annoyed.

"It's a large?" He asks skeptically.

"Yes….a large…"

"Then it's the wrong size."

"C'mon man, we're about the same size. It'll fit you just fine." I say, a real snappiness creeping into my tone.

"No. Large is the wrong size."

That seems to be his final word. As I'm turning to go, almost benevolently he says, "Good luck to you and your shirt. Best regards to those unseen forces". Is that a little smirk I see on his face?

I'm getting pissed. Moving at a good clip I'm about twenty yards off when I hear him calling again, "Hey you! Shirt man. Come back." I turn around, holding my ground there, just looking back at him. He can see I'm not up for getting played again, so this time he forces a bit of a smile, gesturing for me to come sit on the bench next to him. A theatrical display of mock warmth. "No. Really. Come back, come back. It's important. Urgent even."…slightly pleading.

I'm mostly of a mind to just keep walking, but seeing how things worked out with Molock last night, I figure in his honor I'll do the opposite of what I want to do here just to see how this plays out. He's studying me hard as I approach, as if he's decided something important and is looking for some kind of confirmation on my face. He leans forward and under his breath whispers, "This hideous shirt. The one in the pretty box. Is it long sleeve or short sleeve?"

Sigh. I sit down on the bench and unfold the shirt. It's a long sleeve shirt, which is a plus, it being cool weather and all. "Long sleeve." I say, half pissed, half hopeful that this will seal the deal.

He nods, again as in affirmation. "So it is."

"So, do you want the shirt?" I'm getting impatient here. He says nothing. "It's cold out here. You're wearing a t-shirt. A long sleeve shirt would be much better than that. You'd be warmer."

"No, I wouldn't." he replies, somewhat dismissively.

"Suit yourself. But this shirt is better than the one you're wearing. You're gonna regret not taking this shirt." I get up and huff off. Twenty yards away I hit a little hitch in my stride, waiting for him to call me back again, but he doesn't. This time he waits until I'm almost out of earshot.

"Hey! Shirt man. Come back. Come back. I got a question for you…"

I turn and, now a good distance away, I see him alone on that bench beckoning me back. All of a sudden, although it's the last thing I expect, I start laughing. Why am I laughing? I have not the slightest fucking clue. Then it dawns on me—of course, the bum, he's an agent of the Unseen Forces, just like Molock probably was last night, and this deal with Cousin Loser's shirt, it's a game the Universe has arranged for me to play. I've been slow on the uptake and therefore I'm losing. I nod, maybe to myself, maybe to him, maybe to the Universe and the Unseen Forces as well, then walk back, simultaneously wondering how to get back in the game here, and what remaining detail this blue-eyed lunatic can possibly think of to ask about the shirt.

"That figure on the pocket?" he asks with genuine interest, "Would that be a stallion or a unicorn?"

I search for some glint of whimsy lurking in his eyes but see none. I show him the pocket. Again he nods knowingly. "Ah. Yes. A unicorn. Pity." he says, staring off into the distance, placid, untroubled. I study his implacable countenance. He's much better at this game than me. Big surprise. I rise, intent on walking away for good this time. "I'm going now." I say.

"Apparently so." he nods.

"I know who you are," I tell him as I'm turning to go, referring to him being an agent of the Universe.

"As do I." a tight little smile of affirmation.

Twenty yards off, right on cue, he calls out, "Hey! Shirt man. Come back. Come back."

What else is there to ask? I have to find out, so back I go.

"Cotton or polyester?"

This is followed by another rebuff, followed by me walking away, followed by him calling out "come back, come back", then...

"Block tail or contour cut?"

Then, another rebuff, followed by me walking away, followed by him calling out "come back come back", then...

"Pleated back?"

Then, another rebuff, followed by me walking away, followed by him calling out "come back come back", then...

"Double stitched seams or single?"

Then, another rebuff, followed by me walking away, followed by him calling out "come back come back", then...

"Neck size?"

Then, another rebuff, followed by me walking away, followed by him calling out "come back come back", then...

"French cuff or standard?"

On and on it goes. Now that I understand it's a game, it's absurdly hilarious. At first I think I can wear him down, that he'll run out of questions, but eventually I get it; him being powered by the Unseen Forces, this game can go on forever. Only I can stop it—but how? It has to be done right. If I just keep playing along I'll never prevail. But I can't just give up either. So what to do? Keep on walking the next time he calls out to me? Or keep on returning and answering questions until something magical happens?

But wait. At the point where he's been stopping me each time with his calling out, to my surprise I observe something. How did I not notice this before? Here in the middle of the path beside me stands a perfectly functional, totally empty wire mesh garbage can.

Here it is and here I am and there he is.

A lovely, exotic triangulation seems to have taken place. Without a nanosecond of paralyzing deliberation, I turn, wave at him, hold the box high in the air so that both he and the Unseen Forces can see it clearly, then, as if performing Shakespeare, I release it—gravity does its work and into the can it plunges. I smile, studying it laying in the bottom of the empty orange bin. The world's ugliest shirt has left my gravitational field. I salute the bum, take a bow and triumphantly depart.

As I stride away I hear him calling out, "Hey! Shirt man. Come back. Come back. I got a question for you…" but do I look back? No. I just keep walking, with every step feeling less and less under the jurisdiction of anything other than my own free will. It's exhilarating.

His words echo across the park until I'm out of range. It isn't until I'm all the way home that I accept that I won the game, that I got rid of that goddamn shirt the right way. And who's to say this is a mutually exclusive proposition? Maybe both me and the bum won. I smile, thinking of him being a winner too. Like Molock, there was something deeply endearing about that homeless man.

What's most significant to me is how at that moment in time and space throwing the shirt in the garbage can constituted the right solution, despite it being the wrong answer just minutes earlier with the preceding garbage cans. Something to consider in terms of paradigms; avoid rigid interpretations and general dogmatism.

At peace with myself and the world of shirts, soon after returning home, I fall into a deep peaceful sleep. I'm awakened for a second time on my thirtieth birthday by someone knocking at my door. I look around, surprised to see night has fallen. This time it's Balzora's wife, Elizabeta, a sweet, rosy-cheeked Slavic babushka. What a cheerful, nurturing person like Elizabeta is doing with that creep Balzora is a perplexing mystery—it must be some kind of eastern European thing. Slung over her shoulder is a heavy duty garbage bag loaded so full it looks like it might bust at the seams. She glances around furtively then sets it gently on the floor. Her English is spotty. She touches my arm, smiles sadly, then nods over at Smolynsky's door.

"Smolynsky. Friend for you?"

I nod.

"Yes. Him tells me. Him say you play this music?"

I nod sadly.

"So, Smolynsky dead. Ah, I cry so! For this good man. This friend. Bye-bye." Elizabeth rubs a tear away, then collects herself. "So, Balzora, he say clean apartment, throw in dumpster. But why throw? Maybe you like?"

As she offers me the bag I hear the telltale clatter of musical instruments bumping around emanating from within. I happily accept, both because I love musical instruments and they'll remind me of my friend.

"No word to Balzora, okay? Our secret."

What a sweetheart. There she stands in her peasant dress and kerchief, a figure come to life out of some nineteenth century Millet painting. She has no idea it's my birthday, and yet here she is, bearing this mysterious gift. She's in the right place at the right time, which has happened with her and me before occasionally, albeit in lesser forms. It's like maybe some people are just locked in to the dance of life, knowing where they're intended to be without the burden of being aware of it.

"Our secret." I say, "Thank you, Elizbeta." She smiles, laughs one of those laugh-because-I-don't-want-to-cry deals, then tip-toes away, tossing me a theatrical, impish grin before waddling down the stairs.

Inside the garbage bag I find violin bows, random instrument parts, several battered violin bodies, an exotic mandolin looking instrument missing the tuning pegs, a parlor sized guitar with a hole in the back and two complete violins, one of which looks like it's been through a fire. Having seen the expert shining his penlight into the f-holes earlier, I get curious so I follow suit. I spot the maker's sticker inside—sweet Jesus, don't let me die of heart failure!—inside the slightly charred violin on the ancient looking hand-printed label it clearly reads "fabricat en Cremona 1763, Antonious Stradivarius."

Holy shit, now that's a birthday present!

And hour passes, then two but I can't take my eyes off of it. Could it be? Am I suddenly a very wealthy taxi driver? I sit studying the burnt violin sitting on my fold-out bed, knowing there'll likely be no sleeping tonight.

And there isn't.

Dawn comes rolling around and I've got this important appointment with the scholarship people over at New York University. I'm trying to finagle (read: weasel) a little more scholarship money out of them so I don't have to drive the taxi as much. Of course in light of last night's events, hell, I might not need their goddamn charity. But I keep the appointment anyway, intending to locate an instrument appraiser later in the day to see just how rich I am. After all, even slightly charred, it's still a Stradivarius.

So I'm at this financial aid counselor's desk, the one in charge of scholarship fund dispersement. She's painstakingly detailing why filthy rich NYU can't possibly give me even one more slim dime, intoning on and on, blah, blah, blah. I'm utterly exhausted from two days of little to no sleep and, well, just weird shit happening. I'm sagging both mentally and physically. Listening to her bullshit rejection becomes an unbearable chore. Finally, my eyes drift away and go soft focus in the air over her head. I don't know how long I'm in my little trance, but suddenly I notice she's smiling warmly at me, saying "Oh, are you a fan of his too?"

Lost, I say "Sorry—what?"

So she repeats, "Are you a fan of his? I just love his work."

She swivels around in her chair, pointing at a poster hanging on the wall behind her cluttered desk. I've been so laser focused on connecting with her that I didn't really notice it. Now I do. It's a three feet by four feet poster and features a photograph of what appears to be that bum from the park yesterday, the one who I tried to give the world's ugliest shirt to.

What???

I rub my eyes, wondering, what, am I dreaming here? Dreams sometimes play out like this, right? So maybe I'm just dreaming. But, no, I look around the room and everything appears to be real and tangible. I pinch the fold of skin between my thumb and index finger and distinctly feel pain, signaling this is probably not a dream—there is no pain in dreams, after all. The scholarship lady's studying my face, puzzled, waiting for my response, which is clearly way overdue.

"Are you….a fan..? She asks, slightly impatient.

"Of him? Uh, I dunno. Who is he?"

She laughs then playfully taps me on the arm. "Silly, only the greatest playwright of the twentieth century, Samuel Beckett."

"Samuel Beckett??? No…no, that guy's a bum. I talked to him in the park yesterday," I report.

"In the park???"

"Yeah, Tompkins Square Park. I tried to give him an ugly shirt but he didn't want it."

She laughs mirthfully, (was that a wink she just offered up?) saying, "An ugly shirt? Oh, that's very funny. Very…Beckett-esque…"

"No, I'm serious. It was him."

"You…you're saying you talked to Samuel Beckett…here in New York…yesterday??"

"I guess I did. I mean, I didn't know it was him… but that's the guy." I say, pointing at the man on the poster.

"Oh, but that's impossible. He's dead." she smiles, somewhat patronizingly.

"Sure looks like him" I say, shrugging slightly. I know but one slim fact about Samuel Beckett; he's some kind of famous writer. That's it.

But now she's not so sure. "Is he dead? Maybe he's not…I'm pretty sure he's dead. No, no, no. Definitely. He's definitely dead."

She's a Beckett fan and I'm not, so I take her word for it. Like I said, I know squat about Samuel Beckett. But her interest is peaked about this bum, so I tell her the whole crazy story, starting with Molock, Balzora, Smolynsky and on to Cousin Loser and the world's ugliest shirt.

To my surprise, instead of looking at me like I need a double dose of Thorazine, she rolls with it, reveling in every bizarre detail and twist. We share a few laughs, she asks a few more questions about cab driving and my weird religious back story, then, smiling, she says in a hushed conspiratorial voice, "Well, look. I'm not supposed to do this. But actually there are some resources available. The film school maintains a special account earmarked for emergencies. I'll see what I can do to funnel something your way."

Happy birthday indeed!

ENSLEY, FLORIDA, JUNE 1998

Letter Two wraps up around dawn, weighing in at a meagre two pages. I make no mention of the music box—thinking such talk might tip fate's scales in misleading ways. As best I can I've sidestepped all that manic hostility that fueled Letter One. It's a chore aiming for high roads and soft tones without flat-out lying, so I speak about my fears as a personality disordered parent and what I do say is vaguely conciliatory and apologetic. Generalized. I take the pages to the back room and read them aloud near the music box, relieved it doesn't activate any mechanical devices nearby like the first one did. I take that as a good sign.

As I'm depositing the letter in the mailbox, I spot the postal truck come around the corner, so I hand the carrier the letter and she hands me a post card. It's from my record label. All it says is "Call us" and that's it. I got no home phone, so here I go, schlepping four blocks up to the 7-11 on Highway 29 to use their outdoor pay phone.

As I'm walking up there a bunch of typically depressing scenarios cross my mind, thinking probably they're gonna cut me loose because my debut record bombed. Granted, the material was praised by some highbrow critics, even the New York Times singled it out as noteworthy, but you can't eat reviews. When all was said and done, the record came and went and I sold a meagre few thousand copies. I remained both destitute and unknown, eventually coming to rest here in Ensley, the unemployment and crime capital of Florida.

I lay a stack of quarters on top of the phone box, drop a few coins in and dial. The beautiful Australian receptionist at Luaka Bop puts me on hold, then the label head comes on the line. He's kind of nonchalant, chatty, asks how I'm doing and all. Eventually he gets around to the reason he contacted me: he explains that nothing's settled yet, but a song on my obscure record somehow attracted the attention of this high profile Hollywood film starring Drew Barrymore. It's in the final stages of post-production and if they decide to use my song in the soundtrack, it'll mean some money might finally be coming my way. He asks am I okay with this, to which I all but scream oh hell yes. I'm almost scared to ask how much money are we talking about here? I'm hoping for five hundred, maybe a thousand bucks. Turns out it's a closing credits placement deal, he explains, so if it goes through, the payday will land somewhere in the vicinity of forty grand.

Shit. I about choke.

But don't get your hopes up, he quickly adds. There's two other songs in the running for the same slot. The film people can't decide which of the three to use. I sigh, then ask about the other songs. The label boss clears his throat then gingerly, reverently murmurs the names of the other contenders. Yeah, okay. Got it. I offer a rueful hangdog style laugh, then thank him for his time and hang up. I grab those coins from atop the phone and set to trudging back home, more depressed than ever. No sense wasting precious quarters chit-chatting about my chances of beating out Eric Clapton and Chris Isaak, right?

But oh my, my, my, this Universe, how it will fuck with you if you dare it to. Dare the Universe wrong and you end up dead. Dare it right and, hell, apparently just about anything can happen.

It's two weeks later. I'm walking down to the 7-11 for the third time today just to call the bank and hear that mind boggling balance—each time I hear it I cannot believe my own ears. The puzzled teller says, "Forty thousand and thirty seven dollars, just like it was three hours ago." I keep thinking this has gotta be some bizarre practical joke. But unless the people at the bank are in on it, it's not.

Instead of walking home, I opt for a stroll up the highway past a couple of car lots and pawn shops. I get to fantasizing about waltzing into one of those places, throwing down a wad of cash on the counter, and walking out the door with some choice Gibson guitar or low mileage second hand pickup truck. But no, I just keep on walking. There's that baby girl due in a few months and in my mind this magic money is as much hers as it is mine.

On the way home, passing the payphone I think to call a few old friends to share the good news with, but then it occurs to me—fuck this payphone at the 7-11 bullshit—I can now afford my own damn telephone. So I dial the Southern Bell service lady, who reports it'll be three hundred bucks with the installation fee and deposit, saying I can pay the service technician by check when he's done installing it. I hang up and say to myself, "Shit, now I only got thirty-nine thousand seven hundred and thirty-seven dollars."

Walking home, I'm still trying to puzzle out the cause and effect at play. Is it that simple? I listened when the Universe spoke to me via the form of that music box, so it sent me a massive reward? In the form of forty grand? Jesus. I wish I'd have figured this out earlier.

It's one week later. The Crazy Maker's guarded reply to Letter Two just arrived in the mailbox. I sit down to write her back, aiming for the way of the music box again, and thus begins our tenuous conciliatory correspondence; two personality disordered souls desperately trying to strike postures of sanity. The back and forth covers the final months of her pregnancy and, buddy, every time a letter comes or goes, I make damn sure I read it standing in that back room, keeping an eternal ear bent for any more outbursts from the music box. It's a stupid, superstitious practice; everyone knows lightening never strikes in the same place twice. I know too, but I do it just the same.

NEW YORK CITY, DECEMBER 1989

Breakfast rush at my favorite Ukranian diner, Leshkos, on the corner of 7th and A, grabbing a bite before I head out to classes at NYU. There's no booths available so I plop down at the counter. The Con Ed worker next to me takes big gulp of coffee, drops a fiver on his check, stands and offers me his copy of New York Newsday. It's not my paper of choice, but it's free and I'm poor so, que sera sera, I thank him and grab the Newsday. He winks at the waitress, saying, "Keep the change, honey." then struts out the door. I like his style. He will surely beget many fine children.

I check the headlines. Nothing major brewing so I flip to the back pages where they tend to bury the best stories and lo and behold, what do we have here? Mr. Samuel Beckett's name in bold print accompanied a photo of him. Turns out he died just yesterday in Paris. What?? So that means the scholarship lady was wrong, and he was alive two years back?

Eating my eggs and hash browns, I study his face and it damn sure looks like that bum from the park. Could that have been him? What are the odds? I keep circling around to the bizarre tenor of our exchange that day. Whoever that guy was, he was flying at a high level mentally, plugged into some strange, brilliant energy. You could feel it. So who knows?

Either way, thanks to the world's ugliest shirt, Cousin Loser and possibly Mr. Samuel Beckett himself, my scholarship money got doubled. Not having to drive the taxi constantly, I've been able to concentrate more on making films. My adviser says I'm actually developing a minor cult following at the school, but he's a little stumped about my success because, like everything I do, the results are typically back-asswards.

Case in point, in my first NYU student film festival appearance the experimental film I made won best narrative film. In the most recent festival, my narrative film won best experimental. Further evidence of a life that's a study in irrational inversions. It's like with that Stradivarius. I took it to the appraiser the day after my NYU appointment. How much was it worth? Twenty bucks—it was a forgery. And not even a good one. And yet, it was an integral part of that big story I told the scholarship lady that landed me an extra five grand a year in tuition assistance. Something about that tickles me, I mean, how blessings masquerade as curses, and curses as blessings. Shit like that keeps you on your goddamn toes.

Wolfing down my eggs I do some meta assessments: if that was Beckett who I spoke to, then what, if anything, was the Universe trying to teach me via one of its shining exemplars? What moral can I glean from the knowledge that for my thirtieth birthday I received the curse of an ugly shirt which then mysteriously transformed itself into the blessing of a scholarship deal at NYU via an encounter with one of the luminary minds of the twentieth century? And what about Cousin Loser? Was it a good thing he sent me that godawful shirt? Clearly so. Would I still have met the bum who was probably Beckett and then landed the scholarship money if Cousin Loser hadn't sent the shirt? Or, for that matter, hadn't broken his arm during our half-assed crime all those years ago? Or if he'd forgotten my birthday? Or if he'd sent me some other gift, a stink-assed bottle of cheap cologne instead of the world's ugliest shirt?

There's only one conclusion to reach here; the fabric of reality is way way way more intricate than we in our myopic hubris could ever envision, even in our wildest imaginings. The logical extrapolation on that goes as follows: anyone claiming to have an authoritative handle on the true disposition of this miasmic whorl we call reality—preachers, gurus, pundits, presidents, kings, even me—is full of shit.

As such all there is is this wondering.

TALLAHASSEE, FLORIDA, DECEMBER 1998

Transferring busses. The Greyhound station's jammed with a verdant slice of humanity, impoverished Christmas travelers for the most part. It's your typical sad sack procession of society's cast offs; single moms dragging scruffy looking kids named Tiffany and Colt by the arm, broke down grandpas and grandmas with thrift store suitcases off to visit distant kin, runaways and stumble drunks, everyone headed from here to there.

Passing a bank of pay phones, I hear shouting, then spy a raggedy old codger in his nineties on one of the phones. He's about stone cold deaf, owing to how he's yowling into the receiver, "Tell her…it's a collect call…from Norvelle…" he slowly, deliberately informs the operator, "Norvelle Brains!".

Praise be to the wonders of Deep South taxonomy!

Me, I'm en route from Ensley to Valdosta, waiting for the transfer bus to pull in. Why Valdosta? Well, uh, I'm fetching the Crazy Maker and our brand new baby daughter to come live with me. And since that woman does not travel light, I'm gonna have to rent us a giant U-haul to convey her boatload of priceless, indispensable antique junk.

And yes, I do wonder just what in the high holy hell am I doing here. Often. Blame it on the music box, I guess. This could all go terribly, terribly wrong if…

Don't wander, fitful mind, for many are the land mines in yonder fields of doubt. Prime directive here is to pound as many upbeat notions into my head as is humanly possible before I make landfall in Valdosta. That said, waves of second guessing are hitting me pretty hard at present.

Once the exchange of letters between her and me got rolling full steam did I take liberties in my mind fleshing out the story arc of me and the Crazy Maker, fluffing it up with a few too many pie in the sky details? In the new improved version of my magic music box life, me and her, we start acting sane and work things out, all for the sake of the baby. We both become great parents to our infant daughter and learn to love and respect each other just fine.

I cozied up to that notion with such a blind vengeance that soon after the baby was born I sat down at the Smith Corona and earnestly invited the Crazy Maker to move in with me there in that spooky house in Ensley. And she agreed. I guess I'll find out in a couple of hours here how viable this conceptual model is.

The bus comes wheeling in, transfer passengers shuffle off, the early winter light hitting them just so as they de-bus, giving all, great and small, a mythic, cinematic appearance. On days like today, you catch reflections of yourself in every passing soul. Me and a handful of others board the bus and off we go, rumbling north toward our first stopover up in Thomasville, just over the Georgia state line. Do I feel confident about this transition into family man mode? Oh hell no. But the music box spoke, so I guess there's no disputing that.

Weaving our way beneath the I-10 underpass, I keep coming back to the cause and effect of that music box incident. Some tangible force of energy triggered that mechanism, but where exactly did said force originate from? My mind? Hers? Some commingling of our psyches, like when you mix nitrogen and glycerine and things go kaboom? Was it her daddy's ghost, or our unborn child sending the pulse into that mechanism? Or maybe the agents of the Universe, Unseen Forces and such, or just some bored poltergeist? Bottom line here is there just ain't no way to tell. Anybody says different is a liar.

The bus chugs up HWY 319, the north/south two-lane blacktop that crosses over into Georgia. Tallahassee invariably leaves me feeling skittish, as it, like Pensacola, is a realm overrun with old, worrisome energy. Its early settlement years were marred by outrageous massacres of Seminoles and blacks at the hands of greedy white interlopers. Such travesties were commonplace. Treaties were signed, solemn promises made over and over, then flagrantly abandoned during brazen land grabs by the whites. Such legacies of bad faith linger like radioactive contamination, the half-life of civilized savagery being considerably greater than that of more rudimentary forms of violence.

A few rows back some toddlers are on the move; one fussing, one crying, one beating a plastic spoon against the window. The crying one spies me looking over my shoulder at him and promptly notches up his wail a couple decibels. Children…and soon I will have one of my own. Yow.

The loud, dull-witted mom is clearly overmatched. "Destiny! You stop that! Stop! I'mon smack you a good one! Kyle! Put that down! Don't you! Eating off the damn floor! Stupid! Lukey, you get back here and sit your hynie down! NOW!!" Destiny, the oldest, is maybe five, her name sadly prophetic. Perhaps the younger ones will fare better.

I do my best to tune out the litany of insults the clueless mom hurls at her pitiful offspring, focusing on the scenery sailing by—zip, there goes the Auto Zone, zip, there goes the Hardees, zip, there goes the 7-11, then, zip, there goes the Olive Garden, McDonalds, Lowes, and TJ Maxx. But then lo and behold, zip, the daisy chain of crushingly generic roadside franchise America gets disrupted by an old time north Florida AM radio station, WFNF, a good sized pillbox affair perched atop a low hill.

Judging from the fish logo, it's one of those insipid Christian Praise type operations. What manner of soul could DJ at such an establishment? Can you imagine? Sifting through, then programming endless hours of droning, saccharine drivel, then monitoring the drek that's emitted from that transmitter day after day, year after year? Jesus, what a life—no pun intended. I study the majestic old antenna towering above the tree line, imagining the dismal waves of invisible signals emanating from it. Then zip, like the others it's gone, the view now giving way to a wall of monotone green, intermittent kudzu outbursts and orderly rows of long needle pines.

Welcome to the rural South.

Ever since that music box deal, I keep circling around to a quote by Nicola Tesla, "My brain is only a receiver. In the Universe there is a core from which we obtain knowledge, strength and inspiration. I have not penetrated into the secrets of that core. But I know it exists". Amen, brother Tesla.

Seeing WFNF go whizzing by gets the cognitive wheels turning, triggering ruminations about that core and the secrets Tesla alluded to. If he's right about the human brain being a receiver, then how might said secrets received by the brain be transmitted to it? As the Greyhound settles into its highway groove disparate threads of thought mesh and out pops a full-fledged crackpot notion, a theory based around something I'm gonna go ahead and call "Psychic Antennas".

So, Psychic Antennas; in this theoretical paradigm everyone's got one. But some folk's Psychic Antennas pick up a whole lot more information than others. They just do. Like mine, for example. Trying to wrap my causal mind around this conundrum it occurs that receptivity is likely predicated by, for lack of a better term, antenna size and shape.

The folks with the biggest, most elaborate antennas—mad spiraling Dr. Seuss style structures towering into the stratosphere of their minds—they pick up everything being broadcast on all frequencies, so let's just go ahead and call those poor souls schizophrenics. They're perpetually besieged by an incessant barrage of random, multi-tiered transmissions, but aren't configured to process even a fraction of what's 24-7 bombarding them. As such they spin and twist wildly in eternal whirlwinds of reckoning and misreckoning.

What a life. Lord.

Living in New York, I've met my fair share of schizophrenics, a couple who fashioned tinfoil hats, hoping to shield themselves from the onslaught of stimulus flying in, another who pried the metal fillings out of his teeth, believing the amalgams to be conduits for bad energy.

Sounds crazy, right? Maybe, maybe not. It turns out rotting amalgams can in theory generate the ingredients necessary to create a diode, a primary component for AM radio wave signal reception. And where one finds a commingling of signals and receivers one finds what? Right— information being transmitted. So who knows, maybe the schizophrenics are on to something here.

Then on the other side of the spectrum there's the mainstreamers, the ones with minuscule one channel Psychic Antennas. These simple souls don't pick up a whole lot of information, have never heard footsteps in the darkened hallways of their minds, never felt the tug of the esoteric undertows or the irrational nudge of Unseen Forces via bizarre birthday gifts and randomly playing music boxes and such. They'll scoff loudly at the prospect of invisible wavelengths carrying paranormal data, speaking with certainly that the finite scope of their perceptions is an absolute measure of all that is. Their only exception to this one-dimensional dogmatism might be data emanating from the wildly rigid constraints of their ancestral religion.

Prayer and angels, occasional miracles…that's the outermost limits of acceptable magic for most mainstreamers; they're conservative through and through and will do backflips over mountains of flaming dog shit to avoid engaging in any activities that might challenge the primacy of their tiny antennas. "God forbid!", they often say, that notion becoming a self-fulfilling prophesy. But hey, they don't know any better because that's just how they're designed, with antennas unable to process complex esoterica, so what's there to criticize here? Not much. In fact, at times I find myself envious of the mainstreamers and their small, tidy lives.

Me, I'm a big antenna type—thankfully not so oversized to render me a raving maniac crippled with a bad case of the crazies, but certainly personality disordered enough to raise alarm bells in most mainstream psychological contexts. True, I've never actually been diagnosed as mentally ill by a certified healthcare professional—no, I just worked on getting better on my own, sorting out the math and myth of my purpose here earth. But it's always been obvious to anyone with two eyes in their head that something ain't right with me.

Tesla's quote leads me to the lesser known Guglielmo Marconi. Who's that? In the year 1909 Marconi won the Nobel Prize in Physics for discovering wireless telegraphy. Shit, think about it, that was just a little over a hundred years back. My, how far we've come.

Guglielmo was an electrical engineer obsessed with the disposition of sound waves, which was how he stumbled upon the phenomenon of radio transmissions. Historical fact: when Marconi first went public with his revolutionary theory of radio waves, he was universally ridiculed.

"You can't snatch human voices out of thin air Guglielmo! Patso Italiano!" People said.

Then when he submitted further proof of his discovery to the Italian government and asked for funding for more research, did they hail him as a genius and embrace this world changing discovery? No, they deemed him a mental case, even threatening to throw him in the infamous Lungara Asylum. But he persevered and proved all them small antenna mainstreamers wrong and later became known as the much-venerated Father of the Radio.

Flash ahead to this new invention they're calling the internet. Can you imagine what any self-respecting early twentieth century rationalist would have said if you'd suggested you possessed a portable machine that allows instantaneous connection to anyone in the world, that can store unimaginable amounts of information; films, photographs, books, etc in a wallet sized hunk of metal and plastic? And with a little digging, said device can provide said person with the answer to ANY question—math, geography, history—known to man.

You want the GNP of New Guinea for 1977? Gimme a minute, it's floating in the air swirling around our heads this very second…along with all other information ever recorded in human history. Pitch that idea to mainstreamers even fifty years ago and they'd have locked you up and thrown away the key for-ev-er. Yeah, what in previous epochs was unimaginable is now ho-hum daily bread, so, as far as I'm concerned, the sky's the limit when digging into the prospect of Psychic Antennas.

Back to my theorizing: the bus just passed WFNF, which, via that big antenna, is presently emitting invisible sound waves out into the atmosphere all around Tallahassee. Transmissions of WFNF's broadcast are in fact present in this very bus at this very moment, as they are in barber shops and bathrooms and penthouses and crawl spaces of ratty old duplexes all over the greater Tallahassee area.

The signal flies everywhere, riding those same omnipresent radio waves that Marconi discovered, albeit on differing frequencies, commingling with myriad other diverse signals, chock full of competing fields of information; rap, country, oldies, right wing talk shows, left wing NPR operations, all out there in the ether just waiting to be apprehended, right? All a person has to do is adjust the knob on that radio until they land on the frequency that best suits their personality, and whoosh, words, ideas, music and more are snatched from thin air—literally.

So, now, take that foundational thought then imagine you're listening to a different kind of radio, one that picks up more esoteric transmissions, ones that you and only you can receive. Since it's your own personal station, let's just go ahead and call it WYOU.

WYOU's programming features up-to-the-minute news about everything YOU-related: YOUr hopes, YOUr fears, YOUr sins and self-deceptions, YOUr prayers, dinner plans, YOUr preference in socks, how that taco YOU wolfed down at lunch is digesting, how YOU feel about YOUr neighbor's cat peeing on YOUr hydrangea bushes, YOUr toenail fungus, the high deductible on YOUr home owners insurance, that damn Mickey Mouse wristwatch YOUr uncle gave YOU for Christmas when YOU were five that never kept time right—every minuscule concern that might cross YOUr mind, it's all being transmitted on the wavelength generated by an imaginary station called WYOU, and from womb to tomb, each and every human soul is tuned in to their own personal version of WYOU.

But what happens with us big antenna types when out of nowhere other stations intermittently break through the WYOU broadcast and start delivering their own signals on the same frequency?

And the information being broadcast? At first it's all jumbled, like short wave radio gibberish—mind clatter, as one therapist friend dismissively described it—but if you keep listening, just as distant lightning and thunder foretell the coming of a storm, when those additional stations start broadcasting and bleeding over onto WYOU's broadcast it often foreshadows the advent of serendipitous events in your life that will soon thereafter come sailing in from unexpected directions—yeah, like movies appearing on the sides of buildings, stolen cars appearing before your disbelieving eyes and music boxes springing to life at propitious moments.

Pattern recognition kicks in and you start to realize the value of those renegade transmissions and so increasingly you perk your ears up for them. And since you're receiving compelling information, and it recurs, let's go ahead and give those other enigmatic intervening stations names, WHAT, WOAH and WWTF. Okay? Which circles back to that song I wrote called Static on the Radio:

> *Now there's a church house, about a stone's throw down*
> *From this place where I've been staying.*
> *It's Sunday morning and I'm sitting my truck*
> *listening to my neighbors sing.*
> *Ten years ago I might have joined them,*
> *But don't time change those inclined*
> *To think less of what is written*
> *than what's wrote between the lines…*

NEW YORK CITY, FEBRUARY 1985

It's a small time drug dealer making drops in the restaurant bathroom. That explains the loose tile behind the toilet tank. He's chiseled away the grout and carved out a nice little hidey-hole compartment for his transactions. I found the loose tile at closing time last night while mopping the bathroom and was stumped by it. Joan the night manager, she figured it out.

Joan's a trip. She's regularly visited by incubi. Last week she held a seance at her apartment, trying to contact Elvis. They didn't reach The King and ended up spending an hour talking to an embittered South Vietnamese soldier who was pissed about having died so young. Joan finally told the solider he was complaining too much and to get over it, whereupon she ended the seance. Joan's a gamer. With her tipoff, we commence to surveil the bathroom.

An hour after we open, sure enough a known dope dealer in the neighborhood appears. He first very casually orders a cup of coffee, sits down, takes one theatrical sip then heads to the bathroom. He's there all of two minutes then leaves, clearly scoping out his surroundings as he exits. And here's the kicker; as he goes sailing past his table, full cup of coffee sitting there, he nods surreptitiously to this yuppie type sitting at the next table over, then heads out the door.

The yuppie pops up and heads to the bathroom then comes out a second later patting his pocket and likewise checking his surroundings. I guess it's safer than conducting business out in the open on the street corner but this ain't no dope house. Joan being Joan, she decides to have some fun with it. She asks me to cover for her while she's gone.

It's twenty minutes later and here she comes with a big luminous grin on her face, waving a small paper bag at me. From the bag she extracts a tiny toy police car, just big enough to fit in the hidey-hole. She carefully positions it there, returns the tile to its place and glows with mirth. I love Joan, but not romantically. She's typical of the freak show of folks who work here.

Food Restaurant is apparently some sort of famous Soho landmark. Having come from a Southern Pentecostal background, I know nothing of art or the NYC hipster scene. I know vaguely who Andy Warhol is, but not Jean-Michel Basquiat or Keith Haring, but apparently they all used to eat here, and some even created dishes for the menu.

The day manger's a dancer named Charles. He's stunned when I don't recognize names he mentions: Vincent Minelli or John Coltrane or Alvin Ailey or Martha Graham. He's a tender soul who often brings me books he thinks I need to read. He also makes compilation tapes for me to listen to. Charles has never hit on me, so I guess I'm like a project to him, and he just wants to help me learn. Thank you, Charles Richardson.

Most of the music he offers I've never heard of, downtown scenesters like Meredith Monk and Laurie Anderson, but last week he gave me a tape I recognized. It was that strange repetitive piano music that I heard on the BBC back when I was hiding out in Amsterdam trying to reassemble this busted mirror I'd found, spooky minimalist stuff by some guy named Phillip Glass. I mentioned how I'd heard it before and uncharacteristically Charles bragged on Phillip Glass, reporting he used to be one of the co-owners of Food Restaurant back when it was an artist co-op. That's how Food became such a famous eatery, folks like Glass and Warhol being part of the show.

But now Soho is turning into a fine art ghetto. Daily I make sandwiches for wealthy shoppers who flock to the area to partake in the newly gentrified scene. At present Tom Waits is standing outside the restaurant. I'm a big fan, owing to our shared underbelly sensibilities and his penchant for fashioning lovely mosaics out of the flotsam and jetsam of humanity. In my book, Tom Waits is a fringe avatar, so I'm watching intently as he carries on a long involved conversation with Hank, the grizzled schizophrenic homeless man who lives in the boarded up doorway of the failed clothing store opposite Food on the northeast corner of Prince and Wooster.

Hank's my friend. I sneak him meals from the restaurant fairly often. Sometimes he eats them, sometimes he doesn't. For all his raggedy charms, Hank's a stinking, toothless, disgusting wreck of a human being whose sole possessions consist of his soiled clothing, a grievously battered box guitar bearing just two strings, cowboy boots and a filthy cowboy hat. Hank regales passing well-to-doers, fashionistas and jaded hipsters with revolting, unintelligible grunts that he confides to me are brilliant songs of his own devising. He claims to come by his musical genius honestly, being the illegitimate son of Hank Williams, the legendary country crooner. Last week he confided in me that the US postal system recently commissioned him to illustrate a line of postage stamps based on the paintings of Hieronymus Bosch.

Tom Waits seems to have taken quite a shine to Hank's surreal, guttural testimony and appears to be busily transcribing their conversation in a small notebook as they speak. I watch for a while as Tom scribbles away, then suddenly time and space stand still as I consider the contents of Tom Wait's notebook. Imagine what lies within it!

This is an utter revelation—why didn't I think of this before? My shift ends soon thereafter and I make a beeline to a nearby stationary story where I indulge myself in an actual retail purchase, buying the first of many many shirt pocket notebooks. I walk out into the bustling streets of New York City and immediately start taking notes, constructing observational word mosaics.

VALDOSTA, GEORGIA, DECEMBER 1998

The schlep back to the station with my duffel bag over my shoulder winded me pretty good, triggering a yet unborn song to come sailing into rotation on WYOU—this one's a work in progress, my inner DJ reports. It's the day after Christmas and I'm slouched in a filthy corner of the Valdosta Greyhound Station, crying. The emerging song appears to be a chronicle of events transpiring in the here and now as I'm attempting to flee Valdosta and the Crazy Maker and, heartbreakingly, my newborn child.

I've been sitting here a good two hours now, feeling increasingly despondent, waiting on my long overdue bus. To complicate matters, The Crazy Maker's tracked me down and has just come sailing though the door with our baby in her arms. Her infallible radar leads her to directly where I sit over here, cowering in the corner. She's pissed, and crouches before me now, brandishing our infant daughter in my face as if she's a tactical weapon, furiously hissing under her breath, "Get up! And get in that car! You are not running away! This child needs you!"

Goddamn bus, where are you? Leaking out over the crappy bus station intercom I make out a sanitized Muzak version of James Taylor's song Fire & Rain. Jesus, that's some top shelf programming on the soundtrack of my Life there, possibly transmitted via WWTF.

With the arrival of The Crazy Maker the internal radio signals get all jammed up, with WOAH blasting something that sounds like a mix of discombobulated abstract jazz and a cat getting electrocuted, WHAT ebbs and flows with snippets of arguments me and The Crazy Maker had these last few days, while WYOU has programmed an endless medley of entirely suicidal Townes Van Zandt songs, like Nothin', and Waiting 'Round to Die. Then my own unfinished song comes sailing into rotation…

> *Where in the world did you come from my dear?*
> *Did some mysterious voice tell you I'd still be here?*
> *I bought this ticket to Ensley, but I been stranded all day.*
> *The PA said the bus broke down ten miles away from the station…*

I was crying when I stormed out of her apartment, crying all the way walking to the Greyhound station, crying when I bought the ticket from the puzzled lady behind the counter, crying when I found this out of the way nook over in the corner.

What's to cry about?

Plenty. The impossibility of love to start with. And no, I don't mean love with The Crazy Maker—there is no love to be had with that woman—but goddamn, how the fucking Universe spins on its axis every time I lay eyes on this beautiful, helpless child. And now there her innocent face hovers, inches away from mine. She's studying her pitiful father, the weepy-eyed maniac in the bus station corner that reeks of urine.

So what does my all-consuming feeling of authentic love for this child mean? Is it like a square footage deal—you know, in my heart? Like the space reserved for love in my heart is so small that only a child can fit into it? Yeah, that's probably it. And I could love this child. I could change for this child. I could. My heart could grow.

But between her and me stands The Crazy Maker. And from what I gather from our furious negotiations these past few days, unless I bow down and do exactly as she says, there won't be any getting to know this beautiful child. It's a rock and a hard place proposition, particularly since I got no capacity for being emotionally blackmailed. So much for the way of the music box, right? In place of Fur Elise this other song commences to writing itself in my head. It'd be cheating but hell, maybe I'll even call it Christmas Day just to drive the point home. I'd only be a day off.

The burden of love is the fuel of bad grammar.
We stutter and stammer, what a bitch to convey,
the crux of the matter when the words we must utter
are so hopelessly tangled in the memories
and scars we show no one.
So seldom a door, so seldom a key...
So seldom a hit like the hurt you put on me...
but seldom comes happiness without the pain
of the Devil in the details,
since I saw the smile on your face
as I was crying in a Greyhound station
on Christmas Day, in 1998....

I lock eyes with my infant child, her sweet, smiling countenance saying, "Would you leave me to be raised alone by this maniac?"

Shit. I've pulled so many stunts in my life that were stupid and prideful and selfish but suddenly I realize, it's time. Time to cling to love in the face of terrible adversity. I rise and head toward the parking lot, toss the duffle bag in the trunk of The Crazy Maker's crappy little economy car, slump down in the passenger seat and wait as she straps the baby into the car seat. She climbs in, glances over me contemptuously, rolls her eyes and says, "What about your ticket?"

"What about it."

"You're not using it. So go get a refund." her tone is insistent.

The thought of facing the clerk in tears a second time is more than I can bear. "No, let's just go."

"What?? Go in there and get a refund, now!" She scowls at me.

I tell her I will, but I don't. Once inside the station I remove the bus ticket, from my pocket, then tear it into pieces and chuck said pieces in the garbage can. I return to the car, and thus a new fight commences.

I remember quite clearly a sad Muzak version
of James Taylor's big hit called Fire & Rain
Was playing as you crouched down and tearfully kissed me.
And I thought damn what good fiction I will mold
from this terrible pain.

AMSTERDAM, HOLLAND, DECEMBER 1983

Merry lonely desolate Christmas. I'm slumped down in a stained, sagging armchair that sits in the corner of my shitty, sparsely furnished studio over by the De Gooyer Windmill on the outskirts of eastern Amsterdam. I moved in last week. The place reeks of various permutations of decay: physical, moral, spiritual—you name it.

On the floor beneath the chair, like one of those crime scene chalk outlines, lies a rectangle of yellow dust that wasn't there this morning when I swept the place out, testifying to the rapidly disintegrating foam in the core of sunken cushions.

This chair emits a worrisome smell…some unholy mix of ancient bodily fluids and perfumes, masked by the heavier scent of some noxious industrial cleaner, the latter perhaps accounting for the cushion decay. Some poor soul died in this chair.

Was it me?

An Arabic man's garbled mutterings leak through the paper-thin walls from the room next door. This is followed by another man's sinister, mechanical laughter; ha-ha-ha-ha-ha. An occasional creak of bedsprings can be heard and every so often the woman in their company gently sobs. This pattern goes on, cycling in intensity, for several hours. Finally I hear the trio moving around, a door slams, footsteps in the hallway, then all is quiet.

Welcome to my hidey-hole.

A couple years back I hit the wall in that Jesus-riddled, psychic rubble heap known as the Panhandle of Florida, saddled with what my pastor dubbed "a hallelujah breakdown". In plain talk, I snapped and flew the coop, wandering hither and yon before eventually coming to rest in the Sodom and Gomorrah of modern Europe.

I now reside less than a mile from Amsterdam's infamous Red Light District, a sprawling legalized prostitution zone awash with the bottom feeders of Western civilization: third world dope dealers, exotic bands of petty thieves, full-fledged cutthroats, Dutch, Asian, African and Indonesian pimps and hookers, an endless procession of leering American sex tourists, reprobates and gawkers of every shape and form. It's a universe away from that Assembly of God church I fled back in North Florida. Tongues are no doubt being employed here, but for radically different purposes than back home at altar calls.

A mix of rain and sleet's been hammering at my windowpanes all afternoon and evening. It's the dead of winter, so the weather is par for the course, or so I'm told. Since I arrived a few weeks back, the few Dutch folks I've crossed paths with seem perplexed by my presence here, as if the configuration of elements my person represents is fundamentally antithetical to their way of information processing. "But....you were already in Florida…" some actually say, "…why did you come to Holland???"

Holland in winter apparently is a place for leaving and Florida apparently is where the leaving go, or at least dream of going. The shivering Dutch citizens gawk at me like I'm a side-show freak. Their attitude in turn perplexes me—I like it here. The days are short and without shape or form. A relentless grayness saturates life on a subatomic level, soothing ragged edges from every angle of seeing. Nobody knows or has any expectations of me here. There are no conflagrations of searing heat, Jesus, poverty, broken-down cars, withering childhood companions or spooky, drug-addicted romantic interests to devil me here.

Hemmed in by this extended weather event my cabin fever's set in pretty good. I pass the day clenched, trying not to fight the beatdown of confinement, practicing endless rudimentary guitar licks, reading books well beyond my intellectual reach—Camus, Sartre, and of late Celine, who I despise. Back in my Born Again days, it was the bible or nothing, but even studying God's Holy Word I struggled to process the material, what with all the begats and smites and thous and such opacity of antiquated language. It didn't help that my reading comprehension level was hovering around that of a jittery eyed ten-year-old at that juncture.

So now here I am self-educating, trying to make up for lost time, but you can only read so much existential literature before you start formulating plans for a killing spree. Thankfully over the last few minutes it appears that hammering rain's started backing off. I grab my foul weather gear and out the door I fly, in full stride like I'm in a hurry to get somewhere—an important meeting, a date with some attractive young woman, to catch a train to carry me to some magical far-off locality called home.

When I'm troubled, doesn't matter the hour, I walk…and walk…and walk. And day or night, whenever I venture out of my apartment, there she is—that ravaged prostitute, keeping her perpetual vigil on a small, sad patch of weeds directly opposite my doorway.

An outcast from the Red Light District, she tosses me a lascivious grin, rubs her thighs and mutters in raspy, heavily accented English, "Hey…why not…?" like she always does. So far I've managed to resist her alluring entreaties to engage in sexual commerce.

The remnant drizzle softens her appearance like Vaseline on a movie camera lens as she holds her station there in that skin tight mini skirt and bulging, lumpy tube top, clutching a tattered leopard print umbrella, tonight wearing a festive red Santa Claus cap, the sight of which makes me feel like bursting into tears. Fare thee well, dear childhood, fare thee well.

I set a course toward the Muntplein. In my wanders, I tend to aim for populated areas, which I keep telling myself is a good sign. It's healthy to want to be in the company of other humans, even when you lack the basic social hardware that allows any real interaction. How my socialization shortcomings can be remedied is a troubling question, but my core identity appears to believe the solution has something to do with this walking business. Granted, I never actually speak to anyone on these circuits I cover, never make eye contact, but I go where there's foot traffic, weaving my way through the crowds, waiting for something big to happen like I did as a kid when the Interstate Fair would come to town and I'd sprint up and down the freak show aisles dodging gawkers.

At the trendy Leidseplien, I spy a big throng of Dutch hipsters milling around a trendy night spot called Paradiso. It's the See and Be Seen crowd, fashionably attired, smoking, chatting easily amongst one another. It must be some kind of intermission from a show or something. I stop to puzzle out what the big draw is when, through a huge plate glass window, my eye is caught by a strange music video playing on an interior monitor.

Typically, the vibe of this place is that repellent hyper-affected British New Romantic approach, you know, like Spandau Ballet, Dead or Alive, Human League and such pose-oriented acts. But this video playing, while being posey, doesn't quite fit that boring template. No, this video features a palsied young man who appears to be working his way through a series of disembodied, dyskinetic posturings.

I watch, momentarily frozen in place, then feel myself being drawn into the lobby, reflexively recoiling at the thought, but then forging on through the door nonetheless until, rising over the din of the interior crowd, I'm within earshot of the song. From what I can gather this lunatic is singing something about burning down a house. I feel a sudden lightness of being, as if a mild charge of electricity is passing through me.

Nearby, there's a record store I've seen in my rambles. Summoning up an abnormal amount of personal initiative, I march into the place and inquire if they knew anything about this nervous looking man who sings that song about burning down his house. The amused clerk directs me to a section devoted to a band called Talking Heads. I recognize the singer at once. "Yeah, that's him." I say, as if I know him personally or something. The clerk smiles and tells me this strange fellow's name: David Byrne. I purchase a cassette version of the album and take it back home, passing the prostitute, still at her station, still smiling, still muttering, "Hey…why not?"

In the next room the Arabs are at it again, bed springs bouncing, sinister laughing, woman crying. I put the cassette in my little boom box and crank the volume up as loud as it'll go. I listen to David Byrne's songs over and over that night. The storm passes, and the following day still I listen, spellbound, as if beholding one of the magi.

When the cassette is playing and I lock into the groove, synapses get to firing, the notion of burning down the house pin-balling through my psyche, ringing major core identity bells. That's it; my house, it needs burning down. Now. Having abandoned the crutch of religion my house is now uninhabitable in every sense; physically, spiritually, psychologically, culturally. It's time to start over from scratch, time to burn down my house. I play the cassette day and night nonstop for weeks until one day the tape snaps and silence descends.

NEW YORK CITY, SEPTEMBER 1993

Just calm the fuck down. Like, seriously. Like, right now. Calm. The. Fuck. Down.

So what if I'm 36 years old and it's 9/3/1993. So what if today my cab was dispatched at 3:13 and it happens to be cab number 39. So what if I've been inexplicably waking up at 3:33 am these last few nights? So what if for weeks now other clusters of threes have been popping up every fucking where I look; on odometer readings and fare totals, phone bills, change I get at the damn grocery store.

So what if now here I am stopping at the corner of 3rd and 27th after the most beautiful women I've ever laid eyes on has just hailed me. So what if 27 is 3 X 3 X 3 and so I'm basically meeting this luminous creature at the corner of 3 and 3 cubed. So what if it happens to be 9:03—so what! If spooky clusters of threes are what it takes to connect with this transcendent, sorrowful beauty approaching my taxi, then so be it.

Normally, I give such meta-females a wide berth when they hail me, figuring they're surely weary of men throwing themselves at them nonstop twenty-four seven, but as I pull to a stop for this lady, her and me, we lock eyes and there's no mistaking it— she's studying me just as hard as I'm studying her. It makes no sense, me being a scruffy cab driver (cab drivers rating slightly lower than morgue attendants on the romantic attraction scale) and her being whoever the majestic hell she is, but clearly reciprocal sparks commence to flying.

She pops the door open and settles into the back seat as I strain to calm my racing mind. The air is charged with magic, thick and volatile and sensuous. I manage to keep my cool for all of two seconds, until she innocently says, "Hi, I'm going to 313 East 9th Street." And, well, that does it—I let loose an unbridled whoop.

I can see she's stumped, wondering what's so goddamn funny about that address. Fighting to rein in my giddiness, I hold up my hand and say, "Gimme a minute. It's way, way, way too complicated to explain." I jot the address down on my trip sheet. Passenger pick up: 3rd & 27th (3 X 3 X 3). Passenger destination: 313 E. 9th Street. Time: 9:03. Cab 39. Jesus.

I throw the meter, then stomp on the gas and away we rocket. As a rule I drive fast, like I'm always in a rush to get to some magical unknown destination. We bank hard right on 28th Street, then I gun it so as to make the green light way down at 2nd Ave. We've hit fifty mph on this side street, the parked cars shuddering as we hurtle past. I need a distraction so I randomly grab a cassette tape from a pile in the front seat, shove it in the boom box sitting on the seat beside me then hit play as we lean into the turn at 2nd Avenue.

I hear her laughing now as she goes sliding across the back seat, the g-forces kicking in. "I like the way you drive!" she shouts over the roar of the engine, clinging to the open partition to stabilize herself. Then the music takes over and a cloud of sublime bliss settles in as me and this beautiful lady, we just go sailing along down 2nd Avenue, windows wide open, high octane be-bop jazz blasting. It's like we're suddenly characters in that foreign movie I saw at the Film Forum a few weeks back, the French one called "a bout de souffle"…Breathless.

I'm weaving through the tangle of slower drivers when I catch her studying me in the rear view. Good lord, my heart goes skipping pitter-pat. Our eyes meet, she smiles softly, brushing the hair out of her eyes. I say nothing.

There's a palpable charge in the air—we can both feel it. I'm biding my time because somehow I've been hit by a wave of one hundred proof faith that this is the payoff at the end of that weird daisy chain of threes, that the Universe is about to deliver something big and wonderful, that blessing from above that's so long overdue. We've entered a benevolent realm of heightened meaning and opportunity, a realm that is neither of our design nor in our control. We are free falling into love.

Sure enough a moment later she makes the first move. Leaning forward through the open partition she offers a seductive smile, then politely inquires as to what amazing music I might be listening to. I tell her the music comes courtesy of Mr. Art Blakey and the Jazz Messengers. And because this is rapidly devolving into some parallel universe version of the aforementioned exotic French film, she of course beams, proclaiming a near supernatural affection for Art Blakey. She then flashes a longing smile at me, adding, "Thank you! I was feeling so sad, but this music is making things better!"

I study her briefly in the rear view and discover her beauty to be literally breathtaking…like, when regarding her I find myself unable to respirate, and not just because there's no AC in this cab and it's a stifling Indian summer kind of night. At six hours into my shift, I'm more than a bit ripe in the body odor department and approaching rancid in the greasy hair department and yet here she is, this stunning beauty, clearly flirting with me. My head swims a bit, pulse quickening from lack of oxygen to my brain, intense romantic attraction and oblique terror in knowing there are forces afoot here that I in no fucking way even remotely understand. It's exhilarating!

She's waiting for a response, so finally I manage to throw out a story at her—I tend to communicate via stories, not banter or conventional conversation. So I tell her what a truly lovely coincidence it is that she loves Art Blakey because only a few weeks back I had another beautiful female passenger in my cab who likewise offered compliments when Art Blakey came swinging out of my humble boom box. And you know what? When I asked that passenger if she was a fan of jazz music, in reply she gracefully intoned, as if herself singing a jazz line, "Oh yes, jazz is my language. You see, my daddy, he was a timekeeper." Then she introduced herself as Evelyn Blakey, Art Blakey's daughter.

The surprise twist elicits coos of delight from my present lovely passenger. "What a great story! And what a cool coincidence! You're my favorite cab driver ever..." she adds, in a playful tone that suggests she's concealing some wonderful, life affirming secret that she will one day share with me and our children when we're happily married and living in that beautiful split level bungalow at Malibu or the Cote d'azur or wherever.

So since anything seems possible here, I inquire of this magical creature in the back seat if she too might be Art Blakey's daughter. Peals of mesmerizing, musical laughter proceed from behind me, followed by a mock tragic "I wish!".

Oh, how my heart aches! The vibe she emits is utterly disarming, primally connective. We start jabbering about music and literature and film and every little goddamn detail just lines up perfectly, like we're acting out a fast-paced introduction scene in some brainy romantic comedy.

It's a short ride then suddenly we're there, parked outside her apartment door. I throw the meter, which of course reads $3.30, then we sit for a good five minutes, just talking. She's an actress it turns out, new to the city, waiting tables while hunting up her big break. Suddenly a connection between our rendezvous and that Harry Chapin song, Taxi, surfaces in my mind, so I mention the similarity, adding however that I don't smoke weed. "Ha-ha" she says, pulling back slightly, "And I haven't quit acting to marry some rich guy."

There follows an awkward silence. A voice of doubt in the back of my mind starts screaming, "What a stupid fucking thing to say! Why did you say that?? Do something here! Once she exits this cab the spell will be broken and you'll never see her again!!"

And the voice is so right! Once out the door she's gone forever. And on an utterly elemental level I so so so need to see this woman again, so I just start peppering her with quirky questions and off beat stories and she's back orbiting in my gravitational field, laughing that musical laughter, then enthusiastically replying with perfect responses. Oh, thank you God, thank you, thank you, thank you for the mysterious wheels you've set in motion here. And it's all somehow tied into the clusters of threes!

She glances at her watch and with a start and says, "Oh, no! No, no, no—look at the time! Ohh...I'd really love to keep talking but I have to take an important phone call in a minute. But I really enjoyed meeting you..." She leans forward through the partition again, throwing that radiant, pleading smile at me, a smile that could effortlessly dismantle entire civilizations.

My typical demeanor around women who I'm attracted to is hysterical, paralytic silence, but emboldened by whatever cockeyed plan the Universe has cooked up for us here, I blurt out a ham fisted request for her phone number. And although the words sound as if they're formed in the sphincter of a slightly constipated sheep, because the physics of this story aren't governed by any normal casual laws, this beautiful creature smiles ever so sweetly then eagerly jots her phone number down right there on my trip sheet, several threes appearing in the sequence. She pays the fare, thankfully rounding it off to four dollars, then tells me she's so looking forward to my call. Off she goes, turning one last time at her doorstep to wave to me.

Holy shit, what just happened?

We meet the next day and the next and the next and the next. When we're together the air is full of wild-eyed operatic magic. There is sexual catharsis and tearful confession and rampant pathos and revelational secrets revealed and withheld on both sides. We're traveling at light speed through some dark romantic vortex. I fall madly, hopelessly, blindly in love with the actress…even after it becomes abundantly clear that, like me, her mind, her heart, her soul are all woefully afflicted with some virulent form of dark energy. But I just don't care—for this kind of feeling I'm willing to take a fall. Any fall, no matter how hard.

And fall we do.

How long does it take before we start manifesting our respective mental health issues on each other in such terrible terrible forms? A couple weeks? A month tops. We endure lifetimes in brief blinks of an eye. Our worlds go to pieces. We fall apart, then fall back together, the falling becoming an intoxicating pivot upon which the drama called "us" dances.

And then I do what I always do. I totally fuck things up. After a massively bone-headed practical joke I try to play on her goes horribly wrong, the woman I love just flat out disappears—just poof, gone without a trace. Phone calls go unanswered, the lights in her apartment remain darkened. Fearful of embarrassing her by filing an official missing persons report, I jump into detective mode, visiting both the restaurants where she works shifts, asking her coworkers and whatever friends of hers I can locate what they know of her whereabouts.

They likewise are mystified by her disappearance; shifts and theater rehearsals have been missed without any explanation, social engagements broken. The only hint of her fate comes via an actress/waitress friend who she ran scenes with from time to time. She discretely informs me that my beloved's ex-boyfriend from back home had recently come to New York looking for her.

I blanche, but manage to keep my shit together. Thanking her for that information, as casually as I can, I stroll out of the restaurant. Once on the street I find I'm shaking from head to toe, hyper-ventilating, and all I can think, over and over is "Holy shit, holy shit, holy shit. She's dead."

She's told me all about the boyfriend, who'd been doing time for murder somewhere out west. She's terrified of him, fearing if he ever got out of prison he might hunt her down and hurt her for abandoning him when he went up the river. I spend several hours in apoplectic terror, not knowing what to do—do I call the cops? Do I try to locate her fucked-up criminal family to see if they know of her or the boyfriend's whereabouts?

I rush back to my apartment to search through notes she wrote me, letters she sent, anything relevant for some clue that I might have missed. The phone rings! Is it her? No, it's that same waitress I just spoke to, saying she just remembered the name of another actor who's a mutual friend of theirs. She offers his number. Expecting nothing, I call the guy. Real perky like he chirps, "Oh yeah, she's out to LA auditioning for a huge role in a major film. Isn't that great? She'll be back next week."

Blindsided, I can hardly speak to say goodbye to this chipper stranger who knows more about the woman I love than I do, to thank him for delivering me the good news that my beloved is not dead. And yes, I am relieved she's alive. Profoundly so. But I'm also furious that she couldn't be bothered with so much as saying goodbye to someone she claimed to love. Not a note, not a call, not a message delivered through a mutual friend. How do you do that to someone you love?

My hands are shaking as I hang up the phone. I desperately need some distraction to notch down my madly spinning mind. Long ago I swore off booze or drugs of any kind, knowing they'd kill me in short order. Of late, my go-to opiate of choice is the New York Times crossword puzzle—each day, slowly, methodically I work my way through the maze of the puzzle, the process invariably soothing my troubled mind during times, even when walking doesn't.

So down to the local news stand I stagger. I buy a paper and, finding the movement therapeutic, then continue on to Tomkins Square Park. I reflexively head for the row of benches where I, in theory at least, spoke with Beckett some years earlier. I sit on the same shady bench he once sat on, amidst the stumble bums and emaciated drug addicts, and, hands trembling, very calmly, deliberately open the Living section of the Times.

The visual order of the puzzle immediately settles my mind. What a lovely, self-contained grid! And for each and every tiny little square, there is but one and only one infinitely specific letter to go there —if only life could only be so orderly!

It's Thursday, so it's a fairly challenging puzzle—Monday is the easiest, Sunday the most difficult. As is my habit, I pick a clue completely at random, which in this case is fourteen down (nothing with threes, thanks). I've seen this clue before, so know the answer immediately. It's the first name of a famous female gymnast. I should be happy to have a quick foothold, but I'm not because the gymnast shares the same first name as my missing actress. Coincidence, right? It's a common name, I tell myself, even though it's not.

I regroup, my eyes desperately and completely at random landing on the next clue—this time it's number fifty-seven across. It's a longer word, one that should be more difficult to decipher, but to my disbelief I work it out in a matter of seconds—why? Because it spells the word "disappeared", of course. I sit there for a long time staring at the only two clues I've completed in the crossword puzzle, words which inform me that my girlfriend has disappeared.

I blink my eyes, then have to admit the New York Times crossword puzzle is apparently communicating with me. Unreal. What the fuck am I supposed to make of this? Thank you, Unseen Forces, but I already know she's disappeared.

Is the Universe just laughing at me? I can't take this paranormal bullshit anymore and so furiously rip the paper into pieces. An elderly woman feeding the pigeons nearby studies me with a puzzled frown. Sorry, lady, but I'm receiving urgent messages from the freaking Universe and have not the slightest clue what to make of them. Between my missing sweetheart, the profusion of threes assaulting me, the indecipherable messages emanating from confounding unknown sources I'm starting to feel like I'm well down the slippery slope of losing my mind. Is it Bellevue time? Do I need to be committed?

I rise and stumble back toward my apartment. A block away, passing a one of those Puerto Rican spiritualist shops, what they call Botanicas, laid on top of a garbage can I spy the disembodied face of a large plaster saint. His big, soulful saint eyes appear to be staring directly at me, beseeching, asking to be rescued. The ragged edges around his beatific visage, bearded and solemn, tell a simple story; somebody smashed the fuck out of this plaster statue. Accident? Fury? Poltergeist? Inside the garbage can, yep, I spy the pile of remnants from the saint's body, countless shards and pieces. The back of his head's likewise gone but the statue's wizened face is serenely intact. It strikes me this is some form of a talisman, so I take it with me.

A block further on another garbage can lid I find a large rusty iron ring. The two objects coincidentally fit perfectly together. They feel good in my hands and so home they come with me. It's helpful to have a project when you think you're losing your mind, right?

Once home, I use some picture hanging wire to suspend the saint head inside the center of the ring. When completed the halo effect is quite compelling. Hanging the assemblage on the wall over my desk I admire my handiwork, vowing that if I ever do find my missing actress, I'll present this odd assemblage to her as a gift. I lay down on my bed, fretting over my vast array of troubles, studying the assemblage, then eventually slipping off into a fitful sleep.

I'm wakened from a deep deep state of unconsciousness in the small hours of the night by my answering machine kicking on. A voice begins speaking, a woman's voice, a familiar woman's voice—and suddenly I wake up enough to realize—it's her! She sounds high or sad or some combination of both. I'm about to leap up and pick up the receiver when she starts talking about a nightmare she's just had, of seeing an old man's face hanging on a wall inside a circle and how the face turned into my face and flew at her, enraged. She says she's frightened of me and instructs me to stay away from her forever, then—click—the line goes dead.

Fucking hell.

I sit there staring at the answering machine for couple of hours, like I'm waiting for it to offer some explanation, but it never does. I lay back down and close my eyes, praying to drift off, truly wishing to never awaken.

But death is seldom cooperative, so awaken I do. It's nine am, so I dozed for maybe four hours since the call, and though I tend to keep my troubles to myself, this time I realize I'm out of my depth—there's way too much extra-phenomenal information to decipher. I head over to 4th Street and ring the buzzer of my hermetic super-genius computer programmer buddy who, among other subjects, has a passing knowledge of the occult and paranormal topics. I figure he's a good fit for this particular puzzle.

Thankfully, he's home and listens as I confide in him about what's been transpiring. He's a moody recluse, a natural-born scientist with an appetite for the bizarre, someone who can process incredibly complex fields of information at light speed. I once gave him a copy of Sexual Persona, Camille Paglia's six hundred plus page, mind-numbingly dense feminist treatise, just to see what he'd say about it. He read it front to back in a day and dismissed it as fluff, discrediting her controversial premises item by item with lawyer-like precision.

So my buddy, he's flying at a high brainiac altitude. So much so that I figure the information about the clusters of threes, the beautiful actress, the murderer boyfriend, the crossword puzzle that communicated with me while sitting on the bench where I met Beckett, the face on the wall and all attendant ephemera won't freak him out like it would if I mentioned all this crazy shit to my family members or other friends.

Well, he listens, his face drawn and clouded. Halfway through my recounting I can see he's not running with the information the way I'd hoped he would. He's connecting dots that had, in my enthusiastic zeal for a happy ending, thus far eluded me.

He reminds me how couple weeks earlier he was with me when I moved into this new apartment on 6th Street. And yes, of course, it's on 6th Street and the new apartment number is 3A. As we were bringing in the second load of my junk, we discovered a severed chicken foot on my doormat. It wasn't laying there when we brought in the first load, so it was freshly placed there. I laughed, thinking it a cliche signifier—a severed chicken foot, oh, come on, for Christ's sake, really? Voodoo props? Isn't that kind of…theatrical? But his face went pale and he murmured, "That's bad man.". Sucking in a breath, he added, "You're in trouble, man." Just like the handwriting expert said.

Then he cites a second incident last week when I got into that fracas with those arrogant fucking cops in the subway. Him and me were on our way uptown, but when you're in a downward spiral the bad energy is drawn to you and the fabric of reality starts unraveling. So first the turnstile ate my last subway token, then the booth attendant refused to give me a replacement one, then I pleaded with the clerk to be reasonable but he didn't give a shit and finally just turned his back to me like I wasn't there, then I kinda lost it, raising my voice and pounding on the window of the token booth, demanding the clerk turn around and face me like a man.

That's when the two cops came sauntering up, looking to knock me down a notch or two. When the big, cocky cop mocked my truthful claim about the lost token, something just snapped in my brain whereupon I got right in his big meaty cop face and started screaming at him, just ripping this idiot a new asshole—as if he needed an extra one.

My normally standoffish friend promptly laid two strong hands on my shoulders and yanked me away from the cop, then forcibly dragged me out of the subway station. Once on the street, he informed me that it was time I left New York, as it appeared I would not survive much longer if I remained here.

After hearing my recounting of the cluster of threes and this cursed magic woman and all the other mad facts I lay out, my paranormal expert friend goes a little distant, coldly reporting he has no intention of being a spectator to the disintegration of his friend's mind. He pulls a massive dictionary from his bookshelf, locates a word then instructs me to read the definition.

Apophenia: noun. The experience of seeing patterns or connections in random or meaningless data. It may be defined as the "unmotivated seeing of connections" accompanied by a "specific experience of an abnormal meaningfulness", but it has come to represent the human tendency to seek patterns in random information in general, such as with gambling and paranormal phenomena. It is related to Pareidolia, a psychological phenomenon involving a vague and random stimulus (often an image or sound) being perceived as significant, a form of apophenia. Common examples include seeing images of animals or faces in clouds, the man in the moon or the Moon Rabbit, and hearing hidden messages on records when played in reverse.

I read it twice just to make sure I'm getting the gist of it, then say, "That's bullshit."

WARRINGTON, FLORIDA, SEPTEMBER 2004

Damn. These feeder bands are about ready to knock my truck off the road. I go weaving through the deserted streets of West Pensacola on the way home from Crazy Maker Acres as a few heavier squalls from Hurricane Ivan come charging forward, like massive wraiths pummeling the windshield.

I go banking up into the driveway of my house, a tidy little two-bedroom place tucked away in a working class neighborhood over by the Navy Yard. I sprint inside, getting instantaneously soaked, then in the moaning stillness of my house, with no pig to chase, no nagging voice to tell me what a hopeless failure I am, I breathe a sigh of relief. Fuck this hurricane, it's a cat sneeze compared to all that other shit I've been through.

I settle in there in the center hallway listening to the gales come and go, thinking about that magically playing music box and how that particular incident is just the tip of a massive freaky iceberg—it's all just further evidence of that life of stranger truths dynamic. Looking back, I see the patterns now, how these intermittent episodes of synchronicity have been a constant in my life. But it was only this last fifteen, twenty years that I've really become aware of what they represented.

Around age sixteen, I noticed an uptick of otherly energy creeping into my psyche. By that point I was done with being a dope head and had got saved, so I attributed the feelings to a spiritual contact high—conversion euphoria, as it's known. I keyed off that angle to gussy up my inner sanctum, diving inward, so that when most teens my age were addled by emerging sexual fantasies, experimenting with booze, dope and your typical teenage rebellion tropes, I sat alone in my room working up a formula for stacking a deck of cards to deal a perfect hand of Solitaire. In my dreams, I frequently flew over burning cities where I beheld Angels of Darkness crouched in various desolate alleys, engaged in horrific acts seducing innocent children. I devised a theory of eternal life based on actual physics models, applying a cockeyed notion of transcendence of the time/space continuum propelled solely by a perfectly executed spontaneous leap of blind faith.

During this stretch, every once in a while I'd get hit with bizarre urges to act out synchronistic urges in public. Case in point: during one such incident I waltzed up to good friend and, without the slightest bit of provocation, furiously howled at him, "I'm so mad at you!".

My buddy looked confused, hurt. "What??? Why? What'd I do???" He stammered, totally taken aback.

As if possessed, I got right up in his face and said, "You know what you did. You know!"

What was I doing? What was wrong with me? This was my friend. Over the next few minutes, I stood there blocking his path, menacing him with the same cryptic accusation. He quailed, staring at me, slack-jawed, bewildered.

On and on this went. I knew what I was doing was wrong, possibly sadistic, and wanted to call it off but saw no graceful exit. Finally it occurred to me that maybe if I framed my outburst as a practical joke, like I was just punking him, then hopefully we could both just laugh it off—just kidding man!

I was just about to run this gambit up the old conversational flagpole when my buddy, he bowed his head and started crying softly. Then he squared his shoulders and real pitiful-like looked me in the eye and said, "Hey man. I'm sorry. This wasn't my idea, it was hers. I'm really really sorry. Man, I told her you'd find out. I told her."

The "her" he was talking about? It was my good Christian girlfriend, who he apparently was fucking.

Since I was a Born Again Christian at the time, I hung the causal explanation for this bizarre episode on a Christian framework, figuring it was just my buddy Jesus letting me know I'd cast my pearls before the swine. During my Born Again phase that was my go-to rationalization, but up there in New York City, free of all that Holy Spirit and magical religious nonsense, with the perfect storm of desperate poverty, clinical depression, and the constant imminent threat of death aligning, I had no such reassuring structure to hang these oddities on. Events would descend upon me, the bigger ones often taking elaborate forms, like those episodes with Beckett and Woody Allen, the lesser coincidences rolling up in little clusters, sometimes on a daily basis.

And I know, I know, this has all the earmarks of a person sinking into psychosis via a series of manic episodes. Maybe I was/am mentally ill, but even if that's so, something else was/is definitely going on. Apophenia, my ass. By my reckoning, I'd morphed into some kind of highly attenuated paranormal receiver, attracting bursts of wildly esoteric energy not readily accessible to your average mainstream type. But why was I being drawn toward these incomprehensible clusters of meaning? Did my Psychic Antenna have a little growth spurt? Was such a thing even possible?

I saw my big mistake. Early on, once I realized I had some form of whacky psychic gift, instead of proceeding cautiously or doing research to better understand it, I regarded my gift like a kid does an amazing new toy. Whenever I'd feel that paranormal activity energy kicking up—often signaled by that electrocuted feeling— I'd get all giddy and go running straight at it in a "fools rush in" type approach. Bad idea.

Up in New York, I learned the forces that fuel these events are in no way by default benevolent. Nor are these events something a person can control…or even prompt. What comes comes of its own volition—you're just along for the ride. And quite a ride it can be. The best you can hope for is to hold on for dear life, surfing the waves of inexplicable events, making limited use of whatever bizarro revelations the various stations broadcasting in your brain are reporting on. Or you can dig in your heels and deny it all, then promptly go completely fucking nuts.

I opted for the former.

True, the music box incident didn't play out like I thought it would. I kinda got the tunnel vision-y there. Instead of listening to what the Unseen Forces were actually saying, I foolishly imposed my own dumb romanticist happy ending narrative on the circumstances, figuring this music box deal must be happening to facilitate a reunion with the Crazy Maker, presumably so I'd be there to love and protect my child.

Thinking I was doing holy work, I kept psyching myself up for the drudgery of cohabitation with a seriously damaged human being, one whom I felt deeply incompatible with. I kept telling myself it was only gonna be eighteen or so years of me keeping my mouth shut and faking it, then the child would be safe, right? I hunkered down, trying to be a good partner and father. Hell, I even forsook that free rent situation over in Ensley and moved us into this post WWII bungalow in a passable suburban neighborhood, forking over a goodly chunk of that Drew Barrymore movie money as a down payment in the process.

And what of our ill-fated cohabitation? Well, it's a miracle there wasn't a homicide between us during our sixteen months here in this house. I did my best to keep my big mouth shut and my manic reflexes in check, kept aiming for the way of the music box, but our respective personality disorders had the final say.

Right off the bat, she started hoarding animals and running up credit cards willy-nilly and talking shit about me to my face non-stop. There was no end in sight, no reining her in.

Continually insulted and demeaned, I responded with angry, wild-eyed outbursts. We'd fight and yell at each other, at times in front of our child. That's no way to live, so I left her again, just like I did back in Valdosta when she first was pregnant.

Her revenge came in the form of this visitation range war, a dynamic that to this day forms the crux of our interactions. Now any time I ask to see my kid, she responds with a laundry list of onerous chores I need to do at Crazy Maker Acres. If I say no, I get no child visitation. I love my kid, so basically I've become this lady's personal slave. I get summoned all hours of the day and night with bizarre tasks—mostly pet related; a possum's stuck in the wall, the dog got hit by a car and needs to go to the vet, the ferret ate the canary, the raccoons killed one of her fleet of cats. Like that.

Last week, I had to secretly bury that sixty pound pet goat she got a few months back after it keeled over dead in her front yard. She needed the burial done post haste because she didn't want our baby daughter to see it and cry. Then later, I heard an elaborate saga from my three-year-old how their goat was stolen by the crack heads, who ate it. Lord.

Wise friends and family members continually implore me to go to court to establish legal custody of my child, but I know if I engage the court system that'll just make The Crazy Maker all the more hell-bent on punishing me, so I'm stuck seeing my kid according to the erratic whims of a vengeful woman twice scorned. Over the last few years, I'd hoped I could wear her down with kindness. Stupid me.

Wow, that wind's really kicking in now. Amidst this lovely line of rumination, the power flickers then goes out. Shit. It's way too early in the storm for that development. The eye-wall's still hours away. I sit in the twilight a while enjoying the murky stillness, then the phone rings. Crap on a cracker—is it news of my child?

But no, it's only a friend up in Atlanta. She's watching the news and reports that Hurricane Ivan has intensified and they've confirmed it's gonna make landfall after dark a few miles my house. Storm surge could reach twenty feet and I live at fifteen feet above sea level. The icing on the cake is that I'm on the east side of the predicted landfall, where typically the strongest water surges, winds and tornados cluster. I've rode out hurricanes before—hell, I've gone surfing in them—but not a strong Cat 4 direct hit. So apparently I need to get my ass gone.

I think it over, weighing the pros and cons. It's way too late to be evacuating. But what happens if I stay? Power will be out for a week maybe two—then, OH SHIT! With all that pig chasing I forgot about that deadline tomorrow with Hear Music, part of the Starbucks Corporation. They're gonna pay me an unfathomable eight grand to cover that Bill Withers song, Use Me Up, for one of their popular Sweethearts albums. The catch is the material has to be in Seattle the day after tomorrow.

The song's recorded and mixed, I burned the midnight oil last night finishing it up but today got co-opted with hurricane prep and pig chasing and so I forgot to mail it out. Hells bells, if Ivan's scoring a direct hit on Pensacola that means power will be out for weeks and I'm screwed. So, that settles it. I grab a change of clothes, my laptop and a copy of the Withers cover song burned onto a CD, then stack everything else of value I own in the relative safety of the hallway. I lock up the house and hop in my truck, rolling out into the maelstrom. With luck I'll overnight the CD tomorrow morning from Atlanta.

En route to the interstate, I tune in the local news station. Highways are jammed headed west toward Mobile with a horde of panicked last-minute types like me fleeing this monster storm. Since ass-backward is my typical modus operandi, I opt to head in the opposite direction, driving straight at the approaching hurricane, thinking if I can just get fifteen, twenty miles east of Pensacola maybe I can bushwhack my way north from there on back roads.

I'm the only vehicle on the highway when I hit the I-110 spur in downtown Pensacola and go sailing out toward the I-10 junction. From there I modulate east, turning into that ferocious headwind, slowing the truck down to a steady fifty MPH. The roughest stretch comes a few miles up the way when I hit Escambia Bay and that damn two and half mile long I-10 bridge that spans it. It's open water out here with no windbreaks for several miles.

Soon as I hit the bridge proper, mercy, I'm getting blown all over creation. Bang! Crash! Huge waves smack up against the concrete pilings of the bridge, sending plumes of spray sailing over the fifty foot high railing. Ten, fifteen foot swells in the bay? Jesus! I slow it down to about thirty to keep from spinning out and slowly but surely work my way across the span.

Once off the bridge, the strafing gusts ease back down below gale force, mitigated by the wall of pitching loblolly pines that line the interstate. Five miles beyond the bridge I hook north on Ward Basin Road, riding a tailwind now, weaving my way through East Milton, praying no downed power lines or trees on this little two-lane blacktop render it impassable.

Up Hwy 87 I roll, easy as pie, not a soul on the road, crossing up into Alabama, then merging on to Hwy 29 just past Castleberry, headed toward Tuskogee. Fifty or so miles inland I slip loose of the hurricane's spiral. The wind and rain abate and the rest of the trip's a Sunday drive. By the time I hit Atlanta the night sky is gloriously clear, the stars gleaming.

NEW YORK CITY, SEPTEMBER 1984

I'm presently residing in that walk-in closet in the dingy third floor walk-up over the Chinese Restaurant in Queens. It makes that studio I had in Amsterdam look like the damn Ritz Carlton. I'm unemployed and my left hand is still bandaged after that electric saw mishap that befell me a month before I left Florida.

I've run through my meagre savings and am flat-out stone-cold desperate. But today, today will be different. Today I've finally got a job interview, so I'm putting on my best and only suit. Just before I split from north Florida I scored it for four bucks in a St. Vincent De Paul thrift store. I thought it made a real statement about who I was, all baggy and white and funny looking like it is.

Right off the bat I dubbed it my "my lucky suit", figuring I'd wear it during my job hunt once I made it to New York City, but so far lucky is the last descriptor you could apply this goddamn garment. I've been obsessively peddling my dilapidated bike into the city daily for weeks now, combing the midtown streets this way and that, searching for Help Wanted signs everywhere, but in all my searching thus far I've located but one such sign and that was at a damn ice cream parlor. The manager just rolled her eyes when I asked for an application, coldly informing me that I was definitely too old and probably overqualified.

But there's hope; my law professor sister, she used to live in New York back in the late seventies and has a friend here who manages a popular restaurant over on the East side. Sister's arranged an interview, apparently for a host position—not exactly my dream job considering my sundry nervous ticks and array of social phobias, but at this point I'm destitute, eating irregularly (at times out of restaurant dumpsters) behind on my rent and feeling a growing sense of panic—so I'll take anything.

I hop on my rickety bike (also found in a garbage pile when I first got here) and roll over the 59th Street Bridge humming that Simon & Garfunkel song as I go whizzing down Second Avenue. I lock my bike to a light pole at 30th and Second, do a quick lapel and button check on my lucky suit in the window of the Citibank then finger comb my hair roughly into place.

Fully composed, I come sailing confidently through the saloon style doors of the place, aptly named "Shelter". It's mid-afternoon, not a customer in sight. I approach the manager, who's seated at the bar doing some kind of tally, offer her my good hand and politely inform her who I am.

She smiles warmly, singing my sister's praises, then hands me an application and points toward to a back booth. "Just a formality. Fill this out and let me know when you're done."

She appraises my overall appearance for a moment, half smiling, then adds, "Nice suit…very…contemporary…" playfully, almost…flirtatious? She's beautiful and capable and kind. This is going to work out just fine. Perhaps we'll even fall in love.

I set to filling out the application, but just as I'm getting to the dicey part about previous employers and references this midget woman comes staggering through the front door. She's clearly drunk and her two and half foot high frame is decked out in garish attire; a racy low cut top, a severely risqué mini-skirt and black fishnet stockings. Her makeup is smeared and her overall appearance puts me in mind of that sad prostitute who forever stood guard outside my door in Amsterdam.

She sizes the place up, waves coyly at me, then approaches the bar, which towers over her. To my utter astonishment she then launches into an improbable scramble up onto a bar stool, a true challenge for a person of her height. She's less than discrete in her clumsy ascent, shamelessly flashing red lace underwear for the whole damn world to see.

Once she manages to balance herself atop the stool she orders a beer, lights a cigarette, then looks back at me and winks lasciviously. I turn away in terror, but find my eyes wandering back a moment later, as this is an irresistible spectacle developing before me. This time she not only winks but she lifts the hem of her skirt slightly, displaying some sort of garter belt apparatus. As she pretend-fiddles with the belt, she licks her lips and mouths something, which I fear translates to, "Want a date?"

Lord. I throw my eyes back to the application, trying to concentrate; previous employment? Building wooden chez lounges in rural Florida. Reason for leaving employment? Gruesome industrial accident. Every few moments I look up, trying to collect my thoughts, but—damnit!—there she is, that infernal midget lady, taunting me with her drunken midget sexuality. It's infuriating! Doesn't she understand how important this job interview is to me?

Suddenly the beautiful manager lady reappears. She eases into the booth across from me, takes my unfinished application without looking at it and begins peppering me with typical interview questions: have I ever hosted or waited tables before? (I lie and say yes) Am I willing to work holidays? Routine stuff.

Although I suffer from a baseline terror of human eye contact I do my best when answering her to look her directly in the eyes, knowing this is a good interview tactic. But due to the unfortunate angle in which she's seated, the manager lady's eye-line coincides almost exactly with the eye-line of the drunken midget, who's seated about twenty feet behind her, just to the left of the manager's right ear lobe.

Twice while trying to answer some simple question the midget lady blows me kisses and hikes up her skirt to show the fringe of her red lingerie. As such my eyes involuntarily dart back and forth, back and forth between the two of them, my answers becoming garbled and uncertain. The manager, sensing something's amiss, looks at my application and, puzzled, says, "Oh, you haven't finished this yet? Is there a problem?"

Well, that's it—I can't take it any more, so I bark out, "Yes! There's a BIG problem! I mean, how can I finish anything with that damn midget lady trying to seduce me every minute of the day!" I shove an accusing finger in the direction of the bar.

There follows a long, pregnant pause as the kindly manager lady winces, recoils slightly, then slowly peers over her shoulder at the midget woman, who's suddenly become a picture of decorum.

The manager smiles apologetically at the midget lady, who shrugs as if she's just as confused as the manager is. My former future boss then regroups, slowly folding my application exactly, precisely in half. She stands, smiles warmly and offers me her hand with such great poise. "Thank you for coming in." she says, very formally, "I'll be sure to call you if we have an opening!", her tone assuring me that no such call will ever be made.

Back on the street the glaring afternoon light about blinds me. My stomach growls, churning, running on fumes again. I should have at least held out for a severance package including a free side of fries or something.

Damn you, midget lady!

I hop on my bike and go meandering this way and that, hunting for the rarest of rare birds in Manhattan; Help Wanted signs in business windows, all the while muttering "Damn you, midget lady!" under my breath as if it were some malevolent chant.

I end up south of Houston Street in the wilds of Soho. These last few weeks more and more I've come to this area for dumpster diving, digging up items to later sell in the small hours of the night at the Cooper Union thieves market. Soho's an industrial warehouse zone, but there appear to be renovations going on in many of these abandoned lofts. I see theater companies and a scattering of funky boutiques setting up shop here and there. A neighborhood on the rise! I need more rising energy in my life!

I head for a dumpster that last week yielded a box of bakery items still in their wrappers. Major score. Carrot cake and brownies with expired "eat-by" dates, like I care about that. I lived on them for a couple of days, and since then I've been regularly hitting the dumpsters of the various eateries popping up in this previously lawless territory, hunting for more of the same. Sometimes I get lucky, but not today. Dumpster number one is a total bust.

I go rooting around in a new dumpster, this one down near Prince & Wooster Street, finding a suitcase full of old Life magazines that I figure I can sell. I'm stacking them on the dumpster rim when, in an adjacent window across the street what do my two eyes behold? Damn! Some restaurant lady's posting a Help Wanted sign in the window! I ease out of the dumpster, not wanting her to see her future employee lolling in garbage. Just to be safe I circle the block so as to appear from the opposite direction.

It's a cafeteria style joint called Food Restaurant. I compose myself, then go strolling in, very casual and carefree—like all, "Hello, I was just strolling by and happened to notice the sign." I fill out an application, praying no drunken harlot dwarves come leaping out from the psychic bushes of Life.

The manager returns to interview me, introducing herself as Susan Spungen. We shake hands then, stupid me, I mention that her name sounds vaguely familiar. Susan sighs, then grudgingly reveals that Nancy Spungen was her sister. Having no idea who Nancy Spungen is, Susan's then forced to explain that her sister is famous for being murdered in the Chelsea Hotel at the hands of Sex Pistols bass guitarist Sid Vicious back in the late 70s.

My god! This prodigious talent I possess for saying exactly the wrong thing during job interviews. I wince, sigh sadly, then lamely offer up "Oh, wow. Sorry…." whereupon I just clam up, not wanting to make things even worse with more idiotic pronouncements. There's an awkward pause, then thankfully on the interview goes.

There's nothing remotely punk rock about Susan. She's all business, but in a pleasant, chatty, direct way. To my utter astonishment, on the spot she offers me the job! Even with my messed up hand! The catch is it pays minimum wage and there's zero tip revenue, so it's not exactly a livable wage for someone residing in Manhattan. I'm doing the math and thinking it over when she throws in that I'll get a free meal each day and can take as much leftover food home with me as I can carry. Game changer! That means I'll get to the food BEFORE it lands in the dumpster. Well, that seals the deal. I take the job! As I'm standing up to go Susan likewise compliments my lucky suit.

Yes! My lucky suit!

Yee-fucking haw. A job! Food! Rent paid! And absolutely nothing else. Tomorrow morning at ten I'll be officially employed. Hedging my bets, I go cycling around Soho in my lucky white suit, circling all through the East and West Villages searching out remote dumpsters in hopes of finding urban flotsam and jetsam to sell tonight at the thieves market.

And I must cut quite a dashing figure in my lucky white suit, zipping my bike around this dirty, seething metropolis, as I start to notice passersby doing double takes wherever I go, particularly in Soho and the East Village. Interesting—they pull up short and stop in their tracks, brazenly gawking.

Am I just imagining this?

No, look it just happened again. Hip New Yorkers are fascinated by me—and the expression on their faces conveys…what? Favorable appraisal? Hell's bells, that's a commodity I'm utterly unaccustomed to—especially here in trendy New York. I wonder why, and then realize—of course! It's my lucky suit!

I've blinked my eyes and somehow it's three full weeks later. I'm coming off my sixth nine-hour shift in a row, nineteenth in twenty one days, and fuck it, it's Saturday night, I'm gonna go recreate some. My belly's full, my rent is paid and in my lucky suit pocket sits a modest wad of dollar bills.

Tonight I will not transition to the thieves market and aggressively hawk items I yanked from sundry dumpsters. Tonight I will not schlep back to the walk-in closet in Long Island City and serenade the walls of my tiny jail cell.

I've fled the Jesus-happy South to come to this den of iniquity known as New York City to get shut of my dour Pentecostal ways, to become more worldly, more me, so tonight I will don my white suit and bike over toward that little seedy stretch of storefronts in the East Village where I've seen a scattering of cutting edge dance clubs.

Heading north up Avenue A I settle on a popular spot called The Pyramid. The gay cook at Food Restaurant mentioned it, reporting it's the new edgy club in the East Village and as such difficult to get in to on busy weekend nights. I couldn't tell if he was joking but judging from the long line of hipsters queued up outside the door I now see it's true. Damn.

As I'm cruising past I see a cluster of total weirdos in bizarre outfits and exotic hairdos go sailing past the waiting line, whereupon they're ushered through the velvet ropes at the entrance of the club by a hulking, cross-dressing doorman. What gives? Ah, it must be some kind of VIP entrance.

Scattered among the line of garden variety hipsters there's a handful of regular Joes and Janes, all decked out and shivering out in the cold, I guess desperately hoping for said doorman's eventual approval. Since I have no aptitude for the sad and sorry fate of waiting for doorman approval, I decide to give pretending to be a VIP a shot. I lock my bike to a nearby parking meter and come sidling up to said doorman who sizes me up, then to my utter astonishment grins widely, pops the velvet rope gate blocking the door and ushers me in. "Honored to have you, sir!" He inexplicably announces.

The place is packed. The music is loud and aggressive—do they call this style of music punk rock? I guzzle down a few shots of overpriced whiskey, wait for the booze to take effect, then try my hand at modern dancing.

I've never danced, not even as a teenager, so I'm a terrible candidate for this new role, wild and unrhythmic, unfamiliar with the fashionable steps of the epoch. I thrash. I flail. I jerk, all the while preparing myself to be ridiculed and shunned by the gaggle of scenesters surrounding me on the dance floor in this gritty temple of hip.

But surprise, surprise; weaving my way through the pulsing crowd, dazzling counterculture vultures come prancing up to me with huge, greedy smiles on their faces. Huh? And they commence to dancing with me, inexplicably slapping themselves in the forehead and making chopping motions on their arms as they undulate to the mind-numbing beat.

Thinking this to be some new dance craze, I mimic their strange dyskinetic movements, much to their delight. I'm in! I've somehow leaped from the outermost fringe of uncool to the hip center without having to sully myself traversing the soul-crushing middle. What is this? What hand of Grace descended?

It's a few days later now. I'm biking up 8th Street dumpster hunting and as I pass a movie theater near 6th Avenue I'm bewildered to see a poster of my white-suited self in the theater window. What???

I swing back around and examine said image, discovering that, in fact, it's not me at all, it's that palsied guy whose cassette I wore out so long ago, that David Byrne guy. Not only does he have an identical lucky white suit, but he's proudly wearing it in some film called Stop Making Sense. Interesting title!

Studying his outfit I'd wager David Byrne's lucky white suit cost a considerable bit more than mine, which makes me grin a little, having outsmarted the fashion icon himself with my inexpensive, yet apparently chic outfit.

The poster confirms that it wasn't just my imagination when I first saw him through that big picture window in Amsterdam and felt instantaneous kinship. He and I could be related, even brothers—his hair's cut in a fashion identical to mine, his build's also tall, slight and rangy— he's strained and jittery looking like I am and he's got that far away, nervous distracted look in his eyes, just as I've been told I have. And then there's this odd coincidence with the white suit he's wearing in the poster. It's a serendipity puzzle!

I've got a few hours to kill before work and it's the discount matinee, plus I'm one hundred percent gainfully employed so I can afford luxuries like occasional discount movies. I plop my two dollars down and go strolling into the empty theater. The movie starts.

It's some kind of concert film. There's musical performances and quirky, angular, aerobic dancing and immediately the kinship I felt with this lunatic who sang and sputtered about burning down his house returns redoubled. I want to shout at the screen, "Thank you, sir! I too am burning down my house, albeit in a completely symbolic, circuitous, and oblique manner!"

Then about halfway through the film it happens—the eureka moment. David Byrne is singing a song called Once In A Lifetime and he launches into this dyskinetic, emblematic dancing whereupon, to my great surprise he does MY dance, the one I learned from my newfound weirdo friends at the Pyramid Club, you know, where we slapped at our foreheads and chopped on our arms and all.

I'm happily watching my uber-cool doppelganger thrash and gyrate in a manner that I can completely identify with when suddenly it hits me—HOLY SHIT—all those leering, dancing club kids! They thought they were dancing with DAVID BYRNE. I've been mistaken for someone famous! And of course! All those people on the street—the ones who were gawking at me when I rode past on my bike wearing the giant white suit? Same deal—they thought I was that famous Talking Heads guy.

I burst into uncontrollable laugher, but who cares— the theater's empty. Of course, all those style gurus who thought they were dancing with superstar David Byrne, that's why they were so gung-ho about accepting me; they thought David Byrne was doing his signature moves for them! In fact nothing could have been further from the truth. They were dancing with a minimum wage nobody, a mentally ill cafeteria worker, a cipher, an illusion.

The idea of participating in illusions may be alluring to some, but it isn't to me. I'm engaged in an epic struggle to become myself, not David Byrne. As such there and then I vow to retire my white suit forever. I appreciate David Byrne's contributions to my world, but I need to proceed under the steam of my own imaginings, not his.

NEW YORK CITY, NOVEMBER 1993

Thanksgiving? Nope—this ain't no day of thanks, at least not for cab drivers. I make a note that in future years when the urge to work this legendary date on the calendar hits I will give it the hard brush-off, as I would a pile of stale, cyanide-laced doggie treats.

First off, that goddamn Macy's parade wreaked major havoc with traffic patterns, throwing my grid interval system completely off. Then, after the parade ended there followed several hours where the city was frozen with massive logjams at the bridges and tunnels. And by ten pm the party was over and everyone headed home, whereupon the streets went deadly quiet.

It's presently closing in on midnight and I've run forty minutes empty now, not a passenger to be had. In the last two hours I've had two fares that in total brought in a little under twelve dollars. It costs me about thirteen dollars an hour just to run the cab, so I'm working for sub-nothing here, which cranks up big turbines in my ever-increasing reservoir of I-Hate-My-Job inchoate rage.

I'm seething and still have a full three hours left on this damn shift and have maybe cleared thirty bucks for myself thus far after paying the eighty six for the fleet, three for "union dues" (don't get me started) and twenty for gas. My prospects for breaking a meagre seventy-five dollars for twelve hours of grueling toil tonight look increasingly slim.

I've been sinking further and further into a dark mental space of late and the prospect of three additional hours of futility, driving in circles cursing my fate is more than I can bear tonight. So maybe just this once I'll quit my shift early and call the night a write off.

This utterly atypical impulse takes root and suddenly I just decide, fuck it, I'm gonna do it. I'm over on Park Avenue in the Thirties so I bust a move down to 21st Street then bank west, aiming for my fleet garage on 21st between 6th and 7th Avenue.

I'm a couple blocks away when, crossing Broadway literally a minute from ending my night, a young Indian or Pakistani guy, maybe twenty-five years old, steps out of a doorway and hails me. I whip it over to the curb and just have to laugh—ain't it always this way? You surrender and say "I quit" and then what happens? The thing that previously was impossible to apprehend just plops right in your fucking lap. It's like some infallible law of physics. But why is it only with fares? Why not with a good woman? Or a better job?

In my new passenger climbs. He's friendly looking, clean cut, contemporary attire and throws me a bizarre address way the hell out in Canarsie, Queens which is basically an industrial no man's land between Flatbush and Coney Island.

"Canarsie?" I sputter, "What the hell are you doing going to Canarsie at this time of night?"

He laughs, not offended by my outburst. "Yeah, that's what everybody says! It's kind of a weird gig. There's a big TV studio in a warehouse out there. I'm a cameraman and I do the midnight shift." he says, "Uh, ever see Psychic Friends Network? That's…well, where I work.", adding that last bit somewhat apologetically, like he's embarrassed about it.

"Oh…yeah…" I chirp in, "That creepy scam show with Dionne Warwick? What's up with those weird animal print dresses she wears?"

"I know." he laughs, "She's terrifying, but a job's a job, right?"

Right. Maybe I should ask him if they're hiring.

As we work our way out toward the Brooklyn Battery Tunnel we get to talking about the show and his work. It's an eight-hour shift, it pays great and he gets benefits like health insurance and even a monthly transportation stipend. The only catch is there's no subway anywhere near the warehouse and he lives in Manhattan so he has to cab it there every night then get a car service home in the morning. Bad for him, good for me. It's an easy breezy twenty, thirty dollar fare.

I ask about the psychics.

"Oh yeah, total frauds." he admits, "Most of are complete fakes. But there's a couple that, well, I'm not so sure about. They're different…"

He's likable and sane. We have a great conversation as we arrow toward his obscure destination. Jumping off the Belt Parkway near Bensonhurst he guides me through a series of lonely back streets, past shuttered warehouses and the charred husks of stripped cars. It's spooky, urban blight type territory, and were he not such a personable human being, right about now I'd be officially starting to fear for my life. It's places like this that cab drivers go to get shot in the back of the head.

We pull up outside this well-lit warehouse. The fare's twenty three bucks. He throws me thirty, asks for a receipt and says keep the change. Nice guy! As he's getting out he warns me, "Hey, you probably already know, but I wouldn't pick anyone up around here if they hail you. Unless you like getting robbed…" I tell him I know the score but thank him for his advice anyway. I watch him enter the warehouse then roll off, intending to follow the curving road back around to a connecting street.

Well, I curve and curve but find nothing resembling civilization in this direction, then—Jesus—up ahead the street dead ends into railway yard. Great, the perfect place for an ambush! I accelerate and bang a nasty power-sliding turn, whipping the cab around as fast as the laws of physics allow. Backtracking, I start to recognize landmarks then spy the warehouse the cameraman disappeared into up ahead…then something catches my eye—well, someone.

Positioned there under the same street light where I dropped the cameraman stands this petite, gorgeous lady in a full length mink coat.

What???

It's the middle of fucking nowhere in a crime riddled neighborhood and there she stands, calmly posed in the pool of that streetlight wearing a zillion dollar coat. To cap off the surreal vibe, her arm is lifted, casually waving in the air like she's hailing me from outside Tiffany's or the damn Metropolitan Opera House or something. Is this a setup? Women are often used as bait for cab hijackings. Hmmmm. Despite the camera man's warning, I stop.

"I knew you'd be back..." she regally observes as she eases her fur coat shrouded figure into the back seat. She gives me a midtown Manhattan address then leans forward and, revealing a hint of an Eastern European dialect, says, "You have a very strange aura around you. I felt it even inside the building after Ishaan told me you'd brought him here. What is your story?"

Quite an opening pitch. I'm figuring she's one of the stars from the TV show, so I say, "Ah, you're a psychic, right?" She smiles, then commends me on my deduction. "Okay" I continue playfully, "but wait, if you're really psychic, don't you already know my story?"

She laughs knowingly, "No, it doesn't work like that. I only catch flashes, not whole stories. Around you I see many conflicting auras and they are intriguing. It almost reminds me of Krisnamurti—you know Krisnamurti?" And much to her surprise, I do. He's one of those mystical philosophers I read during my lonely self-education stint in Amsterdam, along with other religious lunatics like The Cloud of Unknowing, Meister Eckhart and Teresa of Avila.

I even attended a Krisnamurti lecture once, so I do my best impersonation of him for her, saying very somberly, "Listen! (long pause) Listen!! (longer pause) No, LISTEN!!! REALLY!!" followed by profound, mystical silence, which elicits a lovely burst of laughter from her. "Oh, you really do know Krisnamurti!"

As she's guiding me back to the highway I get to studying her face in the rear view. Damn if she isn't a dead ringer for that beautiful movie star Jane Seymour, from that abysmal mainstream TV series called Dr. Quinn, Medicine Woman. I got me a full blown character weakness for mainstream beauties, so my heart goes pitter pat a bit.

We strike up a lively conversation. I weave my way along the Belt Parkway hurtling back toward Manhattan, the meter churning away, happily finding myself enjoying the best back to back fare I've ever had—in maybe eighty minutes time I'll rake in sixty bucks—hell, that's Mike Tyson level money! And to think, I was ready to turn the cab in! Life pivots on a dime, does it not?

We're mostly making small talk, but then my Psychic Friends passenger, her tone switches, she gets real serious and says she want to know about the sorrows and burdens she feels emanating from me. Hmmm, and there I was feeling all happy and titillated. Good thing she didn't catch me on a bad day.

But still I'm not sure I can trust her, not sure if she's an authentic enlightened being or some charlatan looking for a foothold in my thought realm so she can play me like a cheap pinball machine, so in the end I open up, but only a little, telling her about some of the minor instances of synchronicity that befell me as a kid. Mid sentence she theatrically interrupts me, saying, "Wait. I see something. A woman, very strong face, powerful face, long blonde hair, with a blonde child. Who is she to you?"

Wow. Okay. This sounds remarkably like my one-time friend in Belgium who I experienced an undeniable psychic connection to. We had dreams about each other that often came true and shared letters for many years, pen pal style. But we parted ways a year or so back after a series of crushing misunderstandings, ones my heart still aches about. She's blonde, does have a strong powerful face, and has a blonde son who I was close to for a while. He's maybe eight years old by now. Sigh...

But I'm still skeptical, so I ask, "Is it a boy child or a girl child?"

"Girl," the psychic says without hesitation. So clearly she's off. "Sorry, that doesn't ring any bells.", I say, now figuring she's just tossing out wild guesses here. But the psychic's unfazed by my skeptical tone. "It will. Bells will ring. In the future." she says, making what feels like a ham-fisted attempt at prophesy.

After that little conversational wobble it's a lovely ride. We laugh and talk and she prods more, asking about my past. I'm evasive, which probably just whets her appetite. We arrive at her destination, an apartment on Broadway in the low thirties just a few blocks from where I picked up her workmate Ishaan. As she's digging in her wallet for cash to pay the fare I get to studying her face and can almost see similar conflicting auras around her, like the ones she alleges she sees around me.

She offers me two twenties, adding I can keep the change. That's almost twice the fare! I smile and wave off the payment, "Free ride." I happily announce, "I was coming back to town anyway and I enjoyed our conversation." She thinks this over then smiles mysteriously and says, "No, you must take this cash from me. Otherwise how can you afford to buy me a drink after you turn your taxi in?"

Holy shit. I'm getting hit on by a beautiful psychic!

I'd mentioned how my fleet's garage is just a few blocks away and after I've dropped her I'd be turning the cab in, so she knows I'll be available in a matter of minutes. I study her in the rear view. If she's making a pass at me, she's doing it poker faced. But wait, maybe she's just interested in me as a weirdo, like as a specimen or something? Maybe she wants to interview me on her TV show—who knows? As I'm thinking her offer over she pulls out a business card and scribbles something on the back of it.

"I understand. You're worried about your safety. Here, this is my private phone number. Call me when you get to a bar that you feel comfortable in. Any bar downtown will do. I'll meet you there and you can tell me the truth about who you really are." She hands me the forty bucks and the card then hops out of the cab. I look at the name on the business card; it says simply, "Bahar: Psychic Readings" and lists a Manhattan number.

What do you do? Me, I'm a naturally suspicious person. Paranoid at times. I know if something feels too good to be true, then it probably is, and this particular proposition's definitely setting off some major alarm bells. On the other hand she's beautiful, she's interested in my story and she may have insights about Unseen Forces and psychic undertows that normal human beings don't. Plus, we're meeting at the bar of my choice, so what risk is there?

I shoot down Broadway to 5th Avenue then bang a right on 21st Street and turn the cab in. Two minutes later I'm on my bike headed for my favorite dive bar down on Houston Street next to the Knitting Factory, a watering hole the locals call Tom & Jerrys. I drop a quarter in the payphone in the back of the bar and dial. To my astonishment she answers. I give her the address, then ask what she's drinking. "Chivas Regal, darling..." she intones as if immensely pleased with herself. "No ice."

Ten minutes later a cab pulls up and here she comes sailing through the door decked out like some Hollywood dream girl—you know, that flashy fur coat, sparkly earrings, glittery lipstick, the whole nine yards. The barfly drunks about shit their pants when this imperial alpha female form comes sashaying past them.

I hand her the whiskey and we make a little toast, followed by a round of small talk. Finally she lays her hand on my arm, lowers her brow and says, "Okay, enough of the bullshit. Tell me. You got secrets. I can't see past them but I know they're there and it's driving me crazy. Only you can tell me. I can't help you unless you open up."

Damn, that's some grade A admirable straight talking candor! On the rare occasions when I've opened up about my secret life I've invariably ended up regretting it, as no sooner do I open up than I get abandoned by my confessor. It happened a couple of times back in my church days when I spoke of those dreams of flying over the burning cities, Satan in the alley and all. Over the years it became crystal clear that my past, my inner thoughts, my altered perception of reality apparently just flat freak people out.

So as you might imagine, my first inclination is to clam up. But I've already fallen under this gorgeous lady's spell so my mouth just sort involuntarily starts making noises, sketching out the sundry landmarks of my secret existence. I tell her about Beckett, about Woody Allen and the movie on the side of the building and sneaking into the Princeton Club to steal stationary to send to him, about those dreams of flying over burning cities and more and more and more and with the telling of each passionate lunatic vignette I get a little more agitated and rushed, like some invisible hourglass is running out on our time together and if I don't convey the whole story NOW a terrible fate will befall us both and all of a sudden I start feeling like some goddamn paranormal Cinderella!

At first she's smiling this radiant, triumphant smile, I guess reveling in her power to coax my deep dark secrets out into the open. I get this bad feeling though, like some manner of vanity-based energy is emanating from her as she nods her assents, adding in the occasional, "Of course!" and "Well, what do you expect?" Her cockiness feels like a bad fit for the tone of this confession and I begin to worry maybe I've entrusted the wrong person here, but it's too late; I've been fully triggered and out the tales come spewing, one after another after another.

And as I dive deeper into the exotic tapestry of events in my life of stranger truths the look in her eyes tells the whole story—I watch as the ease and confidence drains out of those lovely eyes like water spilling out of a child's wading pool, all shot full of bullet holes and rapidly deflating.

I'm in the middle of my stolen car story and things are going downhill fast. The smiles are gone. The nods of assurance are gone. My beautiful psychic looks alarmed. I try to make a joke, something to put her back at ease, to show that I don't take my paranormal burden too seriously, but the joke only makes things worse. I forge on with my testimony, hoping she'll find some redemptive plot twist, but remain a helpless witness as a toxic melange of terror and sadness grows and swells in this woman's eyes until she's all but absented herself from the beautiful human form that sits there before me.

Then quite suddenly, as if she's hearing a strident command from deep within her mind, she interrupts, asking me to point out the bathroom. We're at a table way in the back of this crowded little shoebox bar and the bathroom's halfway between us and the front door. I watch as she makes her way through the regulars crowded into the bottleneck around the bar, never looking back at me, and I'm not especially surprised when she sails past the bathroom door and forges on out the front door to the street, now moving at a fast stride. She hits the curb, throws her hand in the air and hails a cab, just like she did with me a scant few hours ago. A taxi screeches to a halt, in she climbs and just like that Bahar's gone.

The drunks are disappointed. They toss me a few sympathy shrugs. I'm left to sit here and work out the math. Let's see, once again I've opened up to a stranger about the bizarre machinations of my whackadoodle inner life only to have them instantaneously flee in terror.

I feel this reflexive urge to go wallow in some mossy green pool of tepid self-pity, to bathe myself in a self-righteous sense of betrayal, or rage, or shame...but it's quickly supplanted by this oddly satisfying feeling of triumph, almost like a backwards validation. I mean, look, this wasn't just any stranger I freaked out with my life story—this was a professional psychic. And apparently the shit I conveyed to her about my life is so bizarre, so eerie, so inexplicable that even a goddamn psychic was terrified of them! Wow!

AMSTERDAM, HOLLAND, JANUARY 1984

This cold clear blustery night. Head down into the wind, I'm nearing home, returning from yet another ghost voyage through the streets and alleyways of Amsterdam. My favorite defeated prostitute welcomes me back with a frostbitten, weary "Hey…why not?" then snaps out of her trance, puzzled by the box I'm toting.

Plucked out of a garbage pile a few blocks away, it's roughly the size of a microwave oven and contains the shattered remnants of what I'm guessing was once a high-end saloon mirror. "It's a mirror," I tell the mini-skirted sentinel, lifting the box for her inspection "Fancy. A broken mirror." She stares as I pass, bewildered, making no comment.

Mounting the stairs I hear the Arabs chatting; just the men this time, no weeping woman, no bedsprings. I silently slip through the door into my place, taking a seat in the decomposing easy chair. Out the window I hear young male revelers passing by, bellowing out Dutch drinking songs, sonic remnants of their sloppy celebrations leaking through the sundry cracks in the walls and floorboards, mingling with the murmurs of the voices next door.

I study the contents of the box. What originally caught my eye in that pile of junk were the etchings on the glass; baroque figures like cherubs and angels and rosebuds and such. It appears to have once been a real status item, and as such its fate as a garbage pile discard seemed unfair, so I went ahead and rescued it.

I sit there a while, my thoughts drifting like my brain was a transistor radio being tinkered with by a slightly stoned chimpanzee. The Arabs are chittering away. The drunken Dutch singers linger outside, yammering on in-between their sloppy song verses. All this foreign sonic traffic is making me evermore lonely, so I switch my cassette player to radio mode and go hunting for one of those BBC stations, hoping to hear some nice English words being spoken. I ease the dial around, hunting a specific broadcast frequency but with the high winds tonight the signal's scattered.

After a few thwarted tries I land on what appears to be a proper BBC station, but the signal's weak, undermined intermittently by snatches of foreign announcements and jumbles of static and such. Minutes pass, the signal stabilizes, then, in increasingly coherent pulses, I catch snatches of this angular piano music playing. The rigid, repetitive scales on the surface appear to be fairly rudimentary, but upon further examination there's more going on, like an interweaving of complex underlying threads, each musical thread a melodic storyline all its own.

Do they call this approach "variations on a theme"? Whatever the hell it is, between the fragments I'm catching of it and the pulsating, interceding waves of static bleeding over from other broadcasts the cinematic dreaminess factor is off the charts. Thank you, Mother Nature and the BBC for whatever the hell this intoxicating melange of ambient sounds and recorded music is.

With this meditative soundtrack elbowing out peripheral annoyances I set to studying the mirror shards in the box. Right away I spy two largish chunks that appear to match up—you know, like Africa and South America do. I extract them, carefully dust off the glass splinters then lay them side by side on the floor—and bingo, a perfect fit. Transformative extrapolations ricochet around in my mind as this box full of razor sharp garbage suddenly morphs into a treacherous, yet exciting jigsaw puzzle.

With the soothing piano music now beaming in clearly, I place the box on the bare floor then slowly, carefully I begin to reassemble the mirror. It's a tricky proposition, but over the next hour I manage to completely reconstruct most of the upper corners and a few lesser regions toward the center of the frame.

Progress!

But these last few minutes I've been increasingly thwarted— the remaining shards being too busted up to work with. I root though the tiny fragments at the bottom of the box with a pencil eraser but, seeing no compatible chunks, I pause my reassembling.

"This mirror is a thing too broken to fix…" I announce to the thin air in the room, that phrase tumbling away down various shadowy rabbit holes in my brain. A thing too broken to fix…sadly, that's a notion that resonates all too well…

Over the next thirty minutes I keep returning to the half-finished mirror puzzle, then the music ends and BBC announcer comes on, all whispery and refined in that all-knowing English arbiter of taste kind of way. He reveals the title of the piano music, something called Einstein on the Beach. I smile, happy at the coincidence, as presently I'm reading a book called Einstein for Beginners, sort of a Relativity Theory breakdown for non-science minded folk.

My smile grows when the announcer names the composer: Phillip Glass. Further synchronicity! Glass, just like the substance I've been hovering over while listening. Wait, it's a sort of accidental life palindrome; while manipulating shattered glass I'm listening to Glass, shattered…you know, due to the intervening radio static. Now it's my turn to mechanically laugh. I do so loud enough for my Arab neighbors to hear, so they know they're not the only ones having fun around here—heh-heh-heh-heh, I go. Heh-heh-heh-heh.

Studying the assembled pieces more closely only now do I notice the myriad mosaic-like versions of my own face reflected back. Well hello, you thousand iterations of self! Which of you poor souls is actually the human being truly known as "me"? Yeesh—let the naval-gazing ponder-spiral begin as I now commence to free-fall into the suffocating abyss of Self.

Yes, okay, Unseen Forces of the Universe, I get it. With an assist from BBC radio, you've offered this healthy dose of ham-fisted symbolism. Yes, I'm a fractured soul with no true identity to fall back on. Comforting message delivered. I feel so much better for that. Thanks a million.

So, now what do I do with this box of busted glass? Tote it back to the garbage pile where I found it? Restore things to their previous order so some other pathetic naval-gazer type can stumble upon it and get all clued in? Sounds reasonable enough. But not now, not tonight. It's late and freezing outside and I'm so enjoying this BBC music show—they've now modulated to some French guy named Satie, also a piano playing dude. I return the assembled mirror pieces to the box then slide it under a table in the corner, intending to dispose of it in the morning.

But I don't.

A week sailed by, as did the next, and the next, and the next. More and more now, for hours at a stretch, in rain, snow, fog or the rare outburst of sunlight, I find myself wandering the filthy back streets of Amsterdam, always alone. But ever since the Phillip Glass mirror shard episode my focus is different; now I have a purpose, I'm a hunter/gatherer, and while trudging this way and that, sooner or later I spy some alluring object among the melting snow and frozen piles of dog shit: a three-legged rocking horse, a stained spiral notebook with Bob Dylan songs transcribed into Dutch in it, a tattered pair of plaid wool trousers with punk rock patches carelessly sewn on. These I tote back to my little studio apartment, where the sad prostitute no longer greets me, averting her gaze now when I pass.

As the weeks have tumbled by and my gathering activity has increased this once monastic cell has become increasingly stuffed to the gills with—surprise—piles and piles of exotic Dutch junk. I haven't given much thought to the issue of my studio's capacity, anticipating no end to my gatherings until just now when, upon returning home with this largish, rusted dial face of an antique clock, I walk in the door and find myself unable to locate a suitable landing spot for it. Strange, but amidst the clutter there's just no reasonable surface available upon which to place it.

I stand in the open doorway cradling my latest precious acquisition, mouth hanging slightly ajar. Normally I just plop things down anywhere then let them migrate around the room until eventually finding their ideal resting place. But today all such localities are occupied. Weird. I fret about this for a while then, cold and tired, finally just give up and discreetly place the clock face outside my door on the Arab men's garbage can in the hallway. Let them cackle about that.

I slump down into the decomposing chair and watch yet another lovely snowfall commence. Are interior tectonic plates shifting? Have I reached some sort of tipping point with my hoarding? Taking stock of my quarters I have to admit it's a possibility. As I scan my cluttered surroundings I spy the topmost corner of the box of mirror shards under the table, tucked behind piles of newer acquisitions. Wow. I guess I forgot to throw that out—but hey, with that thing gone maybe I'd have room for the clock face!

I extract the box, but instead of throwing it out I clear a space on the floor and reassemble the contents again. Interesting! Now, framed by and mirroring the surrounding piles of accumulated junk, the scattered reflections of my face create an entirely different impression than previously. The shards no longer seem disconnected. In fact, the prismatic compound eye effect is quite pleasing, as my reflection now appears integral to the crowded space in this densely packed visual field. Then it hits me: my grim little studio apartment, it's become a sort of a sprawling, accidental mosaic.

Cool!

As if a magic wand's been waved, my previously drab, overloaded room suddenly seems alive with dazzling configurations that'd previously escaped my attention. The mannequin head with the ears painted gold appears to be talking to the big stuffed animal tiger missing—wow—an ear! How did I not notice that correlation before? What else have I missed?

I pass some time happily reassessing my chaotic surroundings, suddenly made aesthetically pleasing simply by being reframed in this new context. I find this discovery especially uplifting because, while I'm obviously the de facto creator of meaning and order herein, said creation has been formed intuitively and is therefore happily free of the clumsy onus of design and deliberate thought. Laying here on my cot admiring my surroundings I feel a weight lift from my weary shoulders, followed by the blessed tug of ever-elusive sleep.

Morning sunlight on this fresh blanket of snow, the city a blinding, angular mess. On my way downstairs I notice first that the clock face is gone, and second that the prostitute is not at her usual station. Something is off…the world feels weighted differently, as if during the night everything's tilted a half a degree.

In a big pile of eviction debris a few blocks into my walkabout I dig a ragged Monopoly game board out of a pile of snow. The iconic addresses have been scratched out and replaced with handwritten Dutch counterparts. Park Place is now Peck & Klopenburg, an upscale Dutch department store on the Dam Square. Baltic Avenue is now a Krank Sex Shoppe. The board's got cigarette burns and cryptic scribblings all over it. It's a major score, familiar yet foreign, manufactured yet handmade, exotic yet commonplace, whimsical, yet slightly terrifying—a true keeper.

I tuck it under my arm and continue on, but long before I head back to the apartment I begin fretting about how this latest jewel will blend in with my existing maelstrom of debris. I try to envision it here or there, but to no avail. The tension builds until a few blocks from home in a fit of panic I fling the beautiful Monopoly board into the Herengracht, the centermost of the legendary canals that form the rib cage of this ancient city.

Watching it flutter downwards, then sink into the freezing brown murk I immediately regret my impulsive action. Hey! I need that! For my accidental mosaic! But like the previous day with the clock, the idea of bringing home additional components is suddenly too painful to consider. Apparently objects can no longer enter my lodgings free of the weight of self consciousness.

Placed here said object will conflict with this, placed there it will conflict with that. Anything new will violate the already pleasing arrangement of that accidental mosaic. What's happening here? What was that passage I recently underlined in that book by that French guy named Sartre, "Consciousness is always consciousness of itself..."? Is this what he's getting at in that unbearably boring Being & Nothingness?

Another wandering day is done. For the first time in months, I brought no flotsam home and as such feel at loose ends. Seated in the decomposing chair I spy the prostitute down below on the cobblestone street. She's back! And look, she's chatting up a drunken stranger! Grinning lasciviously, she goes to tugging at his coat sleeve. And now off they go! Finally! A customer! She looks so happy. I'm happy for her.

A new day. A Sunday. I've done three extended walkabouts today, found amazing objects along the way but returned empty-handed each time. It's like the junk collecting door in my mind has simply slammed shut. I'm back home for a couple of hours now, long enough to eat my pathetic dinner of noodles and canned corn, wash the dishes, then play guitar until my fingertips ache, but suddenly the walls start closing in and so out into the elements I must go. The wind's kicked up pretty good and it's spitting slush. As I slip out my front door I see it's just me out in the elements tonight; even the prostitute has taken shelter.

Since the streets are totally deserted I opt for a stroll on the Nieuwendjke, the winding central shopping lane in the city. Normally I avoid that stretch of Babel like the black plague due to the oppressive commercial vibe and crushing crowds of blissful, doe-eyed Dutch consumers, but tonight the shops are all shut down and the scene is just shy of post-apocalyptic. A few blocks back I spied a dope dealer and then a wandering drunk, but that's it. I now traverse a personless realm, a near ghost-town.

I'm drawing near the Dam Square when I catch a snatch of something carried on the wind. Music? Like Delta Blues genre? It's slightly abstracted by the gusts of wind, sort of like with the BBC broadcast, only I don't have a radio with me and this ain't no dainty piano scales, it's the unmistakable wail of an electrified slide guitar. Maybe it's time to pry out my rotting fillings and get a nice tinfoil hat? No! A body must always opt for the path of sanity, no matter how unlikely the chances of actually apprehending it might be.

I aim in the direction of the sound. A block on I'm catching bits of it more clearly now. See? I'm not crazy! And it's definitely not some trick of the wind, but in the winding labyrinth of cobblestoned streets it's nigh unto impossible to identify either the general location or specific source, like if it's recorded music or something being played live. With one wind gust the music comes from this direction, with the next it comes from that. The only thing I can say for sure is it's wildly accomplished, badass slide guitar and vocals being wailed via some cheap amplifier out into the night air.

I put my ear to the wind and pick up speed, reaching a near trot, then a viable life-notion hits me: hey, if I can't collect jewels in the form of found objects anymore, maybe I can switch to collecting sounds. They take up no space and seem to have a profoundly calming effect on my mood. With that prime directive I press on in search of the sonic source.

But Fate, ever the trickster, won't make this quest easy. I follow the snippets of song down a sequence of narrow winding streets, but to no avail. I keep thinking I'm close, only to turn a corner and be greeted by an empty, dead-end alley, the music floating over the crest of the surrounding brick and stone walls.

The slush is turning to straight sleet, and it's coming down harder now. It's probably close to one in the morning. This game of sonic cat and mouse has gone on for a full forty minutes, the blues lament rising and falling on chimeric winds. Should I just say fuck it and trudge home?

No! I shouldn't!

I forge on, passing a series of small bars, one of them open, dreary Dutch pop music leaking out of the doorway, then turn corner and—lo and behold, tucked back in a shut-down storefront, there he is, the blues guy, wailing out a lament as if his life depended on it while making the wildest, most unhinged slide guitar sounds I've ever heard!

There's an old sauce pot on the ground in front of him with the word TIPS scrawled on it. So, okay he's a busker, but who busks at this time of night? And with not a soul around? In the sleet? And with such unbridled passion? And besides, the visual frame, it's not right. The musician's all crooked looking, seated perched atop a pile of rags and hunched over what looks to be some manner of miniature Hawaiian style slide guitar.

He cocks his head back, sucking down a huge drought of freezing air, filling his lungs so as to properly howl out that next high note he's aiming to hit and now his shape/form issue suddenly comes sharply into focus. His arms are severely foreshortened, his fingers nonexistent.

I've seen others like him, mostly in photographs in textbooks that chronicled the nightmarish saga of a so-called miracle breakthrough prenatal nutrient known as Thalidomide. It was foisted on women in the mid 1950's to early 1960's, hailed as a miracle drug. Before definitive causal links were established between Thalidomide and an outbreak of horrifying birth defects, thousands of babies were born with foreshortened arms and legs, at times no more than flippers like you'd find on a seal. Most didn't fare well in life, much less hang on long enough to play transcendent Delta Blues in a Dutch snowstorm, so before me sits a true survivor.

I step closer, working over the attendant math: behind the thin membrane that shields mainstreamers from the more essential aspects of reality lay exemplars of this variety, this phenomenal musician, this Thalidomide baby who, by all rights should be curled up in a fetal position in some institution, not situated thusly on a lonely street in a foreign land slashing a ragged heart-shaped hole in the veil of reality with his voice, amp and guitar.

But how is he playing guitar?

Closing in on him I now see his methodology; on one flipper he's got a bottleneck slide duct-taped, on the other flipper a pick is likewise taped. His appendages just barely reach the fretboard and that's why his form is so crooked—he has to hunch over to reach the notes, then he comes up for air to sing and breathe in the spaces. It's like some magical scene from a fever dream.

It's just him and me, not another soul around. Either he doesn't notice that I'm there or doesn't care. After a few songs I approach, drop a couple guilders in his cup. No eye contact. Nothing. I walk away without speaking, fearing any utterance would surely shatter the spell.

Arriving back home I see there's a different prostitute on the sad patch of grass across from my door. She's younger, but bears a semblance to the original woman, whose name I suddenly realize I've never learned. She smiles cryptically at me, making eye contact with an agenda of commerce. Is the older prostitute her sister, her mother, her aunt? Am I just hallucinating? What's become of the older woman? What will become of this one? What becomes of those who live on the razor's edge, eternally striking improbable postures in the act of balancing a form not configured to stand?

It's the next morning. I'm carrying a box of junk from my room down to the street. This is my sixth load. I'll continue this ritualistic act until the cell I inhabit is returned to its original monastic status. Load after load will disappear. The new prostitute watches the comings and goings, puzzled, as if my purpose in life is to confuse prostitutes.

It would have felt fundamentally wrong to simply pile all this up on the curb outside my own place. No, there's an order to the Universe and this chore's gotta be done right, so each item gets returned to the various garbage cans and piles around the city where I originally retrieved them. It takes me the better part day and into the night. The last to go is the box of mirror shards.

So long, didactic entity!

When I return home I find my formerly padded cell returned to its original barren state. The decomposing chair, the table, the cot, the mini-fridge, the hot plate. My landlord will be delighted, temporarily at least, for, having run out of objects to salvage, life in Holland suddenly makes not the slightest bit of sense to me.

It's a month later. I'm hunkered down in an economy seat of this Royal Jordanian Airlines flight at Schiphol Airport on the outskirts of Amsterdam, waiting to fly back to the States. It's a cheapo flight, a connecting leg from Mecca and so the plane is loaded with Muslims in their traditional flowing robes and desert garb. I think of my Arab neighbors and wonder if they too are fleeing Holland on this very plane.

The flight attendants are all mustachioed males, burly types who look wildly miscast in their flight steward outfits, their snug little vests, their pleated tailored pants. I'm sandwiched between two hefty Muslim men dressed in traditional robes and have made the mistake of purchasing a conservative American newspaper, the International Herald Tribune, so as to catch up on the US sports scores and goings-on back home.

The burly Muslim man to my left grunts disapprovingly as I open the paper to the sports page. I worry I might precipitate some minor Jihadic incident reading this imperialist rag in his presence until a moment after the grunt he adds, "Man. I been in Mecca a week and them Braves done dropped to third place." I smile. He's a Coca-Cola employee from Atlanta on his first Hajj. You just never know, do you? You think you know, and then the Universe pulls the rug out from under your feet of clay.

Out the window lies an endless expanse of Dutch countryside. The drizzle, the tulip fields, the grey upon grey upon grey. So long, Holland, I will not be seeing you again.

NEW YORK CITY, MARCH 1991

It's my thirty fourth birthday. I'm living in that scary section of the East Village, down near the projects by the Williamsburg Bridge. Over the last few months, from my bedroom window on the third floor I've seen people shot, stabbed, beaten, chased, threatened and more. The operators at 911 know me on a first name basis.

I've been in my outsider film student/taxi driver spiral for four years now and the general trend is downhill. Since no one else seems to care, I've decided to throw myself a birthday party and have invited everyone I can think of, which amounts to fifteen of my fellow lonely, half-crazed cab driver buddies, plus a couple of my weirdo experimental film maker friends from NYU, also of the lonely male variety. They've all showed up at the appointed hour, but as nine o'clock turns to ten, ten turns to eleven, we've gone ahead and accepted the sad truth that none of the twenty or so marginally approachable women we'd collectively invited/begged to come to the party are gonna make an appearance. As such the gender imbalance in the room is putting quite the damper on the general morale of us lonely male partygoers. What to do?

Emboldened by those five shots of vodka I've already downed, I call a party crisis huddle whereupon me and my fellow sloppy-drunk, personality disordered cohorts hastily devise a bold chick-recruiting plan. I break out some vintage birthday cards and colored markers that I dug out of a dumpster a while back and all us cab drivers set to drawing up a batch of crude party invitations. We'll cruise nearby hot spots like The Pyramid Club and King Tut's Wah Wah Hut trolling for attractive young hipster chicks, handing out said invitations in hopes of luring them back to our event.

It's a tall order, right? What self-respecting trendy urbanite female in her right mind is gonna leave a swinging bar to attend some lonely cab driver's birthday party in a sketchy urban neighborhood? So, seeing that our collective social status sits at less than nil, we decide that as we hand out the invitations maybe I should just go ahead and pretend to be someone famous...like a celebrity.

My resolutely demented, self-harming buddy Clayton giddily suggests I dress up as Anthony Perkins—I'd once mentioned to him how back in my fashion modeling days some of the photographers commented that I resembled the infamous serial killer portrayer—but I nix that suggestion strictly on a strategic basis. What streetwise hipster chick is gonna come to an anonymous party with a Psycho theme?

Remembering that movie poster from those years prior, I suggest David Byrne. Everyone cheers, agreeing that the Talking Heads frontman is a superior chick-magnet type celebrity. Now we're rolling! I dig my white suit out of the closet and in giant letters we hastily add David Byrne's name to the invitations, scrawling it willy nilly on the already madly emblazoned cards.

Off we go, a doomed romantic SWAT team, my staggering faux David Byrne-self leading the charge. We make a beeline for trendy East Village nightspots like Save The Robot, Horseshoe Bar, The Pyramid—all cutting edge joints overflowing with young, fabulously disinterested Gen Xers decked out in black on black on black on black, as is the fashion of this time.

I hit the various dance floors and bars in my now well worn, slightly stained white suit, my pockets bulging with the home made invitations, I chop my arms and slap my forehead but strangely no grinning hipsters leap up and join me—what gives here? Has the whole white-suited Talking Heads scene come and gone? Not one club-going hottie mistakes me for David Byrne anywhere.

After striking out in a series of clubs packed with the East Village scenesters, the demoralized romantic SWAT team gives up and heads back to the apartment to drown their inner loser in a bathtub or two of gin. I stick around this last place, called The Horseshoe Bar, and after some triangulating devise a secondary ingenious plan to salvage our first ingenious plan; I station myself directly adjacent to the door of the lone ladies room in the crowded bar and there strike up conversations with various women impatiently waiting in the long, slow moving line for the single toilet!

Brilliant!

But even then, with a captive audience, as I pass out invitations and do my spiel, not one woman is willing to join me/David at my/David's birthday party. This is a new low! I can't even get noticed as David Byrne! I walk home, dejected, feeling lower than whale shit. Happy birthday indeed.

It's the next night. And again the world of popular music provides me with a clue as to my forward path. I'm driving the taxi, running empty down in Chinatown when I'm hailed by this foppish looking punk rocker and his hyper-sexualized Asian female companion. Turns out he's Mary Byker, the lead singer of a popular British band called Gaye Bykers On Acid. Mary is headed to the Hotel Pennsylvania, just across from Madison Square Garden where, he boasts, he's playing a big show later tonight.

Both of them are high as a kites and after commenting favorably on my hyper-aggressive driving style, he begins to soliloquize to his adoring companion how cab drivers and rock stars are really essentially practicing the same art form. Right. He happily listens to himself riff on this line of utter horse shit for the entire ride. I listen too, but not so happily and only because I'm a captive audience. On and on it goes, until mercifully we arrive here at his hotel.

As he's disembarking he leans in the passenger window and mutters, "Oy, mate!

What's your name? I put you on the guest list!" I point to my hack license, which presently is about four inches from his face. He reads my name, then scowls mightily, barking, "Nuh-uh! No! That ain't you! You're not HIM..." pointing at my hack license, "You're…you're…" suddenly it comes to him like a bolt of lightening, "Travis Bickle!".

Mary then points across the street at Madison Square Garden. "RIGHT! Travis, I'm putting your fucking name on the fucking guest list! Right? That's it! Consider it done... TRAVIS!" He shouts, leaning back into the cab, again screeching Travis Bickle's name grandiloquently, I guess waiting for some thankful response from me.

I offer none.

"Yeah, that's who you are, right Travis??" he continues, drunkenly peering in the window, slightly imploringly, searching my face for some confirmation of his wonderful compliment. I look away, adding, "The fare is four-twenty, sir."

He sneers, digs in his grubby jeans pocket then chucks a ten dollar bill through the passenger window onto the front seat, grinning conspiratorially. "Keep it Travis! And that's the name that'll be on the guest list, right? Travis Fucking Bickle!" he slurs, not just to me but also to the garish Asian woman who laughs and coos as if she's heard the funniest goddamn joke in the universe. As they stumble past the stoic doorman arm in arm, the singer jabs a finger back at me and sneeringly howls out, "Travis Fucking Bickle!"

I suppose Mary is, in his own obnoxiously repellant way, trying to be helpful, but I resent his remark and so do not attend the Gaye Bykers On Acid concert at Madison Square Garden. The last person in the world I want to bear any semblance to is Travis Bickle, the psychotic, homicidal stalker portrayed in Martin Scorsese's depressing film Taxi Driver.

The shift wears on with a similar off-kilter vibe as scenes from Taxi Driver return to me again and again. I get home around three and drift off into a bout of manic dreaming, but I'm not flying over burning cities, like usual. Tonight it's a series of scenes involving machinery gone amok. The vignette I recall best involves a charismatic young black woman named Janet Mallory whom I know vaguely from one of my writing classes at NYU. Janet's a rising star, an eminently likable person, a highly articulate inner city exemplar, self-assured and full of hard won dignity and salt of the earth humor.

I wake late, exhausted from the night of tumultuous dreaming and have to scramble to get to classes over at NYU on time. Entering 721 Broadway who do I cross paths with but Janet Mallory herself. Interesting coincidence! Universe? Are you calling me?

Seeing coincidence at play I plunge forward, conveying the details of the dream to her. She's a writer so I figure she'll appreciate the absurdity of the imagery. The action takes place in a gloomy swamp. I'm myself and she's a huge yellow bulldozer. I climb into her cockpit, start her engine then drive her into the swamp, jumping off at the last moment as the slimy green water pools around my ankles. I swim back to shore as she plows ahead driverless, disappearing into the mire.

"Uh-huh. And that's it?" Janet asks, lowering her brow.

"Um, yeah. Not a long dream. But an interesting one…" I add, hopefully.

Janet clears her throat, then informs me that I am not to have any more dreams about her. Me being me, I don't quite get why. We stand facing each other for a long awkward moment, then I finally connect the dots then—oh shit—Jesus, what a train wreck of Freudian archetypes!

My faces flushes red—God, what did I just say to this kind, intelligent woman, and WHY? The ensuing silence is utterly agonizing, so, stammering nervously I apologize then, wildly casting around for some deflection, I blurt out a bewildering excuse, blaming my indiscretion on the fact that I'm too pathetically white.

"Say what???" she asks, doing a double take.

Jesus. As usual I'm just making things worse. I forge ahead, just winging it, hoping to put all that bulldozer/swamp/slime/sexually-charged dream imagery behind us.

"It's like this: I've been thinking about opposites more and more." I tell her, "And in relation to that, since I'm white, I've been listening to all kinds of black musicians lately, you know, like Don Cherry, Brownie McGhee, Fela Kuti and John Lee Hooker, and well, they just get it. It's like they're connected to the pulse of the Universe, you know? Like in some integral way. I've compared their performances with the works of parallel white musical exemplars like Monte Alexander and Dave Brubeck and Joe Jackson but it just seems like the black musicians come much closer to the foundational truth that music conveys."

"Uh-huh…okay, so?" she says, still wary, but interest piqued.

I plow ahead, "Me, I'm awkward and possess no such integral rhythmic connection to the Universe, but I'm hungry for one, like down in my soul? The catch is that every time I try to emulate the mannerisms of those exemplars of soul, you know like Cherry or Hooker, instead of becoming more soulful and rhythmic and…well, black, I become the opposite—like…more pathetically white."

"Oh no, you can't do that." she agrees, "White folks trying to act black? You know what we call them? "Perpetrators"."

"Yes. Amen. And there's nothing more pathetically white than a "perpetrator", right? So it occurs to me that if there's, like, a spectrum between, for lack of better terminology, "blackness" and "whiteness", or maybe "soulfulness" and "soulessness", then me being like I am, you know, so incredibly uptight and awkward and constricted and, well, white, maybe I'm positioned so far out at the uttermost end of the white spectrum that no amount of hard work or determination could possibly get me anywhere close to a zone of even moderate soulfulness—it's just too far to go from where I'm starting from. So does that mean I'm stuck in the white zone forever? Like there's no hope for me to ever be cool?"

My writer friend snorts, then shakes her head ruefully. "Oh, my..." She mutters to herself, looking away. "Oh my, my, my...."

"No, listen. I don't think it does. Since I'm unwilling to accept a fate of mediocre whiteness, it occurs to me that maybe instead of making these endless feeble attempts to cross that vast expanse of whiteness that lies between me and the beginning of the cool spectrum, you know, where those black musicians I admire reside, maybe I'd be better off just setting out in the opposite direction—you know, endeavoring to become more and more white."

This idea she thinks over, "Oh right. Yeah, like that Jung thing...enantiodromia." she adds, nodding approvingly. I stare blank-faced at this brilliant young woman until she elaborates, "You know, where a person takes some aspect of personality so far that it becomes its opposite..."

Wow. Wow-wow-wow. "Actually, yes! That's exactly it. I need to become my opposite. But I know I'll never accomplish that goal by simply trying to act oppositely, you know like feigning cool black jazz cat status. No. That approach only makes you more pathetically white—like a perpetrator. So my only hope lies in embracing my whiteness and venturing far enough into the furthest extremes of uptight white behavior that I come to the end of white. And maybe there, like blinded by that vortex of whiteness, I might accidentally stumble and/or fall into a rhythmic, soulful black modality. I guess, like, sorta by Grace?"

Until this point she's been listening with pursed lips, seeming to follow this line of reasoning. There's a moment of formulation on her part, then, instead of rejecting the paradigm she goes with it, "So, correct me if I'm wrong here.' Janet reasons, "What you're trying to do, then...is become...super-white...?"

SUPERWHITE!

Scientists refer to breakthroughs like this an "ah-ha moment". As soon as she utters the term, a halo of definition's suddenly rendered to the whirlwind of confused thought projectiles that've been crashing and clunking around in my psyche for years and years and years. Of course, I'm trying to become Superwhite! It's that simple. That explains my affinity for droning, whining white gospel hillbilly music....and my compulsion to button the top button of my shirts and coats, and my irregular dancing style and my inexplicable affection for activities like drag racing and bingo and Polish parades! I'm simply becoming Superwhite! This is suddenly going very well.

"Right! Exactly!" I excitedly agree, "I'm trying to become Superwhite!"

Janet pats me kindly on the shoulder and in parting says with a hint of whimsy, "Well honey, if anyone can become Superwhite, it has got to be you. So long, Mr. Superwhite!"

I'm unable to properly reply to her compliment because this time when she utters the name "Mr. Superwhite" a face suddenly appears on the big movie screen in my mind. Whose face is it? Carl Jung's? Woody Allen's? NO! It's David Byrne's. There he is, staring intently at me through his geeky black glasses, in his big white suit manically chopping on his forearm, dyskinetically slapping his head with the palm of his hand. Of course, David Byrne! Yes! He's the epitome of Superwhite. He's so square that he's cool, so white, that he's black. He's Superwhite!

No wonder I felt that intense kinship with him! We're both pursuing the same destiny—a state of soulfulness called Superwhite! Of course he's clearly far far ahead of me in his metamorphosis, and so likely knows much more about the disposition of this quest than I do, but we're fellow seekers! How exciting it is to belong to a movement!

I decide there and then that if I ever come face to face with Mr. David Byrne, I'll neither introduce myself, nor offer any preamble or apologetic explanation, I'll simply, boldly, with a knowing smile utter the term "Superwhite" to him. And if the Universe is the place of mysterious order and meaning I so hope and expect it is, he'll instantly both understand and embrace my codified utterance.

Janet heads off to her next class and as I watch her go suddenly all the unlikely angles of my existence nestle into place.

It's empowering knowing who you are!

With this newfound anchor in my consciousness the day sails by. Once home I go about my evening routine then sleep like a baby, no flights over burning cities, no incarnations of Beelzebub in darkened alleyways seducing innocents, no bulldozers or dismal swamps.

It's the next morning. I wake with a clear vision of my future—it's time to realign my identity in relation to this theme of Superwhite. But rather than try to imitate David Byrne's appearance, which would just make me more pathetically what I am, I first aim for my own personal coiffure landmark. A quick check in the mirror shows that my hair, coincidentally looking very similar to a photo I saw recently of David Byrne's present hairstyle, has grown long and floppy and modern looking, like some hipster collie dog's.

A conservative, anachronistic haircut would likely be more in keeping with a Superwhite approach, right? So, time for a makeover. But this proposition is slightly problematic, as a costly trip to some trendy New York City hair salon is flatly out of my minimum wage reach. I may walk the hallowed hallways of NYU with a bevy of plutocrat offspring and sneering trust fund babies, but, aside from my meagre scholarship money, which barely covers tuition, I live well below the poverty line, paying my own damn way with slim pickings gleaned from driving that infernal cab. But hey, no biggie. In true Superwhite style, I'll just undertake this new haircut mission on my own.

I grab my shaving kit and dig out that sixties era electric hair trimmer I found in a dumpster last year. I start low, working the sides at first. Things are going well enough until a stray wisp of severed bangs hair tumbles into my eye. I jerk a bit and—damn! The snap-on comb attachment pops off the trimmer, exposing the bare cutting blade, which comes to rest directly on my scalp just above my left ear. Shit! I've just gouged out a massive chunk of hair!

Jesus, there's no good way to cover up a mistake of this magnitude. I gingerly attempt to even that side up, trimming off a little bit of the surrounding area, then a little bit more, and more, until by the time I've blended around the bald spot, the entire left side of my head is essentially shaved clean. Sigh. An inauspicious baptism for my new Superwhite persona!

There's only one way to fix this; I'll just have to shave the right side the same way—but hold up a minute! This amended hairstyle, if done properly will look a little like what they called "whitewalls" back in the 50's, so maybe I'm on the right track here after all!

I start working on the right side aiming for a retro buzz-cut flat-top style, but as usual I get too much in a hurry and now realize I've made the transitional line between bare skin and stubble much higher up on the right side of my skull than on the left. Damn! Subsequent efforts to even out the sides just make the two lines all the more asymmetrical.

In the ensuing series of reductive miscalculations my manic reflexes kind of kick in and I go a little crazy with my new Superwhite haircut. By the time I come to my senses and put the trimmer down there remains only a scruffy median of hair down the center of my skull. I study it in the mirror and think, "Well fuck a duck, I've given myself a god-damn mohawk." I examine the end result of my efforts and sadly admit that the obnoxious stoner guy from Gaye Bykers On Acid was right. I am Travis Bickle.

Is this what psychologists refer to as a self-fulfilling prophesy?

It's a work day, so after giving up on my hair I sadly hop on my rickety bike and head off for the taxi fleet. No hipsters gawking at me today, just a scattering of mainstreamers wondering who the scary looking freak on the old bike is. Arriving at the shape up room I notice Marty the evil dispatcher glaring at me, then remember my bizarro haircut. I nod and smile. Marty being Marty, he scowls, mutters an obscenity and then limps away.

I take a seat on the bench at the center table where fifteen or so veteran drivers have already gathered, waiting for a cab to free up. I pick up a stray Daily News that somebody left behind but before I can even open the damn thing I hear several of the veteran drivers suppressing guffaws. When I look up everyone's staring at me. The whole room busts up, offering up the obvious catcalls about my haircut.

Larry Zaitz, a regular Joe from the Bronx, leads the way, making a grand show, greeting me as "Travis", asking me to stand so he can pat me down for concealed weapons, then seeing I have none he offers to get me a great deal on some zip guns. Further hilarity ensues.

I'm in no mood for teasing, so I stomp out the door, opting to wait outside in the early fall chill. I catch my mohawked reflection in a storefront window. Jesus, I can't really argue the point, as not only do I now look like Travis Bickle, I'm starting to feel like him.

Ninety minutes later I finally hear my name droned out over the PA and, after I've paid my obligatory five dollar "tip" (bribe) to Marty, I'm handed a set of taxi keys. It's a crisp blue early fall afternoon as I drive out into the city, drawing ever closer to my inner Travisness.

MILAN, ITALY, SEPTEMBER 1981

Damn man, those gold and red brocade curtains are getting on my last nerve and making me twitchy. But then I always feel a little off-kilter in the presence of wildly over-the-top pomp and circumstance interior design. So does that make me some kind of minimalist?

Either way I'll just have to tough it out, being that I'm presently sitting on my hands in this classy ante room, waiting to be summoned by the advertising director of Georgio Armani's clothing company here at Armani's World Headquarters. I'm two weeks in Milan now, doing this male model gig, and am on what's known as a "casting call", this one apparently being a big-ass deal. My agent pulled some strings and arranged for me to swing by, as Armani's mounting a big fall campaign and they're looking for a young Anthony Perkins type. I don't quite see the resemblance but my agent damn sure does.

Fashion photography legend Fabrizio Gianni is shooting this campaign and my agent says I've got a bonafide chance of landing it, as I'm on a little bit of a roll since arriving here in Milan a couple weeks back. Day one I landed a couple of small editorial jobs, high fashion work for legit magazines, which generated a little "buzz". Then along came that four-page spread for Italian Vogue with superstar photographer Carlo Orsi.

My agent tells me that when that edition of Vogue comes out in a few months it'll beef up my fledgeling modeling portfolio considerably…well, that is, if Orsi doesn't think I'm gay. He's allegedly wildly homophobic and if he suspects a male model's gay, he crops their head off in the image so you can't see their face. This ruins the much-coveted Vogue tear sheet status for their portfolio, as our face is our business card.

Welcome to the bizarro world of high fashion.

It's nigh unto surreal to consider that just a couple months back I was a clinically depressed failed professional surfer, spinning my wheels in that surfboard factory gig back in North Florida, doing mindless piecework ten or more hours a day. I had my crisis of faith and knew I had to get the fuck outta Dodge, to flee the church and my home, but had not a clue where to run off to. The weight of my aimless, troubled lifestyle was starting to eat a hole in the back of my brain when, lo and behold, the heavens parted and into my lap dropped this cushy job in the fashion industry over here in Europe.

Go figure—one day I'm a minimum wage assembly line grunt laminating sheets of fiberglass together, the next I'm in Milan, Italy getting paid serious scratch to mope around in velvet jodhpurs and ruffly pirate shirts, knee deep in supermodels, casting calls, booking agents—the whole nine yards. It's so wildly off the improbable chart that I've just ignored the whole surreal vibe and rolled with it—hell, I might as well have been elected President of Uruguay.

My agent predicts that when the Vogue spread hits the news stands I'll be in demand,

and if the Armani campaign comes through I'll be a bonafide star. Anticipating the Armani go-see, this morning she sent me to her personal hairdresser, whom she gave explicit instructions about how to shape up my limp, straggly surfer hair. I went there in good faith, figuring these people were experts, but buddy that lunatic barber all but shaved my damn head in the process. But I guess these people know what they're doing, right? Please tell me so. Now here I sit in Armani World Headquarters looking like some miserable plucked chicken waiting to show my portfolio to the various haute couture big shots.

Walking in the building a minute ago I paused in the foyer, gazing heavenward at the garishly opulent gilded-filigree adornments crisscrossing the vaulted ceiling and said to myself, "Goddamn, this is it. I'm set for fucking life."

Well hello! In comes the drop-dead gorgeous receptionist all smiles and elegant charm. She beckons me into the conference room which features a sprawling wall mural, like a fresco, of some manner of erotic medieval pastoral scene—think galloping nymphs and satyrs and other such agents of Satan.

I've seen pictures of Fabrizio Gianni before so I recognize him right off. The others look like your basic weasel-eyed fashion snobs. I smile and offer my hand to the lady nearest me, she studies it for a second, repressing what appears to be extreme revulsion, then gives it a tepid shake, as if she were handling a soiled diaper or some similarly unappealing item.

The two art director types shy away, so I slide my portfolio across the table and take a seat, watching as it makes the rounds at the table. There's some conversation in Italian. Tones are skeptical as they discuss my few meagre tear sheets and test photos, looking up at my face, then to the book, back and forth.

Okay, so I'm a specimen. I can work with that provided it keeps me from having to go back to the psychological crucible of rural Florida and that minimum wage factory work. Finally Fabrizio Gianni himself leafs through the portfolio, frowns a little, like he's puzzled and says, "Your hair…..is very short. But in pictures…is different…" I nod enthusiastically. He sighs, then talks a bit more to the others in Italian, then closes my portfolio and dismisses me.

On the way out I catch a glimpse of my haircut in a plate glass window. Shit, did this goddamn haute couture haircut just kill the deal? The one I got this very goddamn morning? Because I was told to? Is this just another case of one of those fingertips an inch away from a legitimate foothold on the stairway to heaven type of deals?

It is. The next morning my booker informs me it's official—I didn't land the big Armani campaign.

As the week passes I get turned down for two more campaigns. Same with the next week. And the next. Fashion being the arbitrary shell-game it is, it takes me a while to work out the subtext. The castings I'm being called for are less and less prestigious.

It becomes clearer and clearer that either my rising star is now plummeting, the style paradigm's been scrambled or it's some lethal combination of both.

I notice that the malnourished, brooding types such as myself are no longer being sent out on the best go-see auditions. We're now vying for pajama jobs and hokey advertising shoots for shaving cream and baby soap. Meanwhile I watch with increasing dismay as swarms of wholesome blonde, dreamy-eyed, super-buff beachcomber types come storming in by the planeload. They all have test shots from this buzz-worthy New York City photographer named Bruce Webber and they commence to gobbling up all the choice campaigns, elbowing me right out of the business.

It's a month later and I'm officially desperate. I got no plane ticket home, no money for food, and I'm way behind on my hotel bill. I'm hanging on by a thread here, waiting the last week before that Vogue spread comes out, not that it matters since all the clients in Milan now want blonde beach boys. I'm living on the third floor of a squalid boarding house called the Albergo Trieste over by the Luna Park, a working class amusement park type setup. The area's blighted, populated mostly by hookers, drunks, poverty level farmers and factory workers, produce peddlers, day laborers—you know, the scruffy folk.

The first floor (prima piano of the Trieste is a whorehouse, and floors two and three are the cheapest rental rooms in all of Milan. Me and a few other desperate models reside here. When things get boring we go sit in the lobby and time the tricks. Eight minutes is the record; a tee-tiny farmer who stank of onions and the big mama prostitute. She was twice his weight so he may have just thrown in the towel out of self-preservation.

On Sunday the friendly prostitutes attend Catholic mass with the owners of the Trieste, then they all sit down to a big happy dinner in the lobby afterwards. It's tragically beautiful, and such a far, far cry from the puritanical Pentecostal realm I fled a few months back.

I'm down in the lobby timing tricks when I start confiding my dire situation to a fellow fringe model who's been on the circuit for several years. He comes down to Milan from Germany twice a year in hopes of landing a few coveted tear sheets from Vogue, Linea Italiana and such, which he then parlays into high dollar catalog work up in the northern European markets.

Up in Germany, he confides, the work is boring, you model ugly suits and pajamas and do necktie ads for mainstream clothing companies, but the pay is great and the work is steady.

He takes in my desperate story then does some mental triangulating. He's a savvy survivor type and after a bit of deliberation grudgingly reveals he knows of a couple of secret small market towns that he works further up in northern Europe where it's easy for any American model to find work. He figures with those Vogue tear sheets I'll be sitting pretty—they're like gold up there. He offers names and numbers for agencies in the towns, but only if I promise to vamoose whenever he shows up, so I don't take his livelihood from him.

Wow, bless you, handsome stranger. He names a couple places: Stuttgart, Zurich, Amsterdam. The next day I'm on a train headed north, hotel bill settled and railway ticket paid for with cash borrowed from the owner of the Italian agency, who sees I'm a sinking ship. In an act of true altruism, she's bailed me out, knowing full well that she'll likely never recoup the cash.

NEW YORK CITY, APRIL 1994

The afternoon wears on. I'm a week into my new Superwhite lifestyle with this goddamn Travis Bickle mohawk. It's actually scared a couple of potential passengers away—they leaned in, took one look at me and made some lame excuse and walked away. Great; that's all I need, even less opportunity to make a living. I keep thinking about Janet Mallory and her comment, wondering if maybe the Mohawk will draw me closer to or further away from my inner Superwhite status.

Passengers come and go. It's nearing sunset and I'm hunting fares down in Greenwich Village. At the busy intersection of Houston Street and Washington Place this angular, quirky looking dude sporting a coonskin cap and mirrored sunglasses jaywalks in front of me. I brake, then slowly inch forward studying the jaywalker—there's something oddly familiar about his herky-jerky gait. Wait—could it be? NO! It's him—it's David Byrne! Walking right in front of my cab! Just a few days after my Superwhite epiphany!

The moment's choc-a-bloc full of ill-defined portents. Obviously the Universe has spoken! I have to convey the word Superwhite to Mr. Byrne somehow RIGHT NOW, whereupon something pivotal will probably happen in return—but what? I sit at the red light there at Houston Street, trying to calm my frantic mind and formulate a viable plan.

What do I do? Park and approach him on foot? Make eye contact? Or just stay in the cab and shout "Superwhite" at him from behind the wheel? Yeah—that's better, more dramatic and theatrical.

And what will he do in return? Break into a palsied dance on my behalf? Or maybe bark out some equally surreal non-sequitur in my direction, a corollary to Superwhite that only he and I will understand? It'll be like Albert Einstein bumping into Thomas Edison in a doughnut shop. We'll swap ideas in the secret language of uptight white geniuses. This is going to be a defining moment in my life, a meshing of wildly disparate threads, a magical nexus between ignominy and fame.

I need time to formulate a foolproof approach, and, knowing the lights are all in my favor I go racing past David Byrne, circling the block, banking right on Bleeker Street, then zipping around Mercer, then two more corners, gunning it on the straightaways, making all four lights with time to spare. Maybe a minute's passed and I find myself back on Washington Place heading north and there he is on the sidewalk, dead center in my crosshairs, David Byrne himself, jauntily strolling along. I ease the cab up behind him, roll down the window and stick my head out, preparing to shout out the magical term "Superwhite". I go so far as to open my mouth, but no sound comes out.

What…?

Indecision? Do I doubt the integrity of my message? No. I certainly do not—I just want to make sure I'm doing this right. I take a deep breath and relax, letting my mind clear. Yes…good advice; when in the thralls of some life changing paranormal event, take a breath and collect your wits before you go leaping into action.

So instead of shouting, I study David Byrne as he walks. He's a bit shorter than me, has better posture and seems to be affecting some kind of post-modern cowboy look with his outfit. Is that a look I'll adopt further along in the Superwhite self-realization arc? Who knows?

I think about that night a few years back in the Pyramid, all those hipsters dancing with me. Do we really look that much alike for people to mistake me for him ? Really? I'm a dozen feet behind him, just crawling along and some little hint in his body language suggests maybe he's become aware of my presence. Somehow he knows he's being followed—is he picking up my vibrational energy? Yes! He stops and shoots a furtive look over his shoulder at me. Contact! It's time to shit or get off the pot, so I lift my chin at him in greeting and confidently call out, "Superwhite!"

There are those magic moments in life, moments that you dream of, where opportunity intersects with dreams and desire and preparation. This is not one of those occasions. Sadly, my utterance blurts out somewhat louder and more aggressively than I'd intended. So aggressive and loud in fact it echoes all along the nearby street, causing sundry passersby to turn and gawk my way.

David Byrne flinches, stopped there in his tracks staring at me. I wait for some welcoming response after the flinch, but there is none. Wait, is he even looking at me? With those damn mirrored sunglasses he's wearing I can't be sure. What's he doing? Is he processing my message from the Universe or isn't he? He appears to be thinking it over, and yet he's made no gesture signaling either understanding or confusion. Now—what?? He wheels back around? He continues on his way???

What the hell?

I speed up. Drawing nearer to him, I shout more emphatically, "SUPERWHITE!", fighting the urge to add "Hey David Byrne, turn around! This is important!" or "Hey! Slow down, big shot, and listen—this is a special message from the Universe and it's just for you!". No, as was the case with Woody Allen, I feel a seminal need to avoid contaminating this enigmatic message with the burden of explanation. It seems axiomatic that if I have to in any way explain the concept of Superwhite to him, it will invalidate the magical power of the term.

"SUPERWHITE!!" I shout a third time and now he reacts. But instead of turning around and addressing me, he hunches up his shoulders and quickens his pace forward so that he's moving at something between a canter and a trot. This is not at all the desired effect I was hoping for and as such is both confusing and infuriating. Does he think he can outrun a motorized taxi cab? If so he's mistaken! I hit the gas, matching his increased speed and further closing the gap between us, shouting over and over the word that he and only he should not only understand, but welcome.

Suddenly David Byrne breaks away from the curbside and sprints toward the open doorway of a nearby photo store, disappearing inside. What's he doing? Does he need to buy some film? Is he a camera buff? I stop for a moment, then spy the mirrored sunglasses peering out at me from behind a tall rotating rack of photo instruction manuals. What? He isn't buying anything at all! He's avoiding me! I call out SUPERWHITE! to him several more times more, but to no avail.

Somewhere in the growing abandonment of my calling, in the plate glass window of the photo store, I catch a blurry reflection of myself leaning out the taxi's window. I'd forgotten about my recent defacto mohawk, but now see my reflection clearly as I furiously shout out that secret code word to my world famous doppelganger.

The sight stops me dead in my tracks. The visual scene's a garbled inversion of my first encounter with him all those years ago, the one where I watched him through a plate glass window in Amsterdam, dancing as he ranted in that video about burning down his house. In this reflection though, I'm now the person ranting. In fact, for all appearances, I'm a raving lunatic, perhaps to him even…a stalker?

No!

To make matters worse, in the reflection here and now, in this go-round on the roller coaster of Life it's not David Byrne I visually resemble, it's Travis Bickle. Oh, the indignity of it all. My house is so-so-so burning down, and there isn't a damn thing I can do to stop it.

I speed away, defeated, demoralized and furious that the Unseen Forces of the Universe have failed me so miserably.

GULF BREEZE, FLORIDA, DECEMBER 1980

Lurking in the darkened church foyer. Nary a soul around—not yet anyway. In a couple hours this Assembly of God tabernacle will be packed wall to wall with mourners. Checking the time I'm startled by the color of my new velcro wristwatch band. It appears to be bright red, not turquoise blue like I always purchase when the old one wears out. When I walked into that surf shop on the beach today I could have sworn I purchased the normal turquoise color. So how did I end up with this red wristband instead? What could it mean? Is this red wristband a sign? Is the Universe trying to tell me something here, like maybe it's time for me to go? Run far far away from here, from this church, this town, this job, from Jesus Christ, from everything I know. Run like a scalded dog and don't look back?

A quick tally: my surfboard business is bankrupt, my girlfriend and I have split up. I found out she was cheating on me with the smirking moron who sits behind us in our friendly little Assembly of God church here. Over the last month my sweet, tame little house cat and four adopted feral cats one by one went the way of dust, the last one drowning in a storm sewer after that torrential downpour yesterday—I tracked his little cat footprints to the drain, culminating with long sliding paw prints disappearing into the black hole below. It was like a cartoon illustration, only not funny.

Two of the feral cats got decapitated during cold spells a few weeks back after crawling into various parked car engines seeking warmth. It happened once to me, once to my ne'er do well business partner—we turned the ignition switch and heard the heartbreaking howl. The other feral, he got hit by a semi out on the highway. The house cat died of feline leukemia. When it rains it pours.

Topping off the dead list is Brent. He's not a cat, he's my friend, a member of this church—hence the impending mourners. God, did you not hear our prayers? Apparently not. Apparently you're not listening. Or don't care. Or don't exist. So what's there to stick around here for?

Brent, he exited this celestial plane last week, aged twenty three. I would gladly have taken his place. Many would have. With all the knuckleheads in this town who wouldn't be missed, God, why did you pick him? Was it part of your glorious plan to get Brent T-boned by that maniac with the steel plate in his head? That deranged miscreant not even supposed to be driving a car? Was it your plan for Brent to languish for weeks in that coma? Only to slip away from those he loved and who so fiercely loved him back? He was the best of us, but look, the best of us is gone. Brent is no more.

Hey Jesus, buddy…you listening? I'm trying not to hold a grudge here, but I'm not feeling so sanguine about the twenty or more prayer meetings we held on Brent's behalf during this stretch here since Brent's wreck. See, if you are in fact the Alpha and Omega then you knew that miserable collision was in the works, right? So why pray-tell did you not lift one finger to stop it? And you knew the prayer meetings would likewise fail, right? As instructed by both scripture and our sweet pastor, as Brent lay comatose in the ICU for those excruciating weeks, we gathered in this very church and in fervent prayer claimed Brent's miraculous healing in your glorious name, Lord. We did so over and over. Vigorously. With faith, and knowing our faith was strong, our prayerful voices resounding and full of insistent, unimpeachable love. Some spoke in tongues, everyone sang and cried, one received a Word of Knowledge that Brent would be healed and, oh, how we all rejoiced, claiming that assertion as fact! Hard claim!

We considered his return to us a done deal, so what exactly did we do wrong? Did we not claim his healing correctly? Was there some technicality in the paperwork we overlooked when we invoked Matthew 7:9, "Which of you if your son asks for bread will give him a stone? Or if he asks for a fish will give him a snake?" We begged for bread and fishes, Jesus, but here I stand alone in this lonely church knee deep in stones and snakes. And so I must go. I should stick around for the memorial service, I know I should. But I just can't.

Besides, if I am to flee this town in the coming days I've got orders to cover at the factory before I depart to try my hand at that fashion modeling nonsense up in New York City. I go rolling down Highway 98 toward the surfboard factory listening to a wobbly 8 track Steely Dan tape called Can't Buy A Thrill. And yes, pastor, I know you warned me about the perils of godless, secular music but these particular unholy words make a whole lot more sense right now than any of those hymns you tend to call out come Sunday morning. That Donald Fagan, when he sings about the fire in the hole, well, I can relate. When he sings about nothing to left burn—yes, that resonates deeply. And like his protagonist in the song, I'd damn sure love to run out now, because there's clearly nowhere left to turn.

Oh yes, with Steely Dan I can identify—there's definitely nothing left in me to burn. But truth be told pastor, when you really think about it, if sung right and heard just so, at the end of the day can't any song be a hymn?

I ease up to the row of cinderblock pillboxes where me and my party-animal business partner have been building surfboards this last ragged hem of a year. We're an odd couple, me the pious Christian servant of the Lord, him the raging heathen doper who fosters an unhealthy adoration for Jim Morrison. As for our "factory", it ain't much. In some distant epoch this isolated enclave was a roadside motor court, the office now serving as our work quarters, the semicircle of smaller cabins tucked behind the office still vacant, overgrown with weeds.

I stumbled on this choice spot last year cruising up down the highway hunting for cheap rent possibilities well outside the city limits, far beyond the watchful eyes of those pesky city code enforcement types. And there it was. I asked around and found the owner—he runs the hardware store down the highway a bit. We met up here an hour later and when he unlocked the office door to show me around, lo and behold sprawled out on a soiled mattress lay a raggedy drifter, half asleep.

The owner man studied the drifter thoughtfully, then as if talking to a friendly pup said to this scruffy soul, "Fella, what are you doing in here?" The groggy man sat up and rubbed the sleep from his eyes, replying, "Living, I guess." The owner gave it a moment's thought, then in a calm, measured voice said, "Well, you best gather your things and get on. You ain't living here no more." The man nodded forlornly, stood, picked up his bedroll and out the door he walked, never to be seen again. And with that the place was mine…well, ours.

My hotshot partner, he's a board shaper who made his name in Hawaii crafting surfboards for famous big wave riders there. Shapers are the rock stars of the surfboard industry. They sculpt the form of the board out of bulky polyurethane foam blanks. It's a fine art, like regular sculpting only with complicated hydrodynamic design involved.

It felt flat-out serendipitous how he moved back home to the Redneck Riviera right at the same time I did. I took it as a sign from the Universe and so we joined forces. On paper it looked like a good match: him the high-profile shaper type and me the steadfast, blue collar laminator—kind of a yin-yang deal. But lately I've come to suspect he's concealing a hefty drug habit, as a couple of times now funds from the company bank account have gone missing. He's twitchy and always has some bizarre excuse at hand as to why the books don't balance out quite right.

Me, I'm the foot soldier in this business partnership. There's no glamor in laminating. I toil long hours daily bonding layers of fiberglass cloth with liquid resins which, when properly catalyzed, turn hard as stone in a terrifyingly brief window of time, creating the surfboard's protective outer shell. Over-catalyzed resin can go so far as to catch on fire, emitting deadly fumes in the process, so laminating is a tricky proposition. Plus, on your average day I inhale in an exotic cocktail of toxic fumes and airborne carcinogens, the latter in the form of fiberglass cloth shards that are eternally floating around in the room.

Then there's the extensive exposure to noxious solutions like Methyl Ethyl Ketone Peroxide, Acetone and of course wildly carcinogenic materials like Styrene and DMA. For such a wholesome, natural sport surfboard manufacturing facilities may just be the number one most unhealthy workplace environment in the whole of the USA.

This is what, my twentieth day in a row working ten, twelve hours a day? There's no pay for me anymore, hasn't been for weeks. I'm just trying to fight my way back to a financial zero to pay off the loans I took out to start this black hole of a business. My feet are swollen, bleeding in places after getting swarmed by fire ants yesterday. I'm so lost in the swirl of disasters going on I had no idea I was standing in a huge ant bed while that elder from my church stopped by the factory here to have a heart to heart with me.

He spoke of his concerns for my walk with the Lord, which was touching until he put his arm around my shoulder and real firm and paternal-like informed me it was my duty to not forsake the gathering of the brethren, aka the Church. He said whether I felt like it or not he and the pastor expected me to attend every service. His slightly threatening tone suggested it unwise to dispute the point and I was so furiously intent on holding my tongue while a barrage of fuck-yous to him bounced around in my head that I failed to notice the swarms of venomous creatures assaulting my feet. I guess the ants had the final say in the matter, particularly since I'm allergic to insect stings.

Limping along prepping the boards to be laminated, laying down my tape lines and such, I get to thinking about my recent forsaking of the promised lands of both California and Hawaii. I had connections in both idyllic locales, yet I couldn't find any measure of peace in either so-called surfer's paradise. In Hawaii I was a made man; I had a car, a coveted job at the best surfboard company around, inside connections in the surf world and of course perfect surf to ride every day. I was a top amateur competitive surfer and had just turned pro, posting respectable performances in the first few prize money contests I entered—nothing sensational, but I progressed through the early rounds where the wheat gets separated from the chaff. By all indications I was on my way to a legit surfing-centered life, but inexplicably I fled that world, and not once but twice.

Why?

Hard to say, other than something big was missing—some primal connection to Spirit. It being a God-related ache and Pensacola being a town overrun with rampant Christian energy I figured the Lord was calling me back the mission fields of home. So home I came, to the armpit of the South and the crappy Gulf of Mexico surf, home to start this surfboard company with an unstable megalomaniac, to join this dinky little Pentecostal church and do my best to truly settle in and finally belong somewhere.

On the Spirit front, I'd been to plenty of those sprawling, touchy-feely hippie-fied Southern California megachurches and was bored to tears…all that low key "mellow" religious pageantry, the preacher wearing flip flops, the congregation singing rounds of new age Kumbaya-sounding songs like Great is the Lord and Everybody Ought To Know.

No-no-no, not my cup of tea. See, once you've sat on a pew in some hard boiled old-time Spirit-filled Pentecostal church, once you've heard tongues spoken and prophecy uttered and the air filled with inexplicable supernatural magic, it's just a stone cold chore sitting through most mainstream milquetoast services. And doesn't the bible say in Revelations, "Because you are lukewarm, neither hot or cold, I will spew you from my mouth."? That's basically it; I left those other places because they felt lukewarm, so I came home to be on fire for the Lord. Now two years later there's nothing left to burn.

I start laying out fiberglass cloth on the three boards I have to laminate tonight. By now that little church will be filling up. The pastor, he's not one of those flashy, puffed-up evangelist types. He's a good man, a kindly soul caretaker. He'll start in with consoling the congregation, doing his best to reconcile what the bible professes should have happened with what actually transpired.

As for all that nonsense we believed about our prayers miraculously healing our friend, he'll say something like the Lord just loved Brent so much He decided to draw Brent to his bosom a little early. And can we blame God? No, for Brent's leaving is just further evidence of just how truly anointed a person he was. So anointed the Lord called him home at age twenty three. And wouldn't we all like to be in Brent's shoes? Walking the streets of gold and jasper, cleaving to the bosom of the Lord?

The congregation will answer with many tearful amens, amens that I can in no way authentically utter, so better to absent myself, despite admonitions to the contrary by various elders and deacons and the pastor. Besides, my girlfriend, she'll be sitting in the pew right behind where her and me used to sit, with her slimy new born-again beau.

I finish laying the tape lines on the three boards then mix up my resin buckets, adding tints, catalyst and a drop of DMA, then grab my squeegee and go at it. For boards in the six to eight foot range from the moment you add the catalyst it should be no less than fourteen minutes, no more than eighteen for the resin to commence to gel. Add too little catalyst and the gelling takes too long, causing the liquid resin to seep out of the fiberglass shell and down into the foam core, making the board weak and heavy. Add too much catalyst and halfway through the process suddenly the resin changes from fluid to solid prematurely. That's a costly disaster, requiring the cloth to be frantically yanked off and the glassing process, if salvageable at all, to be started over. Resin and catalyst ratios are alchemic, wildly sensitive to humidity and temperature, so every day is different and to some extent a guessing game. Though not by disposition the methodical craftsman type, I've learned this trade with the hopes it'll provide steady employment in the years to come.

I toil for several hours laminating the bottom surfaces of each board. Once the resin properly sets I carefully trim the excess fiberglass cloth from the seams along the rail line. Again, it's a tricky business. I let the bottoms cure until hard to the touch then flip the boards and set to laying tape lines on the other side and repeat the process on the top.

It's well past midnight when I get home. The answering machine lights are blinking and I've got a good idea who the calls are from so I don't bother listening to them. I just lay down and try to sleep.

I toss and turn until morning grey creeps through the shutters. Today they'll lay what's left of the human being formerly known as Brent down into a hole in the cold January earth. Out the window I spy flurries of snow falling, a rarity for this Florida Gulf Coast town. I fix myself a bowl of cereal, grudgingly eyeing the blinking light on the answering machine. I know that sooner or later I'll have to listen to those messages.

Screw it. I press the replay button.

It's mostly church people asking where I was, why I wasn't at the memorial. Accounts of how the Lord was moving in the crowd, how everyone felt Brent's presence.

But the final message is secular in nature, from a stoner friend of my business partner. He's a party animal like my partner and sounds strangely apologetic, "Hey dude. Uh, not sure if you heard, but Ricky…uh…he tried to kill himself yesterday. He was like, really high and threw himself in front of a car out on Highway 98. But it's okay. He would've been toast but, man, lucky for him he was in that twenty zone by the elementary school. So, yeah, that saved him. I mean, the car that hit him, it was only going, like maybe ten miles an hour? I guess he was so high he didn't notice the cars were going super slow, but anyway, yeah, Ricky's got a broken arm and all, but he should be okay. You should give him a call, dude."

I don't know whether to laugh or cry. I look down at my red watchband and realize the answer is neither. I need to run.

NEW YORK CITY, OCTOBER 1984

I'm rolling. Just one slim hour ago I plucked this battered three speed Schwinn out of a garbage pile a few blocks north and further west on 9th Avenue in Hells Kitchen. Thank you New York City, I am so done with this endless walking, pounding the pavement in my daily job search.

A super was emptying out a basement as I passed by. He'd just lugged the dusty bike up the steps, leaned it against a big garbage pile, saw me eyeing it and said, "You want it, take it." Just like that. The tires were flat so I giddily hefted it over to a nearby gas station with a free air pump. In went the air, the tires firmed up and away I rode. Yes!

Now I'm peddling east on 14th street, when I hear a sort of strangled howl. Out of the corner of my eye, over on the east side of 5th Avenue, I catch sight of an eddy in the river of passing souls, a clump of spectators forming on the sidewalk. In between their tangled forms, flashes of that jumbled body commotion particular to street fights are evident—arms flying at odd angles, erratic, illogical body movements. I hear more shouts. Someone's angry—a man, then another, the second a bigger man's voice.

I'm new to the city and hungry to see, so this is an enticing aberration of patterns. I double back and pop up onto the sidewalk, weaving through the river of pedestrians.

The gathering crowd is your basic urban blight cheering section—asshole construction workers, pimped out guidos from Brooklyn Heights with gold chains and greased down hairdos, drab file clerks sporting knockoff Rolexes on their wrists, sweet little old latino matriarchs shopping for carpets bearing anthropomorphic renderings of poker-playing dogs or clocks bearing semblances of El Senior, Jesus Christos. There's an Indian nanny in a sari holding a slack-jawed rich kid by the arm and two withered old ladies simultaneously horrified and agog with bloodlust, all of them hoping against hope for some real carnage.

As for the fighters, what a mismatch. In this corner stands a hulking, pissed-off Puerto Rican gangsta type (wife-beater, jogging outfit, gold earring and "whassup whassup, poppy?" pimp roll). In that corner, one very scrawny, refugee looking, skeletoney-boney hollow-eyed loser. Gangsta dude, he's a six-foot, two hundred plus pound train wreck of furious muscle and greased back hair. And this other guy, he's a pitiful, bald child's puppet. So the impending fight sets-up like an IQ test for the mentally impaired. "In this picture, can you point out which man is about to get his ass kicked…?"

A fancy mountain bike, which the little man has apparently just been yanked off of, lays sprawled out on the sidewalk between them. Deciphering gangsta dude's howls and taunts, I gather that it's his bike and he's just now caught this bike thief in the act of stealing it.

I start edging my way to the front of the throng just in time to see some dancing around and scratching at the air by the combatants. "What! What you are doing? What you are doing? What? What?" the little refugee shouts in thickly accented English. The fighters' faces are thus far unmarked, although the little man has a red welt on his neck, presumably where he got clotheslined by the big guy while trying to flee on the bike.

Petty theft 101: if you get caught stealing a bike, ditch the merchandise and run like hell. Don't look back, because chances are slim you're gonna get chased by the bike owner, who will have his hands full retrieving his property. That's the logical out in a situation like this. But inexplicably the little refugee eschews flight and stays put. He digs his heels in and fights for what isn't his. Probably the story of his life.

Gangsta dude, he's in no hurry, and seems to be triangulating the finer semantic points of this proposition. Fact one: bike thief is a little scrawny refugee. Fact two: thief is not cooperating. Fact three; a violent act will be required take this bike back. Fact four: acts of violence without risk of physical or legal ramifications equal free entertainment.

Once he's got the whole picture, gangsta dude warms up to the task, hanging a little smirk around his lips and eyes as he goes into his fight dance—a crablike shuffle—which he uses to slowly hem in his quarry. "What up, B! It's getting REAL! Uh-huh. That shit is MY fucking bike! You want it? Uh-huh! Okay, go ahead— take it! Just try! But you ain't gonna like the price, motherfucker." he smirks.

"What? What? What you are doing?" the little man repeats furiously. Perhaps these are the only English word he knows.

Something about the glazed glee in gangsta dude's beady eyeholes sets alarm bells off in my brain. I flash back to a mismatch of similar proportions that I spectatored over in Amsterdam once, and judging from the variables here this is shaping up to be a replay of that scene—one which ended up being so profoundly lodged in my memory that to this day I'm still tripping over the mental baggage it left behind.

It happened that time I ran off to Holland. It was late and and I was on one of my lonely rambles when I stumbled upon a street fight featuring this big, drunk rugby player type who, mid-fight, locked his meaty paws around this equally drunk skinny guy's chest. He got the skinny guy in a bear hug and gave him three hard yanks. It was a mystery to me what the big guy was up to, hugging and yanking on him that way, but I guess skinny guy knew the score.

He started desperately clawing at the big one's eyes trying to break away, but couldn't quite get his adversary's eyeballs gouged out in time. On violent bear hug number three, even all the way across the intersection where I was standing I could hear it, the snap. Skinny guy went limp all over, his eyes rolling up in his head.

The big one, noticing the dead weight in his arms, seemed puzzled by this instantaneous loss of adversarial resistance. He dropped skinny man onto the paving stones, busted rag doll that he now was. Big guy taunted him, daring him to stand up and fight, not quite getting it. The skinny one, he didn't move. He couldn't—his back was broken. Once that fact became clear, the big guy started running his thick meaty fingers through his hair, letting out a string of fretting and whining sounds, then he took a swing at the air, shouting some Dutch expletive that probably translated to fuck. With that he ran like hell, disappearing in the maze of cobblestone streets.

I was the only witness. Of course I felt like a piece of shit for not stepping in. It was a mismatch. So call me stupid or an egomaniac or whatever, but from that back-breaking moment on, I've always told myself, that, given dire enough circumstances, I won't just stand around spectating. I'll try to step in and do something, anything, to disrupt a juggernaut of irreversible violence. So here he is, gangsta dude, circling his opponent, using the crowd to slowly back the little man up against the dark marble wall, where on either side the refugee's trapped by a tangle of goggle-eyed gawkers.

Things are going south real fast for the underdog, so I start scanning the immediate vicinity, hoping to locate some useful prop from a nearby garbage pile; a busted umbrella, a discarded bra, schematic drawings of a vacuum cleaner, some agent of confusion to distract gangsta dude, should worse come to worse. Maybe I'll just rush into the fight circle and commence shouting words that start with the letter Z. Z words always confuse people. I don't know what it is I'll do just yet, but I gotta do something.

I'm so busy scanning my whereabouts that I almost miss the big man throwing the first bonafide punch. Had I missed it, I might have assumed the worse and rushed in, yowling about zebras in Zanzibar, but I hold back, because something's puzzling about that punch. Even though it doesn't land, an instant after the big guy's fist whooshes by the refugee's deftly bobbing head, little man lets loose this blood-curdling wail, like some ungodly shriek, then grabs at his head like he's been poleaxed, or struck by lightening or had a brain seizure or something. He staggers, then collapses against the wall, crumpling into a little pile on the sidewalk.

Now gangsta dude, he's all turned around. He knows he whiffed on the punch, so why all the moaning? Why all the crying and dying before his eyes here on the 5th Avenue sidewalk and shit? Being the big dumbass that he is, he leans forward, sort of leading with his chin, and gives the little man's ribs a little exploratory nudge to see what gives. Is he dead or what?

This, of course, is all the refugee could hope for and more. One tiny opening. Erupting with a rabid howl, that brand of grotesque fury best observed in wild animals cornered and ready for mortal combat, the little man lunges upward, wrenching his stubby little fingers around gangsta dude's throat in a cartilage-crushing death choke. It catches the big guy completely off guard. Big man goes rocking onto his heels and as he starts to tumble backwards the little man lets loose of the throat and starts swinging, unleashing a flurry of furious punches that hit their mark with a series of sickeningly hollow thuds.

Gangsta dude, he swats at the air, trying to deflect the blows, but fast as he tumbles backwards the refugee follows, white on rice, just raining blow after blow around big man's face, head and neck, until, boom, down gangsta dude goes, sprawling out on the sidewalk, cheek to the concrete, legs aspraddle. Without missing a beat the little man rears back and kicks the big guy in the side of the head.

From the crazed look in his eye he'd probably keep kicking but someone shouts "Cops!" This gets the refugee's attention. As that inevitable "oooph" of defeated wind escapes from gangsta dude's big deflating lungs, little man snatches up the bike, hits a seam in the crowd, and, whoosh, like the wind, he's long gone.

We in the crowd are momentarily stunned. Gangsta dude, he's lolling around on the sidewalk clutching at his windpipe and temples, making choking sounds, sputtering out intermittent coughs and gasps as a sundae of spit and blood leaks out the corner of his mouth. Sirens are gathering in the background, closing in. Despite our appreciation for the physics of this miracle turnaround, the respectable passersby have no real interest in getting entangled in the vagaries of police reports, so the crowd quickly scatters.

Everyone hurries to go about their business but me. I'm unemployed and curious, so I figure I'll stick around and see the drama through to the end. Here they come, three yowling, whooping cop cars. Gangsta dude, he's playing Hamlet, waving a pathetic, pity-me hand in the air. Zoom-zoom-zoom, the cop cars come and zoom-zoom-zoom they go, not even stopping—they've apparently got bigger fish to fry.

Once they've passed, gangsta dude's alone on the sidewalk with no script. He sits there gawking this way and that, touching his bloody lips, rubbing his throat, disoriented, puzzling over the brief but incredibly violent exchange.

Hanging over the whole of this scene is a sort hologram of violence generated by little refugee's diabolical assault. Etched foremost in the picture place in my mind is that portrait of the fury tattooed on little man's face as he pummeled his adversary. It was like some terrifying mask of savage bloodlust. And to think I was about to intervene to save his ass. Risk my own skin for that murderous little thief.

I listen to myself running out that line of indignant bullshit and try to recognize it for what it really is. What is that? Skulking around back there in the shadows? Is it hatred? Is it fear? Loathing? No, after a bit of introspection I confront the shadow and correctly identify it—it's envy. I envy that little fucker. Envy him in his moral abandon. Envy him in his capacity for controlled mayhem. Envy him for being able to communicate his fury so succinctly, to employ it to some concise tactical end, wielding his rage like a common tradesman's tool. But why would I envy that pitiful human being? Probably because somewhere inside of me a similar inchoate rage lies trapped, unacknowledged, undefined, unrealized and unemployed.

All along, even back in those Pentecostal churches, proned out at the altar weeping and praying to sweet baby Jesus, I knew that deep inside my heart something was wrong, wrong, wrong. That somewhere there in the wilderness of my soul, there was a huge black yawning abyss with a gravitational field all its own, a malignant dwarf star spitting out the inexplicable antimatter of hunger for self-annihilation.

When I was doing hard drugs in my early teens, there were times I'd found myself teetering at the edge of that terrifying abyss, toying with the allure of it, peering over the edge, dreaming of submitting, just pitching head first forward and falling and falling and falling and falling. In fear of my own malfunctioning mind, I recoiled, fleeing into the comforting arms of Jesus. I guess that's the obvious reflex for an immature personality in the Deep South, it's the black hole of amorality or Jesus. No exploration of any theoretically grounding territory in between.

So here I am, climbing on my bike on a street corner in New York City, identifying with a sneaky little murderer. What the hell? I decide the exploration of middle ground needs to officially begin, right here right now with me moving at a rate of eight miles an hour on my new piece of shit bike that I didn't steal but now sorta wish I did.

I circle the streets hunting for Help Wanted signs until it gets dark, then I deadhead it back over the 59th Street Bridge, hungry, tired, demoralized. Ensconced in my closet, on my tiny black and white dumpster TV that night there's talk on the news of another sensational New York City murder. No big surprise there, except that as soon as the news lady utters the word, the little refugee's grimacing face pops into the picture place in my mind. And every time she says murder, it happens again; I see the little man's face, his raw, rugged, strangling hands.

Over the ensuing days every time I see or hear that murder word, he's there, visiting me, that little thief, the one who I pathetically envy. It's got my thinking all fucked up, to where I come to associate the very word "murder" with his contorted visage.

Like anyone I guess I'd prefer to imagine myself incapable of murdering another human being, but replaying that scene in my mind over and over, seeing his face screwed into such rage, the exuberant exhilaration of his conscious-less strangling assault, it's like he's teasing me with his amorality. Dark ideations come wandering into my mind, constructs that suggest that if I'd simply abandon my own suffocating moral code and follow the little refugee's lead, maybe for the first time ever I'd feel a sense of something truly authentic in me, not the charade of poses that have thus far kneecapped any shot I might have had at making sense of my messed up existence.

It's two months later. While prowling the streets each day dumpster diving, I've kept my eyes peeled for the little murderer but there's been no sign of him. Understandable, it's a big city, easy to get lost in. A few weeks back I landed a minimum wage cafeteria job down Soho way at this trendy eatery called Food Restaurant. So far so good with this bout of gainful employ. The managers approve of my hyperkinetic work ethic, which is probably attributable to some sort of manic personality disorder—hey, you gotta make the best of the hand you're dealt, right?

So yesterday the slime-bag drifter dishwasher Randy quit and I'm back there in the pit running the Hobart AM-15 machine, my new job until manager Susan locates a suitable societal dreg replacement. Dishwashing's not what you'd call my favorite gig, nor is it what I hired on to do, but a job's a job and today's slow so dishes I will wash. Of course my present occupational status is quite the far cry from a few years prior, sitting in Georgio Armani's opulent foyer waiting to be "discovered", but that's life, right?

It's mid afternoon, not a soul in the place. I've come out to the counter to get a cold drink. Susan goes sailing by with a Help Wanted sign like the one that got me hired a while back. She tapes it to the window then heads back to the office. I'm just watching the world go by when lo and behold, through a plate glass window, a mere thirty feet from where I stand, there he comes, the little refugee, "The Murderer", trudging along the sidewalk.

He slows, peering suspiciously inside the restaurant, surveying this hipster joint with its famous quiche offerings and Zagats recommended brie sandwiches. A trendy, bullshit artist hangout, it seems all wrong for "The Murderer" to appear hereabouts. Due to the optics, I'm apparently invisible to the little man. But I see him just fine.

It's mid-afternoon, mid-week. The restaurant's dead so, there's no distractions. I got nothing to do but study this odd coincidence as it unfolds. And how will it unfold? Has he come to deliver his own brand of evil to my little world? Is he planning more crimes? A robbery? A murder perhaps?

Or is this little episode something paranormally personal to me? Is he invading my psyche? Using me the same way I've been using him, as a mental landmark? Have I been appearing in the picture place in his mind like he has in mine? If so, then what word do I represent to him? Am I "The Spectator"? Is he aware of the dark qualities I've been attributing to him? If so, is he angry…offended…flattered? Has he come to clarify some error in my assessment of him as a murderer? Would he like me to be his understudy?

He paces outside the door, gazing in fretfully now and again, like he's casing the joint, hooding his already hooded eyes with those crude throat-crushing hands. It's cold and he's wearing a grimy down vest under a long, tattered trench coat, like a duster. His appearance is that of a small but fearsome ghost.

Despite the fact that I'm a head taller than him, behind the counter, just out of his sight, I've instinctively reached out and am now clutching that ten-inch knife the sandwich maker uses to slice open baguettes with. I'm frozen, buddy, just immobilized with fear. I'm fairly certain he didn't notice my presence during the fight, but somehow it feels like he knows me…like he's been seeing me in the picture place in his mind.

Then suddenly, like he's received some telepathic command, he pivots and…here he comes shambling through the door! The compact, spooky looking bald-headed man approaches the counter where I work, stands before me glancing this way and that as if fearful of being followed. He lifts his eyes to meet mine (a chore) then points back toward the entrance with his stodgy little throat-crushing fingers. "I will take it." He whispers, very softly, like this, "Hi wheel tak heet".

The words are without context…nonsensical. I study his face, grip the knife, ready for anything. But his look is in no way threatening, so likely he's not talking about taking my life or soul or the cash in the register. He waits for me to respond, so finally I say, "Um, you'll take what'?"

He points to the door again. "The sign" he says, "The sign."

It's a philosophical conundrum. I start working over the notion of signs. The sign. The sign. Finally, seeing I'm stumped, he says "Deeshvasher. I…I can be…will be deeshvasher."

It's like some kind of magic trick where Sinister gets transformed into Banal. Now I see, that Help Wanted sign Susan hung out there, it's says "Dishwasher Wanted. Inquire Within", so a slightly different sign than the general one she hung that day she hired me. I bust up with jittery, nervous laughter, I guess because this twist is so completely averse to my expectations. He smiles, wanting to laugh too, but not knowing what the joke is, not knowing what I'm thinking, having no window into my mind as I do into his. He's no paranormal entity, he's just a terribly violent little strangler who wants to wash some dishes.

It's like tasting milk when you're expecting Kool Aid. You spew it out and start laughing. I notice Susan, the manager, standing not far off. She's heard the exchange, witnessed my incongruous reaction to his greeting and is studying me, head tilted to the side in puzzlement. She already thinks I'm crazy, so it's no big deal—my incongruous response.

She breezes up and says, "I'll handle this." then ushers the little man away, shooting me a chill-out look as she goes. They settle in at the same table at the back of the restaurant where she interviewed me. What can I say to her? "Wait! Don't! He's a murderer. Not even "a" murderer, he's "The Murderer.""

Time to collect my jangled wits. Could there be some manner of skullduggery afoot here? I've been tricked before and am trying to expand my awareness in my new role as a secret agent of the Unseen Forces. I take a couple deep breaths and set to spying on him once more, this time via his reflection in the plate glass windows that line two sides of the restaurant. When I squint my eyes just right, The Murderer appears to me as a transparent specter at a table in the corner—it's like watching a silent movie on a sheet of cellophane.

Manager lady sits him down, then heads to the office to fetch an application. What's his plan? To rob the place? With a thousand dollars or more in the office safe? But how does he know about the money?

No sooner does she disappear around the corner than he rises, surreptitiously scanning the empty room. He tiptoes over to the pastry cooler, a huge vintage display case loaded with exotic cakes and desserts. He leans heavily against the glass and sighs, staring longingly at the sweets until the manager returns.

I think about how the manager herself was involved in that sensational murder, how her sister's grisly end captivated the New York headlines for weeks. She'd suffered greatly at the hands of the tabloids, the greedy, unfeeling media, the whorish movie producers, some of whom who called just days after the killing at the Chelsea Hotel, waving cash, hoping to acquire movie rights to recreate her personal nightmare on the silver screen. Now here she is sitting face to face with "The Murderer".

Don't get me wrong, Susan's a tough cookie and sets to grilling him with her standard ball-busting dishwasher spiel—where he's worked before, what his qualifications are, what machines he's worked with—can he run a Hobart? Like he's applying for the Nobel Prize or something. He speaks quietly, answering her questions, strangling hands folded calmly before her on the table.

Now he's filling out the application. He hands it to her then shakes her hand, turns and shuffles toward the door. He stops, turns and offers her his best smile, which has a slightly unreal, forced quality about it, then calls out, "I would…to be happy…to have this job. I come back. Tomorrow." He waves—the compact strangling hand passing through the air a mere ten feet from where I stand. With that he exits, disappearing on foot around the corner.

No sign of the stolen bike.

The manager lady's headed into the office, the application folded in her hands. I rush over and ask if she's going to hire him. She thinks she might. I suggest she might not. I launch into my little tale, how I know for a fact he's a bike thief, a vicious street thug, and possibly even….a murderer. She pales at the very mention of the word. "That little guy?" She gasps incredulously. "I just shook hands with him!"

I captivate her with the whole sordid tale. She goes silent for a moment, then shudders all over, mortified at the thought of being in such close proximity to someone capable of such evil.

We sit down and look over his application. His name is Andras Groff. Under previous employment he lists a kitchen job at the highest of high brow dining epicenters in New York City, a swanky joint called Tavern on the Green, which is utter bullshit—no way he's ever worked there. We search for the telltale signs of irrational criminality but there's not much to go on. Just some words and letters childishly scrawled here and there, a skeleton of lonely, meaningless data.

A few customers come drifting through the door. Time to get back to work. I ask Susan if I can keep the application as a souvenir, something to remember The Murderer by. She's happy to be shut of him and his murderous ways. After my shift ends I take the paper home and stash it in a box full of weird shit I've found in my daily garbage foraging. I keep it safely stashed under my bed. The box is marked, "Strange, But True".

Needless to say, Susan's not calling Andras Groff back. As I lay on my crappy cot in the walk-in closet strumming my guitar suddenly it fully dawns on me what I've done. I've betrayed "The Murderer"…kept him from that job he wanted. I wonder if he knows of my complicity in this affair? Will someone be murdered due to my actions? Will it be me?

PENSACOLA BEACH, FLORIDA, FEBRUARY 1994

Way down South I know a girl who is blind.
She walks alone along a lonely highway each day.
She dreams that one day a man will pull up in a car.
He'll open up the door, she'll climb in and he will say…
he'll say "Hey babe, whatcha know? Hope you're ready to go,
'cause today's a perfect day to chase tornados."

I wake to a hellacious roll of thunder and incessant flashes of lightening as a howling gale bows in the closed window just beside me. Shit! I yank back the blinds and crack that sucker open to equalize the pressure. I know the drill—this is tornado season on the Redneck Riviera. Another gust hits, sending the tattered curtains billowing into the air.

I check the grey-green predawn sky, spying an approaching array of ominous squall lines. A massive, violent cold front is bearing down on this thin meridian of sand separating the intercostal waterway from the Gulf of Mexico. In the coming hour the tempest will rage, the temperature dropping anywhere from twenty to forty degrees as said squall line surges past, rampaging out over the raging topsy-turvy surf in the nearby Gulf.

It's February, the apex of winter storm activity hereabouts, so this approaching maelstrom won't be neutralized by warm Gulf air any time soon. By dawn the huge, sloppy storm-tossed waves will be pummeled into submission, flattened into demure, orderly little feathering ripples as the north wind howls, the cold front marching ever southward, headed on toward Puerto Rico and Cuba.

I force myself to sit up, watching as the tempest passes. I'm feverish and my gut aches like hell, as it has for months now—this crippling mystery illness has spread to my legs and left me unable to walk any great distance, unable to pass food. Fevers come and go, I eat little bits here and there but, well, frankly, nothing much ever comes out, begging the question if not out, where does the stuff going in end up? I'm clinically depressed, destitute, critically ill but lacking that crucial survival ingredient known as health insurance.

Simultaneously I both fear and hope I'll soon die. Seriously, I've made peace with the notion of moving on, disappearing from the face of the earth. More and more I've come to accept that I just ain't cut out for life on this particular planet. It's time to go, but I can't quite get a fix on how to gracefully exit stage left.

I feel strangely grounded, centered, watching as the weather goes code red outside. It mirrors the wild raggedness of my thoughts, I guess, like some form of psycho-barometric equalizing. I always enjoyed my kinship with such storms. As a kid, when those late summer hurricanes came bearing down on my town, I locked into a higher gear of consciousness, feeling extra connected to the proposition of being. While the reasonable folk were scurrying hither and yon, fearfully preparing for the worst, I'd be giddy with excitement, hoping the damn roof would get ripped off our house. As teen I often surfed in raging hurricanes, the Civil Defense crews and sheriffs, bullhorns in hand, lined up at the end of the fishing pier commanding me to return to the beach for my own safety.

But once I got to New York City, I truly landed in the catbird seat—driving that taxi in white-out blizzards. On such catastrophic snow days fender-benders were all but inevitable and therefore a threat to your minimum wage career, as anyone who incurred three collisions in a year's time got blackballed by all the major taxi fleets. As such, on inclement days upper management types were fairly sanguine about drivers no-showing, fearing they'd lose too many of us minimum wage worker bees to collision attrition.

As for me, I never missed a major storm. When the roads were slick with black ice and visibility was reduced to near zero, when die hard New Yorkers were skiing down 5th Avenue and the only vehicles in the city moving were a handful of yellow cabs and a few scattered cop cars, that's when I felt integrally placed—like I belonged. I drove a sixteen-hour shift in what Hollywood would later dub The Perfect Storm, or what at the time the local newscasters dubbed The White Hurricane.

Busting it up down the avenues that day it felt like I was buzzing on top notch drugs, so at one with the elements was I. Subways and busses shut down, thousands of stranded passengers lined the streets with a mere hundred or so cabs in service, moving at a crawl here to there, there to here.

Typically haughty uptown types were deferential as they sought sanctuary in my back seat, as if they were in the presence of some storied Zen master. Announcing their swanky destinations on utterly inaccessible uptown side streets, ones with exalted names like Riverside Drive or East End, I'd correct them, explaining we'd go no further than their cross street on one of the primary avenues. From there they'd simply have to hoof it, as the side streets were impassable. Some tried to sway me, wielding threats or sweet talk, but I held firm, asking if they'd perhaps like to catch another cab. Nobody did. Along the way I'd point out the side roads littered with stranded taxis, buses, delivery vans, and invariably they'd get my point and cave.

The squall lines draw near. Hurtling sheets of rain now pummel this beach enclave. Over the roar of the wind and downpour, just outside the front window I hear a faint, familiar thump against the glass. I catch a glimpse of Dopey Don, the feral polydactyl cat who's adopted me. Over the howl of the wind I catch a snatch of his faint mewling, pitifully begging for shelter so, on unsteady feet I rise and make my way to the living room to let him in.

He's a stray, like those ones I cared for at my doomed surfboard factory all those epochs ago, so named Dopey Don due to this inability to distinguish when the window is open or closed. Early on in my stay here I'd hear a gentle thunk, then find this young tuxedoed tomcat lying dazed in the sand outside this pillbox cottage that my kindly sister rented for me after my life fell to pieces up in New York.

I tried to keep my dire mental and physical health details from her, but she intuited the degree of my spiral and promptly wired me enough cash to cover train fare home and three months of off-season housing in the cheapest bungalow on Pensacola Beach. Once here I figured I'd quickly convalesce then land some temporary work, but I fell deeper and deeper into this malady, ending up all but crippled and unable to walk, putting the notion of landing anything approaching gainful employ out of my reach.

The cinderblock place I'm staying in, it's musty and dim, one of those early 1960's efficiency deals; kitchenette and living room all rolled into one common space measuring maybe twenty by twenty. Fluorescent lights. A small bedroom with a battered dresser, sagging bed and the usual crappy sea oats on a sand dune acrylic painting on the wall.

The cheap linoleum floor, louvered windows, cheesy tropical motif breakfast bar and exposed ceiling beams supporting a low, flat tar-and-gravel roof vibe puts me in mind of those places my tippler grandma used to rent for us out here those Christmases back in the mid sixties when I was just a kid. To this day I carry mixed emotions about such dwellings—nostalgia wants to win me over, but it's a hard sell, family dynamics being what they were.

Spartan pillboxes of this variety were once a regular fixture dotting the dunes of the barrier islands along the Gulf, but most of this breed are long gone from the coastline, flattened by hurricane storm surges or bulldozed at the hands of greedy developers who threw up gaudy three-story stucco and concrete obscenities in their place: manatee mailboxes, motorized window shades, minimum wage yard crews triangulating quantum stratagem to maintain those verdant carpets of lush green Kentucky Fescue grass planted in the nowhere and nothingness of fallow Florida barrier island sand.

Dopey Don scampers through the open window and takes refuge in an armchair, hunkering down. Sporting his best dim-witted expression, he obtusely regards the apocalyptic storm passing by. And oh, how I envy him in his simplicity. I close the window and ease down on the old couch, then pick up this ridiculous purple electric guitar I've been loaned by my step dad and, accompanied by the enigmatic tempos of the storm, set to work on the song that, when finished I expect will be called A Perfect Day to Chase Tornados. I'd finished verse two just before I drifted off to sleep, and then here comes this storm waking me up, so clearly something is in the air presently.

> *Hey what about that preacher man on the run from the law?*
> *He killed a girl in Memphis, then ran 'till the dogs tracked him down.*
> *They shot him by the river and as he lay dying in the mud,*
> *someone asked him, "Hey preacher, where's your soul going now?"*
> *And preacher say, "Well, I do not know. But wherever it is I'll gladly go,*
> *'cause today is a perfect day to chase tornados…"*

Just prior to waking I was dreaming of yet another iteration of that long train ride down to Florida. A plane ticket was out of the question, so my tactical retreat from New York City came via a discount ticket on Amtrak. In DC this deranged white woman, likely a meth-head, boarded and loudly plopped down in the seat beside me, high as a kite and ranting about this "coal train", I guess meaning the riders were mostly black. I ignored her as much as was possible, but it's no small feat avoiding a meth-head when they're situated in the seat next to you.

In the small hours of the morning somewhere south of Richmond with most everyone asleep, one disoriented traveler a few rows ahead of us rose and called out, "Where are we? Where are we? Are we in Raleigh yet? I fell asleep!" Someone hollered, "Shut the fuck up. People be sleeping here!", then another joker howled out "We in Georgia. Just passed Atlanta!", this even though we'd only just pulled out of Richmond. The disoriented man all but shrieked, "Atlanta! Lord! I oughta got off at Raleigh!"

The wild-eyed woman beside me cackled, then shouted, "Well then drop your ass in a envelope and mail yourself home!" Everyone laughed but me. I studied her rutted, haggard face then burst into tears.

The leading edge of the front pushes through. So far there's no telltale roar like a train, so tornadic activity seems unlikely. A hefty gust pummels the house, billowing the curtains out as the ranks of colder air descend on the barrier island. The lightening's easing up now, the wind settling in at a steady twenty-five knots from the north as the sea oats in the front yard bend hard toward the Gulf waters, submitting to this arctic blast washing over the beach.

Here I sit with Dopey Don, a creature who just like me appears not quite configured to make it in this world. I sympathize with those who keep blindly diving at holes, never knowing if there's glass or not.

The storm may be passing, but my nemesis sleep won't return. Despite only a few hours of shut-eye I'm now wide awake, so I sit watching the sun rise as I work over the variables of the final verse of this tornado song. I try this, I try that, over and over until, suddenly, there it is; I stumble on the appointed arrangement of images and notions.

> *Sometimes I feel like the sky is a prison and the earth is a grave.*
> *Sometimes I feel like Jesus in some Chinese opera.*
> *Sometimes I'm glad I built my mansion from crazy little stones.*
> *But sometimes I feel so Goddamn trapped by everything that I know.*
> *And I wish it wasn't so, 'cause the only thing that anyone should ever know…*
> *is today is a perfect day to chase tornados.*

With that there they go, my guts start twisting and cramping. I rise and limp to the bathroom, hoping the change in barometric pressure might break free whatever it is that's been tormenting my insides for months now. Long shots are all I got at this point. Sitting doubled over in pain on the toilet I get to thinking about her, the actress and how she disappeared, just like the crossword puzzle said. It occurs to me I may be the only man on earth presently doubled over on a toilet lamenting a lost love while considering issues involving digestive disorders and synchronicity. But you never know.

After her rambling late night answering machine message I never heard from her again. It was a trial letting go but I managed to stabilize my psychological state for a while and get on with my life. Then six months later, walking out the door of my latest studio apartment in the East Village of Manhattan, one I'd just moved into the week before, there she went, strolling past my place. I was half hidden in the foyer and, as is my wont, didn't call out her name, just stepped back into the shadow and observed her stride purposefully by, dressed in a sexy new outfit, all aglow with her enigmatic charms and paralyzing beauty.

I'd hoped she might turn, climb the stairs and ring my buzzer, but no, she just went sailing on, not a care in the world. It lifted my spirits to see her looking so free-spirited and confident. I felt happy for her. Momentarily anyway. Then three doors down she turned and entered that building. What? What? What the hell was she doing going into a building on my block? Maybe…could she be…looking for me?

No. I didn't move to this new place until after she'd vamoosed, so she had no idea I was here. But there she went, just strolling by, walking into a nearby building, so what gives? Was she going door to door on this block searching for me, hoping to apologize, to say she was mistaken, that she had nothing to fear from this person who loved her more than the breath of life itself? There were mysteries to sort out, so I eased down, sitting on my stoop studying that nearby building. Then maybe five minutes later there she came, arm in arm with this scrappy looking punk rock musician type; him with his big florid exaggerated gestures, dread locks and hipster Doc Martin boots. They climbed in this late model Chevy Suburban parked on the street in front of the building, the big engine went boom, kicking over, and away they went.

The real world audio went all hollow sounding inside my head, as if listening to Life through one of those old tin-can-and-string telephone contraptions. I was sort of frozen in place there for so very long. Just totally paralyzed.

What the fuck just happened?

I tried to put it out of my mind. But then a few days later I was minding my own business on my way to buy a burrito nearby, when, passing that corner laundromat on 1st Avenue—goddamn it!—there she was again, curled up in a bright orange laundromat chair, all alone, quietly reading a script, clothes spinning in the dryer.

Bewildered, lost, I stood in the doorway a moment, then as if impelled by magnetism I ventured inside. She didn't notice me approaching. I studied her sitting there, blissfully reading, this luminous soul who claimed to love me heart and soul just a handful of months earlier. I was still a good ten feet from her when she finally looked up. I smiled but got no smile in return, instead she went sheet white, as if having seen the devil himself.

So I spoke. Very soft words. My voice was shaking, but I wore as close a facsimile of a harmless expression as my state of mind would allow. I stammered out that I'd seen her on the block earlier in the week and wondered what she was doing hereabouts. She coldly replied she lived on that block now with her new husband.

There followed an awkward silence.

The situation was a chore to read. Tangled up with all the other data to process was yet another uncanny fucking "coincidence" to decipher. I mean, what are the odds—that out of all the streets and all the buildings in New York City that completely by chance I'd randomly landed an apartment two doors down from that scrappy punk rocker who, it turns out, she'd just married. She coldly informed me of this, then added that unless I immediately left the premises and never contacted her again I would be arrested. Or worse, she would sick her badass husband on me.

So what do you say? What do you do? There was this big roaring sound in my head, like several jumbo jets simultaneously taking off in between my ears. Rendered aphonic, I just turned and staggered out the door, shattered. Eviscerated. Auto pilot impelled me toward the burrito place. Purpose. "I need a purpose. Yes. A burrito. A burrito will fix everything," I thought to myself. I ordered a burrito.

I waited outside the little Mexican take-out restaurant until they called my name.

I paid for my burrito, then began the sojourn back to my apartment two blocks away.

Zombie walking home, bearing the burrito in my arms like an injured child I found the punk rocker husband waiting for me on the corner of 1st Avenue and 6th Street, glint of bloodlust darting around in his shifty eyes, looking not unlike the Puerto Rican gangster just before he got his ass kicked. Me not being an Andras Groff type, I held no diabolical strategies for violence, so I simply attempted to walk past him. No go—he blocked my path, flipping his dreads around in some kind of threatening, ritualistic manner.

He went to barking about me being a psycho, baiting me with lunges and feints, trying to goad me into taking a swing at him. I studied his face long and hard, wondering what he'd been told about me. At the bottom of it all I understood: this man was simply protecting his beloved, just as I would, were she still with me. Twenty yards down the street, hiding behind a sorry excuse for a maple tree I spied her, the actress, playing what I suddenly realized was her favorite role; the cool, detached eye in the midst of the raging storm of life. It was a major mental cluster-fuck to see someone I so loved aiming such hatred at me, but there she was, wishing me dead, smoking a very long, elegant cigarette, calmly assessing the beat down I was about to get.

Punk rocker shoved me once, then twice, shouting words that my brain simply could not process. He reared back as if to cold-cock me, I guess expecting me to defend myself, but I didn't. My spirit was broken, so I just dismally muttered, "Go ahead, hit me. The pain would make sense about now." And I meant it.

He looked momentarily confused, then let loose, his flying fist stopping an inch from my nose, like some action scene in a hokey karate movie.

Why he pulled the punch I'll never know. Maybe he was afraid he'd kill me. I flinched and remember the burrito falling, hitting the sidewalk, sloshing melted cheese and rice all over the place, some even on his trendy Doc Martins. As I gazed downward at the mess for a second I remember thinking, "That looks like a DeKooning painting."

I guess the punk rocker was puzzled by my downward gaze. When he likewise commenced gawking at the abstract art of the burrito splash on the sidewalk I took the opportunity to sidestep him and move on. I have no memory of my footsteps on the pavement as I passed her silently standing there. No words were spoken. Punk rocker didn't pursue me and I truly didn't care if he did, didn't care if he pulled out a shiny black Glock and capped me there and then. I staggered maybe fifty yards on and entered my building, knowing full well they were watching and now knew exactly where I lived. Ah, the complications of this magical life.

I sat down on my bed and shook for a long while. Eventually I got around to practically assessing the situation: I was officially, totally, unequivocally fucked. The woman I loved now resided a few hundred feet away from me with her violently aggressive husband, who clearly regarded me as an imminent threat. I needed to get the fuck out of Dodge. The only problem was I'd just signed a twelve-month lease, was destitute and really had nowhere else in this big wide world to go.

NEW YORK CITY, SEPTEMBER 1986

Andras Groff's dishwasher application resides peacefully undisturbed in the Strange But True box under the latest bed I sleep on in the latest cramped apartment I'm inhabiting. After that day at Food Restaurant I never saw Andras Groff again. He never returned to see if he got the job and the next day we hired this exceedingly streetwise black guy from Oakland.

The first time I spoke with the new dishwasher, as we shook hands I off-handedly greeted him with, "How's life?" Simple greeting, right? But he took the question seriously, coming back with a crooked grin, saying, "I do not know, but it damn sure beats the hell out of death."

Micah Robinson is his name. When he isn't washing dishes he plays trombone in a reggae band. Micah is uber streetwise, cool and utterly connected to the pulse of the Universe. A while back I confided in him that I wrote songs—like as therapy. He asked to hear some of my "tracks", so I made him a cassette tape of a few of my most recent compositions. A week passed after I gave it to him, then another but he never mentioned the cassette, so finally I broached the subject. His grimaced slightly, then tersely came back with, "Oh yeah. I listened to that. Yeah. Damn, brother. You got you a serious intonation problem!"

So six weeks ago, one idyllic fall afternoon, I arrived at the restaurant for my normal shift only to find it empty, the doors chained and padlocked, legal notifications plastered all over the windows. Back by the kitchen door I found Micah and a few of my fellow workers acting all hangdog, milling around in the shadows. The kitchen door was likewise chained shut and they reported they were holding their vigil in hopes of a chance to get inside and grab personal effects they'd left there the day before. Word was that the owner of the popular restaurant was thirty grand behind on her utilities alone and she'd split town with everyone's paycheck—ran off to the Bahamas with some weightlifter type fifteen years her junior. Nice lady.

I was once more unemployed.

Being rendered yet again a worthless workforce bottom feeder I figured maybe I could pass for a waiter. A few days later, following up on a tip from a lady I once knew in the fashion trade, I got hired at this ultra-chic restaurant up on Park Avenue in the twenties. I walked in the door midday for my first shift and, behold, celebrities everywhere; Reggie Jackson, John McEnroe, William Hurt.

The maitre'd was a total prick. The customers were for the most part entitled assholes. I despise talking about food and am not remotely configured for kissing famous person ass ten hours a day and so I lasted all of forty-five minutes there. The dickweed maitre'd barked at me about some petty, trivial concern, showing me his best snooty alpha dog posture so I gave him a good theatrical wink, strolled over to the coat room, removed my trendy-chic waiter apron, hung it on a hook and went sailing out the door. Bye bye, asshole.

Later that day I called a taxi fleet I'd heard of via this cab driver who ate at Food a couple of nights a week. I spoke to a true nitwit there by the name of Ronnie Niedler. Ronnie reported I was in luck, they were hiring. But, as if revealing the intricate workings of the innermost clockworks of the Universe, Ronnie sagely informed me that a man can't simply start driving a cab. No, there are forms to fill out, tests to take, fees to be paid, background checks to complete, waiting periods to be honored. And without a fleet to sponsor a prospective driver, such bureaucratic gyrations take upwards of six months to complete. But I was in luck, because Ann's Taxi Service and he, Ronnie Niedler were there for me, to guide me through the maze.

So it's been a week since I first encountered this Ronnie Neidler. In the mail the next day I received the Ann's Taxi service application for sponsorship, to be completed and notarized. Rent was due yesterday so I borrowed some money from a friend, filled out all the forms then went desperately hustling here and there—taking this bogus exam, taking that bogus physical. It was all just your basic New York hustle.

For the physical the nebbish, pasty-faced doctor came trudging into the grim examination room and, without so much as looking at me, blankly asked, "How do you feel?" "Fine" I said. "Okay. You passed the physical. That'll be fifty dollars. Pay up front." And without another word, out of the examination room he trudged. Took him less than a minute to relieve me of my fifty bucks.

During the english competency test I was asked to explain the meaning of the word "curb". Strangely, I found the task existentially daunting and almost failed. A curb is a curb. What other explanation could a person offer? Each fee ran in the range of fifty bucks. So much pricey blackmail for the privilege of becoming a minimum wage pariah!

I'm back at dumpster diving and thieves market selling to raise funds. The rent's way late and I've run out of dodges and excuses for my landlord. But just now the phone rings. It's Ronnie Neidler, informing me that the final bureaucratic fraud/hurdle has been completed and my hack license has arrived. Ronnie instructs me to report at noon for an official orientation. Fourteen of us will today be welcomed into the cab driving brotherhood!

I grab a quick bowl of Cheerios then hop on my bike and head west. It's a chilly, early winter New York morning. I do the crosstown cycle schlep, dodging yellow cabs all along the way, thinking I will soon belong to that selfsame yellow brotherhood. I locate the anachronistic "Driver's Entrance" sign on West 21st Street and enter the tumble-down brownstone near 7th Avenue.

I find myself in a truly abysmal, gloom-shrouded waiting room whose only distinguishing feature, aside from an overflowing toilet in a privy with no door, is a pair of eye-level window slots set in bulletproof plexiglass. I peer through them, seeing an equally dismal office space in the back. Someone's watching Wheel of Fortune back there on an old black and white TV.

"Hello?" I tap on the plexiglass. After a while a grizzled, elderly dispatcher turns and studies me, scowls, then agonizingly rises from a hidden chair, limps forward and deigns to speak to the me. It's the surly, crippled head dispatcher, Marty. He's like some hideous caricature of an evil old man from a crappy Hollywood B-movie. I tell him that my license arrived and ask where should I go to get my cab. He scowls again then mutters something about orientation, calls me a fucking piss-ant moron, threatens to fire me before I've even started, then he directs me to the room upstairs which, if possible, is even more depressing than the one I've just exited, save the charming toilet and plexiglass slots.

I call it a room, but it's hardly that, it's more just a moldy green wooden box, empty but for twenty wobbly, rusted folding chairs. Along the west wall sit two ill-shaped wooden benches so warped they rock as I walk past them. There are windows in the room, or were. They've been painted over and over and over in the same drab forest green color as the walls— as if the painter was unaware of their presence or the function of windows as he performed his forest green painting duties.

The entirety of this empty room lies hidden under a thick layer of dusty brownish grime. I size up the place then do my usual wallflower routine, weaving my way to the furthest most corner of the room. Hunkering down next to the radiator in the last row of folding chairs, I settle in and wait for something to happen.

Nothing does.

I'm alone in the room for maybe ten minutes, then, bored, I pull out my little Tom Waits inspired shirt-pocket notebook and start jotting down snippets from a dream I had last night. The three wizards…the rain-making apparatus….

I hear soft footsteps. I look up. In the doorway stands The Murderer, Andras Groff. The compact little man studies me, then the room, then me. It feels like another dream, in part because he's wearing the same outfit from a year earlier; the ragged duster, the soiled down vest and jeans, the scuffed up Converse All-Stars.

A blind man couldn't miss the look on my face; the mix of horror, astonishment and delight, a look suggesting that I'm a little bunny dancing madly in the mysterious headlights of Life. What are the odds? Andras Groff finally got a legit job. He's a taxi driver. He applied to the New York Taxi & Limo commission, took the same sundry bogus tests, and then his license arrived here at the exact same fleet as me on the exact same day that my license arrived. The odds of this event happening have to be beyond astronomical.

This time he's seen me before I spotted him. His head's cocked to the side, trying to place me, like where our paths have crossed before. I'm struck speechless. I offer a nod. He continues to stare, then without a word, turns his back to me, easing into a chair in the front row. Creak-creak the chair goes. Creak-creak-creak.

Some minutes pass, just he and I crowding the small room with our silence. Finally, I can't take the pressure any more, I gotta do something, even if it's something stupid, so I flip the page in my notebook and start scribbling covert observations about The Murderer's general comportment and appearance. Short, maybe 5'5". Bald. Multiple scars on scalp. Bow-legged. Rubs his skull often with stubby little murderer fingers. I'm covertly transcribing these notations like an undercover reporter would. Raggedy clothes. Hooded brow. Squarish hands featuring filthy ragged fingernails. I figure I'll paper clip this description to his dishwasher application that I have stashed in that Strange But True box under my bed.

When I'm satisfied that I've done an accurate rendering, I draw a cloud bubble around the words then scrawl the title "The Murderer" above the description in bold print. No sooner do I complete this task than I look up to find Andras Groff staring over his shoulder at me. I flinch like somebody poked me with a hat pin. The look on his face says he knows every ugly, judgmental comment I've just written about him.

He continues to stare, that unwavering amoral, penetrating gaze, as if my notebook words are scrawled in Sharpie all over my face. My pen's still touching the page, the very word "Murderer". I know better than to jerk it away or snap the notebook shut, calling attention to exactly what I don't want to call attention to. So I just nod at him and continue writing—only not really writing now, just pretending to write. After a second I close the notebook and slip it back in my shirt-pocket with a knowing smile. I'm cool bro—just taking a few taxi notes here. The Murderer stares at me a little longer, frowns, then turns back, facing the door. Something's eating at him. He glances back once or twice more.

We sit in silence again a while...a few minutes, tops. I'm trying to remind myself to breathe—the guilty hold their breath! Breathe in. Breathe out.

Without any warning or provocation Andras Groff rises, turns and circles back to where I'm sitting. He's moving purposefully toward me, studying me all the while. My back's to the wall. There's but one exit route in this room, which he's now blocking. He settles into a seat two chairs down, then after a few moments looks over and studies my face. I nod, then look forward. He continues to stare. Or glare. It's a hard look to read.

Now he raises the little stubby strangling hand, starts rubbing his bald head, like something's really bothering him. I got no big sharp knife this time. After a long while he points to my shirt pocket. Sharp, yet sleepy eyes check out my notepad there. Those eyes, little beads of black intensity hidden behind half-shuttered lids. When he speaks, his voice is astonishingly restrained, almost reverent.

He says, "What you…write? What words….in this book."

I nod, not knowing how else to reply without incriminating myself, then I manage a reply, "Yes..." I say, "...words."

His eyes narrow in affirmation, he nods like he knew it all along. He looks away, rubs his head, then looks back, clouds of worry appearing in the midnight sky of his eyes. "Yes. But, what…these papers…you write. What words you writing?"

I'm cornered. The only exit lies beyond him. Next he's going to ask to see the words, to see my unflattering portrait of him. He'll be offended that I think he's a killer, get mad and kill me. Shit like that happens all the time in New York City.

But how did he find me here? It must be like I suspected all along—he can see into the picture place in my mind after all, just like I can see into his, otherwise how did he come to be in this place at this exact moment? He knows my thoughts, has been following me this last year, waiting for the right moment. No one knows I'm here and I have no escape plan. No garbage pile to pluck some broken umbrella out of and make strange Z noises to distract The Murderer. I'm desperately scrambling, trying to think of what would be the least provocative word I could make up to lie about what I've just written, something that would in no way precipitate violence. I'm searching for just the right word when….

"Poetry?"

I hear the word and am fairly certain it's not me who's said it. No, it's Andras Groff. He said it. Poetry? I want to start laughing…thank you, that's the perfect word! When I think of him, I think of the word "murderer". When he thinks of me he thinks, "poetry". He's smiling now, "These words….words you are write…I think…they are poetry? Yes?"

"Yes, okay." I lie, "You caught me. I'm writing….poetry." Puzzling. The word "poetry" comes fluttering out of my mouth and hangs in the air before my eyes like a lovely child's birthday balloon. I have little to no interest in poetry, seldom think of it or god forbid read it, yet here I am professing to be a poet to The Murderer.

And I'm telling him I write poetry so he won't know what I've really written and murder me. So he won't know that invisible hands are steering us toward each other over and over for unknown reasons, maybe so that he can either kill me, or teach me to kill. And yet, in an attractive, obscure kind of way, the story of our entangled paths has the ring of poetry about it.

"Poetry" I say again, just liking the sound of the word. We both study that word, "poetry", as it hangs in the air between us.

"I am knowing you are poet. I see…in your face….(a new thought occurs to him)…is difficult, yes….to be poet." he says. I nod. I don't know—I'm not a poet, but nonetheless I nod. He rubs his skull. His look clouds over again. He rubs his skull more—a self-calming habit, I now realize. He sighs, looking away, saying, "You, your poems…do you….you have been…publish?"

Publish. A strange word to hear uttered from the mouth of a ragamuffin eastern European murderer. I tell The Murderer no, my poems haven't been published. I try to explain in very rudimentary terms that it's exceedingly difficult to become a published poet (especially when you're not a poet).

He agrees, more with his eyes more than with actual words. Something's bothering Andras Groff. His face becomes taut, not with the fury I saw that day on 5th Avenue and 14th Street, but rather with longing mixed with some ancient sorrow. To my utter astonishment he then says this; "You see…I…I too am…I am poet. Every…you see, every day…I send one poem, very good poem—my poem—to this…uh…New Yorker Magazine."

Andras Groff and his little strangling hands writing a poem. English? Polish? Romanian? Serbian? Subject matter?? Maybe murder? Now, placing his poem in an envelope. Addressing the envelope, T-H-E N-E-W Y-O-R-K-E-R. The stamp. Into the mailbox the poem goes. Every single day. It's surreal.

I nod knowingly, saying the full name "The New Yorker Magazine." He sighs sadly in agreement. We've settled on a mutual landmark. He's searching my eyes for an answer. Andras Groff now painfully admits, "But…they never will to…to publish this poem. My poem. How is possible? How these New Yorker Magazine, they will never to….to publish….poem?"

And what do you say? Do you explain it rationally, tell him it's probably a very good poem, but that a magazine like The New Yorker will never publish it, or anything else he might write? Does he then erupt in a fit fury? One similar to the one I previously witnessed? Is he anxious for the truth or does he want to be lied to? Some inquiry is required.

"You send them a poem every day?" I ask.

"Yes, every day." he says, words laden with a great burden of earnestness.

"The same poem?" I ask.

"Yes. Always the same." He thinks it a good strategy.

There's a long moment of reckoning, and I don't know why, but I decide to tell Andras Groff the truth—that no one ever got their poem published by sending it unsolicited to the New Yorker, that to even talk to the editors there you have to have a literary agent.

You have to send press kits and bios and proposals. Most importantly you have to know someone who works there.

This last point seems to hit home, for Andras Groff, it turns out, grew up in an orphanage in a communist country, and connections are everything in such contexts. He looks away and nods. "So…okay. I must know inside person…with this magazine." He sighs and nods. I wait for the backlash, the fury to rear its ugly head, but nothing of the sort happens. To my surprise his eyes glow with a strange tenderness "Yes…you speak…good words. Is hard…very hard life. This poet life." he says.

The door flies open, into the room sails Ronnie Neidler. Ronnie's a mouth breather, a slack-jawed dimwit with milk-bottle glasses, anachronistic Brylcreem hairdo, mama's boy pants hitched up mid-belly and a Beltone hearing aid in his ear, white cord running to the transistor apparatus crammed his front shirt pocket. He's a caricature of a caricature of a total geek.

Ronnie's lugging a ninny-fied briefcase, hopefully containing our licenses. In a loud, whiney voice he introduces himself then improbably launches into a string of ha-ha dirty jokes, like we're his personal adoring audience and it's improv night at the raunchy old taxi garage. Maybe he thinks he's preparing us for the sordid cab driver lifestyle, I don't know, but Andras Groff and I sit in silence and pretend to listen. Ronnie doesn't seem to notice no one's laughing—he probably never has. He's got that hearing aid, so maybe it's permanently turned off?

After ten minutes of his dismal, misogynistic joke-fest it's me who's contemplating murder—Ronnie Neidler's—and I'm starting to wonder if maybe Andras Groff's interested in joining me. Thankfully the twelve other new drivers finally start to filter in. Twenty minutes later the orientation proper commences.

Once Ronnie's done his acutely remedial cab driving spiel we're led back downstairs and handed our licenses, trip sheets and keys. The car is yellow. The bench seat is collapsed in the shape of an acutely atrophied ass. The smell is a sickening blend of fetid body odor and cheap air fresheners. "Welcome!" the cab shouts out, "This will be your home for the foreseeable future!"

As I pull out of the garage, in the rear-view mirror I notice The Murderer trying to ease his cab out of its parking space. It's an easy-breezy straight shot and yet there he is, going back and forth, back and forth. I study him struggling with this task for a full minute then surmise that Andras Groff doesn't know how to drive a car. Jesus.

I roll up to the corner, the light goes green on 7th Avenue, I carefully turn left and I'm off. A block south there's a businessman standing with his hand in the air. I pull over, in he climbs, I throw the meter and with that I'm officially a taxi driver.

It's three weeks later. My intermediate video editing class at NYU ran over and so now I'm late to shape up, likely meaning I won't get dispatched until after five pm, if at all. As a rookie, some days you wait for a cab for two, three hours only to be sent home after drivers with more seniority are given the available cabs. l haven't seen Andras much the last week or so, but less and less the word murderer makes sense in conjunction with his face.

As I scale the brownstone steps, the Driver's Door entrance swings open and here comes Andras, trip sheet and keys in his hand. Attached to his clip board is the dreaded pink slip, an official notification stating that if Andras has one more wreck he'll be fired, meaning he's already had two wrecks in his first weeks of driving. I nod to Andras. He gestures for me to come closer.

Words are trying to come out of his mouth. He's looking around to make sure no one is eavesdropping then leans into my ear conspiratorially. His lips part. Soft warm air seeps out. Finally the words arrive, "Do you…is…..you…..have you know….fat actors?"

I guess my look is so filled with bewilderment that he feels compelled to elaborate, but very secretively. "I am to write…um…(collecting a large memory chunk) a 'broadcast quality situation comedy'…you see?…for television." He lets that sink in. "I must … for to find, maybe five…yes, five fat actors." I'm still unable to speak. He nods conspiratorially, adding "Fat people, they are very funny." He smiles that forlorn orphan smile, as if letting me in on his big secret. "Is true. Fat. Very very funny."

I tell him I know no fat actors. He asks if any of my poetry has been published yet. I tell him no. He gently consoles me, a hand on the arm, a tone of experienced knowing, a veteran consoling a rookie. "Do not for…to be discourage. Is hard life..…poet life. Better…maybe…to write sitcom for television."

As he's about to walk away a thought occurs to him. "Please, but….but..um…what… what…what means—broadcast quality?" I know roughly what the term refers to but I have no explanations for Andras Groff. We've become friends. Daily as we've waited for our cabs he's offered up a scattering of cryptic details about his past: the orphanage in Romania, jumping ship in Port Newark, plans for getting rich in the stock market. How he adores Jerry Lewis and Don Rickles. His sitcom with fat actors, when broadcast to America, will be very very funny and make him rich…very, very rich. I ask him will there be any murders in the sitcom. "Murder?" he says, frowning with confusion, "What...is the meaning of this word?"

I never ask about the stolen bike. He suggests I call him "Andy".

NEW YORK CITY, JUNE 1994

It's a major psychological chore putting that goddamn burrito-laced conflagration on the corner of 1st Avenue and 6th Street in the rear view. I've been entering and exiting my building employing an abundance of stealth. My movements are driven by a singular categorical imperative; avoid any further incendiary contact with the actress, the punk rocker and the slippery slope of madness and violence they so clearly represent. And I've succeeded…for a while anyway. But then a few weeks back, well, the shit truly hit the fan and my big psychosis spiral officially kicked into massive overdrive.

Clinging to the ragged hem of reality, I was passing a news stand a few blocks from my place when a feeling of profound dread and horror washed over me, like I was being watched by ghosts. Or by her. I checked back over my shoulder but found the news stand unoccupied, save for the old geezer working the cash box. It was just him and me, so I tried to shake it off, but the feeling persisted—she was somewhere near, watching me.

Backpedaling and looking closer into the shaded racks bearing stacks of magazines and newspapers I realized she WAS there…not in any biological form—it was just her disembodied face. A near life-sized version of it adorned the front page of the goddamn New York Post. It was like that Woody Allen newspaper deal, only far more personal and terrifying. I figured I must be hallucinating and was okay with that—I mean, frankly mental illness would be easier dealt with than the alternative. But when I picked up the paper and opened it, there she was, sprawled across this huge two-page spread.

What was the story? In the short time since we parted ways she'd apparently become a major movie star. The article chronicled her rise from total obscurity to landing the lead character role in a huge summer blockbuster. I laid the paper down, then looking around, realized she was smiling back at me from an assortment of other newspaper and magazine covers as well.

Holy fucking shit.

And that was it buddy, all bets on me keeping my sanity were officially off. From that point on every time I stepped outside my door, every time I turned on a TV or a radio I was besieged by images of her, stories about her, video clips of her. Billboards! Newspapers! Magazines! She's pasted on the sides of passing fucking busses, for Christ's sake. Just smiling away. At me. People Magazine named her one of the fifty most beautiful women in the world last week.

So it's just a major league mind-fuck. The avaricious gossip columnists can't get enough of her. They report she's recently married—yeah, I've met the groom, real up close and personal, thanks.

I'd just put a grueling stretch of incessant suicidal ideation behind me and my mind was starting to stabilize, and now this. And for the uninitiated, it's a considerable trial tying to forget a person when their fucking face is plastered everywhere: billboards, magazines, on every single goddamn soda cup sold at every single goddamn 7-11 in the USA—hell, the entire world.

And I guess to ramp up the fucked-up quotient to previously unimaginable levels, her and the punk rocker have taken to parking their big rock and roll touring vehicle directly outside the door to my building—who knows why—but now whenever I come or go, there it sits, as if mocking me. Since my first floor apartment looks out onto the street I got no choice but to keep the blinds permanently drawn so as to not lose my fucking mind by looking out at the world through the filter of a virulently hostile Chevy Suburban.

I work night shift after night shift in the taxi, just trying to keep my suffering soul as far from that apartment as possible and my brain engaged in constructive activities, removed from insurgent obsessional, highly implosive thoughts.

More and more I resort to old self-destructive tactics, picking up the occasional clusters of thugs late at night, hoping they'll just go ahead and off me—a quick painless slug to the back of the head would solve all my problems, right? But so far no takers. I know I'm spiraling into madness, find myself weeping inconsolably at times, often with stunned passengers in the back seat.

I come home from fourteen, sixteen-hour shifts and see that goddamn truck of theirs parked directly in front of my building night after night. The gloom of the closed blinds begins to eat away at the last ragged threads of my morale—I'm a prisoner in my own damn domicile.

So, hey, you know what? Fuck this victim shit. I'm gonna take the bull by the horns here and just go ahead and torch the Suburban. Seriously. I'm drifting toward psychosis anyway and figure since they'd been so thoughtful as to deliberately park it directly in front of my goddamn window day after day, week after week, a little arson is in order before I lose my mind completely.

Piece by piece, like a little Carolina wren building a secret nest in some dusty old attic, this elaborate vehicle incineration plan comes flittering into my mind. I round up a stout eight-inch high candle, place it in a shallow tuna can, pouring an inch or so of kerosene in the bottom. I then fill a second much larger coffee can of kerosine and lay a runner line between the two cans so that when the candle finally burns down and ignites the kerosine hours later and in turn it lights the runner line, that'll then ignite the much larger kerosine cache in the second can. That secondary ignition should create a big enough blaze to incinerate the offending vehicle and do so at a time when I can establish an alibi elsewhere. I load up the supplies in my backpack and head out to the taxi fleet for another shift.

I've been running fast and hard all night. It's just past one AM now. I come swinging down my block in the cab, circling a couple times until I find the street completely deserted. With the coast clear, quick as a bunny I double park, slip the assemblage under the gas tank of the Suburban, light the candle and ease away, just another empty yellow cab dropping a fare on a side street in Manhattan.

I bank hard around the corner onto 1st Avenue then go arrowing up toward the West Side and stick to that area so that the entries on my trip sheet will create a foolproof alibi. Sorry officer, at the time the Suburban started burning I wasn't anywhere near that block—just look at my trip sheet! The final hours of my shift crawl by. I don't dare go anywhere near 6th Street to spectate—no, no, that's what knucklehead arsonists do. And I'm no knucklehead, now am I?

It's nearly four am. I've turned in the cab as late as possible, stopped at a restaurant to further establish my alibi and so when I come sailing around the corner of 6th Street and 2nd Avenue on my bike at nearly five am I fully expect to find a phalanx of fire engines and cop cars, plus one heavily charred Suburban chassis.

But….? What...? Where's the emergency vehicles? The cops? The firemen? There the Suburban sits—but it's not the highly anticipated charred black color. My street looks abysmally normal. Something went wrong but I don't dare check under the rear end to see what happened to my little incendiary device for fear I'll incriminate myself. They might be watching.

One thing's abundantly clear—my ingenious plan failed...miserably. Did the candle burn out before it made it to the initial kerosine reservoir? Did the runner line not light? Did everything work, but the fire didn't ignite the gas tank?

I sit in my apartment as the first light of day creeps over the street, staring out my only window for a long time at that Suburban. Considering it. And you know, I'm actually okay with my plan failing. It feels like I've been given some kind of reprieve. More and more this situation is looking like a battle to some grim, pathetic death and clearly I can't win so maybe I need to heed my genius friend's advice and get the hell out of New York.

The only problem is I've got nine full months on that one year lease on this place, so I'll be on the hook for over five grand if I abscond.

And not only do I not have anything approaching five grand, I'm twenty plus grand in debt from the various college loans I took out. But the writing's on the wall—I need to get shut of this place, pronto. So maybe I should try sweet talking the landlord into letting me out of the lease, tell him I'm experiencing delusional thoughts and suicidal ideation—which I am. No landlord wants to clean up a messy suicide, now does he?

Come nine am I lob in a call to his office and speak briefly with the secretary, who wants no part of my sob story. She says I should just come over and talk to her boss personally. I go to retrieve my bike, which I've chained to a parking meter outside the main door of the 9th precinct over on 5th Street between 1st and 2nd Avenues. Whenever possible I park my bike in front of cop stations, figuring nobody steals a cop's bike.

A half block away from the station this young woman randomly approaches me. She looks as if she's been crying and of course singles me out on the crowded sidewalk. "Sir, can you please please help me rescue my cat?" she whimpers, "I've been looking everywhere and I found him, but he's trapped inside an abandoned building around the corner." She's fighting back tears and though the set-up sounds absurdly sketchy, if she's play acting then she's doing so at Oscar caliber level. So I follow her around the corner.

We walk down a run of litter strewn steps toward a boarded-up basement entrance and through the dim, sooty window of this abandoned building on 4th Street I see the outline of a cat and hear its pitiful mewling.

I'm in nadir land, so with pretty much everything my prevailing sentiment is who gives a fuck, but strangely this trapped cat, it seems to matter. I identify with you cat; I too am trapped in the filthy basement of Life. So I bunch up my sleeve at the elbow and smash out a parallel window pane. This is in broad daylight a block from the police station. Crash, the glass goes.

The lady gasps as I break free the shards protruding into the hole, then she starts crying, thanking me, calling out to her cat. But when the poor creature finally emerges from the hole in the glass, she shrieks, "Oh shit! That's not my cat! That's not my baby!" She stares at the cat, then at me, whimpering, "It's not my cat. What…what…do I do with it?"

"Fuck if I know." I say, then turn and walk away, feeling as if my soul is permeated on a molecular level with some vile, deadly poison. When nothing is as it seems, when you hunger for calm lucidity but wherever you turn chaotic nightmares abound the only path left is to just disengage from all hope, all emotion, put your damn head down and let the prevailing winds blow you where they please. Or just check out permanently—it's an either/or kind of proposition.

I fetch the bike and blankly guide it across town to the landlord's place on Hudson and 13th Street. As I'm locking my bike to a light post outside his office a middle-aged mainstreamer passing on the sidewalk pulls up short right next to me, then shouts, "SMOKEY!" at me.

I nearly jump out of my skin, not knowing what the hell he's yelling about. "Smokey???" I ask him, backpedaling slightly, utterly dumbfounded. But this guy, he's too excited. He comes charging toward me, then like he remembered something, whips his head back, waves his arms at a nearby woman. She's wandering around down at the corner as if searching for something. He shouts, "HONEY! SMOKEY! They found him! Look!" whereupon he points at me.

Am I now Smokey?

Thanks, Universe. Just what I need, this totally surreal, utterly alienating New York City moment.

The lady looks as confused as I do, so the guy runs up right beside me and points to the light post where I'm locking up my bike. Then I see it, the lost pet flyer with a photograph of a gray colored cat on it that reads, "CAT FOUND. Gray with green eyes. Yellow collar. Call 212 ……"

I study the cat in the photo. It's a dead ringer for the mystery cat I'd just moments before freed from the basement on the other side of town. But I know that neither that cat or the crying lady's cat can be Smokey because this flyer was posted to the pole days ago, clearly prior to that event just a few minutes gone. So it's just another one of those "coincidences", right? Three identical lost cats, in a city of ten million people, the only connection between them being a suicidal taxi driver who's randomly encountered all of them in the span of twenty minutes.

By this point I'm beginning to finally get it—I've morphed into some highly dysfunctional magnet for psychotic synchronicity, and most of the prior situations I'd been mislabeling as coincidence in my life were no such thing. They were just clusters of subtextual realities that momentarily bubbled to the surface of my perceptive abilities, revealing fleeting evidence of hidden structural forms layered just beneath the surface of conventional consciousness.

Clearly with the cat coincidence I've stumbled into some such meaning cluster, but as usual the message conveyed is one hundred percent indecipherable. What the fuck am I supposed the make of this bewildering configuration of cat elements? Hey Universe, I need a little more material work with here!

The woman runs up and screams joyfully, beaming at me, then seeing I still look lost, tearfully blurts out, "Somebody found Smokey! He's our CAT!" They yank the poster off the light post and sprint down to the corner payphone, where I watch them bang out the numbers on the flyer and joyfully speak with the person who's found Smokey, their lost cat. The man does a little happy dance around, the woman's crying tears of joy. Redemption—apparently it's a sport for others.

Standing there watching them I can't help but wonder how tangible elements in the real world can exist on so many levels, with random cats simultaneously functioning as both actual physical entities and synchronistic signifiers.

NEW YORK CITY, OCTOBER 1994

Your world is in flames there ain't even a name
for the feeling you feel as you watch it all burn.
There's a girl in the distance she's calling your name,
but the name that she's calling is not your name, she calls
The Wordmule!
The Wordmule!
The Wordmule!
But he's plowing the field....

Got this newly minted manic chant ricocheting around in my head. So, what's up with this whole Wordmule angle? I like to think of it as much needed terminology describing an imaginary creature who speaks on my behalf during episodes of apoplectic paralysis like these latest ones that've been grabbing me by the throat and choking me into varying states of near demise.

So how am I doing? Hovering in the general vicinity of fuck-a-duck-struck-outta-luck and careening headlong toward going-down-in-firebally-flames-big-time territory. I daily tussle with sundry health issues—both mental and physical. I'm up to my ears in those student loan debts to Citibank, with bill collectors hectoring me and family members daily.

Sister money has run out and since there was no work to be found for a half-crippled, mentally ill outsider back in my impoverished Gulf Coast hometown the only option was to just suck it up, come limping back up here to New York and start driving that fucking taxi again.

What hurt the most was leaving Dopey Don behind. My heart about cracked in two as I rolled away from that cinderblock pillbox, that goofy feral feline dimly regarding me from the driveway. He had not a clue I'd never be back. Sorry buddy, but maybe sometimes disappearing is the best a person can do. With no place to live up here and the way things are going in my personal spiral to oblivion I'm thinking Dopey Don is probably better off without me.

Last week I snagged a ride north with a friend of a friend. Arriving back in The City I crashed on the hermetic genius's couch for a few days until I landed a room in a tenement way over by the East River in the Puerto Rican section of Alphabet City. This place is a serious ghetto proposition, nestled among numerous large scale drug operations covering entire city blocks, with lookouts and enforcers and cops on the payroll.

I'm told the crack dealing heavies are cool with outsiders like me so long as you don't interfere with their trade in any way, but watch out for the youth gangs from nearby projects who roam the streets all hours of the day and night, especially the ones from that Bandana Gang whose initiation rite is to stab a random stranger while walking the streets. They're well known terrors, so the general neighborhood rule is if you see a gaggle of young raucous Puerto Rican males sporting jaunty bandanas headed your way, run for cover. Fast. That's common knowledge hereabouts.

This dive I've just moved into, it belongs to a cab driver buddy. He's been hunkered down in this same grim little one bedroom third floor walk-up for twenty plus years now. Due to rent control laws he pays virtually nothing for the place—less than a hundred bucks a month, and this in Manhattan! He's got a cot and all his possessions stacked in the living room, then rents out the bedroom, actually turning a tidy profit on his living situation.

I'd left a message on his and dozens of other answering machines my first day back in the city, telling any and all comers I was desperate and scrambling for a room to rent. He'd called back the same day, promising he'd let me know if he heard of anything. So imagine my surprise a few hours later when, on an Avenue A laundromat bulletin board I found his flier offering what? Yeah, a room to rent. So I called him back and asked what was up with the flier.

He hemmed and hawed. I told him no hard feelings on my part, I just desperately needed a place to live. He went all apologetic, saying he felt guilty about charging a friend so much more than what he paid—he was asking triple his total rent, which was still a stone cold bargain in Manhattan—but I tend to disbelieve him on that assertion.

More likely he was just terrified of what I've increasingly come to represent: a sinking mental illness ship. And who can blame him? When you got the stink of psycho-death on you that's just the lay of the land: friends avoid you, calls go unanswered, nobody includes you in any of their reindeer games. And when they're confronted with that fact like this good soul here was, well, excuses abound.

Such depression is hyper entropic—the deeper you fall down the greased chute of your sickness the faster you plummet and greater the inertial forces hurrying you on become, and once you've reached a point of psychological terminal velocity, it's nigh unto impossible to break free of the gravitational field of your sickness. It becomes an entity unto itself, sucking you down, eventually drowning you in a cesspool of your own frailties.

There's clearly a point of no return, and these days I wonder pretty often if I've crossed it….it's hard to say. The bootstrap crowd, the nine-to-fivers who hail from good homes with sane families and non-self-destructive DNA imprinting, the normal Joes and Janes, they'll tut-tut you, say it's all in your head, that you just need to buck up. They don't have a fucking clue. They're like Marie Antoinette saying let them eat cake.

This is my first night back behind the wheel of the yellow torture chamber. I was four months away from taxi driving and battled incessant nightmares about returning. So the nightmare has metastasized into a cancer called reality. Despite my lengthy absence the dispatcher said nothing when I came trudging through the door and handed him my license. He just took my five dollar "gratuity", made me wait an hour then handed me a trip sheet and sent me on my way.

All things considered it's been an okay night. It's after ten now and I was just hailed by this black kid up on Broadway in the eighties. High dollar neighborhood. He's clean cut, well dressed and maybe twenty years old, but he's doing the ghetto hail; wrist broken, fingers flayed apart, hand actively wagging downwards. Any veteran driver knows that hail—it's an instant red flag that your fare's heading somewhere dangerous, some outer-borough hellhole where robberies and ambushes abound. And to be clear, it's often not the person hailing you that's the dangerous part, the real threat comes after the drop, as you're working your way back to the relative safety of Manhattan. In those hell hole areas yellow cabs are prime targets. You can get picked off sitting at a stop light or cruising a side street on your way back to the highway—happens all the time.

I study this kid as he walks toward the back door, easing it open, checking me out just as hard as I am him. He sticks his head in the cab, makes good eye contact and timidly asks will I take him to the Kingsbridge section of the Bronx. No big shock after that hail. He might as well be going to Syria or Chechnya; Kingsbridge being hell on earth. But at this point I give zero shits about where he's going. I've lost interest in my personal safety or what statistics say about the mortality rate of yellow cab drivers who venture into the Bronx. So I tell him to hop in and off we go.

He's happily surprised and clearly relieved. He settles in the back seat, thanking me profusely, adding he's been standing there for over an hour, passed over by yellow cab after yellow cab. The subtle forms of discrimination are many! Can you imagine, watching white people all around you getting picked up no questions asked? But meanwhile you stand there, arm in the air, having to beg and grovel just to get someone to take you where you're going? I'd be permanently pissed. But this kid's not. He's grateful. Thank you, young black man.

He tells me the few yellows that did stop for him despite his ghetto hail promptly terminated contact when they heard the word "Bronx" mentioned. Not me. I hit the West Side Highway and floor it. He comments favorably on my batshit crazy driving style as I weave and zip and bank and lunge between clusters of slower drivers, so I tell him that's how I used to ride waves back when I was a pro surfer.

He gets real quiet, then, disbelievingly, remarks, "No. You? You were a pro surfer???" I confirm this fact and he goes all quiet again, then, as if bewildered beyond words, his voice shot through with pity, he adds, "Oh, shit man! What happened to you???"

It's one of those innocent off-guard kinda questions that arrows deep into your psyche, a question I got no honest answer for.

I change the subject and ask him about his story. This kid, it turns out he's all of nineteen years old and already is the day manager of a chain store back in that swanky neighborhood on Broadway where I picked him up, which is some impressive shit for a dark-skinned teenage male from Kingsbridge. He's on his way home to propose marriage to his longtime girlfriend. He proudly shows me the flashy ring, which he was too scared to carry on the subway, hence his need for a cab.

I ask him about growing up in Kingsbridge, the crack cocaine epicenter of the universe, and he spins quite the tale; death and ruination being central characters. At age seven, seeing his older brother's schoolmates dropping like flies to the ravages of crack, he formed a pact with ten of his closest friends in the project they lived in. The deal was simple, if any one of the ten got caught doing drugs, the other nine had permission to, as a group, hunt him down and beat the fuck out of him, just turn him to pulp. Twelve years down the line only two of the ten went the way of drugs. In the projects of Kingsbridge that's a success story.

I drop him at a row of brownstones and wish him well with his marriage and job and all, then get my conspicuous white ass out of there. As I make my way out of Kingsbridge I feel like a big yellow T-bone steak dancing around in the middle of a pack of starving hyenas and so I roll some red lights and stop signs, doing my best to steer clear of any narrow side streets where highwaymen with automatic weapons might lay in wait.

Deadheading it back into the city via the Cross Bronx Expressway (statistically America's most dangerous roadway), the kid's question keeps resurfacing in the black pool of my psyche. What did happen to me? On paper my CV looks pretty solid: I'm a thirty seven year old ex-pro surfer, ex-European fashion model, ex-New York City fashion photographer, Cum Laude graduate of one of America's finest film schools. Hell, my goddamn thesis film won more awards than any other entry in the NYU student film festival just a few months back.

But behind all that flashy filler I'm a psychological cripple, a serial romantic failure, an economic bottom feeder with serious authority issues, a transportation waitress who takes geo-navigational orders from random travelers, a fringe dwelling service industry grunt who daily gets yelled at, honked at, spit on, talked down to, threatened, harassed and more. Every time I think about the level I've allowed myself to sink to I get to where I'm just apoplectic with rage and self loathing.

I'm hurtling past the steep, foreboding stone walls that frame the Cross Bronx Expressway, rimmed with garlands of razor wire dotted with old shoes and t-shirts and plastic bags and other detritus of impoverished urban experience when out of nowhere verse two of this latest song I'm hammering out comes sailing into my head fully formed.

> *You can't walk on that water—I know 'cause I tried.*
> *It's our spider web thinking, it's just too heavy with holes.*
> *And our thoughts they are made up of red Georgia clay.*
> *We think we know everything,*
> *but man we don't know…*
> *The Wordmule!*
> *The Wordmule!*
> *The Wordmule!*
> *But he's plowing the field….*

It's always like that with these "aha!" moments; they tend to come sailing into reach when your thoughts drift and your subconscious takes over. Try to lay hands on them via an A to B act of conscious will and they're nowhere to be found. When they do materialize out of thin air, if you're smart you drop everything and document the revelation, lest the nuance of the phrases slip beneath the surface of your addled, erratic memory and be lost forever.

Of course it's wildly injudicious to lock up your brakes on the Cross Bronx Expressway for any reason, much less to jot down song lyrics, so I switch to driving with my knees, snatch up that pen on the bench seat and start scribbling out lines on the back of the trip sheet as I drive.

Mid-laying down lyrics I forget my navigational duties and suddenly I'm hurtling toward the on-ramp of the freaking George Washington Bridge—goddamn, have I already traversed the entire island of Manhattan? And the next stop is what—Fort Lee, New Jersey and a five dollar toll? Oh, no-no-no—fuck that!

I bank hard right, jumping over two lanes just in time to hit that last off-ramp before the bridge, looping around under the dismal cloverleaf that's backed by the west-facing cliffs of the Hudson River Valley. I go whipping past a scattering of tattered, spectral figures steering overloaded shopping carts through shadowed passages among the stanchions and pillars that make up the highway superstructure under the bridge approach.

The cliffs of Washington Heights are pockmarked with enclaves of homeless; drug addicts, displaced refugees, maniacs, hard luck cases—all with stories of heartbreak and terror, loss and greed, abuse both doled out and received, on and on. They inhabit a woeful, chaotic cultural tideline formed by an eternal tsunami of hopelessly busted dreams. Campfires flicker here and there on the cliff side, anachronistic encampments as if transported from epochs long lost. The glint of scattered blazes feels mildly threatening, seeing how I live but a slim inch away from succumbing to a similar fate.

So, like the kid said, what happened to me?

No fucking idea. All I know is that via recent reductive spirals of existence these days my life is governed by the One Rule. Make one wrong move, have one bad accident in the taxi, see one slumlord sell the building out from underneath me and boot me out onto the streets, one slip on a sheet of sidewalk black ice where I fall and break my leg or arm and can't work, one more crippling sickness and—boom—I'm homeless, just like these godforsaken souls.

So where would I take refuge were I to lose my tenuous footing in the Puerto Rican slum? Live in a cardboard box under one of these bridges like some modern day troll? Fuck that—each and every bridge in this town is long since overrun with trolls, all of them desperate, some of them deadly. It's a cornucopia of bottom feeders, most of whom inclined to devour folks like me for lunch and spit out the splintered bones, cackling.

So where does a body sleep if not under a bridge? In some piss-stink doorway, huddled around bags of possessions like Hank the bum? A sitting duck for passing bands of drunken frat boys, street gangs, knuckleheads from Brooklyn, various bridge and tunnel thug types to mercilessly badger and harass? Jesus. I follow the banking off-ramp downwards, merging onto the West Side Highway headed southward toward the Upper West Side of Manhattan, chewing harder on that kid's question.

So what happened to me?

PENSACOLA BEACH, FLORIDA, FEBRUARY 1994

Jesus. Something big's gone haywire with my internals. It was festering deep inside me for months now, long before I tried to torch the Suburban, even before the actress appeared on my block. I was oblivious to it, even as my hard-nosed New York City landlord did the unthinkable and let me skip out on that cursed lease. Free of that albatross I made my strategic retreat southwards whereupon that sickness descended full force. I was hoping the change of scenery might help right the internal ship of state. It hasn't.

Soon as I hit Florida the fevers ramped up, getting worse instead of better. Right about now any sane person would be checking their ass into the nearest hospital but frankly I don't see the point. My self-diagnosis center reports I'm in deep, deep shit, beset by some terminal internal malady, a sickness that would require extensive treatment, hospitalization, possibly major operations to cure.

I'm clinically depressed with not a penny to my name and no health insurance, so it's a no brainer here—why should I bother suffering the indignity of trying to get help? I'll just be turned away by various reptilian medical corporations. Or far worse, I'll bring financial ruin on my family by asking them to save me. No, going limp and surrendering to whatever dark forces are afoot inside me makes the most sense presently. Fuck it. Let the fates carry me where they will.

My mom and step-dad, they reside some thirty miles inland in a shabby little ranch style job on a swampy flood plain near a town known to the locals as Scratch Ankle. They're the only family I got left hereabouts. When I first made it back home I rode out a couple of days in the white trash boondocks with them. They saw how sick I was and set in to nagging at me to see a doctor. Like it's just one doctor I need.

They pressed the matter, even sprang for an office visit with a local yokel General Practitioner in Milton, the closest proper town. This folksy son of a soybean farmer tut-tutted then put me on a round of supercharged antibiotics, something called a Z-Pack. Eight day's worth.

He assured me that the Z Pack would do the trick, and as I trudged out his office door I was vaguely hopeful the meds would finally help me turn a corner. Not so. Hell, I was six full days into the protocol before I began to feel even the slightest effects of them. Bad sign, hot rod antibiotics like that taking so long to kick in.

Once the meds ran their course the fever returned redoubled so at this point why bother? I'm committed to resisting any further urgings to consult more doctors, figuring it's time to just lay down in this bed and let the chips fall where they may. If death wants to have its way with me, well then, bring it on and welcome, dark messenger. I'm sick of life, sick of failure, sick of trying to connect with human beings and have them look at me like I'm a vomit sandwich or something.

But herein lies one of life's majestically diabolical contradictions; the more hungry you get to die, to just vanish from the face of the earth forever, the more Death gets all coy and stand offish. I guess It wants to remind you who's the boss before it comes calling. I get it, Death. Thanks for the further tutelage in my resolute disempowerment.

Though I fantasize about suicide non-stop day and night, I can't bring myself to pull the trigger—pun intended—as I see the irreparable damage it would do to good folks who happen to love me. I can't sidestep that pesky mental picture of loved ones destroyed by the anguish caused by my untimely self-generated departure. Nope, I refuse to let their anguished faces be the last image I see before I go skipping off into the shadows.

So accepting that it's not my job to decide the wheres and whens, it looks as though I'm stuck here, waiting for permission to die. So wait I do. And wait. I'm housebound and can hardly stay upright more than a few minutes at a time. Stranded in this little bungalow with nothing to do, no books to read, no TV to watch, days crawl by, the ticking clock and all it represents becoming my mortal enemy.

A couple of days back my mom and stepdad, they swung by my cinderblock beach digs to check on me. I was bedridden and could gauge from their worried expressions that I looked pretty bad. "Your eyes look wrong…" my mom said fretfully. But she won't talk of doctors again because that's already been tried. Fatalism runs deep in the family. I mentioned to stepdad Bill how bored I was, how I wished at least I'd brought my guitar down with me to pass the time.

Bill, he's one hundred percent rural stock, a no-nonsense straight-arrow airplane mechanic from the hills outside of Knoxville, Tennessee, so I was puzzled when he jumped in asking me about my little hobby, saying he had not a clue that I played guitar. Nobody does, I tell him—it's my little secret. A therapy outlet.

Well, the very next day Bill shows back up here with this anachronistic, purple Japanese surf guitar and amp. It's got all the cheapo guitar bells and whistles from the early nineteen sixties, four gaudy chrome pickups and a non-functioning whammy bar meant to look like one of the fancy Bigsby rigs. The brand name's "Prestige". I take one look at it and think, "Damn if this doesn't look like a prop guitar in a Prince video."

Bill's so goddamn proud of this monstrosity. At age twenty five he gathered up a year of his savings, strode into the big city music store in downtown Knoxville and laid cash on the barrelhead for this brand spanking new item, but then never learned to play a lick. After being propped up in the back of his closet some thirty odd years the neck's bowed a bit, leaving it nigh unto unplayable above the fifth fret, but still, it's a guitar. And not just any guitar, it's Bill's guitar, a powerful talisman of lost opportunities to him, so I coo and fuss appropriately, which makes cool cucumber Bill bust out in a bonafide grin.

The ancient, flimsy practice amp miraculously still functions. We plug it in and pluck out a few exploratory notes, the blind leading the blind, musically speaking. It's a gift to me, Bill says, and so after he takes off I mess with the truss rod and the bridge and get it to where I can fret up the neck a bit without it buzzing too much. I've never gone electric before and don't care much for the feel or sound of it, but beggars can't be choosers, now can they? It's been so long since I've played guitar regularly on account of that industrial accident that maimed my fingers that hell, I can't even remember but a couple basic chords.

This day turns to that. A week passes, and now it's two. Confined to this sick bed there ain't a goddamn thing to do but dig in and grind out first one song then another, then a third and a fourth, crafting crazy quilt compositions, mining veins of sorrow and regret, revisiting landmarks of confusion—putting my business in order before I disappear.

And is it just my imagination or is there a shift in the overall aesthetic to my songwriting? One that puts me a bit in mind of that Thalidomide guitarist way back in Amsterdam? Like these songs carry a plaintive simplicity conspicuously absent in my previous, more melodically athletic efforts of years gone by. The tone sounds worn out, world-weary, much less fussy and jumpy than those Frankensteiny songs I cooked up in the past. It's like my ability to express myself is failing alongside my internal organs.

I've taken to calling these compositions "cripple songs" in my head.

It's a month later and today's a fine spring day, the windows are open so there's no logistical concerns for Dopey Don. I've just finished running through four or five of my latest cripple songs, including that one about tornados. I've been writing a full song every day or two now for the last couple of weeks. Most of them are dismal endeavors, dead otters as the saying goes, but there's a couple like those ones I just sang, they make sense. I sing the last verse to the Tornado song again, just because it feels good.

Sometimes I feel the sky is a prison and the earth is a grave.
Sometimes I feel like Jesus in some Chinese Opera.
Sometimes I'm glad I built my mansion from crazy little stones,
But sometimes I feel so goddamn trapped by everything that I know.
And I wish it wasn't so, 'cause the only thing that anyone should ever know
is today is a perfect day...to chase tornados.

Exhausted, I lay down the purple Prince Prestige guitar and reflexively turn my eyes to the invisible roadmap woven into the stucco topography in the ceiling over my bed—by now I know it all too well. I close my eyes and commence to visualizing death as a slow incremental mist creeping up from under the bed. Soon I'll disappear into the fog. Soon I'll….

Wait, from just outside my window….that noise…what is that? Clapping? A solitary pair of hands? Like applause? Am I dreaming here? No, it's real clapping, and nearby—way too close to be emanating from some neighbors house or one of the bars down the road. Clapping? I lift up, hunting around for the source, then I hear a voice just outside my window call out, "Hey! Play another one!".

Okay, surely this is a hallucination. So I call out to the emptiness, "No."

"Aw. Why not?" the mysterious voice says.

Argumentative damn ghosts. "Because the other ones suck. Leave me alone."

"But I just got here!"

Up from a tangle of sea oats and pampas grass outside my open window rises a smiling face. It's not a ghost, or Diogenes or Black Robed Death or the actress. No, it's the face of a friend—my NYU film school buddy, Jim Krieg.

Jim's a talented film maker and tender-hearted soul, an unlikely combination of personality traits considering he's a fast track darling up there at America's most celebrated film school. Most of them fast trackers are predominantly show biz smoothie con artists, but not Jim. He writes heartwarming young adult comedies mostly.

I helped him out a few times on his student film shoots and an unlikely friendship ensued. But what the hell is Jim Krieg doing outside my window in Pensacola Beach…in the offseason? In he climbs through the open window. He plops down on the bed next to me and reports he heard how sick I was and so he came all that way from New York just to check on me.

Who does that? Nobody I know. Nobody I ever heard of. Jim said he wanted to surprise me, but when he was approaching the house and heard me singing he knew I'd stop if he announced his presence. Which is true, I suffer from crippling stage fright. He earnestly informs me that my songs are beautiful, then makes me promise to do two things; one, find a better doctor, and two, record those songs for him so that he can listen to them on his car stereo out in LA, where he's just been accepted to AFI, the top graduate film program in the US.

Jim stays a week. Being a crossroads type, in that short span he instantly makes a gaggle of new friends while touching base with a bunch of my old friends as well. He's playing bingo at the beach VFW post and picking up chicks at the mall. Yeah, he's sort of like anti-me.

It's now his last night in town and he's organized this big shindig at the beach house, sort of a cheer-up-the-dying-man type proposition. Typical of him, he's coaxed a local bluegrass band out to perform. At sunset people start filing through the door, crowding the tiny living room. A pile of crawdads are aboil in a big cooker out in the carport as the band jumps into it hard. There's dancing and hooting and revelry.

Life!

Pretty soon that forlorn cinderblock house is transformed, alive with the buzz of music and humanity. I raise up out of my sickbed and limp into the living room to listen to the lively goings-on, to speak with strangers and old friends alike.

At a certain point with the band banging out some uptempo hillbilly jam, Jim points at me and shouts, "SING SOMETHING!"

Oh, Jesus, no.

I adamantly refuse. No-no-no. Those songs he'd heard me play, they're secret songs. I wrote them as therapy to clarify depressing shit going on in my brain. I wrote them to myself, not to any goddamn body else. They're little musical orations shot through with sorrow and despair, aimed at trying to talk myself into staying here on planet earth—so, not exactly party fare.

But Jim's not to be denied. "SING SOMETHING!" He calls out again and then others jump in, egging me on too. I feel slightly trapped, crazed, about to pass out, but with that band laying down such an infectious, kickass groove, this otherly upwelling takes over, then inexplicably I break into a freakishly impassioned hillbilly hybrid version of that David Byrne song Burning Down The House. Being deathly ill, the choice makes sense, as my house is all but burned down by this point.

The partygoers listen in bewilderment to my feverish ravings. I'm so exhausted by this single act of sonic expulsion that at end of my performance all I can do is collapse into a nearby easy chair. The party rages on around me, and somewhere along the way I drift off the sleep again. The next day the cottage is empty, Jim is long gone and the ensuing silence is at once a relief and wildly suffocating.

It's two days on. Yes, the big shindig has taken its toll on me. The fevers, they're coming harder now, surging and backing off with no rhyme or reason. When they peak death feels close. I'm ready but so far the dark messenger remains elusive. I'm sitting in the easy chair staring out the window when I hear a banging on the door, then enter stage left my childhood buddy, The Count.

The Count's a plumber by trade. He was at the party two nights back manning the crab boil and, seeing how sick I was he showed up earlier today offering to drive me into town to fetch groceries—I got no transportation so this was a solid gold gesture. On our way there he too scolded me, telling me I need to get my crazy ass to a damn doctor. I just shrugged. I got no doctor money, I told him. He offered to pay for one for me but I refused—I been to the doctor already and it did no good. I was stonewalling him and he knew it.

So, after we got back from the grocery run where did The Count go? He beelined it downtown to the public library to look up my symptoms. Now, to be clear, The Count's not what you'd call academically inclined. But there he went, this rural plumber, to the library doing medical research on the digestive system, which coincidentally is the human equivalent of what? Right, plumbing.

So it's a few hours later and here comes The Count, rampaging through the door jumping up and down, shouting he's got my diagnosis all worked out. At the library he found a book that said my symptoms indicated my immune system was in catastrophic failure.

I sit there for a second just bewildered by the overall presentation. Yep, I'm getting a medical diagnosis from a plumber with a high school education. That said, I have to admit his assessment actually makes sense. The book said I need physical exercise to jump start my body's defenses. That too makes sense, but unfortunately I've already tried the exercise route. First thing I did when I got this beach house eight weeks back was take these long ambles along the tideline, sometimes for hours at a time.

In past health spirals walking's always fixed what ailed me, be it mental or physical, so when I left New York I figured a daily constitutional on the beach would be the perfect tonic. But not this go round. Walking hurt—more and more with every step—so after a couple days of diminishing returns I quit. And so what do you do when any form of movement just makes things worse? You go all still, hold your breath and pray, right?

Well, The Count's got a different take on the exercise angle here. Out of his work van he yanks a mountain bike for me to ride. It looks vaguely familiar and then I flash on why: it's a doppelgänger of that bike Andras Groff stole. I sit there a minute staring at it, then have to turn away so as to not just totally lose my shit.

NEW YORK CITY, MAY 1988

A month's passed since I last crossed paths with Andras, AKA Andy, so I ask one of the dispatchers, Big Gary, what's become of him. Big Gary's cool, not a total asshole like Marty. He rolls his eyes and shakes his head. "Andras Groff…" he mutters, "That little psycho. Committed assault and battery on a passenger. First he totaled the fucking cab—yeah, rammed it into a wall up in midtown, then he pulls the passenger out of the back seat and beats him to a pulp. Put him in ICU. So, to answer your question, Mr. Groff is no longer employed at Ann's Service."

"No shit? Wow." I say, then ask, "So…what's he doing? Like, driving for another fleet or something?"

"Another fleet? Ha. Fat chance." Big Gary says. "TLC revoked his license and presently he's a guest of these state out at Rikers."

For the uninitiated, the TLC is the Taxi & Limousine Commission (AKA the Taxi Gestapo) and Rikers is, well, jail.

I stand there for a second with my jaw sagging open triangulating the variables of this story about Andras, weighing his known propensity for violence against the image of my friend, the tender human being looking for fat people to appear in his broadcast quality sitcom. I guess I get a little lost in thought momentarily because Gary taps on the bulletproof glass, then smirks at my stupid pose, making the universal gesture for insanity, finger spinning counter-clockwise at his temple sign.

But is he talking about me or Andras?

It's two weeks later, mid afternoon. l just rolled out of the fleet garage twenty minutes back, ran a quick fare up to Grand Central and now I'm cruising empty, headed south on 5th Avenue in the thirties hunting for passengers. Up ahead, biking southbound who do I see? Andras Groff churning along on yet another ten speed bike. Slung over his shoulder is a bike messenger pouch. I slow down and ease over to his side of the roadway until he catches up, then I pace him. He's pedaling along right beside me but hasn't figured out it's me I guess. Sooner or later he's gotta look over, right? But he doesn't. The window's down so finally I yip out his name.

"Andras!"

He veers defensively, as if I'm trying to ram him with the cab, his furious scowl flashing a glimpse of that inchoate rage I first observed during that street fight so long ago, a fight which went down just a mile or so south of here. I call out his name multiple times, hoping to calm him down, and when finally he sees it's me there's this sudden transformation, an instantaneous hurtling from acute paranoiac aggression to one of kinship, even affection. I pull over and we talk.

He explains about the crash and fight that got him fired. It turns out it wasn't his fault. The passenger was a drunk who'd reached through the open partition and grabbed his shirt collar and started choking him. Andras was just defending himself. That's how the cab ran into the wall. Since he'd already been given that final pink slip warning and knew if he had one more wreck that he'd be fired Andras became unhinged and attacked the man. That's his story. He's just been released from Rikers and some social worker's arranged this job for him working as a bike messenger.

The account seems plausible enough, considering the explosively alchemic relationship between New York City and Andras Groff. His troubles put me in mind of that New Age nonsense theory called The Laws of Attraction, where what and how you think determines what happens in your life. It always felt like so much hippie bullshit but lately I'm grudgingly starting to suspect there may be something to it—like, when things start going bad-wrong and you start dwelling too much on your failures and doomed fate, negative energy levels rise inside your mind creating this overall negative energy suction, pulling darkness toward you. In street vernacular this is what's known as becoming a shit magnet. Andras appears to be in full shit magnet mode presently. I sympathize, in part because by all appearances I'm not too far behind him.

He right away asks if I've had any luck getting my poems published. Sigh. What can I say but no? At this point the truth's too complicated to explain to him. "Keep trying…" he says consolingly, "some one…these good magazine…they will see…you are real poet."

Worn out from the pep talk, he smiles softly then reaches in his bag, pulling out a grimy scrap of paper. He scrawls a phone number on it. "Please, if you can…um, for to call me? Tell him, this man, you are friend. I must have….I am looking for place, just for sleep…nothing else…"

Jesus, that's all I need. Andras Groff as my roommate. I can hardly keep my own troubled self afloat. The image of me and Andras sharing living quarters puts me in mind of that lifesaving class I took as a teenager. The instructor commented that the most common form of multiple death in America is double drownings. They occur when some small, well-meaning individual tries to rescue a larger drowning person and said larger person panics, latches ahold of the smaller one and promptly takes them both down to the bottom of the briny blue.

I take the paper and tell Andras I gotta get back to work. As he's putting the ink pen back in the sack, I catch a glimpse of what appears to be a Groucho Marx mask tucked away among the official looking manila envelopes he's delivering. He spies me studying it and quick-like ducks it out of sight, as if it's some kind of secret personal talisman. I wonder if it's a costume for one of the fat actors in his broadcast quality sitcom.

I slip the phone number in my pocket, having no intention of ever calling it. I'll take it home and forlornly paper clip it to his restaurant application and my murderer description in that Strange But True box that for years and years now I've kept under my various beds in various apartments.

It's a month later. I'm walking north up 2nd Avenue in the low twenties when I hear urgent shouting. Street fight? Accident? Some wild-eyed End Times preacher? No, up ahead, pedaling south on that same ten speed, it's Andras Groff. He looks much worse for the wear, his vest is filthy and torn, his long stringy hair is greasy and unkempt and he now sports a ragged beard. His knuckles are scabbed over, suggesting he's been in recent fights. The capper is he's now wearing the Groucho Marx mask, the one I'd seen in his messenger pouch—not fully, just kinda propped up, half-cocked on his forehead.

As he pedals he's holding aloft a Chinese newspaper which he aims at passing pedestrians. Each time someone meets his eye, he brandishes the paper like a tactical weapon, menacingly howling "READ!" repeatedly at them. Dear Jesus, Andras has totally fucking flipped. As he's approaching me he thrusts the Chinese newspaper in my direction, commanding "READ!"

In return I shout, "ANDRAS!".

He does a little double take then snaps out of his delusional activity and circles back on the sidewalk. My poor crazy friend slips the Groucho Marx mask off and we talk, catching up on what's transpired in the last month. He's lost the bike messenger job and now is unemployed and homeless. He asks if there's room in my place for him. And I truly want to help, I do, but I know for Andras there's no rescue possible. He's too far gone. Like Molock said, "For some home is much further away than others."

I make sad, pathetic excuses. Andras shrugs in defeat, then scrawls out a different phone number to reach him at, this one turns out to be a shelter where he goes to eat. I tell him I'll call him there if I hear of anything, but we both know I never will. I watch him wobble-ride off, Chinese newspaper in hand, Groucho Mask back on. I fear I'll never see him alive again. The world is seldom kind to creatures that far out on a limb in the big rotten tree of this hardscrabble urban life.

PENSACOLA BEACH, FLORIDA, APRIL 1994

The Count's bike riding therapy idea feels roughly tantamount to fighting the armies of Satan with a deflated beachball or a little pink plastic squirt gun or something, but to humor him I climb on the bike and attempt to ride it anyway. I'm shaky but make it out the driveway and about a hundred feet down the quiet little back road that the cottage sits on before my head starts spinning and I have to turn around and get my ass in a prone position post haste before I pass out. The Count cheers me on, gives me a big corny pep talk, leaves the bike in the carport and off he goes to his next plumbing gig.

Exhausted, I sleep then wake a few hours later feeling strangely lighter. It takes a second to realize—wait, has the fever backed off? And the pains in my gut, have they have subsided a bit too?

Could it be? The bike? I figure I got nothing to lose so I drag myself out of bed and go at it again, this time riding a little further down the road.

By midnight I feel a gathering strength in me and so I head out for yet another slow, plodding ride. It's cold—in the upper thirties—and the seaside streets are pleasantly deserted. The canopy of brilliant stars overhead forms a dazzling pinpoint matrix over the whole of the world, and after such a long stretch of involuntary stasis this movement, my legs churning slowly, rhythmically, the wind in my hair, the smell of the salt water in the air, it feels like goddamn heaven.

It's just before dawn and I'm awake and riding again. My gut still aches, but I feel this faint twinge of hope rising up in me that I do my best to suppress for fear this is just another sucker punch in the making. But by midday I've got three rides under my belt. First it's a short distance, then a full trip around the block, then circling three blocks. And there is no question now—I'm feeling increasingly better. My strength and stamina are returning!

It's one week later. For a couple days there I was only managing a mile or two each ride, but now it's five miles. Yeah, I'm still in pain, and yeah there's still something radically wrong inside of my guts, but for the first time in way too fucking long I can walk a good distance without any great effort. Plus, my appetite's finally shown signs of returning. After months of eating little to nothing I managed to get down a full dinner of chicken, rice and peas tonight. But now it's the small hours of the morning and I wake to furious cramps, like something seismic's gone wrong inside me. Bad chicken? That'd be my luck, right? My first damn legitimate meal in months is tainted with salmonella?

Jesus, I'm hit by a series of paralyzing chills, followed by more double-up cramps. Is my appendix about to bust? I keep hobbling back and forth to the toilet over and over screaming out in agony at times but nothing ever happens. I got no phone, no vehicle other than the bike, so I'm about to stagger out the front door and get the nearest neighbor to dial 911.

AAAGH! WHAT THE FUCK IS GOING ON!!

I'm doubled over on the toilet and feel this bizarre shift in my abdomen, there's a jolt of searing pain whereupon I promptly shit out five white calcified stones. Now that's not something you do every day! The pain's instantly cut in half.

I don't need any medical book to tell me what's transpired; I've just passed some sort of intestinal obstruction in the form of those white stones. So that's it; they've been lodged in my gut for months now blocking passage of digested food stuff. The bike riding must have broke them loose. Then it hits me—of course—sepsis! All along I've been suffering from increasing degrees of sepsis.

It's three days later. I'm back on the bike for the sixth time today, moving at a good clip, venturing ever further away from the cottage. It's after ten pm and I'm zipping along nearing the final houses on the beachfront community just before the national seashore territory begins when—what's that? I catch a distant jangle of some worrisome, feral commotion approaching from behind. I toss a look over my shoulder, and... HOLY SHIT!—charging out from behind one of the last beach houses here comes this massive, raging Rottweiler dragging a chain and stake. He goes a hundred and fifty pounds minimum and looks totally berserk, possibly rabid.

Apparently he's broken free of his mooring and now is in hot pursuit of me, foam flinging from his jowls like the proverbial Hound of Hell. There's a split second to triangulate whether I got a shot at getting away clean or not, and if not, buddy, then I need to turn and make a stand ASAP, put the bike between me and him, shield style. Do I stop, or kick it into a higher gear and hope my sickly self has the oomph to outrun his gaping maw? Seeing how crazed this creature looks I opt for the latter, standing up on those pedals and going like hell.

I don't look back. The terrifying pursuit noises are closing in on me fast, those furious growls and gurgles, the chain banging and rattling on the asphalt. I'm in primal flight, the Rottweiler closing in, now snarling and snapping at my back tire. But somehow, enhanced by the adrenalin rush that hits, the mathematics favor me. He snaps at my back tire for a few feet but then lags, falling off. I hear him panting, pulling up short, then abandoning his pursuit. From a safe distance I look back to see, like Cerberus himself, that big black form posed alpha style mid road, chain and post strewn behind him, a look of thwarted fury on his face.

I pedal on.

Yeah, it's a minor incident, but it keeps coming back to me all the way home. That's all I need is to get mauled by some huge errant rabid dog—talk about Laws of Attraction! Then it hits me; this is just another of those parallel realities, like with the cats in New York City that day. The dog is the dog, but simultaneously the dog is some form of meta signifier, an agent of Unseen Forces. I wonder what deeper meaning I should glean from the incident. Much as I hate to tack clumsy morals onto such contexts it damn sure feels like the Universe is saying to keep peddling like hell, you're not out of the woods just yet.

NEW YORK CITY, JUNE 1994

My Florida convalescence is behind me and I'm back driving this goddamn, mother-fucking, accursed taxi. I spot a guy in a wheelchair easing toward the curb at the corner of Lexington and 81st, whereupon he hails me. With the exception of the chair he's your basic wealthy middle-aged white guy in a high dollar Brooks Brothers suit. I jump out and circle the cab thinking he'll need an assist getting in but no, I get a little curt nod from him as he waves me off, "I gotta do it myself." He announces, both to himself and me.

Understood.

He's headed downtown to some lawyer's office. We get to talking. He's a recent paraplegic. A few slim years back he'd been a hot shot wall street broker living that upper crust plutocrat type lifestyle. Then while shit faced drunk one night he got blindsided by a delivery van while crossing Madison Avenue. "It was my own fucking fault…" he admits with an unlikely cocktail of regret and moxie. And thus began his downfall.

There followed an endless series of surgeries, away went the filthy lucre employment gig, away went the trophy wife, away went the swanky uptown digs. He now rents a modest studio apartment on the upper east side. He's suing a couple of people and being sued himself by others, including that ex-wife, hence the trip to the lawyers. Wow, what a spiral. He's remarkably open about it all, so I tell him, "Sounds like life took a major shit on you, man. You must be bitter."

"Bitter? Naw. I'm grateful. At least now I know who I can trust and where my rage emanates from." He says, adding, "How about you? Can you say the same?"

The question carries a conspicuous weight. Okay. This is clearly some meta proposition, a resonant echo of that Bronx kid's question, "What happened to you?" I have to admit I got no authentic response to his poignant question, so I commend him on his clarity and leave it at that. We chit chat along the way before I drop him downtown. As I watch that man wheel himself into the lawyers office building my brain gets to kicking up dark moody rumination dust. Yep, ain't it so; we're all just an inch away from similar abysses.

But what form does my rage take?

A quick tally: Back I came to the city that apparently wants to kill me. Back to the same neighborhood where the actress and her punk rock husband dwell. Back to a landscape overrun with psychic undertows and bewildering whirlwinds of goddamn synchronicity. Hell yes I should've stayed the fuck away from this black hole, at least until I was in much much better physical shape, but what could I do? Sister money ran out, there was no work to be found down there for a half-dead mental patient. Then summer rental rates kicked in hard on the beach cottage, and as of May 1 I was officially homeless. So here I am, thirty six years old and dealing with the consequences of being an existential bottom dweller. Even still, apparently I've got it easy compared to others.

After the white stone purge I'm much improved on the health front—thank you beloved rural plumber/diagnostician! But this cab driving, with all the hurtling for hours on end in vehicles with shitty suspensions over egregiously potholed streets, it's starting to exacerbate my condition again. I've noticed the symptoms creeping back in after working just a three, four day taxi week, and even then only lasting for maybe ten hours a shift before I can't take it any more. Daily I'm on a bike to and from work, but I'm not navigating the calming solitude of an abandoned beach town, it's the chaos of New York City traffic, which frankly ain't what you'd call therapeutic.

It's a few minutes past one AM, I've bagged my shift with two full hours left on the clock. I'm done delivering dazzling New Yorkers here, there and everywhere. Guts aching and slightly feverish I turn the cab in, a slim eighty bucks in my pocket. On my therapy bike I hop, headed home to the Puerto Rican ghetto apartment. A block into my ride that sweet black kid's "What happened to you???" question from a few weeks back comes boomeranging into my thoughts like it has ever since I picked him up. I go into full soul searching mode as I go threading my way past this and that imminent peril; drug dealers, street gangs, muggers, drunk drivers, etc. Soon I'll be safe in my room, alone with the most imminent of all perils: self.

A block away from my place I pass a row of zombified junkies cued up outside that abandoned building housing the big mid-block heroin operation, waiting to drop their dope money through a hole in the cinderblock wall and get their baggie of forgetting powder in return. They'll forget for a while, then the specter of remembrance will return in some dazzling new costume, all aglow with renewed vigor and vengeance. Whatever bad that's happened to me, at least THAT hasn't.

I circle the block once to make sure there's no crackhead muggers lying in wait, then jump the bike up on the curb and beeline it for the door to the building. Safely in my place, I see the light on the answering machine flashing and punch the replay button.

It's Jim Kreig, calling from his new digs out in LA. Thanks to The Count that doctor part of my vow to Krieg was rendered a moot point, but I still had to keep my word to him about making a tape of those depressing songs he'd asked me to send him. So, as soon as I got settled in the Puerto Rican slum I broke out this old, half-busted tape recorder I've had for a decade or more and laid down a handful of my cripple songs for him, singing most of them through a two-liter Pepsi bottle that I'd sawed in half—it sounded theatrical.

"Sorry about the tape quality, old buddy" I wrote with the note accompanying the tape. "I know it's rough, lots of hiss, etc, but who cares? Nobody's gonna hear it but us two anyway, right?"

Wrong.

Jim's all agog about something. His disembodied voice on the answering machine reports—yes, he got the tape. Yes, it's been playing on his car stereo nonstop since it arrived. Yes, he played it for all his Hollywood film friends. Yes, they love it. Yes, his new filmmaker girlfriend, who's some sort of artistic prodigy with, among other accomplishments, an advanced degree in music theory, was so struck by the odd arrangements and lyrics on this crappy homemade cassette that she borrowed it and played it for some woman who's a big shot in the music business out in LA.

Okay....

The big shot likewise gave the material a big thumbs up and sent word that I should contact her ASAP. She wants to get me a record deal AND a gig at some infamous LA hipster hangout called The Viper Room. Jim reports that's where movie stars like Johnny Depp and River Phoenix hang out. That's it. He concludes this long surreal message, voice trembling, by giving me this music industry lady's first name and phone number, and barks at me to CALL HER.

The answering machine clicks off. As the silence ebbs and flows around me, for the first time in a long time, I feel that slightly electrocuted feeling creeping in, like I'm entering a heightened state of consciousness. I'm suddenly aware of distant conversations between neighbors, dogs barking, furniture being moved in apartments typically too far away to register. I listen to his message a second time and it's the same data as the first—loved the songs, record deal, Viper Room, call the lady. I understand every separate word he says, but combined together not a goddamn bit of it makes a lick of sense.

Okay magical non sequitur, welcome to my little slum. After epochs of defeat and discouragement of every known variety on every imaginable front, this weird music I write as therapy, music which apparently has a "serious intonation problem", songs that nobody other than Jim Krieg has ever commented favorably on, suddenly that dismal material prompted this so-called well-connected, music industry mystery woman to offer some lofty, unattainable opportunity?

Ah, wait! I was almost fooled, but no, I get it—it's some kind of setup! Of course! The only sane response to that message is to assume that the fix is in. That's it—this must be life's final cruel joke! This music industry lady'll turn out to be some delusional maniac who'll lure me to a hotel in Wisconsin and stab me to death. My murder will be reported in those small ignominious columns in newspapers that detail squalid human failure and folly. Somewhere a doppelganger mentally-ill fringe dweller type like me will cut my death article out and put it in his own Strange But True box under the bed.

Life is so wearying. I'm tired. So very tired. Time to lay down and try to coax the bear of sleep from its musty cave. I need sleep. Sleep will help sort things out. Tomorrow everything will make sense, if only I can sleep...

It's the next afternoon. I've just spoken with this lady allegedly from "the music industry". She reports she loves my "demo"—a new word to me—and claims to manage superstar producer/recording artist Daniel Lanois, a Grammy winner, no less. Right. Sure. Oh, and her husband is some well-regarded singer-songwriter named Joe Henry.

Right, of course he is.

She claims that she can get me a gig at The Viper Room and has inside connections to big labels.

Yes, of course she does.

So me and this alleged show biz big shot chewed the fat for a good hour. Now I sit in my dismal, claustrophobic Puerto Rican slum room and mull over the unlikely chore I've been tasked with. I'm supposed to now send my profoundly amateurish cassette tape to the A&R departments of huge record labels like Sony Music, Warner Brothers and Matador Records. To do what? For them to actually listen to it? Oh, please—gimme a break. This is ludicrous.

To be clear, my miserably engineered home recording was made employing one cheapo Radio Shack microphone which I picked up at a yard sale fifteen years ago for a dollar. For drums I tapped chopsticks on pots and pans. The whole thing was recorded in the kitchen of the Puerto Rican slum. You can hear my neighbors arguing in the background at times. There's no keyboards, no bass lines, no players other than yours truly thumping away on the ancient purple Prince style surf guitar. Oh yeah, and the recording was done in mono to begin with, but something's broken in the outputs of my old tape recorder and so when the mixed down tape is played on a proper stereo system the sound only emanates from one speaker. Yep. One speaker. It's truly mono. This is my "demo".

Conclusion: this is either some kind of cruel practical joke or this lady's a misguided nut-job. Even still, I sort of want to see where this charade goes. My bitter, broken, mentally ill taxi man life is so dull and soul-killing that I'm figuring such a fool's errand beats the monotonous nothing my life presently amounts to. Something, even if it's something bad, is better than nothing, right? Isn't that what Faulkner was getting at at the end of The Wild Palms when he said, "Between grief and nothing I will take grief"?

The only hitch in going along with this ruse is the practical considerations to navigate—I'm desperately impoverished. To do what this alleged music industry big shot is suggesting I'd have to buy a ten pack of cassette tapes, which would run me ten bucks. Then one by one I'd have to hand-dub all those copies, which would be labor intensive. Also I'd have to borrow a second cassette player to bounce one tape to the other. Then there's the cost of postage to send each and every tape to various luminary destinations.

Now we're talking almost twenty, thirty bucks I'll be out if I do as told. Jesus, I'll have to eat nothing but beans and rice for a solid week.

This I'm sincerely disinclined to do.

Now that I can eat real food again I want to see chicken on the menu at least once or twice in the coming days. But then I think of old Br'er Rabbit fighting that tar baby—the more he resisted, the more he was bound. So maybe I should stop resisting—just play along with the joke, surrender to yonder cruel hands of fate…let them ferry me where they will?

At the bottom of it all one facet of this proposition is glaringly clear, getting pranked by a bunch of LA based mental cases can't be much more depressing than the life I'm leading now. So, debate settled; I'll fight no more. I'll surrender and do exactly as the freaky fates demand. I'll send my shitty "demo" tapes out to sundry music industry giants.

I bike over to a variety store on 14th Street. Hey Korean vendor lady, hit me with one of them bulk packs of cheapo TDK ninety minute cassette tapes! It takes me a couple of days to dub all the tapes, and in the interim I get to work drawing a crazy ass cover for the cassette. It's a cartoon featuring a coffin being carried toward a big mountain range by a bunch of anorexic angels. I got no idea what this drawing has to do with the songs, but I figure at least it looks sincere.

I xerox ten cover copies, then slip the cassettes into tiny cardboard boxes that I fabricate out of the backs of cereal boxes. Between the weirdo covers and the packaging, the bar for that fine art form known as album cover design has been radically lowered. I laugh as I send my little testaments to mental illness off. Have you ever heard sad, bitter, impoverished laughter in the bustling Astor Place post office in the gleaming metropolis of New York City? If so, that was probably me.

It's a few days later. I'm sleeping off my normal shift last night, accessing slumberland at around five am, which is fairly normal. What's not normal is the phone ringing at ten am. That ain't exactly a welcome development. I put a pillow over my head, thinking the caller will give up. Wrong. The goddamn thing keeps ringing so finally I drag my beleaguered ass out of bed and spit out a groggy hello.

It's Jim Kreig's excited voice on the other end. He's all cheery. His girlfriend told him my conversation with Melanie, the so-called music industry insider, went great and she's fascinated by my artistry. Right. Sure she is. Jim launches into talking over strategies with me. Strategies? For what? How to get stabbed correctly? Which motel in Wisconsin is closest to a hospital?

It's time to nip one prominent aspect of this charade in the bud. I break the news to my well-meaning friend that I appreciate his enthusiasm and belief in me, but this music industry big shot friend of his girlfriend's is likely a fraud. She's no music business executive. She's probably just off her meds and this whole endeavor is some sadly misguided folly.

Jim listens patiently, then sighs. He tells me I am so-so-so wrong. He reminds me this woman is Daniel Lanois' manager. "Yeah, so I heard." I say, smirking cynically. So he gets all pissy and adds that her husband is Joe Henry. And this he knows for a fact because he's met them both. I say nothing. See, Jim's fairly mainstream and never had a supernatural curse on him, so he doesn't recognize the warning signs like I do. This set up, it ain't all sparkly and filled with magical elves like he's saying. Finally he says, "Okay, she doesn't like people to know this, but her last name…..it's Ciccone." He pauses to let that sink in, but there's nowhere for it to sink.

"So?" I mutter.

"Um, hello? Does that name ring a bell?" he scoffs.

Like it should? He trots that name out like some obvious truth's on display here. What the hell is the significance of Ciccone? Is that some kind of mafia nomenclature? I got no idea. Jim's officially exasperated. He tersely informs me that Melanie doesn't care much for name dropping in relation to her family pedigree, but that she is, among other things, Madonna's big sister.

I laugh and laugh. "Yeah, and her uncle's the Easter Bunny!" I say. I thank poor misguided Jim Krieg and hang up.

Madonna!

I'm still laughing as I sit down on my bed, but then that electrocuted feeling starts kicking in and weird psychological currents commence to eddying all around me. The picture place in my mind starts flickering to life, then I see it—Jesus, right before I left Florida I had that weird dream. I was drowning in an inland waterway near that little beach cottage. I spied a Miami Vice style cigarette boat rocketing toward me and desperately waved at them to rescue me.

Up zoomed this massive, growling watercraft, but instead of stopping, it banked hard and circled me a couple times. At the helm of said boat was Madonna, wearing this skimpy, revealing bikini. She was sunburned and beamed blissfully. David Letterman was her co-pilot. He wore an elegant silk suit and captains hat and kept bellowing out "Woo-hoo", then guffawing. They circled me twice, waving like we were all best buds, but as I swam toward the boat we heard sinister laughter echoing over the water, whereupon Madonna got spooked and gunned it and away they raced, throwing a huge rooster trail across the choppy waters. It formed a rainbow over my head.

Madonna.

Good god, when will this ever stop? I don't know whether to fight this ever-expanding spiral of delusions or just surrender and enjoy the psychotic ride of a lifetime.

It's a Tuesday a couple weeks later. I got no mail service at the Puerto Rican slum due to a variety of landlord related issues so I'm at the Astor Place post office checking my PO box before I head off to another shift in the yellow prison. Since I got zero else going on in my life here I am, pathetically going along with the "music industry" lady's gambit. But a joke's not especially funny when you already know the punch line, right? All the tapes went out as requested, angels pall-bearing a coffin on the cover and that tidy little form letter introducing myself and name-checking Melanie "Ciccone" early and often.

In goes the key, the PO box door swings opens and what do I find? Four of my shitty demo tape-laden envelopes. There's a rubber stamp over each address that states: UNSOLICITED MATERIAL: RETURNED UNOPENED" and all of them are similarly marked "return to sender". Damn man! And I even wrote this Melanie "Ciccone's" allegedly famous name in BIG letters on the outside of each and every envelope.

Okay, so at least SOMETHING makes sense here. Clearly they don't know this lady. She's just some nut-case suffering from delusions of grandeur, sucking me into her own psychotic vortex, as if I needed an uptick of psychosis in my already psychosis-riddled life. Talk about being in full shit magnet mode! Well, there's consolation to be had here: the good news is my hunch about her was right. The bad news is I just wasted thirty goddamn dollars on nothing.

It's Friday the same week. I stop by the post office. All the envelopes have come back unopened but for one. What's up with that last one? I'm doing my best not to keep my inner hopeless-romantic in check. But here I go, checking my mail again, and all because of that one tape that's unaccounted for. And what magical entity did I mail that final cassette tape to? Was it to Woody Allen or Samuel Beckett? No. Not even Travis Bickle? Nope. That one went to the legendary record label Warner Brothers.

It starts to irk me a little. What's with the delay with these Warner Brothers people? Could the big shots actually be listening to that shitty little tape I sent and discussing it? Snowballs in hell got better odds. I slip the key in the PO box and even though I know better, still my heart goes pitter-patter when the door swings open and, lying in the narrow slot, I see an actual package from Warner Brothers Records, AND it's not the original envelope I sent that's been returned unopened.

Calm down. It's nothing. There is no magic at play here. I take a deep grounding breath, then, hands shaking slightly, open the package, which I now see has my demo tape included in it. There's a letter. The text, it's not War and Peace. It reads as follows:

> *Dear sir,*
> *We have received your tape and listened to it. We feel the material herein is very weak.*
> *We have no interest in having any further contact with you. Please do not contact us again.*
> *Your tape is returned herewith.*
> *Sincerely,*
> *XXXXXX*

I read it twice, three times. Truth be told, I'm kinda relieved, as something here finally makes sense. Really, it does, so thank you for your cruel, candid appraisal, Warner Brothers! And I sincerely mean that. Yes! The ordeal is over! Between the herein and the herewith I now possess hard evidence to confirm that I am officially a zero musical talent entity. So that means I don't have to play along with this charade any more and nurse along that bothersome hope that I kept feeling well up inside of me during this process.

And I don't have to go to the trouble of traveling all the way to that motel in Wisconsin to be stabbed to death by this Melanie "Ciccone"! I can get on with my miserable life, driving the taxi, fending off creditors, working out my plans for a more successful passive/aggressive suicide.

Although, come to think of it, it's kind of a pity. In terms of narratives dovetailing the motel stabbing scenario combined with my plans to off myself might have made for a good little newspaper clipping. But then again, who wants to go all the way to Wisconsin just to get stabbed to death, right? There's easier, less complicated alternatives. Tidier ones!

It's one week and sixty seven hours of white knuckle cab driving later. I'm just back from a run to the grocery store and have made it home without getting robbed or my supplies stolen. Success! The phone rings and I jump, still on edge from being a sitting duck walking with all those groceries.

It's her— this Melanie "Ciccone" nut calling to see how those fancy record labels liked my "demo". I remain cordial as I break the bad news to her: her name on the envelope did nothing—most returned the tape and package unopened. The only label that did bother to listen was Warner Brothers. I relay the details about the rejection letter.

"WHAT?" she barks, "They said that??? Well, you know what? They're wrong! And we're gonna prove them wrong by getting you a record deal!"

I just nod politely and thank her as I say goodbye, telling her I have groceries to put away. I want to add something snide like give my best to Batman if you see him. But I don't. I place my meager grocery store purchase in the roach infested cupboards. Quotidian chores settle a restless mind. I set to washing dishes in the filthy kitchen of this dismal, fetid apartment.

It's maybe twenty minutes later. I'm about done with the dishes when the damn phone rings again. Jesus, what is this, Grand Central Station? Great. It's that pesky Melanie "Ciccone" calling back yet again! Clearly her mania is starting to reveal itself! She tersely instructs me to send my "demo" tape to a certain address on West 12th Street in New York. When I inquire which record label that might be she replies, "Luaka Bop. It's David Byrne's label."

Of course poor Melanie "Ciccone" has no idea why this troubled, reclusive songwriter she's befriended might burst into uncontrollable fits of laughter over such a simple declaration. David Byrne. Good lord. I can hardly say goodbye. I laugh for days and days and days.

And then I send the tape.

But, to prove my conviction that I'm not being fooled by all this nonsense, that I know this is a hoax, this time when I send the envelope to "David Byrne's" record label I include no return address on the outside. Inside, I place no cordial form letter explaining who I am or what this tape is. The only message included is written on a post-it note. It says "Melanie Ciccone said send this, so I did." That's it; no further elaborations. It's fine. You know why? Because no one, particularly David Byrne, is going to listen to this cassette tape. In short, I'm willing to let this joke play out, but not at any great expense on my part.

It's a few days later. I'm about to hop on my bike to dive into another grueling taxi shift when the phone rings. It's this damn Melanie "Ciccone" lady pestering me yet again! God! I'm just about done with this nut. Now she's asking me why I didn't include contact information with the package I sent to David Byrne's record label, Luaka Bop. Part way through my lame explanation, just before I get to the part about her being a fraud and how she can go ahead and cancel that motel reservation in Wisconsin, it suddenly occurs to me; how does she know I didn't include contact info? Simple, she explains: Yale Evelev, the head of Luaka Bop, just called her. He listened to my tape and wants to talk to me about it. The only name mentioned on the Post-It was Melanie's, so Melanie he called.

I'm a little stumped by this twist. I sent that cassette to the New York City address she gave me, so if this joke's going to continue…well, then they'll now need a fake record label here for me to call. Melanie barks out the phone number. This is getting complicated! But I'm intrigued so I promptly dial it. A sexy, yet efficient sounding Australian-accented lady announces that I've called Luaka Bop records. Right. I mumble my name whereupon she transfers me to this Evelev guy.

I warily admit to him who I am and cringe internally, expecting to hear something unappealing in reply, you know, sneering laughter, followed by disparaging remarks about my weak material and how I should never contact him again. Instead, in this kind of skittish short wave delivery Yale Evelev says, "Yeah. I got it—the tape, I mean. Yeah, so we need to talk. When can you come by?"

What do you say? I say I'll stop by around two pm and hang up. This is getting confusing. Do they also have a fake office to lure me to as well? Is this where the stabbing will take place? Their "office" isn't too far from the taxi fleet so it's easy enough to stop by there before my next shift. Maybe I'll regale my fellow drivers with the story as we endure the indignity of yet another two-hour waiting period in the shape up room. I'll tell them this outlandish tale and they'll laugh and laugh, then Larry Zaitz will tell the story about the pimp and the whore and how he stabbed her in Larry's back seat right at the end of the ride, but see, the pimp, he paid the fare anyway, then he dragged her out of the back seat and into the lobby of a midtown flea bag hotel and how he called the cops and the cops found them just by following the trail of blood through the lobby and up the stairs to a room where they busted in on him as he was applying tiny band aids on her mortal wounds even though she was stone cold dead by then. My story isn't as pithy as Larry's but, hey, I got my secret weapon, the Superwhite angle!

I'm weaving my way through the streets of New York and you know what? That niggling backbeat of hope keeps popping up. Like, what do I do if this isn't a misguided joke after all? Like what if maybe there's some other logical explanation?

Oh, wait—right! Maybe they want to offer me a job at Luaka Bop. Like maybe I can be a janitor there or something. Maybe they need their basement repainted and they're looking for cheap labor. They heard the tape and said, "Well, this guy sure ain't gonna get no work as a musician, so he's probably desperate enough to take a nice painting job." Okay! Now that's an exciting prospect because that means there's a chance I'll see David Byrne again! Who knows, maybe he'll come sauntering down to the basement where I'm slapping the paint around. He'll be looking for his camera gear or a lost guitar case and I'll leap out from behind a file cabinet and shout Superwhite at him. Then I'll tell him the whole sad, funny story. Then he'll laugh and laugh. And we'll become friends.

So, into their hip Greenwich Village office I stride. The first thing that catches my attention is a huge poster on the wall behind the receptionist. Of who? Samuel Beckett? No. David Byrne? No. Woody Allen? No. It's a relatively unknown Belgian Afro pop band called Zap Mama, an amazing all female a cappella group. During one of my first major spirals into near psychosis many years ago I saw them play a show in an intimate Brussels, Belgium venue. This was during my modeling days. I'd truly gone off the deep end, and a worried model friend invited me to hear their concert. I arrived a mess, but two hours later left their exhilarating performance temporarily healed of my ailments. Music can do that.

So this is cool, because I always wondered what became of them! It's another one of those disparate life threads merging propositions, as esoteric elements are being drawn together from unlikely angles. So, could that also mean that, like the attacking dog and the lost cat, this poster is simultaneously a poster, and also a message from the past about the future?

Maybe so. But what's the message? That music can heal a soul? That I belong in this world?

I gape slackjawed at it momentarily then tell the drop dead gorgeous receptionist who I am. She nods politely, directs me to take a seat then phones someone and whispers my name and hangs up. Some minutes pass. This suspense is unbearable. Will I be shot? Stabbed? Handed a paint brush? Rendered spontaneously famous?

I'm coiled like a near-snake-bit cat. When I get jumpy sometimes chatty-me takes over. That's how this is—to the point where I almost start blabbing the Superwhite story to the dang receptionist. No! No! I gotta think tactically here—indiscriminate chatting will not do! The Superwhite story is sacred. It's my secret weapon, so probably the first person I should relay it to is this Yale Evelev guy, or even David Byrne himself, should I ever actually meet him in person. I need to breathe. Chatty-me thankfully starts making small talk with the receptionist about the poster on the wall. Thank you, chatty-me! Help me calm down!

Beautiful receptionist smiles pleasantly and the world glows and hums. She reports that the Belgian musical group Zap Mama are recording artists on David Byrne's world famous boutique record label. She asks if I'd like to hear some of their music. Surprise—I tell her I'm already a big fan of Zap Mama! So sure, why not slap their CD on the old stereo system.

In goes the CD, buttons are pressed whereupon hypnotic music commences to leak from a variety of top-shelf stereo speakers around the office. As I sit there waiting to talk to this Evelev guy, tapping my toes along with Zap Mama's grooves, the conflicted feelings of that dismal, lost night in Brussels come rushing back to me, momentarily occluding my thoughts about how to broach the Superwhite story with someone important. A strategy materializes: I'll break the ice by first telling this Evelev guy about that night in Belgium, how I was rendered almost crazy but then that Zap Mama's music served as a balm to my troubled mind. And seeing them represented here in this beautiful office provides a confirmation from the Unseen Forces that I am exactly where I'm supposed to be in the labyrinth clockworks of the Universe!

I sit, and sit some more. My mind drifts, at times venturing into hopeful territory, like, Jesus, what if this isn't a dumb joke...or even a terrible terrible misunderstanding? What if this is real?

No—it's a shitty, shitty, totally unprofessional cassette tape, and cassette technology is wildly outdated. Modern CDs are standard currency in the music industry these days, so this little office visit charade is gonna end up being some manner of bad or disappointing. Fate toys with you that way; big setup and then you end up cleaning out toilets, or worse. The Luaka Bop office walls, in fact, look like they could use a new coat of paint...

But hey, even if they just want to hire me as some flunky, look around! Various beautiful women milling this way and that, filing their important papers, talking in hushed, professional voices, phones pressed to their gorgeous ears. Which one will be my boss? Will point out the cans of interior enamel they want me to slap on the old basement trim? Which one will lead me to the pile of boxes they need moved, or show me that bathtub that needs to be regrouted? I'll do it all! How exciting! With a little luck I'll be a flunky at an uber-hip record label. Serious upgrade from yellow transportational Hades!

I look down the hallway and out of an office door David Byrne appears. This is a surprise. More surprising is how he's now bustling down the narrow hallway holding his hand out like an addled school boy. When it becomes clear that he and his extended hand are moving toward me, that he's about to speak words to me, I rise so as to face him eye to eye, hoping there are no drunken midget sluts in the background to disrupt my concentration.

"What an honor to meet you!" he chirps out, "Wow! I really love your music! Wow!"

Okay.

I refrain from opening my mouth to reply because presently there are no words available to be dispensed. My word bag is empty. I feel like I just got hit by a big old runaway surreal freight train. My head goes to spinning. What the unholy fuck just happened?

Before I can muster up even a feeble response, like some kind of manic pop-music Willy Wonka, David Byrne spins on his heels and, with the back of his head just a few inches from the end of my nose, asks the beautiful receptionist in the same excited tone, "Is there any good mail for me today??" She nods, then hands him a stack of letters which he promptly begins to peruse, humming along to Zap Mama, just tapping his famous toe ninety to nothing as he reads letter after letter.

Has there ever been a moment in your life where events became so surreal that you suspect you maybe crossed over into some bizarre alternate universe? That's exactly how this is. I pass a minute or two staring at the back of David Byrne's head. Nothing critical seems to be happening here so I decide maybe it's time to sit back down. Which is fine—it gives me time to think about what's just transpired. This world famous musician, this celebrity of the highest order, an artist who's appeared on the cover of Time magazine, has just uttered strange words to me. And those words he uttered were said in the exact order and with the exact enthusiasm that I should have said them to him.

I mean, really, come on! It was me who should have told David Byrne what an honor it was to meet him, right? It was me who should have told him how much I loved his music, right? So what exactly is happening here with this inversion of such colossal proportions? Shouldn't there be sound effects? Like some screeching howl to illustrate the rending of the time/space continuum—shit's getting ripped apart here folks! Stand back! At this point one thing is absolutely certain to me; if this IS some kind of cruel practical joke, then buddy, it's getting extremely elaborate. At this point they've got David Byrne involved.

Minutes pass. David Byrne finishes reading his letters then pivots back toward me, saying, "Hey, what about pedal steel??"

Pedal what??? What's that? Some kind of bathroom fixture for handicapped people? David Byrne sees my confusion and adds, "You know…guitar?"

Guitar? I'm reluctant to reveal to him that I'm a reclusive hermit who's never discussed music with anyone, who's never played in a band, never sang in public, who is unaware that such a thing as standard tuning exists. How am I supposed to know that the term "pedal steel" refers to some corny, stringed device that makes those weepy sounds you hear on old-time hokey country records? I just smile blankly, still struggling to process all these surreal non sequiturs.

"Well, then how about singing saw?" he adds, just as enthusiastically.

"Um…I'm not sure what you're talking about..." I finally manage to mutter. My brain's starting to ache.

"For your album!" He exclaims, and with that the legendary David Byrne trots back to his office, leaving me in a state of speechless bewilderment.

Grounding thoughts are necessary. Maybe a quick tally of the situation will calm my thoughts:

- Truth 1: I'm a sickly, impoverished cab driver well down the slippery slope of sanity.
- Truth 2: I write long rambling, self-pitying songs as therapy.
- Truth 3: Very few people—probably under fifteen in the entire world— have ever heard my rambling, self-pitying therapy songs.

Truth 4: Most of those few people, despite being my friends, hate said songs.

Truth 5: There went David Byrne, who loves my songs.

Truth 6: David Byrne said the word 'album' to me…in reference to…what?

So, have I gone completely fucking bananas here? If not, then why is that famous guy saying wildly provocative words to me? "Pedal steel'? 'Singing saw'? "Album"? When is someone gonna ask me to paint the basement? When do I shout Superwhite, and to whom should I tell my whole dazzling, yet cockamamie story? It's all so confusing. The mind clatter this conflagration is generating is all but deafening.

A moment later Yale Evelev emerges from his office opposite David's and casually introduces himself. The old good cop/bad cop routine? Maybe.

Like any capable label head, Yale's certainly much more cagey than David Byrne. He invites me into his office and as I'm taking a seat I notice my pathetic little home-made cassette tape sitting on his fancy Danish modern desk. I study the line drawing of those angels carrying the coffin, the infantile rendering of mountains in the background and realize it screams "mental illness". And even worse—amateur artist. And my-oh-my-oh-my, that little plastic rectangle looks so egregiously out of place sitting there on this guy's crowded, professional desk.

Over in the corner of Yale Evelev's cluttered office I notice a good-sized crate marked "demos"—that same word Melanie kept using about my cassette. It's overflowing with stacks and stacks of fancy looking CDs in proper jewel cases—there are literally hundreds of them piled up there, each one imbued with the appearance of authentic albums, ones done in real studios with real cover art and real performance credits and real everything. I look back over at my shitty, poorly packaged outdated technology offering, wondering what exactly am I doing here?

This Evelev guy jumps into an innocuous conversation—where am I from? How old am I? Stuff like that. Small talk. And then it happens again—the word 'album' gets mentioned. I know I just heard Yale utter the word "album", so finally I just gotta ask, "Um, sorry, but everyone keeps saying album. What's that about? What album?"

This record label guy pauses and gives me the once over like he's truly puzzled by my question. Finally, as if it's completely self-evident, he replies, "Well, your album of course...if everything works out." Then he adds, "The great thing here is that our parent company has a massive distribution network. So when we release your album, it'll get a lot of exposure."

Unable to process the whole "release your album" proposition, I off-handedly ask who the parent company might be, whereupon Yale Evelev, president of Luaka Bop Records smiles and, playing his trump card, confidently replies, "Warner Brothers!"

Warner Brothers. Of course.

In fact, Yale tells me that he and David Byrne plan on taking my "demo" up to Warner Brothers offices at Rockefeller Center for a big meeting that very afternoon. They intend to play it for the big shots up there and inform them how they're going to make an album with this amazing new artist. And yes—the Rockefeller Center office is in fact where I sent the tape that got returned with the 'herein & herewith" rejection letter.

"Warner Brothers. Cool." I say, like I'm familiar with the hep cats up there. "Gonna play it for anyone in particular?" I ask, remembering the name signed on the cruel rejection letter. And of course, Yale Evelev utters the name of that very person.

What are the odds?

This Evelev guy thanks me for coming in, says he'll get back to me after he and David talk to the Warner's big shots, and with that, out yon record label door I am promptly ushered. I stand on the sidewalk staring back at the door. Apparently the meeting's over. Cars are passing. Pedestrians are milling by. Birds are singing. Horns are honking in the distance. I'm so disoriented by this bewildering series of improbables that only after I hop on my bike and start riding away do I realize! Oh no, I totally spaced!

SHIT!

I forgot to tell Yale Evelev or David Byrne the freaking Superwhite story! God damn! A prime opportunity to communicate esoteric, synchronistically connective information just went sailing by.

But…wait, does that mean…that this is real? It's not a practical joke? And this Ciccone lady? She's real too? And she's really Madonna's sister? And what about this new Warner Brothers wrinkle? It creates quite the paradigm shift, for, while this absurd escapade still has all the earmarks of some grand, bizarre prank, it's becoming clearer and clearer that it cannot possibly be a prank designed by any human hand. So who's the joker? Jesus, or his daddy, God, neither of whom I'm in good standing with any more? Anyone who's cracked open a bible knows those two jokers are always messing with poor bedraggled, disbelieving souls like me…testing faith and tribulating on and what have you.

But wait, if I tap into a theological hierarchy then what about the obvious choice? The Devil! Old Scratch—he's definitely a prime suspect! But really there's no fucking way to know. Say for example it's Jesus and/or God, and they're punishing me for betraying them by relocating to decadent metropolises like New York City and Amsterdam and what have you. By cussing and backsliding and drinking whiskey and dancing erratically in poorly lit, trendy night clubs, dancing with cross dressers and on occasion, very, very rarely, fornicating with desperate, marginalized women and such.

Does that make sense? Not really.

So maybe it's the Devil just doing his thang? Oh Dark One, are you luring me ever closer to the brink of insanity so as to gain control of my everlasting soul?

Too much metadata to decipher! I need a freaking mental vacation from myself. But there is no rest for the haunted. Just last week I was working on a new song called The Road That Leads to Heaven. The lines from the second verse now sound damn near prophetic.

> *See the pretty cloud, it's shaped just like a dove.*
> *There's a gust of wind, now it's a famous movie star.*
> *It's reminding me of someone I once loved.*
> *Another gust of wind and now it's just a cloud again.*
> *With so much wrote between the lines,*
> *you can go crazy trying to read the signs*
> *on the road that leads to heaven.*

Oh, shit. Now look— where am I? Jesus, I've gone and ridden the wrong way. I'm furiously pedaling back toward the Puerto Rican slum instead of on to the taxi fleet. I stop the bike and try to regroup. Go to work? Go home and decipher the variables? Go crazy right here in the middle of Broadway and 10th Street?

Suddenly I feel an urgent need to engage in a bit of reality testing. Just, you know, to double check and see if I haven't just flat out lost my ever-loving mind. When you're hallucinating you don't know you're hallucinating, right? Minds are lost every day, especially here in New York freaking City. They just are.

So here I go: I hop the bike up on the sidewalk, park it and begin to touch nearby objects; a wall, a parked car, a phone booth—I press my finger hard on the phone booth glass so that the flesh turns white when I remove it, then watch as the blood floods back into the affected area. By all appearances my physical body is functioning normally. A block south I spy an ad for Crazy Eddie's Electronics Store on the side of the building. Okay, so I write the words "Crazy Eddie" in my notebook then close my eyes and spin around a few times. Then I compare the ad with the words I've written down and— voila—they match. So, it's looking like my mind also checks out. With that reassuring episode behind me I opt to head home and think over this astonishing development instead of going and driving that taxi all fucking night long.

As I'm coming up the stairs to my slum apartment—damn, I hear that blasted phone ringing again. I fumble with the keys, sling the door open and yank up the receiver. I offer big out of breath hello at which point this Melanie "Ciccone" lady screams, "They want to make an album with you!".

"Yeah?" I mumble, "I guess. I mean, they…well, sorta said that, but…I mean, are you sure?"

"I just spoke with Yale. This is fantastic!" Then comes the cautionary follow-up, "The only thing is you have prove to them you can actually be a professional musician. You can do that, right?"

Oh Lord. I hadn't thought of the show biz entertainment angle. What, do I have to wear black leather leotards and guzzle down gallons of Wild Turkey daily? Dye my hair flat black, then tease it into a faux combover and wear loose fitting bathrobes for interviews with Rolling Stone, etc? Truly, how might a mentally ill cab driver go about backing up such a cockamamie proposition? Throw a loser party and introduce the label folks to my cadre of lonely male friends? Regale David Byrne with my sepsis-fueled psycho-billy version of Burning Down the House? Show Superwhite my step daddy's weird purple guitar?

The improbabilities stepladder one on top of the other and are uniformly, pathetically hilarious. I start snickering at the thought of them, which pisses Melanie off. She tells me I need to put on my serious business face here. I thank her and tell her I'll keep her posted, then hang up, whereupon that old Latin aphorism starts pin-balling incessantly around in my brain: "Credo quia absurdum est"—I believe it because it's absurd.

So, the question now is how to proceed? Sigh, I know what time it is—it's time to break down and call my distinguished older sister (the same one who got me the ill-fated restaurant job interview and loaned me the money for the beach house) to seek her wise counsel. She's a respected law professor on the west coast and leads an eminently sane, sensible life. During my recent pyscho-implosion, I've assiduously avoided letting her in on the pathetic, sordid, sometimes terrifying details of my desperate goings-on for fear it would make her sick with worry. But at this point I figure only she can help me sort out the myriad tangles in this mess.

I call her and launch into the saga, starting with Holland and the music video. I tell her about my white suit and that movie where David Byrne also wore a white suit, and later being mistaken for him over and over and about Zap Mama and the failed David Byrne themed birthday party gambit, about the bulldozer dream and Janet Mallory's wise utterances. I tell her about the Gaye Bikers On Acid ride and the defacto mohawk and stalking David Byrne and shouting Superwhite at him and how he ran away and I worried that I was turning into Travis Bickle. I tell her about Melanie "Ciccone" and how she isn't really a mentally ill woman who planned to stab me in a motel in Wisconsin, but in fact actually is Danial Lanois' manager, Joe Henry's wife and Madonna's sister. Finally I explain about the returned "demo" tapes, Warner Brothers cruel rejection letter and the subsequent interview with Yale Evelev and David Byrne at the seemingly fake but apparently real record label.

She takes it well enough, listening silently. At the end of my harangue, in true lawyerly form, she disregards the innumerable glaringly conspicuous indicators of her brother's profound mental instability and calmly advises me to do exactly as she says: "Listen carefully: under no circumstances will you say the word Superwhite to David Byrne, or anyone else at that record label. Got it? You will remain quiet about this until after you have a signed contract in hand. Okay?"

"But...." I say, all confused and muttery, "...but, I mean, that seems like a detail they should know. I mean, that whole deal kinda revolves around Superwhite. It's, well… pivotal…"

"No. The only thing that's important right now is you getting a signed contract. Do you understand? Once you have a signed contract in hand, then and only then can you tell them that story. Until that point you will do exactly as I say. Got it?"

I'm listening, and oddly, there's something about the dry certainty of her response that's calming, grounding. He words catch me happily off-guard. It's like—poof—suddenly this whole surreal, madcap scenario has morphed into an utterly mundane, unesoteric proposition.

And you know what? She's right! This whacko development is in reality just a simple business transaction, and with that eminently sane framing my brilliant sister's categorical imperative becomes a perfectly viable tactic to close this deal. Of course! I'll withhold information, play things close to the vest, just like real businessmen do! And should our progress get mired down in the sloughs of life, THEN, I'll play my ace in the hole—the Superwhite story!

Back my mind goes sailing to the conversations with both Yale and David. Yep, there were ample opportunities for me to launch into that Superwhite story, but for reasons unknown I held back. So what was it? God, Grace, Providence, plain old Common Sense?

After talking with my sister I call Jim Krieg, who likewise does his best to steer me away from the notion that this is some perverse joke designed by God to punish me for backsliding, or for any other equally misguided, myopic reason. Finally I'm forced to accept the facts as they stand—I just met with David Byrne and Yale Evelev. They want to make a record with me and this isn't some cosmic practical joke.

No, it's a just simple business transaction!

It's two weeks later. I'm headed for that Chinese take-out place over on the relative safety of Avenue A, just trudging along when—oh shit! Here them fuckers come—that dreaded Bandana Gang! I'm square in their path, but so far they haven't spotted me.

I do some quick triangulations. If I bolt right and cross the street they'll notice and run me down. To my left is your garden variety row of silver garbage cans. The cars are parked snug, one bumper up against the next and are all likely locked, so no escape route by hiding between them or diving into the back seat of an anonymous vehicle. I got no choice but to work with the garbage cans.

I blindly lurch out and yank the lid off the nearest one then go frantically rummaging around inside it while mumbling a stream-of-consciousness monologue featuring cigarette butts, kitty litter and a Catholic priest named Father Fathead.

It occurs to me there's an added plus with this crazy-man garbage can tactic: should the gang initiation stabbings commence I can wield the lid as a makeshift shield. But first and foremost I'm hoping yonder approaching miscreants will mistake me for a loony tunes homeless type. Muggers, they tend to steer clear of the mental cases—too hard to control and typically impoverished, no big fat wallets to plunder. Dear Jesus, let them regard me as a deranged bum wholly unworthy of their finely honed mugging/stabbing skills.

As they draw nearer I commence to jabber at a cigarette butt on the ground by my shoes, then I ask Father Fathead do I have to say the rosary in Swahili again! And again! And again! I stay solidly in character until—whoosh—the deadly pack of punks go sailing past, all loud and braggadocios, likely hunting trust fund hipster prey with soft underbellies.

The ruse works—no stabbing initiation gauntlet to run today! No mugging! I keep mumbling and digging in the garbage can for a few extra beats, lid in hand while side-eyeing the gang as they move away. I'm about to lay said lid back in place when, inside the garbage can, who do I behold? Woah, fucking Nellie, what???— Hello David Byrne and Yale Evelev. What? What? What?

I reach down and retrieve a pristine studio portrait 8 X 10 black & white image of Superwhite side by side with Yale Evelev. Perched atop of a pile of reject photographs, it's a two-shot featuring both men in three-quarter profile, gazing confidently into the camera. I just stand here, my jaw hanging down, stunned, trying to tally up the variables; I am at present negotiating a magical business deal with these two exact human beings. This week alone I've zipped past what, thousands if not tens of thousands of similar random garbage cans, cans that I did not lift the lid on, cans containing no synchronistic material whatsoever in them. Then along comes this swarm of pestilent gang bangers, in desperation I lift this one single lid and voila'—Yale Evelev and David Byrne. What are the odds? Astronomically incalculable.

Okay Unseen Forces, you got my full attention.

And here's the kicker: I was just thinking about them two suckers. They've been trampling around in my head a whole bunch after that not so encouraging follow up face to face with Mr. Yale Evelev yesterday wherein he commenced to give me the third degree about my backstory and lack of performance experience. Yale didn't seem to like what he heard, describing me as a problematic prospect, seeing how I've never played live anywhere ever and don't even know what key I'm playing in or how to tune a guitar correctly or assemble and lead a band. He got all the more jittery when I let it slip I'm not real keen on becoming a public person, you know like a stage performer.

That kinda stuck in his craw. He sighed, pointing out that, should Luaka Bop offer me a contract, they'll be investing tens of thousands of dollars making my fancy debut record and they'll want assurances of at least a fighting chance at recouping their investment. So I'll need to perform, he informed me flatly. I kept my big mouth shut after that, listening for clues to see if this whole performance angle was just some manner of bargaining chip or if he really meant it. Business is confusing like that.

I study the mysterious photograph. Hey Universe, what gives? Is this some magical gift from the Unseen Forces? I mean, this ain't some crappy xerox reproduction or wrinkled page torn out of a music magazine, it's an actual black & white darkroom proof in pristine condition. I scrutinize the realness of it, holding it reverently at arms length. Yep, it's clearly a talisman of some sort. This chance find is no chance at all—it's fated. I'm clearly being given this photograph for a specific purpose. But what is it?

My mind's gets to buzz-buzz-buzzing with the swarm of esoteric variables at play. I've lost my hankering for Chinese food so I beeline it back to the slum.

But see, here's the most confusing component; since the Bandana Gang precipitated my picking up that garbage can lid in the first place, does that mean they're somehow complicit in the overall magic plan here? It sure looks that way, right? Because if there's no gang, I lift no lids. I just go sailing by the magic garage can with the photo in it totally oblivious to its presence there.

So does that mean the Bandana Gang is likewise influenced by the mysterious powers of the Unseen Forces? Were they guided to that point in time and space on that sidewalk exclusively to menace me so I would then find this photo? If so, the implications are astonishingly myriad.

And aside from the Bandana Gang angle, like the cat and the dog signifiers, I can't escape the notion that this photograph is functioning on at least two levels; it's a material object, but also a thread in some larger fabric of meaning—that truth is indisputable. I tote the photo up the stairs and lay it on my bed, studying it for a good long while. What in the high holy hell am I supposed to do with this thing?

Okay. An hour's passed and just now the clouds parted. Stupid me—I forgot to heed my sister's wise counsel! There's no need to over-think this particular serendipitous find—after all, this is just a garden variety business transaction, right? And so shouldn't I just look upon this discovery as a practical windfall, like a bargaining chip? Hell yes I should! Think about it; my prospects with Yale Evelev and David Byrne have been nosediving of late, but now thanks to the Unseen Forces I have in my possession a second secret weapon alongside the Superwhite story.

But how to deploy said weapon effectively?

I dig in, really studying the picture. You know, something's familiar about the framing and lighting…but what is it? Neural points go a'leaping, connections are made and suddenly I see! It's the angle of their faces, looking up into the camera like they are.... the simple key light contouring their features. It rings a visual bell...HOLD UP! I got it! I yank out the other box I keep stashed under my bed, sitting next to the Strange But True box. This other box contains old stories, drawing, personal documents including piles of my old modeling tear sheets and set cards. And what do I find? Yep, a head shot of me from my modeling days that's a perfect match to the portrait of Yale and David Byrne. Black and white, same size, same lighting, similar clothing.

The relationship is uncanny. And, since the garbage can photo is a two shot of Yale and David featuring a sizable black space between them, my face fits perfectly in between. Snip-snip-snip, I carefully cut out the head shot of myself and lay it in place. Jesus, it's a perfect fit. I grab both images, stuff a bunch of pencils, markers, Scotch Tape and White-Out in my coat pocket and go bombing out the door, headed for the copy shop over on St. Marks Place.

It takes me a good twenty xeroxes to render the image seamless, but ultimately there it is; a single, seemingly unretouched image featuring the three of us. Some passing hipster looks over my shoulder and chirps, "Cool album cover, bro." I wince, then hunch up my shoulders and recoil at being "bro'd"! But wait! Hipster's right, the new improved picture's got a trashy seventies album cover look to it. Of course! An album cover!

A band name, I need a band name. "The Stars", comes flying into my head, so I cut some letters out of a copy of the Village Voice left on the counter and overlay them on the image—thank God I brought my Scotch Tape! So now I need an album title. I study the image—we look locked and loaded, drunk on our own rock and roll excrement, so the words "Hot Shit" come popping into my brain, asking to be added.

Snip-snip-snip and there we go; Yale, Superwhite and yours truly in our own little retro seventies band. "The Stars present, Hot Shit!" It's hysterically funny. I make a viable final print of this on nice stiff card stock then head over to Astor Place Post Office and mail this fucker anonymously to Luaka Bop in care of one Yale Evelev.

I use my left hand to address like I did with the Woody Allen letter so Yale won't recognize my handwriting. Hoo-hoo! Can you imagine Yale and David's surprise when they receive an alternate version of their fancy magazine picture now adorned with campy hostage-note style text on it and that crazy cab driver, the one they're thinking of signing a record deal with, posing right between them? They'll be freaking mystified.

It's two days later. The phone starts ringing. It's ten am. Doesn't anybody know that I work the goddamn night shift? It's that Yale Evelev calling, and he doesn't sound happy. Oh, yeah, I forgot about that little package I mailed. He wants to know about the picture—how I came into possession of it. For reasons unclear to me I act like I haven't the faintest idea what he's talking about. What picture? I ask groggily.

He forces a laugh, then presses me for info. He reports the source photo came from a fancy shoot they did for the cover of some big music magazine cover some years back. What he's confused about is that the cover image had text all over it, so how exactly did I get my hands on an original proof?

I'm not about to jump into the magical story about the Bandana Gang, you know—pretending to be crazy and lifting the garbage can lid—and thereby disable my secret weapon, so I just keep acting dumb, telling him I don't have the slightest clue what he's talking about. He's getting pissed. He tells me I'm not in trouble or anything, he just needs to know how I got ahold of that photographer's proof, like for legal reasons. It's hysterical. And I just keep playing dumb, which gets him more and more wound up. As he vents and cajoles and tries to get me to admit I sent that thing my mind wanders, coming back again and again to the odds of any of this happening.

Yale huffs, frustrated. He instructs me to come into the office to inspect the picture. So, on my way to the taxi fleet a few hours later I stop by. Why not? He shows me the fake cover, asking am I sure I don't I know anything about this? I act surprised, laughing as I gawk at the image, asking him who made this? He hrumphs, waiting for me to divulge that I'm the perpetrator but I never do. My lips are sealed, just like with the Superwhite story. I'll spill the beans when I got a signed contract in my hot little hands.

Why keep it a secret? Because I'm a businessman creating an aura of mystery around my product!

Weeks pass, it's almost unbearable not being able to tell anyone at Luaka Bop all my secrets; the garbage can incident, Beckett and Woody and of course the whole Superwhite saga. I wait and wait for some kind of contract to be offered, but even with this new fake album cover twist Yale Evelev seems to grow increasingly distant and cautious about proceeding.

Why??

Was the fake album cover a bad idea? Or is it because I got zero experience as a performer? Or that I've never been in a band? Or that the parent company hates my music? It could be any or all of the above. What can I do to allay his fears? Is it time to break out my ace in the hole—the Superwhite story? Hmmmm. No. Not yet.

Summer's hit and the Big Apple turns into one big, stinking, greasy frying pan. Most of these cabs don't have AC, so I can't bear more than four scorching twelve hour shifts per week.

In the interim I'm figuring I might can assuage Yale's fears about me by writing more songs. He's telling me to aim for that Beck guy but if you tell me red I think blue. I never succeed in hitting my target. Case in point: a few weeks back I aimed for Beck and hit Bob Dylan instead. It's this quasi-mystical saga called Still Waters, and vaguely reminds me of Dylan's Tangled Up in Blue. I finished it ten days back, the last verse resonating deeply with my plight as a haunted soul:

> *There are projects for the dead and there are projects for the living.*
> *Though I must confess some times I get confused by that distinction.*
> *And I just throw myself into the arms of that which would betray me.*
> *I guess to see how far Providence will stoop down just to save me.*

After I put the finishing touches on Still Waters I recorded it on the crappy Fostex four-track player and right away sent it to Melanie Ciccone for approval. Owing to recent developments she's now categorized as a non-hoax entity. In fact, she's helpfully guiding me through the process of "getting signed", typically chiming right in with advice and counsel about the new songs I've sent her. But recently she's dropped off the radar, which isn't like her.

So I'm sitting on my bed working over a chord progression on my step dad's purple guitar. The phone rings and it's finally Melanie. But she's sounding a little irritable. I bring her up to date on our negotiations (omitting the fake album cover story) and such, then make some small talk but she says nothing about the new song, so after a minute or two I ask her did she get that tape with Still Waters on it. I get a terse "Uh-huh, I got it."

She pauses like something's eating at her, then asks, "You mind telling me where you got the idea for that song from?"

Jesus, what's with that weird tone in her voice?

"It's just, you know, I mean, it's about things that happen in my life." I say, "You know, my crazy little dance with synchronicity..."

She thinks that over, "Look….give me your word—swear to me you haven't heard a song called Still Waters recently…"

What? Is this a cult or something? So I say, "Swear to you?? Why? What's going on? You're acting strange…"

"I'm sorry but I need you to swear to me you haven't heard a song called Still Waters recently…" she's holding firm.

This is weird and uncomfortable and slightly uncool. It takes a second before I can respond. "No. I mean, yes—I swear I haven't."

She chews on that for a long beat, then comes clean, "Okay. Dan (Daniel Lanois) has a new record coming out in a couple of months. There's a song on it that he's really fond of. It's also called Still Waters, so I was worried that someone had leaked it in advance and somehow you got your hands on a copy. But I guess it's just a weird coincidence."

"Yow." I say, then I just can't help myself, I bust up laughing—I mean, it's flat out hilarious how this runaway synchronicity train just keeps plummeting down the big hill of Life. "Sorry. I guess it's not funny to you, but, you know, welcome to my world. I can't explain it, but shit like this happens to me constantly. Sorry if it's causing you problems. I mean, I can bury the song if you think it'll make trouble for you with Dan's label." I say.

And being that my version of Still Waters feels like one of the best songs I've ever written, the offer to bury it stings considerably, but this lady has gone to bat for me, so I need to return the favor. We sit and listen to each other breathe for a few seconds, then I hear her sigh.

"That's sweet, but no. It's a good song. If Luaka Bop signs you, you should definitely record that one. I can handle explaining it to Dan.", she adds.

Dan, this legendary Grammy winning producer/musician guy who I'm now having quotidian conversations about. Each time I hear her say Dan or David or Yale in that first person informal way I come to accept a little more that this incredibly kind, thoughtful human being is for real, that she won't be stabbing me to death in a motel room anywhere, much less one in far away Wisconsin.

We finish up and I wish Melanie well. After hanging up it hits me; she said "if" Luaka Bop signs me, not "when." And she's right, this is not a done deal, it's a conditional situation. With all this crazy magical energy swirling around it's nigh unto impossible to decipher where the hell any of this is actually going.

I'm up early and needing some fresh air, so I run up to Avenue A, intent on digging a newspaper out of a garbage can or off a restaurant counter. Some days it's the Post, some days the Daily News. Today it's the highbrow New York Times, which I prefer due to them having the best crossword puzzle. I head over to Tompkins Square Park, coming to rest on that bench where I likely met Mr. Samuel Beckett himself.

It's a short walk from the slum and this newspaper in the park ritual has become a habit lately. I go flipping through the pages and my eyes land on a little column about a cow that escaped from a slaughterhouse in Georgia a couple of days earlier. This cow, it lead the local townspeople on a merry chase, hither and yon, high jinx abounding before eventually being cornered in an alley. There the friendly townspeople shot the cow dead, basically executing it, then they dragged it off to the slaughterhouse to be chopped up into little tasty pieces of something called "meat".

Likely the story was intended to be a lighthearted fluff piece but it strikes some deep sorrowful inner chord, whereupon I just burst into tears. It's like that damn cow is calling out to me from the grave, and, just like I did all those years ago seeing Mr. David Byrne through that Amsterdam window, I feel a sudden, profound sense of kinship with this poor, doomed creature. Just like that cow, I too have been running for my life. Just like that cow, I've been cornered and terrified. The more I look the less I can discern any real difference between me and the cow.

Then, like some mysterious hand has thrown a switch deep inside my mind, the very thought of meat is rendered repellant to me and there and then I know I'll never eat another bite of it. Never. I'm struck down, like the Apostle Paul on the road to Damascus. Only instead of getting hit by the Holy Ghost, I get vegetarian.

To prove my conviction I go storming back to the slum, march into the tiny kitchen, dig out a costly package of ground beef that I just bought the day before and chuck it down the toilet. I watch it spin away, then wonder what the fuck have I just done! Ground beef is a tasty luxury item!

The fledgling vegetarian that I am needs to calm his nerves. So I sit down and dig into verse two on a song I'll likely call Book of Angels. Verse one came easy enough but I've been beating my head against the wall for a couple of days now on the follow-up verse. But now, free of my carnivore onus, suddenly the lines come flying into sight up there in the sky of my mind. Words coalesce. Sense is apprehended.

> *This gloomy old house in a spooky town.*
> *You make that light, better just keep going…*
> *higher still, climb the mountain.*
> *Of course what you find there you can't be certain.*
> *'Cause when you're free, you're just free.*
> *Ain't that scary? Ain't that wild?*
> *Don't you feel, feel just like*
> *chucking freedom out the window?*

Thinking I'm on a roll I move on to the final verse but hit a brick wall. Final verses are the bane of my existence, what with having to tie up all those esoteric philosophical loose ends you introduce in the first stanzas.

I blink my eyes and, boom, after moving words from here to there, then there to here, then back again, on and on, ad nauseam it's two hours down the line. Jesus, I get lost in these songwriting rabbit-holes. The damn walls on this twelve-by-twelve cell of mine are closing in hard. What I need is a break from all this musical triangulation melodrama.

I set the purple guitar down and head for Kim's Video, a sprawling hipster-centric movie rental store located in the relative safety of Avenue A. Yes! A movie! That's what I need to transport me far far away from this psychic quicksand I'm presently mired in.

Kim's registers a full ten on the hipster Richter Scale. Punks and goths and rockers, plus a few fringe types like me, all mingle together browsing the titles. I go wandering down this aisle and that, spotting nothing especially inspirational. Eventually I migrate over to the art film section of the store. At eye level I spy a familiar face—it's David Byrne on the cover of a movie. Goddamn, this fucker's everywhere.

I study the empty video cover of True Stories, Byrne's directorial debut. His outfit looks like something I might wear on a dare: cowboy hat, tight fitting suit, bolo tie. We're similarly angular, all elbows and knees. Out of a sense of loyalty I briefly consider renting True Stories, but then remember it's the world of David Byrne that I'm presently trying to escape. So thanks, but no thanks, Superwhite.

I drop the video cover back in place on the shelf and wander around some more. A full twenty minutes later I settle on an obscure French film called Playtime, by director Jacques Tati.

I mosey up front and hand the empty video box to the cashier, who disappears into the back where the actual tapes are stored. He comes cruising out, clear video case in hand and starts to write up a receipt, but when he pops open the plastic case to double check that the tape in the case is what it's supposed to be, he studies the title then frowns and shakes his head.

"Sorry....wrong movie. We've been wondering where this was." he says, waggling the video cassette, adding, "It's not Playtime. So that means Playtime's probably in the lost tape box. Gimme a second."

He walks away, leaving the video that was wrongly placed in the Playtime case sitting on the counter. I absently glance at the title and about choke. Out of some three thousand movies at Kim's Video Store what cassette was in Playtime's case? David Byrne's True Stories, of course. I just sit there shaking my head. It's raining fucking synchronicity here. Is there no escaping the gravitational field of this magical cluster fuck? It's undeniable that some divine huckster is at work here. Jokes are being played, but by whom, and to what end?

I head home and disappear into the Tati film. It's a bizarre, beguiling structuralist dreamscape offering serious respite from the burden of Life's maddening complications. I adore the clumsy, well-meaning protagonist, Mr. Hulot, am enthralled by the banally surreal, totally artificial world as he endlessly blunders through a series of serendipitous encounters with a cast of archetypal yet incidental characters who continually intersect and re-intersect with him as he bumbles pointlessly along. It's sorta like a stylized, symbolic version of my present life!

The credits are rolling when the phone rings. It's Yale Evelev on the line. In his typical terse manner he says, "Got a minute?" I mention that I just now finished watching a movie. "Which one?" He asks. I tell him it's Playtime, to which he, of course, replies, "Playtime? Jacques Tati's Playtime? That's my favorite film...." Of course it is, I think to myself. There's a long pause, then he continues, "Look, can you come over? We need to talk."

Bad vibe. Worrisome tonality to Yale's voice, especially with that "We need to talk." line. Ominous.

But truly, was there ever any doubt that this long-shot miracle would fall to pieces? Nope. I hop on my latest crappy bike (they're crushed by vandals or stolen every few months) and sadly, like some New York City version of Monsieur Hulot, weave my way over to the West 12th street office where I find Yale in the process of locking up. He apologizes about having to leave, but asks would I mind taking a cab ride with him over to Brooklyn where he's supposed to meet some music industry hot shot for dinner.

He suggests we talk along the way and offers to cover my subway fare home. I'm a fatalistic cheap date, so I say, "Sure, that's fine." In the back of my mind I'm already triangulating on the restaurant angle, thinking maybe I can at least weasel one free meal out of this idiotic record deal charade.

Yale flags a cab and away we go, diving south into the gaping maw of rush hour. After spending ten long years exclusively in the front seat of a taxi it nigh unto freaks me out riding in a yellow car but not having my hands on a steering wheel. I'm thusly disoriented as Yale Evelev launches into this formal sounding pitch about what lies ahead for "us". He talks all cool cucumber-like, a true businessman, which is equally disorienting. I do my best to pretend like I'm a businessman in return but, well, I'm badly miscast in that particular role.

We're running down 2nd Avenue. Home turf East Village streets go whizzing by as Yale outlines his major issue with signing me; it all boils down to my complete lack of experience as a live entertainer. That's a deal breaker, he bluntly reports. He's been after me for months now to book some live shows so he can see me perform, but landing a show at a hip venue is easier said than done; a couple of years back even Beck himself was forced to busk on the streets around here—that's how hard it is to book a venue in Manhattan.

Okay. I need to just breathe and stay calm. I explain to Yale how I've tried, but without a real record to show various snooty venue bookers none of these hipster joints would even consider stooping to allow some unknown weirdo taxi driver musician to grace their celebrated stages. I got zero tools to work with in this proposition: no convincing demo tape, no band, no following, no connections or music buddies who might put in a good word for me. Hell, I don't even do drugs, which seems to be a universal common denominator with most of these edgy musician types.

Yale listens to my various excuses, shaking his head skeptically. "Look, if you can't even book a simple gig, how are you ever gonna make it in the music business?", he gripes. Fair question; one I got no answer for. I'm stumped, so I just stare at him, waiting for the official kiss off. But instead he starts in brainstorming about "strategies" to jump start my career.

"What about this..." he says, "...you find some other record label to release your first album, then if that record sells, then Luaka Bop can release your second one..."

Huh?

He continues, "Or what about joining a punk band? You know—tour relentlessly for a couple years? Just so you can really learn the fine points of performing..."

Huh again?

So here it comes. I act like I'm giving his suggestions some consideration, thinking if I resist these truly idiotic, deal-breaking suggestions then the axe man is surely lurking in the wings, chomping at the bit to come out a'swinging. And frankly, it's no big shock though that this whole fairy tale music proposition is primed to unravel. It's just like everything else in my life. But should I just passively accept my inevitable fate, or fight? Is now the time? Do I launch into a preemptive Superwhite attack?

As we've been talking the taxi's modulated onto the Williamsburg Bridge. At the end it'll bank south on Broadway. Although Yale just gave the driver a street address I already know where he's meeting this guy—there's only one viable restaurant in this blighted neighborhood: the anomaly known as Peter Luger's. Arguably the best steakhouse in the whole damn USA, Peter Luger's is surrounded on all sides by high-crime, drug-infested slums. Amongst the shells of burned out, abandoned buildings and hollow-eyed addicts somehow Peter Luger's flourishes. Over the years I've dropped dozens of fares at Peter Luger's—mostly high rollers, mafioso types, celebrities, tycoons and what have you.

But wait—Peter Luger's! Of course. It's a freaking top-shelf steak house and I'm a freshly minted vegetarian. Thank you, oh great benevolent Universe! I can't even bum a free dinner before I get the official kiss off here. Well, there you have it. What's that old line, "If it wasn't for bad luck I'd have no luck at all."?

As the cab eases to a stop in front of the restaurant canopy, I decide this is as good a time as any to make myself scarce. Yale Evelev can go on to his carnivorous dinner appointment and I'll just hop a subway home and gnaw on some nice raw kale or something. And who knows, maybe I can dodge a bullet here, like maybe in the meantime he'll reconsider dumping me.

I'm on the sidewalk side, so I throw open the cab door and say, "Okay Yale, good talking with you. We can pick this conversation up later I guess." Yale looks puzzled "Hey, we're not done here."

"Yeah, well, we're here. You gotta go and, um, I need to get home. So just go ahead." I tell him.

Yale frowns, "But…we're still talking here." to which I reply, "Look, the L train's just a few blocks away. I can hop that back to Manhattan. Have a nice meal." He studies me like I'm some kind of freak, then abruptly says, "Yeah, but why not come inside—we can talk over dinner. The guy I'm meeting, he probably won't mind."

I just kind of stare at him. Thank you fucking cosmic jokesters of the Universe for hauling off and converting me into a goddamn vegetarian this very goddamn morning, just hours before I'm offered a free goddamn meal at the best goddamn steak house in all of the goddamn USA by a guy who holds my fate in his goddamn hands, a guy who will probably be seriously insulted if I decline.

So what do I do? I bust up laughing. Life's just too fucking hilarious. The twists. The turns. The unexpected trips to legendary steak houses. Good lord. Yale stares at me, puzzled as all hell.

I try running my escape line through my mind before I dare say it, "Sorry Yale, but, see, I…uh, this morning, well, I became a vegetarian…"

Oh no, no. There's no way I can utter those words with any conviction. Even as a fledgeling non-meat eater I'm well aware of the scorn vegetarians elicit. Besides, I'll sound like even more of a complete flake than I already am and any slim thread of hope of salvaging my record deal will be severed.

And truth be told, explaining my newfound dietary status in some reasonable fashion isn't even really an option—there's nothing to explain. I never gave this massive lifestyle choice one iota of thought, much less tried to frame my decision in words—it just happened. This morning! While I was sitting on the bench where I met Samuel Beckett! Why-why-why does everything in life have to be so goddamn complicated?

But Yale persists, "Come on. I'll even pay…"

Hmmm—menu options at Peter Luger's? Meat, meat and more meat. Meat and meat alone—bright rosy chunks of sundered cow parts. Ribeye and Prime Rib and Sirloin and Tenderloin and T-Bone and countless other legendary cuts. I try to envision myself sitting in Peter Luger's dining room, being served up a heaping plate of dead cow flesh, which yesterday I would have deliriously devoured but today I can't bear the sight of.

But, so, say I do accept this dinner offer…what happens when I try to consume the meat and then freak out? Like if I think of that poor slaughtered cow and then suddenly retch and puke all over Yale and his music industry friend? Who knows! Anything's possible!

And wait—what if they serve me the actual flesh from that actual runaway cow in Georgia? The actual cow who I felt such kinship with just this morning? That meat had to go somewhere, right? So it's within the realm of possibilities it ended up right here at Peter Luger's.

So, my options are as follows: eat my friend the cow and violate a sworn oath to Self, or not eat my friend the cow and proceed to insult this record company big shot who Jesus, God, Beelzebub and various other utterly perverse deities are clearly using to torment my sorry ass? It feels like some kind of New Age music business version of that philosophical conundrum called the Prisoners Dilemma.

I collect myself, then offer up lamely, 'Um, yeah. I mean, thanks and all. I appreciate it, I do, but, like, I gotta…you know…like, run some errands..."

Yale can tell I'm lying. What he can't tell is why. I'm half out of the cab when he grabs me by the sleeve, "No really. Come inside!" he says, "I'll pay."

"Really, thanks, but like I said, I'll just go." I come back with, slightly chippy-like.

But I can't go, because Yale won't let go of my freaking sleeve. And frankly I don't like being detained like this. I want to yank away, but know if I do so that'll be the end of this whole sprawling inexplicable music industry charade. Yale gives me a little nudge in the direction of the door and half growls. "Look. Just go inside. They're waiting…"

Yale's gone slightly flushed, looking back at the cab driver, who's got not a clue what the hell's going down. He just wants to get paid and get the hell out of this spooky dope-head neighborhood. I climb the rest of the way out of the cab, closely followed by Yale, who tosses the driver a ten spot, then starts guiding me toward the door. I don't want to fight this guy, but shit, this is getting way too weird. Who's he meeting for dinner for Christ's sake?

Okay, I figure I'll just say hello to whoever it is then duck out. Yale can't shove me around with one of his big music industry buddies watching, now can he?

We go stumbling through the door. A quick survey of the various opulent dining areas reveals countless plates adorned with heaping piles of giant steaks. Meat everywhere! Great.

But then directly ahead, seated at a long banquet style table, whose familiar face do I behold? Shooting me this wide, mischievous, beaming smile like Jezebel the Pig grinning out from the brambles? It's Superwhite, of course…surrounded by his staff of glamorous assistants: beautiful ladies, handsome young bucks, all of them likewise grinning ear to ear. What the hell are they doing here? What?

"Congratulations!" Yale grumps, huffing a bit, "You're now a recording artist with Luaka Bop. We drew up the contracts today." He points at a manilla envelope with my name on it sitting on the table in front of the empty chair opposite David Byrne. "Now take a seat and order yourself a nice big juicy steak!"

And you know, the irony of, well everything at play here: the practical joke Yale played to lure me here, the envelope, the restaurant, the meat, Superwhite himself seated directly across from me.

Fucking Life!

I spectate as David Byrne orders his own big juicy steak. Words are being said but I'm tripping so hard I can't make out the meaning. The air is thick with that electrocuted feeling and suddenly here's the waiter asking me what I'll have. What will I have?

I just start laughing. And, you know, suddenly it hits me; I've been doing more and more of this laughing business lately. My sad, doomed existence is suddenly full of inexplicable jokes and mysteries. The puzzled waiter is invoking his namesake—waiting—as his perfunctory smile gets stretched thinner and thinner.

Okay, I get it—in honor of the innumerable contradictions surrounding me, I'll do the opposite of what seems right here—I'll postpone my decision to forever give up eating meat for one last meal. So I order the most expensive steak on the menu, then burst back into discrete hysterics. It'll be the best and last steak I'll ever eat and once that last forkful goes down the old drainpipe, well, then the so-called forever I swore to this morning can begin anew, this time not to be reversed by the meddling hands of the Unseen Forces.

Dinner's served. Everything happens in slow motion, as if this is some strange, drug-induced dream. I'm half-heartedly munching that last bit of savory cow flesh, staring at the animated face of David Byrne as he relays some exotic anecdote to his beautiful assistants when—wham—suddenly I flash back years earlier to that moment when I first howled out Superwhite at him. I remember him running, hiding from me, remember how disappointed I'd been because he didn't seem to accept or comprehend that crucial enigmatic message I was so hellbent on conveying to him. It seemed as though the Unseen Forces had failed me yet again...right?

But here I am, aren't I? Sitting down to an elegant dinner with Superwhite himself. And he's paying! And a recording contract sits on the table before me. So maybe he did hear what I shouted out after all? Maybe the mechanics of hearing are far more intricate than I've imagined? Maybe at times we hear in ways so incremental as to elude understanding? Maybe we burn down our houses not all in one fell swoop, but sliver by sliver, nail by nail, until we find ourselves sitting atop a mountain of astonishing ashes that we can truly call our own.

I eat in silence and as I swallow that final chunk of world class steak, as it lodges firmly in my gut, for the first time ever in this endless cluster-fuck called Life, I feel in complete control of my destiny.

PENSACOLA, FLORIDA, JUNE 2001

Damn this van. Something in my accelerator linkage just broke loose. Half a mile back the pedal wobbled and shook. A minute later it flopped to the floor, dead. I stomped on it twice but got no push back, so I cut the motor and coasted onto the shoulder. I'm way the hell out on Gulf Beach highway, five or so miles west of Pensacola proper. It's closing in on dinnertime and I need to get my ass home or there'll be hell to pay with the Crazy Maker. I yank the engine cover off and am about to unscrew the air filter bolt when a caterwaul of hollering erupts from somewhere nearby.

"GOD–DAMN!!!GOD—FUCKING—STUPID—MOTHER—FUCKING—COCKSUCKER—!!"

Woah, somebody's righteously pissed. I lift up, warily scanning the surroundings, intent on steering clear of whatever random act of violence is about to take place—West Pensacola can be a dicey proposition on the best of days.

There. Other side of the chain link fence at the construction site. It's just that burly, red-faced foreman. Jesus, look at him go, all puffed up, punching the air, strutting around that concrete foundation they just poured yesterday! And why's he wagging that big sheath of blueprints around?

"WHERE??? SOME–GOD–DAMN–PISSANT–WANT–TO–TELL–ME–WHERE!! WHERE THE FUCK IS IT??" he howls, tantrum style at nobody in particular. He furiously scans the surface of the freshly dried slab for something, checks the blueprint, stomps his boot down, points at the ground and howls "WHERE'S MY GODDAMN STAND PIPE?!?!"

Okay, so that's it. When they poured that slab yesterday nobody bothered to check on if the plumbing lines were laid according to spec. Somebody's ass is grass. The carpenters and day laborers sheepishly skulk away. The foreman jabs the blueprints at one of them and barks out, "YOU! DRILL A HOLE IN THAT SUBSTRATE AND TELL ME WHAT YOU SEE!"

I'm a good fifty yards off from the action, but when I hear the words something magical happens—that phrase he says, it kind of materializes in the air over his head, sorta like a cartoon caption, and just hovers there. I study the words as they glow and hum, floating just above his hard hat, then, for reasons totally unknown to me, I bust up laughing, like nervous, skittish laughs. I got no idea why—I just do. What the hell's so funny about those particular words?

I'm late so I get back at it, still chuckling as I work the base of the air filter free and spy the problem; a spring in the accelerator linkage has snapped. It's long gone so I dig up a rusty paper clip and a rubber band from the glove box and thread them through the eye-holes on the two dangling links, successfully reconnecting the accelerator to the carburetor. I give the gas pedal a few exploratory pumps then twist the key. The engine fires up, the improvised spring thankfully holding.

As I'm pulling away I glance over at the construction site one last time and spy the seething foreman now supervising as his laborer chips away at the foundation with a jackhammer, hunting for those missing pipes. That imaginary caption's still hanging over foreman's head, which starts me in to laughing again, and it's that same edgy laughter like before, like there's some resonant truth concealed behind it.

On the short ride home that foreman's words keep deviling my thoughts, "DRILL A HOLE IN THAT SUBSTRATE AND TELL ME WHAT YOU SEE!", he shouted. And I can't get that expression out of my head—every time I hear it, I bust up.

I'm still laughing when I walk in the house, but that passes soon enough. The Crazy Maker is lolling on the couch, dissecting the latest issue of some au curant fashion magazine—one of the many she subscribes to. She shoots me a scowl then asks how I got my clothes so dirty. I tell her the van broke down. Crazy Maker rolls her eyes, flips the page on the magazine then sarcastically mutters, "Mr. Rock Star himself. Go wash up for dinner. That van…god…"

Jesus, here we go again. I aim for the bathroom, hoping to avoid yet another Nick Cave diatribe.

Too late.

"It's just so embarrassing—" she moans, laying the magazine in her lap, "You think Nick Cave drives some old clunker like that? I can assure you he does not. He's got style, and people with style don't drive clunkers, they drive a Porsche or a Jag or a BMW. I don't see why you can't just get a…"

I tune her out as I wash up. This last hour is a microcosm of my fucked-up life: cars and women—I never had one bit of luck with either. That dynamic's hit a new low here with its present incarnation. Between what's parked out in the driveway and what's parked on the couch, I got my hands full with shit that don't work.

Her and me, we met a few years back at a hipster hang-out up in New York City. I was playing one of those open mic deals, which was the only performance opportunity I could locate since no bonafide venue would book me. I waited my turn then played three of my best implosive story-songs about Jesus, loneliness, poverty and death in the South. The small crowd of tipsy scenesters could have cared less. When I finished it felt like nobody's even noticed me, or so I thought.

But then there she came, weaving her way though the tangle of jaded souls, calling out to me, all aglow, asking who I was and cooing how she loved, loved, loved my songs— loved how they were so dark and troubled and deeply Southern. She was easy on the eyes, stylish in a New York kind of way, but with a hard, poor-white southern twang.

She asked where I was from and lo and behold it turns out we grew up about a hundred miles apart down in North Florida. We even went to the same damn summer bible camp as kids, or so she claimed after I mentioned I'd gone there.

We talked a bit about home as I packed up my guitar. I was headed for the front door, whereupon she squared up to me and asked, "Hey, did anyone ever tell you you look like Nick Cave?" I half-noticed the hungry glint in her eye but at the time didn't think much of it.

I vaguely knew who Nick Cave was, but no one had ever connected me to him before. David Byrne? Sure. Anthony Perkins? Occasionally, but no Nick Cave. When she mentioned it, though, it sort of made sense. I guess if you were to squint your eyes real hard we might pass for some kind of relations—cousins, half-brothers. Throw in the fact that my songs plum similar themes as his—you know, that Southern Gothic, doomed love, existential despair, base criminality kind of approach, and her question sort of made sense. She acted shocked when I told her nobody'd ever connected me and him before. Then with this rabbit in the headlights look on her face, she added that I reminded her of Nick Cave A LOT.

As a rule women have always shunned me, particularly attractive ones, so the math of this lady didn't quite add up, but I didn't much care. I was coming out of that long death dance with the actress and my mystery illness and, despite my newfound musician status, I was still mostly a broken, lonely loser type. And there she was, this fine-looking, fashionable woman who was clearly throwing me a line. It'd been a long while since a woman had paid any sort of attention to me whatsoever, so hell, if looking like Nick Cave was at the root of her interest in me, I had no problem with that and no offense taken. Having spent most of my adult life battling bouts of crippling depression and extended stretches of self-imposed isolation, I knew I wasn't much of a catch.

After signing my big six record deal with Luaka Bop they'd insisted I get busy learning the craft of performing. Eventually I found a few of these open mic deals in Manhattan, this one up in Hell's Kitchen being my go-to venue. I'd mumble-sing a few of my rambling dirges and usually nobody seemed to take much notice. But there she was.

As I picked up my gear and headed out the front door she came trotting out and handed me a scrap of paper with her phone number on it and said, "Call me.", then sashayed off into the bar. I stood there watching her go, my feet frozen to the sidewalk, gripping that little scrap of paper in my hand like my damn life depended on it.

The next night we had ourselves a proper date and from there on it was a no turn back proposition. Despite her refined appearance this woman was one off-kilter human being. She could flat-out drink two linebackers and a husky stevedore under the table and trotted out an endless succession of exotic stories about her own troubled past in the South; tales brimming with demented kinfolk, cruel preachers, murder, thievery, sorry relatives, shotgun weddings and suicides galore. I just sat there listening, bewitched, as she went on and on. It was like listening to my own darkest imaginings, only on steroids, so her and me seemed like a match made in heaven. In hindsight she did mention Nick Cave a little too often, but by then I was too addled to notice.

We saw a lot of each other for a couple weeks, then a month or so into our courtship she phoned, frantic, telling me she was getting evicted and asking could she move in with me.

The Universe was up to its old tricks, as just that morning my roommate had informed me he was moving out, so in my reckoning that meant the Unseen Forces were telling me they wanted this deal to go down—suddenly I needed a roommate, and suddenly there she was, this good looking, totally bizarro Southern woman in distress. The timing of this coincidence spoke of vast, universal mechanics at play, of some enigmatic blueprint of fate to which, stupid me, I felt typically obliged to surrender to.

So out roommate went and in she moved, with her dazzling array of priceless shoes and fashion magazines and clothes and clothes and clothes and bizarre antiques and morose paintings of murdered and decapitated women and urns filled with dead cat ashes. Our first week cohabitating, while I was out driving the taxi, she redecorated my quirky Brooklyn man-cave in a style that called to mind some weird hybrid between a whorehouse and a funeral parlor.

Shortly thereafter the Nick Cave digs commenced. At first they were playful rebukes, but as one day slaughtered the next the tone shifted and they came with greater and greater frequency. In her eyes I couldn't do anything right; I was a miserable excuse for a man, for a boyfriend, for a musician—nothing like the majestic Nick Cave.

A month into the cohabitation experiment, even though I'm typically the "left", not the "leaver", I was just about to do the unthinkable and break up with her when she announced she was pregnant—this despite her having sworn all along that she was on the pill. And there you have it; you're promptly plopped down in one of those crossroad moments in life where your entire future will soon be rendered fundamentally changed, all due to one tiny element in your trajectory being altered.

By then I knew—there was something fundamentally wrong with that woman. But no matter how bad I wanted to get the hell out of Dodge, I couldn't see walking away from this theoretical child. I just couldn't. So I tried to make things work.

With a baby on the way her and me decided to move back home to the South. On the trip down we fought and split up, me heading on to Ensley in the Panhandle of Florida after abandoning her with her family over there in Valdosta. Then came the music box incident and the rest is history.

Shortly thereafter my star began to rise as a musician. There was a lot of fuss made in the highbrow music press about my debut record. I started to slowly but surely build a "following", doing exhaustive tours with David Byrne, then later with Ani DiFranco, the Bare Naked Ladies and more. I sold that song to a big Drew Barrymore movie and boom, I was a bonafide professional recording artist. There followed major network TV appearances in France and England, then the US. A few weeks ago my second album was released and hit the top twenty on the Amazon charts. Nick Cave sits at number twenty four, so two years into this circus ride of the music business I'm neck and neck with my nemesis.

I tour a lot now and in general am treated with a surreal reverence out there on the road. But when I come home I'm greeted by my own personal rock and roll Xanthippe. The causal chain as to why we're together is clear; I tend to long-term commit to the first woman who says yes to a date. She's obsessed with Nick Cave but has zero shot at getting access to him, so she's grabbed me as a sorry surrogate.

For my kid's sake I've tried to get used to her exotic ways but, buddy, that's a tall order. Aside from the animal hoarding and serious credit issues, not a day goes by that I don't hear Nick Cave's name and wince. I'll be sitting on the back porch working on a new song and she'll step out of the house, frown and say, "I don't see why you can't sing that song more sexy like, you know, like how Nick Cave sings…".

A few weeks back she said "Why can't you write a real love song, like Nick Cave does?" She's got this worrisome affinity for murder ballads and from time to time reminds me how she knows that one day someone will murder her and cut her body up into little pieces then cram said pieces into old mayonnaise jars. That demented mindset is the full time lay of the land hereabouts. Moral to the story? Fictional shit is fun, but only so long as it stays fictional.

In the real world I'm slowly gaining ground on Nick Cave, but, as far as she's concerned, no matter what I do, it's never enough. Last month I landed the musical guest slot on The David Letterman show. Afterwards all she had to say was, "Why do you have to look so stiff all the time? Can't you move more like Nick Cave does when he's on stage? Swing your hips around. Look dangerous." She means well I guess; all she wants is for me to be perfect, like Nick Cave.

It's gotten to where, although I loathe touring and all the associated nonsense with being an on-stage personality—you know, night after night getting gawked at by throngs of adoring fans—I now actually look forward to the long hauls on the road. Three weeks crammed in a dilapidated van with a bunch of smelly side-men? Fine by me, so long as nobody plays any Nick Cave cuts on the car stereo…

—Jesus, the sink's about to overflow! I hear the Crazy Maker calling me to dinner. I finish washing up and sit down to eat, dining on her fine, southern home-cooking, sadly laden with the psychic grizzle of my misbegotten fate.

It's morning now. I head over to Jimmy Tuck's place. He's my shade tree mechanic buddy. Pulling up in the driveway I notice Jimmy's sporting a black eye, which, if you know Jimmy informs poorly on whoever it was that hit him. I'm guessing that sucker presently resides in an ICU somewhere. I ask him about the shiner and he just grins, rolls his eyes and mutters, "Family reunion."

He replaces the busted spring in the accelerator linkage and does some fluid maintenance and belt tightening. When he hears I'm headed toward the Rockies he adjusts the carburetor for high altitude combustion, then spins donuts in his front yard to show off the new pep in the engine.

Woo-hoo. Good times.

I'm slated to leave on a big coast to coast dream tour in two days, so seeing the old van in fighting form is a big relief. I'm taking a bigger band than previous outings, which means more gear, more suitcases, more overall weight, so it'll be a major chore for this old clunker.

I beeline it home and while I'm doing tour prep she starts in. Nothing new here; every time I'm about to go on the road, her standard goodbye posture starts with picking fights and such. Then come the premonitions: the van will hurtle off a bridge and I'll be trapped inside and drown, a lighting rig will collapse on me, snapping my neck, I'll contract a deadly brain-eating fungus from soiled sheets in some dive hotel. I shit you not, these are actual scenarios she's voiced to me.

At first her bizarre fears seemed quixotically tender, but eventually I've connected the dots; her fretful imaginings have little if anything to do with concern for me. She just covets the notion of some grotesque descending horror and hungers for it to manifest on someone other than herself.

Two days have passed relatively quietly. Thankfully there's no further Crazy Maker premonitions of death to process and it's time to hit the road, leaving her and the ever-present specter of Nick Cave behind. Good riddance. It's ninety-one smoking degrees as we roll out of Pensacola, six of us packed into that fifteen year old Ford Econoline van. I built bunks in the cargo area so four can sleep while the other two drive and navigate. We're pulling a 4 X 6 cargo trailer for our amps, gear and suitcases. I picked it up from a redneck repo man out in the sticks. The back door'd been pried open during the repo operation, but a few whacks with a sledgehammer and a twist or two from a pry bar fixed that.

This is my first run in this vehicle, so I'm breaking in both the van and the new band. Fully loaded like this, as soon as we hit the highway it's crystal clear the engine is woefully underpowered. Under the hood sits a meager 302 small block Windsor—hardly ideal for the demands we're making on it. Out on the highway it tops out at around sixty mph. As we go putt-putting down the interstate an endless procession of lavish tour busses blow by us, Prevosts costing a million bucks or more, sporting five hundred horsepower diesel engines, hauling big name acts like Jewel, Wilco and REM.

Thankfully it's a short hop today. We're aiming for the legendary House of Blues over in New Orleans, less than a two hundred mile jaunt to the west. From there it's a long haul to El Paso, Texas, opening for guitar wizard Junior Brown, one of the hottest acts in the music business presently. After El Paso comes the high cotton: a string of headlining dates in clubs up the West Coast, then on to Boulder, Colorado, Kansas City, followed by a slew of Midwestern and Northeastern cities, an appearance on Conan O'Brien, then capping off with a four-night stretch opening for Dave Matthews at a twenty thousand capacity arena outside of Philly. Goddamn, this sure looks good...on paper at least.

A hundred miles west of Pensacola the air conditioning sputters and dies. Compressor? Freon leak? Mechanical suicide? Late summer in the deep South in a big metal box crammed full of sweaty men—hello, world of stink, you are present and accounted for!

No time to stop and get it repaired so we crank down the windows and soldier on. An hour later the alternator starts acting tweaky. Every time I touch the brakes or flip on the blinker the engine stutters, nearly cutting off. Fun stuff. We spot a you-pull-it junkyard west of Biloxi and ease off the interstate, downshifting into lower gears to slow us since we can't fully engage the brakes without the motor cutting off.

Me and Clint, the keyboard player, yank a replacement alternator from a junked van (a newer model than ours, ironically), bolt it in place, tighten the belts and say a prayer. The replacement alternator holds and we miss our sound check arrival time badly, pulling up to the House of Blues just twenty minutes shy of our first big show's actual start time. Whew and damn.

Double whew and triple damn—check out the huge crowd milling around outside! It's a freaking mob. I'm thrilled, as are the bandmates. The sea of fans part as we ease into our designated parking space right behind a giant Prevost tour bus. I make my way through the swarm and locate the stage manager. He points out a second door back at the rear of the building and informs us they got us performing in what he calls "a smaller listening room" off to the side.

Pretty good crowd, I note to the stage manager. "Oh, yeah, they're here for the main room act." he reports. So who's that? Some kid by the name of John Mayer. The stage manager mentions Mayer's show in the eight hundred capacity main room is sold out and ours in the seventy-five capacity room isn't, so maybe we'll get some overflow. We're escorted to the smaller room, hustle to set up our gear then play to a teeming crowd of seventeen Jim White fans.

I sell a handful of CDs then we grimly load the gear back into the trailer. Everyone's depressed, settling back into the hot, stinky van. We're waiting for our guitar player

Chris to finish his idiot check of the dressing room when, through the open side door of the van, four gorgeous coeds come leaping in. That damn sure gets everyone's attention. They're frisky, young and sexed-up, half-to-three quarters drunk. They go to dropping flirty bombs, asking can they come back to the our hotel with us.

Huh?

My lonely loser bandmates are officially rendered shit-your-pants, deer-in-the-headlights addled, but I've already worked out the groupie math here. I call out to the leader of the debutante crew, asking her whose van she thinks she just jumped in. She looks a little confused, then lamely offers up "John Mayer's???"

I smirk as the band members recoil, crestfallen. I nod at the massive, shiny Prevost bus parked directly in front of us and say, "Honey, if you were looking for John Mayer, where would you expect to find him, here in this crappy old van, or up there in that million dollar tour bus?"

She scrunches her nose, offering up her best confused cute-girl pose, then shrieks and leaps out of the van, followed in quick succession by her mortified entourage. Off they skitter, skootching down their miniskirts as they triangulate invasion plans to sneak onto Mayer's bus.

Good lord.

I laugh and laugh about it, but my band mates, they might never forgive me. Sorry fellas, there's a couple human beings on this earth I might be willing to impersonate, but, like Nick Cave, John Mayer doesn't make that list.

PENSACOLA BEACH, FLORIDA, FEBRUARY 1994

"Shavette Shingle? Are you back at it again? Hireman Bargainer? You been prowling around with that no good Mobutu Tony Hines? Oh no. No, no. You two got no business hound-dogging together. Probation officer gonna have your ass in a sling. Cotton Crabtree, I hope you learned your lesson this time."

I'm talking to the criminals in the newspaper. It's my fourth week here laid out on this impoverished sick-bed and I'm one-hundred percent stone-cold bored.

You might ask what does a body do when they're deathly ill, flat broke, with no transportation other than their own two feet, which at present aren't cooperating? The answer is not much. I wish I had a book, or a radio or a deck of cards to play solitaire, but I don't. Other than strumming this crazy purple electric guitar my sole form of entertainment comes via the old codger in the beach house next door. He's took pity on me and brings over the newspaper each day when he's done with it.

The Pensacola News Journal is your basic Gannett Press soft-core right-wing propaganda rag featuring an agonizingly narrow spectrum of mainstream bullshit. That first week I was stranded here I daily forced myself to read the few actual articles scattered among the countless mall ads. As the hours crawled by and boredom ramped up to unbearable levels I'd read and reread the paper front page to back, plodding through the same mind-numbingly conservative screeds, combing through the local news, then on to the inane op-eds. By late afternoon each day true desperation would set in, whereupon I'd move on to the classifieds: junker cars for sale, boats to trade, a precious few minimum-wage jobs. I'd get to counting typos and noting contradictions in previous stories.

But then, near the end that first week of bedridden perusings, tucked between the classifieds and the public legal notifications a name in a narrow column leapt out at me: Vonkish O'Day Gellman. It was a bonafide nomenclatural puzzle; was this man a Slavic-Irish-African American-Jew? Vonkish's name was the first listed in that discrete back page column, one I'd not noticed before, something called the Felony Report. The write-up included a brief description of Vonkish's crime: drunk and disorderly, plus indecent exposure while playing his guitar naked on the shoulder of Highway 29 North up by Car City. I laughed, thinking, "Well, hell, if I was named Vonkish O'Day Gellman, I too would be playing my guitar naked on the side of Highway 98."

That solitary laugh went echoing down through the shadows of my weary psyche, and, laying there staring at that man's name, I felt a tiny hint of that electrocuted feeling inching up my spine. It was almost as if in Vonkish I'd found some manner of long-lost kinfolk, one with similarly spectacular loser superpowers.

And then it happened again—another such name at which I busted up laughing in the form of Brown Vesey Rainwater. I read about his crime, then, among the list of thirty or so other arrestees, spotted the names Buster Quarrels and Royal Hand. Well, I whipped out a pen and documented those names in my latest Tom Waits inspired pocket notebook. I studied them there, and the manner in which those names called out to me is difficult to explain. They felt like signal beacons from some long-lost promised land.

So each day now when the paper arrives, I skip the foreplay and flip straightaway to the Felony Report. To date I've compiled a tidy list of hundreds of exotically named felons: McSteve McQueen, Pharaoh Lolovanhan Drain III, Gussy Tippy, Biplob Dash, Buckle John Cherry, Ultra Dyna Lucas, Dominique Givehand, Venus Uvodka Mitchell, Gaylord Tisseboo.

Accompanying the Felony Report lies the equally fertile column called Obituary Listing, which is inexplicably placed alongside the felons, as if the act of dying were some manner of crime.

With the Felony Report there's three basic categories. You got your garden variety criminals with garden variety names and typical crimes like burglary and assault. They warrant no entires in the notebook. Then you've got your exotic named citizens committing ordinary crimes. Their names are added to the list. Then you have my favorite category, the criminals whose names seem to inform on the crimes they committed.

Take, for example, the case of Miss Myrtlene Wink. She got herself arrested for stealing a collection of priceless antique glass eyeballs from a display case up at the local drug store.

I'm especially partial to repeat offenders. I'll flip open the News Journal and—lo and behold—there they are again, those Dortch brothers (Step and Wall, two of five brothers, all named after building parts). And occasionally I'll recognize some childhood friend, like Catman Windeguth, who I did a shit-ton of dope with in my early teens before I got saved.

This roster of lowbrow miscreants has become my defacto extended family during this crippling health spiral, so much so that this morning, after reading the Felony Report, I got so inspired by that burgeoning list of luminous names that I started working up a song about them. I mean, if I don't highlight these misbegotten souls, well, who exactly will?

For the time being I'm calling this one "The Felony Report Song"—who knows, the name may stick.

I'm back behind the liquor store,
chatting with some ne'er do wells.
Swapping tall tales, just killing time.
It's a lazy old morning, then without warning,

the trash talking starts as fisticuffs break out.
First Blueberry Johns slugs Ramjam Jones,
then Vonkish O'Day jumps on Titus Stone.
Red White runs, as does Guppy Troop.
Jimmy Ray Speaks howls at Kizzy Koop.
I guess irrational names
sometimes…
lead the name bearers
to commit…
irrational crimes.

The second verse all but writes itself…

And what were you thinking, Miss Myrtlene Wink,
stealing those glass eyes from the drug store display?
And Catman Windeguth, you been charged with petty theft,
plus criminal mischief for ransacking your best friends place.
Royal Hand, what a grand old name you have.
But you've been an inmate far too many times.
And Romeo Maytag, your name made me smile,
'till you got arrested for molesting a child.
I guess irrational names
sometime…
lead the name bearers
to commit…
irrational crimes.

I smiled this morning to find Catman's name listed there and wished him well. Things are bad, but they could be worse. There but for the grace of the Unseen Forces, go I.

EL PASO, TEXAS, AUGUST 2001

Up till El Paso the Texas topography slanted in our underpowered van's favor; uniformly flat. But as we near the westernmost corner of the state we're running into a few gentle inclines, whereupon said already slow van begins to drag, going slower and slower. Even with it floored, we're now topping out at around forty-five miles an hour. The engine's running pretty smooth so all indications are we're experiencing some kind of drive train failure—lovely. Transmission? Torque modulator? Differential? We're hardly a thousand miles into a six thousand mile nonstop tour, shows booked almost every day, with no time budgeted for breakdowns and subsequent repairs.

We come limping into the big venue parking lot where Junior Brown's impressive tour bus is parked, running late on account of the slow van. No time for dinner—after a quick sound check we roll right into our performance. Halfway through the set it's clear Junior's mainstream leaning fans could care less about us. We do our thing, then clear our gear off the stage as Junior and Tonya Rae proceed to tear the roof off the place. I dutifully man the merchandise table, selling not one CD afterwards—a true index of a show's failure.

First New Orleans, now this. So much for the initial leg of our dream tour. But tomorrow we got a day off and guitar player Chris has mechanic relations here in El Paso. That gives us thirty-six slim hours to remedy this van situation before we're due in Taos.

I rise early and meet up with Chris's kindly step-dad Al, a retired homicide detective. Al mechanics on the side and has offered to help out. I break down the symptoms for him, the smooth running engine but loss of power, the alternator, the AC going out. He jacks up the rear end of the van, takes some measurements and, to my surprise, quickly diagnoses the problem as being a differential with "tall gears", meaning the back axle gear cogs feature a ratio designed for economically running on flat land—think of riding a 10 speed bike. It's fine until you have to pedal uphill in the highest gear. Combine the underpowered engine and heavy load with these alleged tall gears and you get low torque, which is Al's explanation for why the van slows significantly on hills. Makes sense I guess.

With the Rockies looming ahead of us, Al suggests we rebuild the rear axle, swapping out this differential for one with a better gear ratio. Okay. Since there's no time to order a new replacement part I'm about to call around to some junkyards to hunt up a used differential when Al remembers that Chris's Uncle Kemal once owned a similar make van, so he gives Kemal a shout.

Kemal resides in a gutted double-wide out on a godforsaken stretch of land sitting astraddle the Mexico/US border. The uncle is contacted and reports his van's still around, sitting on some cinderblocks at an abandoned gas station a few miles down the road from his trailer. The year, engine size and model match, so he says if the gears in it suit our purposes we can have them no charge.

It's a long, dusty drive to the middle of nowhere. When we arrive Kemal greets us warily, and by warily I mean with a pistol in hand. A very large pistol. Bullet casings litter the walkway to his trailer. He looks to be in his fifties, big and brawny, cut from mountain man stock. His filthy Levi's cutoffs more resemble a loincloth than any other form of apparel, and that's all he's wearing.

He walks us into the double wide, instructing us to take a seat, adding a stern warning to watch out for the skunk and rattlesnake he shares the trailer with. There's a skittish young Mexican woman lurking in the back room. She looks to be no more than eighteen and is off-handedly introduced by Kemal as his "latest" wife. She looks scared, more of him than us.

We visit and make small talk about beer, guns, cars, and, inexplicably, Mother Teresa, all the while on the lookout for that rattlesnake, which he reports often sleeps in the coils of the various recliners scattered across the living room, some of which we're seated in. Eventually an expedition is mounted to retrieve the gears.

At the abandoned gas station there's no sign of the van. Scrape marks leading from the cinderblocks where it sat to the two lane blacktop testify to it having been recently dragged off by someone. Kemal seems unperturbed. He suggests we sift through the many piles of cast-off auto parts that litter the interior of the defunct service bays to see if we might locate some usable gears there.

It's a fools errand, but hell, I figure I'll humor him—might as well, right? After all, he's armed and clearly insane. I flip over a rear end assembly with a dusty whomp whereupon Kemal howls furiously, scolding me for disturbing the rattlesnakes. Then, as if offering a benediction to them, Kemal lifts his ropey arms toward heaven as if praying, and shouts, "Mother Teresa says: if-you-love-some-damn-body, by-God-set-their-asses-free…SET-THEM-FREE!!" He pauses for dramatic effect, then adds, "THEN, hunt them sorry sons of bitches down and KILL…THEM…DEAD….DEAD!" This is followed by Kemal's trademark whiskey-soaked cackle.

Good times.

No matching Ford gears are found, so, at crazy Kemal's insistence a second expedition is mounted to another gas station some twenty miles up the road. The Mexican mechanic there also humors Kemal, but, like the present wife, seems terrified of him. He disappears into the back yard of the station, which is littered with rusting vehicles, returning ten minutes later with a differential bearing a suitable gear ratio. He offers it to us free of charge, clearly happy to be shut of the big lunatic and his entourage.

By the time we drop Kemal back at the double wide and return to El Paso it's late. No way to do a rebuild on the rear end tonight. We need to pull out early for Taos, so we'll just have to limp our way there and hope to locate some mechanic along the way to drop in the new unit. Not ideal, but that's life on the road as an entry level musician.

Ten-thirty am. We've hit true hill country halfway to Taos. On inclines even floored the van incrementally loses speed to the point where we're just crawling along the interstate at thirty or so. On that last steeper incline it dropped to twenty, then fifteen pitiful, wimpy miles an hour. Shit. With the RPMs holding steady around five thousand it's clear we're gonna blow this fucking engine if we keep pushing it like we are.

Ten miles ahead lies a bonafide mountain. Great. We're in the middle of fucking nowhere. Perfect. There's a lonely exit ramp up ahead so we take it, thinking it's better to be stranded up there than on the side of this busy interstate. We exit, and hitting the rise at the end of the ramp what do we behold? A tidy little four-bay auto repair joint that, to our utter astonishment, appears to be open for business.

Hallucination? Nope, it's real.

We limp in and convey the long tale of our journey to the young, taciturn mechanic who runs the place: the lack of power, the tall gears, the mountains ahead, our tight schedule. He listens stoically as he loosens the bolts on the intake manifold of a beat-up GMC Jimmy. After a long pause he asks to see the differential given to us, so I dig it out. He gives it a cursory inspection then hands it back to me, shaking his head disapprovingly. "Nope. No good. Teeth are scored—see…?" He points out several irregularities in the notching pattern on the gear.

Perfect.

"Pull it in number two," He then says flatly, discretely nodding his ball cap brim toward the second bay. I drop the trailer and ease the van into the bay. He cranks the engine on and off a few times, listening, sniffing at the air like a coon dog on the scent of something feral. He pops off the interior engine cover and begins to quickly, methodically adjust the gas-to-air ratio on the carburetor. It takes him all of eight minutes.

He replaces the engine cover then says, "Try it now." I ease out of the bay, hit the gas and—WOW! This crappy old van about leaps out of its skin. So much for Al's tall gear theory and Jimmy Tuck's carburetor adjustment. It's suddenly a completely different vehicle, one with power to spare.

No time to consider the miracle. We're running late so I hustle my band members into the new, improved Econoline and head in to settle up with the young Zen cowboy mechanic. He's sitting there with his boots up on his desk, on hold with an auto parts store, expressionless, just staring out the window at the vast expanse of prairie behind the station. I thank him and ask what I owe. He shrugs, saying, "No charge. You fellas look kinda hangdog."

I give it some thought, then drop a twenty on his desk. It may be laying there still.

Hello San Diego, city of my birth! And hello West Coast, the best coast so far as my fan base in concerned. The van's surmounted first foothills then mountains, getting us to Taos and Tucson on time without breaking a sweat. In each city we were met with great crowds, energy and most importantly CD sales. But tonight in San Diego there's a weird vibe present; attendance is light and during the show there's an air of uneasiness in the audience of thirty or so. I can feel it, the band can too.

As I'm breaking down my gear a few fans come moping up, sporting disgruntled looks.

"Hey, where were you last night?" one guy asks.

"Tuscon." I reply, coiling guitar cables, "Played the Hotel Congress, why?"

"You were supposed to play here last night. At the Civic Theater."

"Really? That's news to me." I say, half-listening.

"Yeah," Another one chimes in, clearly disappointed, "We went to see your show but you weren't there."

Puzzling. "Huh?" I'm distracted trying to get my damn cables coiled right.

"And I was really looking forward to seeing you play with Nick Cave…"

I freeze. A strange, choking sensation seizes my throat and chest. Dropping the cables on the stage I square up opposite the guy, who now looks slightly fearful of my apoplectic expression. I sputter, "Did you…just…say….Nick Cave??"

"Um, yeah…you were billed to perform with him here at the Civic Center last night…what happened?"

I get all queasy feeling, like I'm the target of some sick, sick prank. I want to think this is just some joker the Crazy Maker sent to punk me, but then a couple more fans corroborate, saying that not only did Nick Cave perform in San Diego last night, but the show advertisements listed me as his special guest.

What? What? What? Why has my psychic antenna suddenly switched the station from WYOU to WWTF without anybody telling me?

———————————————————

It's two am and I just rolled into my hotel room. I jump on the internet and grudgingly pay a visit to my nemesis Nick Cave's website—and lo and behold! It turns out that the legendary rock god Nick Cave will be playing a goddamn show in every single goddamn city on the goddamn West Coast exactly one night before I'm scheduled to goddamn play there. Seriously? Are you shitting me?

And who's his special musical guest every show? Jim White, of course. That's the kicker. I do a little digging and discover that this Jim White is a celebrated drummer from some Australian band called The Dirty Three.

Oh please no, Universe, you gotta be kidding me!

For a moment I feel exactly like that foreman back on Gulf Beach Highway, screaming and hollering about his standpipe. Fucked up blueprints are in my hand and I'm howling like a maniac. From there on out, my big West Coast tour goes as follows:

LOS ANGELES: Pulling into LA, as we go rolling through the trendy Silverlake district headed toward the venue, what do we see? Yeah. Posters everywhere advertising the Nick Cave/Jim White show last night.

Unfuckingbelieveable.

Again the strange vibe from the smallish audience makes playing the show a chore. Again when I'm packing up my gear a group of confused fans approach, asking where I was the night before. Again I'm told Nick Cave and my namesake played to a sold out crowd in a much larger venue a mile or so away.

Fucking fantastic.

SAN FRANCISCO: As I'm standing around after the show explaining to a scattering of fans in attendance why I wasn't with Nick Cave last night, the opening line from that song of his, the one that the Crazy Maker plays incessantly on the home stereo, comes popping into my head. The line goes:

I don't believe in an interventionist God.

Well Nick, old buddy, if you walked a mile in my shoes, or drove a mile in my 1984 Econoline van, you probably would, because clearly there's some kind of divine organizing principle at play here, laid out by the Unseen Forces. Otherwise how else could this bewildering coincidence be explained?

Nope, God, or Jesus Christ or whatever magical deity's working here is up to his old tricks and, just like with the stolen car and the record deal and various other metaphysical sleights of hand, this deity appears to be looking down upon me, saying, "Let me royally fuck with this little pissant's mind and see how well he acquits himself." Mission accomplished, big man. You split my strongest fanbase slap down the middle like Moses parting the Red Sea, ushering Nick Cave down the exalted center path that lies between severed halves.

PORTLAND: Light attendance? Check. Confused fans? Check. Nick Cave's name being reverentially bandied about? Check. Posters dotting the landscape featuring my name side by side with Nick Cave's? Check. Over and over I hear, "Hey, where were you last night?" and with each repetition of that line, more and more I hear the words as if delivered through the filter of the Crazy Maker's grating, accusatory voice.

SEATTLE: See Portland.

VANCOUVER: See Seattle. But wait! There's a light at the end of the Nick Cave Tunnel!

A fan just informed me that Nick Cave's sensational sold out west coast tour officially ended last night in Vancouver. Good riddance to you, hard rocking pathos master!

We load up our gear after Nick Cave Groundhog Day number six and go barreling back in the direction of the US border, hunkered down for the fifteen hundred mile schlep over the Rockies to Boulder, Colorado, where two days ahead of us there are absolutely zero Nick Cave/Jim White shows scheduled, where there are no misleading posters featuring our names side by side, hence no disappointed fans to console, hence and, most importantly, where there are no reminders of my dismal home life. We aim south and east, weaving the Econoline first through Washington state, then across the big sky country of Idaho.

Since we're due in Boulder for sound check early the following afternoon we got no choice but to duck our heads and deadhead nonstop, Bataan Death March style. The van's running like a top thanks to the Zen cowboy mechanic's magical healing powers. Everyone takes a turn behind the wheel. Day turns to twilight, twilight to darkness, darkness to deeper night. Sixteen, eighteen hours of continuous driving. Presently the band members are snoring away on the bunks in the back as me and Bishop, the bass player, take turns piloting the Econoline across high prairies ringed by distant mountains.

It's coming up on midnight and here's my problem; for the last twenty minutes or so, out the corner of my eye I keep seeing, like…well, like, flying lights. They appear intermittently; spooky moving specks of white way out in the middle of the empty expanse of prairie where there are no visible roads.

What's even weirder is they only appear in my damn peripheral vision—every time I whip my head to snag a clear view of them, them fuckers just flat out disappear. It's not reflections on the window—I know because I already tried rolling it down below eye level and noted no difference. The notion of UFOs jumps to the mind pretty quick, as do the possibilities of Highway Hypnosis and insanity.

Ten minutes of fruitless head whipping later I hear Bishop say, "Hey…um, Jim, um….. are you….um….well….seeing…"

"FLYING LIGHTS?" I all but shriek. "You're seeing them too?? God! "

"Man, whew…" he exhales, laughing softly "I thought I was losing it there…"

We discuss the phenomenon as rationally as possible, I mean, Idaho's one big Minuteman missile range, right? So we settle on writing off what we've been seeing as somehow military related. Inexplicably, no sooner do we mention the lights than they disappear. We keep our eyes peeled from here on out but the flying lights officially go AWOL.

It's past one in the morning now. I'm trying to settle into the rhythm of the late night drive but this proposition just got a little more complicated because directly over the highway stretching out ahead, way up high in the western sky what do I see? White darting lights? Nope. How about a monstrous semi-transparent green blob? Yep. I blink my eyes a few times—blink-blink-blink—hoping it's some weird reflection on the windshield. But no, no matter how hard I blink, the green blob not only remains, it continues to grow…bigger and bigger and bigger. After a couple of minutes it fills roughly half the vast, western sky ahead.

I look over at Bishop, who looks scared. "You see THAT, right??" I blurt out, jabbing a finger at the giant blob.

"YES! God, I was beginning to think someone slipped a roofie in my Big Gulp at that last truck stop…"

So the good news here is we're both not going insane, but that still leaves us with the troubling conundrum of this massive green blob in the sky. But wait, the green blob's now slowly turning red? Now purple? What?

Bishop points ahead and says, "Look!"

Along the side of the highway there's cars pulling over, small clusters of travelers beside them admiring the phenomenon in the sky, visuals that call to mind cheesy science fiction special effects. YES! It's not just us!

There's a rest stop coming up so Bishop eases off the highway. It's jammed with parked cars galore in there, passengers out in the clear night air oohing and ahhhhing, pointing at the sky. Then it hits us—it's the Northern Lights! Us being from the South we're new to this phenomenon.

I wake the band members and me and the boys join a crowd of travelers who've gathered around some picnic tables, everyone watching the sky reverently. Truth be told, after about five minutes of green/purple/red blob action I'm rendered just this side of flat-out bored. This particular iteration the storied event amounts to a series of colored patches floating in the sky. I'd rate it a "so-so"…I mean, gimme a flashlight and a tie-dyed t-shirt and I could create the same effect on any relatively flat surface.

We've got a tight deadline to meet in a fan-friendly town where Nick Cave will not be playing tomorrow, so it's time to put the rubber to the road here. I round up my band members but they buck, saying we gotta stay and watch this once in a lifetime experience. Well, too bad, I herd them into the van anyway. Grumbles filter in from the back bunks. I hear the word "killjoy" muttered.

What a tour.

It's late and I'm exhausted anyway so here's the compromise I offer: the first exit we come to I'll pull off and get us motel rooms. They can do as they please during the interim five or six hours while I get some shut-eye.

We roll a good twenty miles before I spy an off-ramp sign for a town bearing the slightly surreal name of Bliss, Idaho. I ease the van off the highway, cruise up to the end of the off-ramp, finding a lone motel called The Amber Inn.

Bliss is less a town, more of a way-station. The front lawn of The Amber Inn is littered with travelers sitting on blankets watching those boring Northern Lights. It's Saturday night, busiest night of the week so, as expected there's a NO VACANCY sign blinking in the window. I trot into the lobby anyway, hoping the clerk can recommend a motel nearby.

He can. I'm directed to an old mom and pop place a couple miles down this little two-lane blacktop that intersects with the highway. We motor out into the lonely high prairie, a good four miles from the interstate and find the motel, a low-slung, fairly defeated looking cinderblock structure plopped out in the middle of nowhere. There's not a car in the parking lot, not one room rented.

We are officially off the beaten path.

An episode of Star Trek is playing on the ancient black and white TV in the empty lobby. I ring the night bell and this groggy middle-aged lady emerges from a bedroom attached to the office. She's dressed in a bath robe sporting a recurring UFO motif, her hair up in curlers. She greets me warmly, hands me registration forms then starts humming the Star Trek theme as I fill them out.

The vibe is weirdly cinematic, but not unpleasantly so. As she's grabbing our room keys I notice a rack of post cards showing comical images of archetypal western situations—cowboys, wagon trains, cattle drives—all of them featuring crudely photoshopped images of UFOs floating in the sky. Captain Kirk is talking in the background about intangibles like faith and love and kismet and clearly there's some kind of psychic trade wind present and blowing at a good clip here— I can feel it, like I'm standing on the edge of some surreal abyss about to be lifted off my feet.

I get us three rooms and hand out keys to band members. A couple of guys grab sleeping bags and wander out into a nearby field where they'll lay down and take in the event. Been a long day for me, a long week, month, year, etc, so I turn in, the night sky ablaze with colors. Sleep comes quickly tonight—a rarity for me. In my dreams Nick Cave appears and disappears, an ever-silent figure watching in the distance.

I'm in the middle of some complicated dream where I'm trying to fit sixty-three stolen pork pie hats into a vacuum cleaner bag with a hole in the bottom when I'm wrenched awake by a desperate pounding sound. That's…that's…wait, that's not dream pounding—that's REAL! Shit! I sit bolt upright in bed, look toward the window and see it's morning. Who the hell's beating on my door? Wait, I know that voice. Who is that? Is it Chris, my genius level, albeit slightly ADD riddled guitar player? It is. What's he saying?

"JIM! WAKE UP! Come outside! You gotta see this!!"

I wrench my eyes fully open, pull on a pair of jeans, leap up and about go blind flinging the door open. When my eyes finally adjust, for a second I think I'm seeing double. Parked parallel to our beige 1984 Ford Econoline ban is an identical beige 1984 Ford Econoline van also pulling a trailer. Same year, same color, same engine size. They're automotive twins. It's confusing. These are the only two vehicles in the parking lot at this remote motel. And what's stranger is that second van was definitely not parked there when we pulled in last night around 2 am.

But Chris isn't done. He yanks on my sleeve, dragging me toward the other van.

"I see, Chris, I see. The vans are identical." I say, slightly pissed at being woken up for such a minor coincidence.

"NO! LOOK INSIDE THE VAN!" Chris barks out. I stroll over and do so. No crudely constructed bunks in this one. No sir. Instead, in the cargo area of this doppelgänger van I see a standup bass, a Fender amp and a couple of vintage keyboards. So, a further coincidence. Identical vans. Identical professions.

"LOOK ON THE BACK SEAT!!!" Chris all but shrieks.

I do so, and whose face do I see staring back at me from a stack of show posters piled on said seat? Why, Nick Cave's, of course. And under his face are the words, "Nick Cave, appearing with special musical guest Jim White". I blink twice to make sure this isn't some optical trick. But it's not. It's real.

Here I am presently situated at what is arguably one of the top ten most remote motels in America and yet that fucker has tracked me down here. Thank you interventionist God, you have certainly outdone yourself this time.

I turn and check the line of rooms at the motel. Only four of the rooms feature closed curtains, meaning they're the only ones occupied. Three belong to me and my band, so that makes the room adjacent to mine ground zero for this mystery. Whoever owns this Nick Cave themed van sleeps in that room, a room which sits a few meagre feet from where I slept, dreaming about Nick Cave. Such intricate intertwining elements to this latest synchronistic mosaic! But to what end?

I'm standing there frozen in place, studying that door when again in the back of my mind I hear the furious voice of the foreman on that slab in West Pensacola. He's howling, "DRILL A HOLE IN THAT SUBSTRATE AND TELL ME WHAT YOU SEE!!".

So, I'll drill a hole, but then what happens next? What will the hidden meaning reveal here? In this go-round I guess I'm the foreman, right? The beleaguered soul brandishing a sheath of messed-up blueprints in my hand, following the outrageously intricate lines of this meta-construct, lines that've lead me to a motel room door in Bliss, Idaho? And behind that door what will I find? A missing stand pipe in the form of Nick Cave? And with that will the disparate elements of my psyche finally entwine in a coherent manner?

I march over and stand in front of that door for a long time working over the possibles. If it is Nick Cave in there, then what does that mean? What do I do? Hand him a phone and tell him to call the Crazy Maker and let her know that in fact he drives a shitty Econoline too? Do I buddy up, or seek vindication? Revenge? Or do I maybe take the Zen road and not knock at all, just walk away and let it be? You know—revel in the mystery?

Fuck that latter consideration.

No. Now over the foreman's call, it's Kemal I hear, triumphantly exhorting me, "Mother Teresa says if you love someone, SET THEM FREE! Then hunt their sorry asses down and KILL THEM DEAD!" Yep. The Unseen Forces seem to approve more of Kemal's messaging. It's hardly eight am—way early by rock and roll standards. Even still I commence to banging on the mystery door. No response.

I wait a few seconds, then bang harder. Finally I hear some shuffling around in the room. The door cracks open and out peeks a groggy young woman. She's clearly none too happy to be roused at this ungodly hour.

"What?" she says, blinking at the glare, "What happened?"

I crane my neck, checking for Nick Cave's presence therein. It's a double room and some hipster-looking guy who's not Nick Cave lies sprawled out in his street clothes, asleep on the bed next to the one this unhappy woman has clearly just risen from. He lifts his head and regards me wearily.

No Nick Cave, unless he's hiding in the bathroom. Nothing makes sense. I look back at this attractive young woman and in a befuddled tone demand, "Okay. So...who are you?"

"Who are you??" She shoots back, bowing up a tad.

"Fair enough." I say, "I'm Jim White…"

"Bullshit!" she fires back, "I know Jim White and you're not him."

"No, I am Jim White. You're thinking of the other Jim White." I say. Jesus, this is getting weird.

"What?? What do you mean, the "other" Jim White?? "

"There's two of us. Probably more. Um, is Nick Cave in there?"

"Nick? Nick went back to Australia."

"Oh, so…who are you?" I ask her.

She studies me. Long hard gaze. This is no shrinking violet.

"My name's Neko, Neko Case."

Okay, so the name Neko Case is so close to Nick Cave that it sounds slightly sleight of handish, like an anagram-based pseudonym, like it's really Nick Cave passing as a woman or something. But see, I've heard of Neko Case before, so I know it's not a joke, and least not a joke of any human origins.

The guy sleeping in his street clothes sits up and says "Oh yeah, he's the other Jim White. You know, the Jesus guy." at which point Neko says, "Oh right. Weren't people asking about him on Nick's tour?" The street clothes person says, "Yeah. He's the guy."

"Oh, so you're the guy…" Neko says.

I smile. Oh, buddy. This is just whacko. Why have I been led to bang on this random door in the middle of fucking nowhere by something, some intricate extra-phenomenal design laid out by some superior form of consciousness? Why am I here and what is this blueprint I hold? Upon closer inspection, really what I'm dealing with here is less a blueprint and more a fucking three-dimensional temporospatial Rubik's cube of intertwined, utterly dazzling and completely incomprehensible intersecting lines.

So me and my new pal Neko Case, we share a friendly laugh about this baffling coincidence. And baffling it is; it turns out she's been playing keyboards for Nick Cave on his incredibly successful West Coast tour. Her groggy roommate? He's been sitting in on bass. They cut away after the final Vancouver show and are on their way back home to Tucson, just coincidentally following the exact same route as us. Nick Cave, Neko informs me, is on an airplane, flying home. I envision him lolling in a first class seat, sipping cognac, reading Baudelaire or something while dreamily contemplating the deep meaning of the ripples far below in an ocean known as "Pacific".

The arcs and trajectories here are legion. Start with the Crazy Maker, who's obsessed with Nick Cave, then add the van that I bought for this tour that turned out to be identical to Neko Case's van, throw in the various breakdowns and delays that synchronized our movements, allowing our paths to not only cross, but to cross in an observable manner, for, much like the photo in the garbage can, an unobserved coincidence is devoid of meaning, right?

Had either of us bypassed Bliss, had Neko been driving a different vehicle that my guitar player did not feel inclined to go snooping inside of, had there been a free room at the other motel or a million other variables, this meeting would have never taken place, thus we would never have become aware of our proximity to each other.

Then throw in that, months ago these shows were booked by disparate agencies wherein the random routing of parallel West Coast shows led us to this convergence at an utterly remote locality in a town provocatively called Bliss, Idaho. That's already fairly mind-boggling, far more so than that little display of Northern Lights last night.

But as we talk the schematic for serendipity only becomes more intricately wrought. For a full day now we've both been driving at roughly the same speed on the same highways. They were ahead of us first, but we passed them somewhere along the way. Last night they'd seen the same mysterious darting lights over the prairie, the same green blob which turned into the Northern Lights. They'd pulled off at the same highway exit and asked the same motel clerk at the Amber Inn if there was another motel nearby, then drove to this same tiny motel out in the middle of nowhere. They'd arrived at said remote motel not long after us, unwittingly parking their identical van side by side with ours, then Neko Case and her friend had slept and dreamed in beds roughly three feet from my headboard.

I just sit there shaking my head. So, interventionist God, here we are. What can we do for you?

Once we've covered this bizarre backstory we struggle to make small talk—"How was your tour, Neko?"

"Okay. And yours?"

How do I explain my tour without sounding mentally ill? The conversation quickly runs out of gas, so we shake hands and the motel room door closes. Neko presumably goes back to sleep and, standing there in that parking lot in the middle of this colossal anticlimax where nothing makes the least bit of sense I find myself inexplicably laughing again, and as I do, suddenly it hits me.

Of course. That's it. The slab with the missing pipes. That's the reason I laughed that day in West Pensacola. It was a gift from the Universe—the perfect metaphor for my psyche. My whole damn life the pipes haven't come up where the blueprints said they should. And I've spent pretty much every waking moment of the last forty years drilling holes in my mental substrate, trying to suss out why nothing was as it should be. This begs the big question; was the blueprint in error, was I simply reading it wrong, or have I done just fine, and am exactly where I need to be here in the wild, wooly wilderness of the Universe?

My mind leaps to our frantic search in Texas for the replacement differential for our van with Kemal the feral madman. We searched among ruins and rattlesnakes, hunting in vain for some crucial missing piece, the apparatus which would make things right. But of course, it wasn't what we needed at all. We thought the blueprint said go out to Kemal's and lay hands on the solution. The fact is, the blueprint took us out there for other reasons, ones that made zero sense until the answer was delivered to us completely by chance, first in the form of a Zen cowboy mechanic, then later here in Bliss.

So is that it? When it comes to understanding this manner of such enigmatic schematics maybe we're all just pissing in the wind? Is that what I'm doing here Bliss? Pissing in the wind then shaking the soggy yellow hand of my own ignorance? Who knows? Maybe so.

I wake the band members, herd them into the van and on we roll. Boulder lies many hours ahead. It'll be another long day on the road.

Pulling out of the parking lot in the rear view I catch a glimpse Neko's van adjacent to the room where she now lays sleeping. As I hit the interstate onramp at Bliss, Idaho laughter finds its way into my mind again. But this time it's not that worried, nagging laugh I had that day back home by the construction site, it's a laugh free of burdens. This time I got a pretty good handle on why I'm laughing—I'm drunk on the sheer physics of magical connections, and am happily rejecting the temptation to decipher what, if any significance I can glean from this experience in Bliss, Idaho.

As the highway stretches out before us, as I push the Econoline to cruising speed I recall an article I read somewhere that stated one of the greatest attributes of the human brain is its ability to recognize complex patterns—the apophenia angle, but with a positive spin. The flip side to apophenia is our reflex to reject complex fields of variables because they present themselves absent of conspicuous threads of decipherability. When we encounter such a configuration we call it chaos, right? But is it chaos, or simply a limitation in our own seeing? Is the blueprint in error, or are we just reading it wrong?

Jesus, there I go, groping around for some tidy bow tie to seal off this bizarro incident. Is it a sin to suggest that once the universe has spoken its secret incoherent language that no further commentary is necessary? Maybe so. After all, us human beings are essentially clueless, because so far as knowing goes, all we have to work with are shadows of meaning, phantoms that we lunge out toward in the darkness with this frailty we so boldly refer to as intelligence.

I want to tell somebody that. That's what I want to shout, out loud for all the hear, but I don't. I understand the futility of vocalizing such contradictions, for my, how they lose potency when spoken of.

NEW YORK CITY, FEBRUARY 1990

Snowflakes falling. Nothing major, just flurries. I've seen him a few times over the last months, chugging along on that damn ten speed, Groucho Marx mask on, the Chinese newspaper aimed at random souls like some supernatural holy tablet. Uptown, downtown, there he goes. Most times when I pass him there's a passenger in the back so it gives me an excuse not to stop. I keep telling myself I can't stop or I'll lose my job. I drive by because I can't afford to end up in the same boat as Andras Groff. But that's a lie. I'm avoiding him because I'm terrified he'll ask to move in with me again. And I'll have to tell him no again. I just will.

It's a little after 1am and I've just spotted Andras huddled in a shutdown store doorway on the corner of 16th and 5th. The temperature's hovering in the mid teens. I got a passenger in the back headed way out to Bay Ridge, Brooklyn so there's no chance to stop and check on my friend.

Over the next ninety minutes my fares carry me far and wide. At ten to three I come rolling into the fleet lot on 21st Street, pay my shift fees, hop on my latest rickety bike and aim for my present hidey-hole in the East Village. I swing by the storefront where I saw Andras earlier and find that he's still there. Something seems familiar about the context and then I realize it's just two blocks shy of where I first encountered him in that fight six long years ago.

He's huddled under layer upon layer of filthy coats, and rightly so, bitterly cold like it is. As I hop off my bike and approach he seems vaguely comatose. I call out his name once, twice, then on the third time that forlorn smile of his lights up his face. I sit with him, talking long enough to learn that he's lost his bike. A thief took it.

Sigh.

He retrieves a box of black pepper and a bottle of Listerine from his rag bags and offers me some, telling me a doctor prescribed a special diet for him. "This is medicine… good medicine," He tells me, "Do you want take some?" Perpetually sane person that I am, I decline.

He takes a swig of the Listerine, then pours out a handful of the pepper and tosses it back. Tears come to his eyes as he swallows. Mine too. Is that the point? When no more tears are available, do you manufacture them with Listerine and black pepper? Andras mumbles incoherently. He says I should call him "Captain Andamich" from now on. I offer him my gloves and scarf. He first refuses, then grudgingly accepts.

It's the next night. Another fourteen-hour shift is behind me. Andras is still huddled in the same doorway—I passed his wrecked form several times during my shift, so this time before I visit him I stop by a deli and grab him some real food—tuna on rye and a side of chips. He refuses it. He'll die if he abandons his special diet, he weakly asserts. The doctor, the doctor. The black pepper will make him strong.

There's not a lot to say. He pleads, asking don't I have some room at least on the floor in my apartment for him? I tell him the hard truth—I'm a guest in the place I'm staying and I'll be evicted if I bring him there. "Why not go to a homeless shelter," I ask.

"No!" his face clouds. "They…these bad mans…they kill you…for…steal your shoes—your shoes! When you sleep. Like that."

I ride away on my bike feeling like I'm missing some crucial part of the picture. I can't let him live with me and I can't help him live elsewhere. The Listerine and black pepper are taking their toll. As I weave my way home I pass that corner where I first encountered him. Then in my mind's eye I see a dim semblance of that fight—not the one between Andras and the Puerto Rican guy two blocks south, no, the first fight, the one in Amsterdam so many years before, the one where that man's back was broken.

It's a week later. A bonafide blizzard's in the works. The snow's just started coming down hard as I turn in the cab at the usual 3 am. The streets are hushed as they can only be when heavy snow falls in New York. I hit a deli and grab soup for Andras, then ride my bike down 21st Street, watching out for patches black ice hidden below the white frosting. I bend south on 5th, heading to the shutdown storefront where Andras has been residing. I find him asleep, covered with a light dusting of white flakes. No two flakes alike.

I wake him up to warn him about the blizzard, urging him to find some shelter. He's incoherent. He swings his hands at my face, telling me, no, it's too late, the doctors lock the doors after a certain hour. It's unclear if he's talking about a shelter or a hospital or maybe some orphanage back in Romania.

He scolds me, then it seems it's not me he's scolding but a nun. He tells me I shouldn't have become a man—that hits a little closer to home. Now Andras is rambling in an unknown tongue. I know if I take him to the tiny place where I live, the living room I've converted into my bedroom, my roommate from the affluent family, the one whose apartment it is, she'll kick me out. I'll be homeless just like Andras.

Again I try to get through to my friend—you have to find some cover! Go to a shelter! But no, he's too far gone, the secret diet, the orphanage, the Groucho Marx mask and Chinese newspaper, the sad spiral of events leading here have severed any ties with his ability to reason clearly.

I get on my bike, searching for a few blocks until I find a discarded cardboard refrigerator box in a dumpster. I drag it back to where he sits and try to force him to get in it, but he resists, shoving me and the box away. What can I do? I know what fury awaits me if he gets mad enough. So I just stand there, rationally explaining to him how he'll die if he doesn't get in the box. After twenty minutes I give up. I give him yet another scarf and ride away.

By morning ten inches of snow has fallen. The box is gone. And so is Andras.

KNOXVILLE, TENNESSEE, OCTOBER 1998

"They was a-fighting and a-fighting. Just right out yonder, rolling in the gutter. And that little one, he snatched that butcher knife out from under his shirt and went to jabbing with it, just a-jabbing away around the other'n's neck. And the two of them, they rolled this way and that. Then come the law and hauled the both of 'em off. Never did hear if that big one lived or died."

Walter's putting the finishing touches on an unsolicited account of a stabbing that took place directly in front of his barbershop on Central Avenue in downtown Knoxville, this particular incident having gone down some sixty years prior. "Saturday nights. Back then—ooooh-eee buddy, they was like the Wild West." Walter sighs nostalgically, seated there in his ancient barber chair, whittling a small owl out of a stob of white pine.

I find myself here in Knoxville, Tennessee as the opening act on David Byrne's big East Coast tour. I'm a guest artist, riding on David's big fancy tour bus, and we rolled into town earlier in the day. With time to kill before sound check, David and I went exploring the seedy old downtown area around Gay Street. Here we stumbled upon Walter's train wreck of misguided commerce: part barbershop, part thrift store, and, due to the presence of dozens of crudely carved, unpainted wooden owls of all shape and size scattered willy-nilly around the forward area of the shop where the barber chairs sit, part folk art emporium. The rear of the rundown storefront is crowded with chaotic shelving stacked to overflowing with what appears to be utterly worthless junk.

It's just me and Walter now. Poor David fled the premises a scant few moments into our visit after being accused by Walter of conspiring to commit petty theft. Upon entering the shop, in his inimitably quirky fashion, David enthusiastically asked the old man if he minded us looking around that back area where "all those cool piles of junk" were. Walter scowled, then flatly suggested we remove our persons from his establishment, announcing we had a shifty, shop-lifting look about us. David Byrne, unaccustomed to such rough handling, thereupon nervously excused himself from the premises.

But I stayed, and after a round of friendly jawing, Walter's grudgingly allowed me to browse. The forward aisles feature piles of cheap, wildly outdated clothing, 70's fashion rejects—many items still bearing their original discount tags. Everything's covered in a thick coat of dust. Further back among the jumbled shelves of gee-gaws and clothing I unearth an old Hohner chromatic harmonica under a pile of polyester blue jeans. I hold it up. "How much you getting on this, sir?" I ask.

Slumping a little further in his barber chair, pocket knife in hand as he continues to whittle, Walter regards me dimly. "What? Oh....that? Harmonica is it? Oh, well. I need that. It's not for sale." He recommences whittling. "Now this other time..." he intones, and there he goes, launching into another gruesome recollection.

This pattern repeats itself a dozen or more times over the next hour. Nothing, it turns out, is for sale. As I meander this way and that Walter offers up a steady stream of dreamy, horrifying monologues recounting cataclysms transpired thereabouts: stabbings, shootings, bar fights, kidnappings, patricide—scandals and heartbreak of every imaginable variety. He's a walking compendium of true crime stories and has just now finished up that tale about the small man with the butcher knife under his shirt.

Through it all Walter continually whittles. By all appearances it's an autonomic activity for him, like breathing or digestion. He was slowly, methodically whittling when we first peered in the shop window, whittling as he succeeded in running David Byrne off, whittling during his various monologues, whittling in the spaces in-between.

"You whittle all these owls yourself?" I ask, just trying to make friendly conversation. Walter sighs. He did. He whittles to pass the time he says, complaining that business is slow lately. Last ten, fifteen years.

He asks my name. When he hears the White part he cocks his head to the side and says, "White? Quite a few Whites hereabouts. You any kin to that Farrell White? Married that Harwell girl? Locksmith by trade, like his daddy was. He come downtown that Saturday afternoon with his little daughter, gonna buy her an Easter dress…" and with that Walter drifts off into his next reminiscence.

In my left coat pocket is a dog-eared copy of Cormac McCarthy's novel Suttree, which happens to be set here in Knoxville way back in the fifties. I'm not much of a planner, so to some extent or another it's sheer coincidence that it ended up in my suitcase as I packed for a tour taking me through Knoxville. Likewise I'm no great bibliophile, certainly not one of those types who might find it exhilarating to locate and use, say, the exact toilet that Jack Kerouac took a shit in while he was writing On The Road.

That said, I've read Suttree front to back many times, usually when events in my life have gone spiraling out of control and that clinical depression that's dogged me off and on for much of my adult years rears its ugly face. Things are going pretty well for me presently though, so the inclusion of Suttree in my suitcase is an aberration.

"And that poor soul, he died right there, leaning agin that light post just out yonder. His little girl by his side. Spoke not a word, did she. Cried not a tear. You any kin to that Farrell White?"

I tell Walter I'm not from Knoxville.

"Well, Knoxville. It's a good town for leaving, some say. I never left. Suits me fine."

The tenor of Walter's tales are so eerily reminiscent of Suttree's general tone that I can't help but wave the novel in his direction, asking if he's ever read it. Walter beckons me over, takes the book with shaking, liver spotted claws, studies the cover through his bifocals with some puzzlement, then replies, "Suttree?? Well, would you look at that? I'll be. Suttree wrote a book?"

Walter seems to have misunderstood my question. This is understandable. He's somewhere in that eighty to ninety year old range, one foot firmly planted in the world beyond. "Old Sut" he murmurs to himself as he returns to whittling. Likely it's a mild touch of dementia—the joys of becoming unmoored.

"No, Walter," I say, "This is a novel by a famous author. It's set here in Knoxville. The main character is called Suttree but he's not a real person."

"Suttree? Not a…what?" Walter sputters. Slouched down there in his barber chair, Walter considers this as he reaches for a new stob of white pine from a large plastic bucket next to the cash register. He's intent on whittling yet another owl I guess. "Why, of course old Sut was real. Real, as you. Real as me. Sat in this very chair, he did. Many a day. Can't cut a man's hair if he ain't real. It don't work thataway."

I'm rendered momentarily speechless by this bizarre claim.

Walter notices my silence. He gouges a considerable chunk out of the latest owl's backside then adds, "Old Sut. Paid me with a catfish one time, he did. Big old thing…" Walter gestures widely with his hands to show the length of the fish. "About yea long. Used to run his trot lines down on the river."

Trot lines.

Trot lines. The world momentarily hums and glows as I study the two words hovering in the air. Trot lines—it's an obscure fishing term, one I've heard referenced nowhere other than in McCarthy's Knoxville-based novel. Trot lines. Is Walter exhibiting some kind of second sight, or could this claim somehow be true?

"You're telling me you knew a fisherman here in Knoxville named Suttree? Cornelius Suttree…"

"Cornelius? Oh, my. Is that right? Cornelius. Hmmmph. Well, they all called him Suttree, or Sut. Course I knew his head better'n I knew him. Natural part on the left. Brush cut. Lived in a houseboat down to the river. Kept to himself. Folks said he was troubled and I guess he was. But he wasn't never no trouble to me."

Walter returns to whittling as I silently process this information. Whittle-whittle-whittle. Scrape-scrape-scrape. A scene from the novel where Suttree stops to get his hair cut springs to mind. Likely it was…here?

Good lord.

Somehow I've stumbled into the pages of my favorite novel. It's like standing in line at the supermarket and discovering the customer ahead of you is, say, Holden Caulfield, or Hazel Motes, or Boo Radley. I stare at the doorway. Suttree walked through that door. There's Walter's ancient barber chair…and so Suttree sat in that—hell, got his hair cut in that chair. I'm apparently poised at a threshold between the factual world and the fictional one.

BROWNSVILLE, FLORIDA, MAY 2003

Drenched, just soaked head to toe in this suffocating Deep South sweat. And, hell it ain't even officially summer yet—we're still weeks away. So who's idea was it for me to be slinging this bush axe for hours on end in this heat, hacking furiously away at hundreds of yards of hyperbolic Florida brambles? Not mine, that's for damn sure.

As usual, the genesis of this colossal folly stems from the mind of the Crazy Maker. After yet another incursion of crackhead zombies came ambling across her property last week she's decided it's high time to install a proper fence around the whole of her sprawling, vine-tangled acreage here in the poorest urban neighborhood in Florida.

But after receiving a minimum estimate of ten grand by a legitimate fence company to first clear a swath in this hell growth, then partition off the four acres of rolling terrain with field fence, she flip-flopped on her stance of me being Satan incarnate and, in a voice dripping with saccharine tones of affection and conciliation, informed me of her need for a secure perimeter. The fencing and posts only would come in at around $700, she coyly reported. Would I mind installing it? And would I be okay loaning her the money for the supplies? Just until her income tax check comes in…

Well aware if I say no, I'll not get to see my child in a timely fashion in the coming weeks, possibly months I grudgingly agree. And realistically speaking, a fence will enhance my child's safety, so it makes sense to just bite the bullet and dive in. But by doing so am I setting myself up for further blackmail and manipulations?

Just last week I was her sworn enemy when, after she called demanding I take off work to help rescue a stray peacock she'd heard about fifty miles due north in the middle of an Alabama swamp, I said no, that I was too busy with work. Well, she slammed the phone down halfway through the final word—how dare I refuse her? And with that my daughter became inaccessible. That's just the typical daily circus ride with Crazy Makers I guess; up we go, down we go. Rag doll this way, rag doll that.

I look back at the first hundred or so yards of cleared ground I've spent the last four days clawing/sawing/hacking my way through. Normally clearing such a dense, jungle-like expanse of foliage would require the wonders of hydraulic mechanization and internal combustion engines: bulldozers, bush hogs with chomping, grinding blades and such, but this being a discount operation, I go the old school manual route, courtesy of bush axe and machete, going at it like a some hellbent extra from Raiders of the Lost Ark.

I lay back into the wall of green, hewing further into uncharted territory as if it were some metaphor for the mind. Is it just my imagination or does this foliage, when severed with bush axe, ooze and spit, at times hissing at me as if possessing sentience and a goodly dose of antipathy at my presence here?

Though only ten in the morning the thermometer's already topping ninety fucking degrees, replete with that legendary humidity that sent the Spanish conquistadors back peddling to the Caribbean with their tails between their legs—the same pussycats who later went on to conquer a sizable chunk of South America.

It's been hand-to-hand foliage combat for these four long days, matching wits with the evil octopus of Ma Nature. Just to make matters worse, into the mix these last two days the Crazy Maker injected that horny, snaggle-toothed cracker neighbor of hers, the one who pines to get her in amorous clinches. So here I am stuck working alongside him. Maybe he views me as competition for her hand, or maybe he's just a natural-born dick, but right off he's taken to contrarying every other word I say, like he's elected himself my own personal Sheriff John Brown (see Bob Marley).

I'll say, "Tree sure is tall.", he'll look at me like I've lost my mind, then grunt "That tree? Shit. That tree ain't nothing." Or I'll say "Look at that red tail hawk". And without even looking up he'll say "That ain't no hawk." His comebacks don't appear so much to be corrections as they are rebukes for violating the manly silence with the painted whore called "talk".

Then yesterday I borrowed his snips to cut loose some rusty barbed wire from the ancient fence line collapsed in antiquity, and somewhere in the process said snips fell out of my pocket and promptly disappeared beneath the underbrush.

I went rooting around for a good half-hour hunting for them, but to no avail—it's not an orderly floor here, you drop something, it vanishes quick-like. So grudgingly I let him know. And buddy, that's when any pretense of cordiality expired. You'd think I just stabbed his favorite coon hound in the eye with a rusty ice pick.

"You know how long I had them things!" he bitched, all pissy like. "Christ! You lost my tool!" Like I misplaced his reproductive device. He stomped off, shaking his head—red-faced with heat and frustration, with having to cut fence lines with a moron. "I'm damn near sixty years old…" I heard him grumble to himself as he went lumbering out of earshot. "…I gotta put up with this shit."

Him being part Cherokee, all redneck and wielding a machete in hand, I erred on the side of caution and went wading off through the underbrush to the far end of the plum line where I commenced to defoliate in solitude.

He's steering clear of me today, so I can work in relative peace. In my head I start turning over the lyric to that song I'm working on, a morbid tune called Objects in Motion. I've been rereading this book called Einstein for Beginners, and am grafting physics theories onto romantic and emotional subject matter forms, coming up with the songwriting equivalent of a truly fucked up musical bonsai tree. I got the first verse. It goes:

Objects in Motion, tend to stay that way.
You can't waste the whole damn day
loving what you need to cast away.
Case in point, just yesterday I found
a suitcase full of love letters
floating down a cool brown river.
Unsigned and undelivered
they set my mind to wandering
as to the history of the unknown writer.
Did she marry? Did she run?
Was she old? Was the she young?
Was her heart undone by the cruel business of loving?
These objects in motion.

The song vibe feels meditative, so I decide to make that first line the hook in the song then repeat the pattern, like Jimmy Webb did with that song Galveston.

And so the day goes; hours of slinging and chopping and yanking and tugging, all the while miserably failing this paradigm of southern manhood. I go wandering further down the fence line hunting up where to dive in next when out of nowhere—OW! DAMMIT! A singularly rusty, up-facing nail attached to a ruinous rotting plank lost under the dismal carpet of moldering underbrush introduces itself to the sole of my discount work boots, penetrating through the sole and far into the deep flesh on the arch of my long white boney left foot.

Cracker hears my howl, eye rolls theatrically, then clomps over, opaquely regarding my insufficient footwear "Them ain't real work boots, you know". He mutters, showing me his manly boots just to drive his point home.

I remove the boot, bloody nail still intact in it, and study the ragged puncture wound. Cracker sniffs condescendingly, asking, what, do I need an ambulance? Hard to tell if he's serious or just jerking my chain, so just to show him I say fuck it and limp on, toiling through the rest of the afternoon.

So now it's just past midnight. I'm in the ER, my foot aching pretty bad. The nice lady ER doc gives me a little chastising head-shake, then breaks the news to me that dirty wounds do best when promptly probed and cleaned—her line delivered like some Aesopian moral. She then commences with an extended round of said probing and cleaning. I limp out two hours later half crippled—the cure far worse than the affliction.

53.1424° N, 7.6921° W, APRIL 2007

Am I the only misbegotten soul on the whole of this giant aluminum sausage not constituted for sleeping on fast moving airborne objects? Apparently so. I ease up the window shade and study the horizon. The creeping hand of dawn appears off in the east, just now working its fingertips around curvature of the earth. An hour ahead lies Glasgow, Scotland, where they got me lined up to play some high profile Americana music festival tomorrow night.

These folks are paying top dollar for sixty minutes of my off-key singing and generalized bullshitting, so I been working up a few musical rabbits to pull out of various hats.

I'm not sure why, but when I wrote up the setlist I decided it should include that river song, the one I wrote back there when I was hacking out the Crazy Maker's fence line. The dark fatalistic story-song lyrics to Objects in Motion came in a rush, fully formed over a brief span of an hour, but the musical accompaniment never did add up to much.

Around that time I was having another one of my occasional musical nervous breakdowns where, excepting variations of A and E chords, I could not for the life of me summon up a succession of notes that sounded right one up against the next. So the melody just rocks back and forth between those two utterly rudimentary guitar chords. Despite the lackluster melody I recorded Objects for my last proper studio album.

Ah, the hilarity.

As fate would have it, my producer buddy Tucker wrangled legendary guitar virtuoso Bill Frisell to play the guitar part, which was tantamount to buying a supercharged Lamborghini to ride out to the end of your dirt driveway to check your mailbox once a month. Hats off to Mr. Frisell—he did just fine rendering those A and E chords, but nobody seemed to care much about that song. I never heard any mention of it in album reviews, nobody ever called out for it during a show.

The album it was on, Drill a Hole In That Substrate and Tell Me What You See (yes, named in honor of that furious foreman who couldn't find his missing standpipe), came and went, forgotten under the avalanche of modern music that besieges the average listener's ears daily.

But I'm proud of those lyrics and always wanted to play that tone-poem style song live somewhere. Problem is, in rehearsals it tended to sound more like Othello recited by Pee Wee Herman, instead of Paul Robeson, so I mothballed it. But I figure it can't hurt to trot it out for the Scots. They talk funny to begin with over there, love a good morbid tale and have always been forgiving of my many musical shortcomings.

I set to work trying to formulate a presentable live shape and form for the song using loops and echoes. Being that I'm not a natural born performer and often can't recall my own damn lyrics, I've made myself a CD with the show songs on it and have been listening to the final rehearsal version of Objects in Motion incessantly over and over during this long commute to higher latitudes, driving the song deep into the recesses of my psyche until the words get fully committed to muscle memory. I close my eyes and quietly sing along…

> *Objects in motion tend to stay that way…*
> *or so I learned on the riverbank just yesterday*
> *for shortly thereafter I beheld as if in a dream*
> *the body of a young woman adrift*
> *beneath the surface of the cool brown water.*
> *My friend, so unnerved was I by this cruel apparition*
> *that I let loose of that suitcase and it tumbled right back in the river.*
> *Then spellbound I watched as a halo of love letters*
> *formed a circle on the surface of the water right over her body*
> *then drifted away.*
> *These objects in motion…*

Of course the genesis of this particular song is no big secret to me. I got my fill of Ophelia-dead-in-the-river imagery during those eighteen arduous months of cohabitating with the Crazy Maker. Romanticized variations of Hamlet's lost love as a river-borne corpse were everywhere in our house, imprinting onto my already wildly damaged psyche.

When we split up and she was moving her considerable inventory to the crack neighborhood house I put out a call for helping hands to load out all her exotic and highly fragile antiques. This old friend I hadn't talked to in years, now a hard core fundamentalist preacher, stopped by to help with the hefting. He took one look at all her morbid interior decor and promptly shivered head to toe, proclaiming the house marked by signs of witchcraft.

Ah, home.

In the distance as the sky brightens I can just make out the dim outline of Scotland and know Glasgow is now only a handful of minutes away. Better hunker down here and get to my silent mental practicing. The final verse coalesces well.

> *Objects in motion tend to stay that way*
> *you can't waste the whole damn day*
> *loving what you need to cast away.*
> *For from the flame of love*

comes the cinder of regret…
sometimes the thing you cling to most
is the thing you'd best forget.
Yes sometimes the thing you cling to most
is the thing you'd best forget.
These objects in motion….

The big aluminum sausage alights in Glasgow with a gentle thump. Jet lag's nipping at my heels already, but thankfully I go sailing all easy breezy through customs and am greeted VIP style at baggage claim by one of the music festival organizers. First class treatment! It's a far cry from those ignominious New York cabbie days. Now I'm the client!

The festival's putting me up in some posh hotel downtown and on the way in from the airport the friendly promoter gives me the rundown of my schedule: time of performance, press obligations, guest passes, catering options. He's excited about me seeing the very special venue he personally picked for my show, a new operation called The Renfrew Ferry.

The mention of a ferry puts me in mind of that iconic Gerry & Pacemakers song Ferry Cross the Mersey, and as that sublime melody goes dancing through my head, opening doors in dusty back rooms of consciousness, just offhandedly I ask him why they named it The Renfrew Ferry.

The promoter cheerfully reports it's an actual decommissioned ferry boat docked at a pier on the River Clyde. River Clyde? My ears perk up at that, as that river song I'm doing is wedged in my mind and such incidents are seldom simply random. I don't burden him with the backstory, but mention how it's interesting that I'll be playing my river-themed death song for the first time ever live and it's coincidentally on a stage in the middle of a river. He's not especially impressed.

Promoter drops me at this highbrow hotel. My swanky room up on the Executive Level is a top shelf fifteenth floor palace, a spacious, airy room with a view featuring modernistic surfaces of impersonal, highly polished planes and geometric forms amidst tastefully restrained textile patterns. I'm a blue collar musician twenty-four hours into my commute and so could give a shit about what the room looks like. What I'm interested in is a thing called sleep.

I beeline it to capacious shower then hit the sack, flicking on the TV in the process, hoping to unwind a bit with the local news channel before I nod off. Not much happening in Glasgow. Wee this and wee that. I listen for a while then nod off. Sleep is good. Even at eleven am…

Where am I? Oh shit, Glasgow! But what's that sound? Sirens? It's night time and I'm waking to the sound of sirens? That can't be good. Near? Is the hotel on fire? Maybe. In the distance, sirens now drawing closer, closer, then whoosh, on they go, racing on past this hotel. Whew.

Out the window I spy several cop cars converging a half mile or so off on a quay alongside the River Clyde. In the background now I hear on TV the news lady saying something about a murder, a body, and the river. As is often the case, I wonder am I dreaming.

From the eerie glow on the TV screen, I behold a jumble of images; rescue boats, flashing search lights, a bridge, and in the distance, a ferry boat docked at the quay. Could that be the Renfrew Ferry where I'll be playing in a few hours? Framed in this surreal criminal context? Goddamn, it is. The broadcaster reports the searchers have recovered a young woman's naked body, found adrift in the river a mere hundred yards from the Renfrew Ferry.

Holy shit.

She's someone's daughter, sister, wife, lover. Was it her I saw in my mind's eye four years earlier as I was hacking away at the vines on The Crazy Makers property? If so, that's beyond baffling, mainly because that means the fictional song I imagined in my head was actually reporting on something…real?

Holy shit again.

Then—ba-bing! A huge quasi-mystical schematic comes flying fully formed into my head.

Picture this hypothetical:

Part 1: In the here and now you're reading page so and so of this book, right? So at this exact moment your eyes are moving in a linear fashion left to right over a series of shapes and forms called "letters" written in a language called "English". Your brain is effortlessly converting these abstract forms into clusters of meaning, right? Let's just go ahead and accept this as a baseline reality. You just read the term "baseline reality", right?

Part 2: Now imagine you're reading a slightly different book. It's called The Book of Your Life. Presently you're reading page whatever (depends on how old you are, and how much life you've led) of said book, which chronicles this exact same moment that you're reading the lines I just mentioned in this actual physical book.

But here's the twist: in Part 2 you're seated by an open window and it's a gusty day outside. Suddenly an unexpected blast of wind comes whipping through said window and—whoosh—it ruffles the pages of the Book of Your Life, you were on page 142, but the gust flips the pages ahead a couple of chapters to, say, page 397.

Your eyes alight briefly on this new page featuring text just chock-a-block full of details describing some random moment that exists in your future. It's a fleeting glimpse, happening so fast you only manage to catch one little fragment of a passage on this new page. It's some innocuous passage, like maybe, "And then the yellow cat jumped off the roof of the moving car and…" whereupon the wind backs off and the pages in The Book of Your Life flip back to the here and now; page 142. All contextual information surrounding the yellow cat from page 397 has vanished and you've resumed reading in a linear fashion these lines that I've written in this book called Incidental Contact. Got it?

Part 3: Regarding the gust of wind and glimpse into the future it afforded you: you know something important has just occurred, that somewhere in your future there's a yellow cat on a moving car, but the implications are wildly unclear—why? Because you have no contextual foundation to integrate that vignette into your understanding, right? All that you know is that eventually in the future the significance of this yellow cat on the moving car will be revealed, but only after, in a linear fashion, you work your way up to page 397 in the Book of Your Life. Since you're sure that up to this point there's been no mention of yellow cats jumping off moving cars in the story of your existence, you accept that this information is some small piece of a mysterious future based puzzle.

But here's where things get complicated: the little computer in your brain, that wondrous entity that likes to believe it's controlling your actions, it now insists on reconciling and integrating that previsioned tidbit of future information into your present understanding. So what do you do with the information fragment about the yellow cat and the moving car? If you're like me, like most artist types, you fabricate a narrative that aims to make sense of fleeing images that you briefly glimpsed. So is that what the Objects in Motion song is, me making sense of a premonition of this woman's death? It's possible.

Part 4: For most sane human beings the notion of such temporospatial jostling is unsettling, unwelcome, and so the grounded, mainstream folk, they tend to avoid such psychic windows, particularly on windy days, to insure no further gusts ruffle the pages of the Book of Their Life. They build houses without windows and unerringly gravitate toward a typical linear approach to information gathering and processing. And so, line by line they continue consuming the story of their lives until suddenly they reach page 397 and—bing-bang-boom—there it is; the yellow cat, the moving car and the denouement.

As for me, I've always lived in a house with many open windows. And so the wind has always blown my pages. And frankly, I wouldn't know how to move to a sheltered position, some Valhalla free of such winds, if my life depended on it. I'm just not made that way.

So, did I envision some stylized variation of this poor woman dead in the river all those years ago? And so was it the same when I saw that scene from Crimes & Misdemeanors on the side of the skyscraper and then later that day crossed paths with Woody

Allen? And what about with Beckett and David Byrne and all the other events I've spoken of? Has "future me" been in contact with "present me" and slipped him little tidbits of guidance, related information that lead me to this daisy chain of exceptional coincidences? It's possible.

But wait, is this even a viable metaphor? Can a person's life be like a book, already written from conception to extinction, no change, no choice, just and endless stream of words locked in place from womb to tomb? Sounds vaguely like old fashioned fatalism, right?

Well, sorry friends, don't blame this whackadoodle theory on me. This notion comes to you not via my screwy cranium, but courtesy of folks like Albert Einstein, Richard Feynman, and Steven Hawking, all of whom posit that all time exists simultaneously. It's their works that I'm riffing on to substantiate the supporting mechanics of this far-out Book of Your Life hypothetical.

Some physicists call it Spacetime Theory, others prefer Block Universe Theory and it's not just Einstein and the other two. According to a broad array of freaking geniuses, both past and present, time is not linear, nor is our three-dimensional reality configured as we perceive it to be. It only appears as such to us due to the severe limitations of our tiny human brains.

This new paradigm posits that reality is in fact, a four-dimensional structure, where every event, past, present, future, has its own coordinates in the enigma known as "Spacetime". And all points (past, present, future) in "Spacetime" have always and will always exist.

Strangely, when I read about Block Universe Theory my brain leapfrogs over to that Bible passage in Revelations where God is proclaimed to be "the first and the last, the Alpha and the Omega" which is an interesting set of qualities when considered in a "Spacetime" context. And in Luke we read, "Every hair on your head is numbered...", meaning what? Predetermined? Hmmmm. Basically it sounds like the Bible's describing God as a four-dimensional construct.

So, if I'm understanding this concept correctly, then the implication is that everything—the day you're born, the day you die, every thought you'll ever have, every hiccup or windfall you'll ever experience—it's already in existence, written there in the Book of Your Life.

That flat tire you'll get three years from now? It's already happened up ahead on page 412. But you won't know about it until you're reading page 411 and hear the whomp-whomp-whomp sound as you're tooling down the highway. And unless some chimeric gust flips the pages of the Book of Your Life and you catch a glimpse of the future pages, that's how the experience will unfold for you.

The vast majority of human beings perceive time in a singularly 3D, linear form. But are there people who are wired differently? Ones who are capable of, for lack of a better term, 4D perception? Maybe like psychics and mystics and mediums and such?

Is there some way to flip forward through those enigmatic pages in the Book of Your Life or other individuals' books and catch glimpses of respective futures? And could a person possibly somehow engineer psychic flashes by purposefully situating themself near one of those mysterious open windows where unsettling winds come blowing in? Wait for the gusts to come, then take notes on the flashes of information on the future pages they behold? Is that what oddballs like Nostradamus did?

This line of thinking circles the conversation back around to Marconi and the notion of WYOU, WWTF, etc. Alongside his radio wave theory Marconi posited that, since sound waves never die, every sound ever made still exists, albeit at radically diminished levels that no creature can apprehend. And were humans able to develop the technology, we could in theory still apprehend, say, the Sermon on the Mount, or the final song played by the orchestra on the Titanic as it sank, as Marconi dreamed of.

Extrapolating on that idea, that means not only are folks like me picking up broadcasts from WYOU on our own personalized frequencies, but we're also recipients of random future-based broadcasts emanating from other stations, WOAH, WWTF, etc.

The tricky aspect lies in the fact that such esoteric broadcasts are not conventionally accessible. You can only hear those freaky esoteric stations when you have a few mental wires crossed, and even then only when conditions are just so.

Which brings us to the Dr. Demento Show.

As a teenage counter-culture dope head, on weekends me and my pot smoking buddies would drive out to the tall bluffs overlooking Escambia Bay and there attempt to dial in the Dr. Demento Hour midnight radio show broadcast.

The Doctor Demento Hour came via a distant 50,000-watt station called KAAY, broadcasting out of Little Rock, Arkansas. The signal only reached as far as the Florida Panhandle on certain random clear winter nights.

Being offbeat hippie types, me and my buddies were hungry to get clued in on counter-culture movements and entertainment existing elsewhere in more progressive areas of the country via these distant broadcasts. But the only way to apprehend it back then was this quasi-alchemic approach of waiting on the bluffs on cold clear winter nights when the transmissions could travel further than normal.

This childhood memory is likely the origin of my previously mentioned psychic antenna theory. My guess is that I possess some manner of antenna that every once in a while picks up enigmatic transmissions, and that's what accounts for my frequent encounters with synchronicity.

Back to Scotland. I watch as another pod of police cars come racing past as a line from Static on the Radio comes flying into my head…

Now there's a church house about a stone's throw
from this place where I've been staying.
It's Sunday morning and I'm sitting in my truck
listening to my neighbors sing.
Ten years ago I might have joined in
but don't time change those inclined
to think less of what is written
than what's wrote between the lines?

Yep, maybe that's it: maybe my internal receiver is configured more to receive what's transmitted between the lines than the primary signal.

Suddenly in my mind's eye, there she is, Bahar, that beautiful psychic I picked up in my cab. Remember how on our ride into Manhattan, mid-sentence she suddenly closed her eyes, concentrating real hard then said, "I'm getting information about you…"? Then she spoke about the blonde woman with the blonde daughter. But at that point the only blonde woman I knew who fit the description had a blonde son, and since that didn't coincide with her vision I labeled Bahar a fake. But flip ahead ten years and here's the Crazy Maker, a blonde woman, with my daughter, who's a blonde girl. Hm-mmm. I figured Bahar was talking about my past, but who's to say she wasn't seeing into my future?

So now here I am in Glasgow, watching this news report chronicling the recovery of the dead woman in the river. And there's that dead woman in the river song I inexplicably decided to sing for the first time at my upcoming concert.

And rivers—of course! Rivers are a recurring theme in the Book of My Life saga. Most of these coincidental events I've described happened in Manhattan, a city surrounded by rivers. So is that locality my own personal "open window" where the winds fluff pages?

During my darkest days in New York I'd forlornly walk the banks of the East River in the New York, sit on the promenade railing and wistfully regard the furious swirling currents below, all the while working out the math of my potential suicide by drowning. The river was calling…I could all but hear it.

And that book that saved my life, Suttree, it begins on a river in Knoxville with a body being pulled from it. Yes—rivers are somehow integral to the physics at play here, both literal rivers and figurative ones.

Once in the cab at the peak of a hellacious blizzard I picked up a passenger headed over to Brooklyn Heights. It was past midnight and by then there wasn't a soul on the road other than me. I had to drop the guy several blocks from his place because the streets were becoming impassible, then I eased around, avoiding the snowdrifts and such, and deadheaded back toward Manhattan.

Halfway across the empty Brooklyn Bridge suddenly I got hit by a crazy urge. There was no one around. Not a soul. So dead center in the middle of the bridge I stopped the cab and got out. I was immediately immersed in the muffled stillness. The view was breathtaking.

I walked over to the edge of the roadway, stepped up on the I-beam that formed the outer arc of the bridge and peered over the edge, down-down-down, watching the snowflakes go dancing onward toward the pitch black surface of the East River far below. The urge to follow those snowflakes was so powerful. I so deeply desired to just go, become one with the water below. I stood there a couple minutes, running the suicide scenario through my mind then laughed about the idea of my empty cab being found—how inexplicable! That would be some serious front page news. What outrageous urban myth would arise from my exotic departure? Aliens? Cult? CIA?

But I didn't jump. The laughter brought me back, so instead I opted for a secondary route at becoming one with the water. I took a piss, watching as the yellow stream exited my body and drifted downward, disintegrating into the haze below. I stood there a minute afterward then heard a fully formed phrase uttered in my mind. I'd never read it, never heard it before. It just materialized out of the ether.

"Can an echo move backwards in time?" I heard that inner voice ask.

It seemed ludicrous at the time. I had no idea what it even meant, but after reading about Block Universe Theory, it turns out the answer is actually yes, an echo can theoretically move backwards in time.

See, presently the universe is expanding, but since the theories of The Big Bang and entropy have been proven and are widely accepted, we know that the expansion of the universe will one day cease, and at that point scientists are betting it'll start to contract. When it does, time will commence running in reverse and hence, echoes will move backwards in time.

Freaky shit.

NEW YORK CITY, JANUARY 1986

Old timer Larry Zeitz is holding court in the shape-up room, blasting out one bizarre taxi story after another, made all the more gritty and surreal by his good-natured, yet cynical tone delivered via that heavy Bronx accent: cons, assaults, babies being born, half-naked lovers hard at it in the back seat, passengers hurling human excrement at him ("They carried it around in a fucking baggie!" he howls), celebrities he's picked up, then celebrities who actually once drove a cab at this very fleet.

There's Danny Sullivan, the Indy car racer, who honed his chops racing up and down the streets of Manhattan in an Ann's Service cab, then a string of minor actors I never heard of. The Coen Brothers used to tend bar around the corner. He calls out a string of visual artists and musicians that sound vaguely familiar but when he chirps out Phillip Glass's name my ears perk up.

Really? That guy I heard on the BBC? And who also worked at Food restaurant? Do I feel my psychic antenna twitching to life here?

Larry dives into a story about how "Phil" was still driving a taxi at Ann's when Einstein on the Beach debuted and became a smash hit up at Lincoln Center. Larry claims "Phil" used to sit outside Lincoln Center when the performance was letting out and pick up highbrow New Yorkers then eavesdrop on their reaction to his masterwork. Larry claims an aristocratic lady leaving the performance once noticed "Phil's" name on the hack license and said, "Oh, driver, what an amusing coincidence. You have the same name as an exciting young composer. I've just been to see his opera. It's breathtaking. You must go see it!" To which "Phil", ever the minimalist, is reported to have replied, "Oh."

So, here's that damn Phillip Glass again. He was in Holland playing on the radio as I tried to reassemble the broken mirror. He worked down in Soho at Food Restaurant, where I was employed for a couple years, and now here I am, following along in another of his geo-points. So…what's the connection—is it random chance? Am I coasting in his slipstream? Are we fated to meet? Will I one day run over him in my cab? Is this apophenia, synchronicity, fate, or just my imagination?

I jot down Phil's name in my notebook, then attempt to sketch out a diagram of our mutual paths. Let's see, first contact was in Holland, but only sonically—does that count? Then we were both physically in Food Restaurant and Ann's Taxi Service and subsequently circling the streets of New York in similar patterns at similar speeds. How would you diagram that? The two-dimensional sketch fails to even remotely capture what interests me in our interrelationship. Geographically we've been in similar exact locations, but our socioeconomic and cultural status is disparate; he's way up there, and I'm sitting on the bottom of the world.

I'm frowning at the insufficiencies of my sketch when I hear Marty, the misanthropic dispatcher, grunt out my name over the PA. I give up on the diagramming. Marty shoves me a set of keys and a trip sheet through the grimy slot in the bulletproof glass and off I go, arrowing into the uncontrolled mayhem of rush hour.

It's a Tuesday night in the early fall and so the city isn't especially lively. Fares come and go until around 11:20. The streets empty out and I find myself crawling around the semi-treacherous side streets of Alphabet City where I resort to fare hunting only when the main avenues are massively overloaded with empty yellows. I run South on Avenue B, then, banking west on 7th Street by the Horseshoe Bar, I spy a prospective fare.

She's on foot on the sidewalk, heading for Avenue A, where cabs are more abundantly available. She's clearly moving at that determined, "I'm looking for a cab" pace and as I slow to get a better look at her, I see that I actually recognize her—she was my passenger once before. I picked her up on this very block six months back. Just like last time she's dressed head to toe in combat fatigues. I slow as I pass, giving her a little toot on the horn. She pulls up short, sees that I'm stopping for her, raises her hand in the hail position as she beelines it for the back door.

In she hops, and just like the previous ride, right away the spiel kicks in. "Driver," She says, "I'm going a very short distance but I'll make this trip worth your while…" So, she doesn't remember me. I slide open the partition and kinda bored say, "Like how? Asking me the definition of the word funambulist?"

She's wearing the same mirrored aviator glasses and ball cap as last time so it's hard to read her expression, but she sucks in a breath and winces slightly, apparently not liking that I got the jump on her. Yep, I remember from last time how she likes to be in control.

"No…" she comes back, somewhat warily. "You correctly defined that word last time and it cost me some money…"

A few months back this same exotic fringe-dwelling human being hailed me right here and gave me a similar opening line, only she was headed up to midtown. "The destination is 45th and 9th." She said in a clipped, clinical tone, adding, "At the beginning of the fare your tip is ten dollars. For every red light you hit along the route I subtract one dollar from that sum. If you hit more than ten red lights you get no tip. That's it. Now, let's go."

I like games and so did a quick tally in my head, counting roughly fifty traffic lights along the way. Since it was late and the streets were empty I knew using my crosstown interval system I could get to 45th St. and 9th Avenue hitting maybe one or two red lights max, the first being the transition from 7th St to 1st Avenue, just a few blocks ahead.

So I said, "Okay, hang on!" and gunned it up to 1st Avenue, turned north there and hit that first red light at 8th St. "Your tip is now nine dollars…" She calmly reported, an undertone of superior satisfaction in her voice. I thought, "Uh-huh. We'll see how long that lasts…"

I ran with the wave of synchronized lights up 1st Avenue, which is no big deal—the lights on most of the big north/south avenues are roughly synchronized. But rather than just roll straight ahead unimpeded to 45th St then head west, thereby hitting five to seven lights moving across the island of Manhattan, I banked left on 17th St and floored it, hoping for no obstructions or slow drivers.

"Hey, why are you turning here?" She said, real chippy like.

"You never said what route I had to take, right? So I'm taking the most expedient route. Get ready to fork over that nine dollar tip." I said, laughing.

Momentarily stymied by my self-assured tone, she quickly regrouped. Then, seeing me make the light at 2nd Avenue and watching as the light at 3rd went green just as we hit it, she realized I had a system and so tried to distract me.

"Okay. Second game. We're going to do some definitions. For every word you correctly identify I will give you a dollar. For every word you get wrong I subtract fifty cents from your tip. Agreed?"

I like words and was feeling pretty cocky, so I said, "Sure, fire away."

The first word was "valetudinarian". I had not a clue what it meant. I stalled, buying time so that she couldn't whittle my tip down too fast. We raced through the green lights at Lexington and Irving Place whereupon I reported I didn't know that word. She delivered a remarkably succinct definition as I blasted across Park, and Broadway, then said, "Your tip is now $8.50."

The second word was "Xanthippe" which I thought I meant "philosopher's wife", but it didn't. She fired off the corrected definition then subtracted another fifty cents off my tip as I hurtled across 6th and 7th Avenue. Hitting that long 7th to 8th stretch I saw the crosswalk lights start to blink early—is that 8th Avenue light out of synch? You typically get eleven blinks crosstown and nine blinks uptown/downtown. I counted, one… two…three, did the triangulations and knew it was gonna be tight. If I got caught by that stop light that meant it would cost me two red lights, because I'd turn the corner and then hit the light on 8th. That's two dollars lost, plus it'd give her two more minutes to ask me definitions to bizarro words I'd never heard of.

Just as I floored it she chimed in with the third word, "funambulist". The light was switching from yellow to red just as I banked hard around the corner at 17th and 8th. I slowed slightly so the light at 18th and 8th could pop to green just as I hit it then smiled and said, "Funambulist: tightrope walker." That puts my tip back up to nine bucks and there's no more red lights in our path.'

She sat silently watching the synchronized lights on 8th flip green, green, green until I banked left on 45th and, pacing myself on the block, I approached the corner slowing slightly until that signal turned green. I pulled over and threw the meter. The fare was $6.75, but with the $9 tip the total was $15.75. I did the tally for her and she coldly handed me a twenty then counted her change twice after I passed it to her, leaving the cab without another word. Sore loser?

So here she sits in the back of my cab again just these few months later. What are the odds? The intervals wherein people are looking for cabs is typically fairly short and there are thousands of cabs in motion, so this is likely more than just a coincidence.

She studies me hard, as I do her in return. She's shortish, slim, nicely proportioned, rugged looking with high cheekbones and full lips. Under all that camouflage clothing, ball cap and teardrop sunglasses I detect an extremely attractive woman lurking. "The destination is 137 1st Avenue. Do you know where that is?" She asks pointedly.

Of course I do. It's three blocks away, mid-block on the East side of 1st Avenue. "Don't feel like walking tonight? That's just around the corner." I throw the meter and start rolling west toward Avenue A.

"I have another game for you.", she says, ignoring my question. "Are you interested in playing?"

"Sure. Especially if it gets me a nine dollar tip." I say, already nearing 1st Avenue as she launches into the new spiel.

"You're a woman and you live with a dangerous man—a man many people fear. He's a paid assassin and has killed many people. He's a friend and ally to powerful individuals in government and on the police force. He's your boyfriend and is beating you regularly. You're afraid for your life and want to leave him but fear he'll kill you if you try to go. So, what do you do?"

We're rolling up to the doorway of 137 1st Avenue as she finishes this hypothetical. Clearly she's talking about herself in some thinly veiled form. If true, this kicks the stakes of the conversation up pretty high. I sit for a second, then say, "Shit. I'm sorry—there's no easy answer to that question. I guess I lose this game." I throw the meter adding, "That's a buck-fifty."

She studies me a moment then hands me a ten dollar bill and says, "No, that's a good answer. Keep the change. Your tip is eight dollars and fifty cents. If within a period of thirty minutes you can think of a better answer, return to this address, ring buzzer 1B and ask for Cheri—that's me—and tell me your improved answer. If it makes sense I'll give you another fifty dollars on top of this. Agreed?"

What?

I agree and then, like the wind, she's gone.

Off I drive, arrowing up 1st Avenue, merging into the huge, ravening pack of empty cabs hunting our next fare. The city's dead—everyone's home for the night, so I zig-zag left and right, slow and fast all the way up to 55th Street but nobody hails me, so I bank left and bust a move west toward 2nd Avenue. 55th between 2nd and 3rd is badly backed up, a dozen empty cabs stuck behind a garbage truck, so no choice there—I bang another left and find myself heading straight back toward where I just came from—the East Village. I lay at the back of the pack of cabs, running with the changing yellow lights down 2nd Ave, finally catching the red at 34th Street.

No fares materialize out of the Murray Hill theater or from any of the businesses around it, so I keep heading south. Twelve, maybe fourteen minutes have passed and suddenly I find myself cruising empty a few blocks from where I dropped this lady, Cheri. I'm a little scared of her, scared of her apparent insanity, terrified of her imaginary hitman boyfriend, but I feel an inexplicable magnetism pulling me back to 137 1st Avenue. Is it really just that promise of $50?

No, it's attractive because it's mysterious and I'm not doing anything productive anyway, so why resist? I have no new improved answer for her, at least not in words. But simply by returning am I providing her with an answer? I guess I'll find out.

I double park the cab outside the building, run up and ring buzzer 1B. A brusque sounding woman who's not Cheri answers. I tell her I was Cheri's cab driver and need to talk to her. "She's crying and can't come right now." the woman flatly reports. There's a pause as I hear mumbled discussion in the background, then she adds "Can you wait a few minutes?"

Of course I can.

Three or four minutes later Cheri appears. Her face is red and flushed. There's telltale signs of tears running down her cheeks. She climbs in the back of the cab. "So? What's the answer?" She asks.

"I still don't have an answer," I say, then an idea pops in my mind. "...but I thought it might help you to see the river. Sometimes seeing moving water helps me think."

"Water's a negative ion environment.", she remarks off handedly, as if this is the most self-evident fact in the entire universe. "It stimulates the pituitary gland to create endorphins. I studied negative ion theory when I was at NASA. Part of an effort to reduce pilot error."

Okay. I can honestly say that's the last thing I expected to hear. "So…then you're okay with me driving you down by the East River?"

She thinks it over then says, "Okay. You're on. Water. You want me to see water. But that won't get you the fifty dollars, understood?"

"Yeah. I'm okay with that." I slip the cab in gear and aim for 14th Street.

As I ease back into the traffic flow she says, "So you're too smart to be a cab driver. What did you do before this?"

I first report that I was a fashion model in the early 80's, to which she replies "Back in the seventies I was in the fashion business. Too short for runway and editorial so I did hand modeling mostly, for big cosmetic campaigns. My rate was $650 a session. No hourly rate, just a flat $650 take it or leave it. What agency were you with?"

Lots to process here. If she was a hand model making $650 a session in the seventies then she was a top shelf model. I tell her I was with an offshoot of Wilhelmina, which at the time was one of the biggest modeling agencies in the world. Cheri knows all about Wilhelmina, knew Wilhelmina herself before she died, knows all about my little offshoot agency and names a couple of bookers there just to prove it. She knows modeling rates for catalog versus editorial, casting protocols, the whole nine yards. In other words, she's not bullshitting here. "But modeling is for suckers. You've had some excellence in your life. Not modeling. What was it?"

Jesus.

So I tell her about being a pro surfer and my time in Hawaii. Cheri asks which island I lived on so I tell her. She knows Oahu well enough to give me a vivid description of the block I worked on, Piikioi Street, in downtown Honolulu.

She asks more questions and it turns out Cheri knows a lot about everything. It's fucking scary. She fires a few more rounds at me cross-examination style then, after answering them as best I can she starts berating me for using poor logic forms in my replies. She confidently tosses out a string of phrases like "risky epistemic" and "conditional claims" and "impeccable inferences."

By way of explanation she says her second husband was one of the world's foremost linguists and taught her the various logic forms and fallacies said forms point out. My language, she claimed, was full of fallacies. "But you show potential…" she added cryptically.

I roll down 14th Street and bank left on Avenue C, hitting on-ramp to the FDR Drive, which runs along the East River. As she catches sight of the moonlight on the water she sighs and says, "So. Water…at NASA we developed this negative ion protocol in conjunction with a nutrient called NRSL. It's secret. Nobody knows about it. We found that increasing catecholamine levels combined with a diet high in soy based proteins enhanced alertness levels and, when properly integrated into a diet and exercise regime, reduced pilot error to nearly zero."

She goes quiet for a second then says, "Ralph would kill you if he knew we were talking like this. He's very jealous."

Oh yeah, so Ralph is his name. But is Ralph real? Or is this lady completely fucking nuts? Or could it be both? Hard to say. I keep coming at her with questions about random remarks she makes about places people, but she's infallible. It's beyond uncanny—it's verging on supernatural.

We roll south from 18th Street on the FDR down to Grand Street, a distance of a couple miles, then I circle back through Alphabet City as Cheri alternates between reminiscing about various NASA projects and firing off more personal questions about my life, like she's interviewing me for a job. It's the most intense grilling I've ever experienced and it's starting to eat at me in a worrisome way.

Side by side I also feel an intense sense of connection to Cheri, like our stars are somehow crossed—not romantically, more like our meeting is fated. Twenty minutes into our ride I roll up to the place I picked her up initially by the Horseshoe Bar and ease to a stop.

"What? Why are we stopping?" She asks, bowing up a bit.

"A circle. We've come in a full circle. We're back to where we started and I still don't have an answer for you, but I need to get back to work. I figured seeing the river might ease your mind."

Cheri says, "Look at me." She leans forward and removes her mirrored teardrop glasses. Despite the black eye and bruises, she's quite beautiful. Almost breathtakingly so. "I'm not lying. And you're such a chickenshit, do you know that? You know who I am and I know who you are. You know as much as I do that we need to talk, so—okay, look at it this way; take this as a business proposition. What do you gross for an hour of driving?"

"Twenty, maybe twenty-five if I'm lucky."

"You're such a chickenshit!" she barks out, exasperated, "Just say twenty-five, okay?" I shrug. This is getting way beyond my ability to process. "So I'll pay you twenty-five dollars an hour to continue to talk with me. But we'll need to find a discrete place. I want to sit somewhere where I have your full attention, not driving a cab, so it needs to be far away from here so Ralph won't find out. If Ralph sees you with me you're dead."

Fuck that, I think to myself. If I hide then I'm complicit in a deception, and therefore opening myself up to the consequences. "But, if we go far away, then Ralph will definitely see us." I say, "That's just how things work. What about if we go up to the corner here and sit in that big picture window of the Sidewalk Restaurant where everyone can see us. If we're obvious enough, then maybe we'll be harder to see. Right?"

She's thinking it over. She laughs sadly—like it hurts, like a cough—then says, "You know what? I was right. You do have potential."

It's just past midnight when we take our seat in the bay window of the legendary Sidewalk Cafe, her in her camo attire and me in my sweaty, stinky shabby cab driving clothes. We're two furiously out of place souls plopped in the middle of hipster central. The Pyramid Club's directly across the street, King Tut's Wah-Wah Hut's just down the block, and sailing by the window is and endless counterculture cavalcade of punks and mods and cross dressers in platform shoes. There's sexy bar hoppers and club kids and aging losers who got stranded in the hipster mode too long and all of them are just breezing by. But I take no great notice of them, nor does Cheri.

We order some fries and drinks then dive into deep focus verbal communion. I do my best to hold up my end of the conversation, but increasingly get shut down every time I try to make a salient comment.

It's got to the point now where I'll open my mouth, about to speak, and she'll anticipate me breaking her monologue rhythm and say, "I know, I know, I know what you're going to say…" then she'll tell me exactly what I'm about to say. It's just utterly uncanny. She's channeling some kind of psychic nitroglycerin and has just now gone on a ten-minute jag about the origins of fine art photography, which I actually know a thing or two about.

I'm tired of listening so I interrupt her, asking her if she's familiar with The Light Gallery, the first art gallery in New York to regard photography as an art form rather than simple mechanical representation.

She half-sighs, half-scowls, calls me chickenshit for doubting her, then explains how she helped co-found The Light Gallery, whereupon she drops the names of all the luminary photographers associated with the place, facts I know from my photo history studies; Garry Winnograd, Andres Kertesz and more, describing them intimately, closing out with a bit about her friend, French photographer Lucien Clergue. I'm familiar with Clergues' sublime black and white portrait work with nudes so I ask Cheri if she's ever seen them. Not only has she seen them, she was one of Clergue's models.

Of course.

Pretty soon I just give up and it's only her talking; long elaborate jags, the information flying at me pop-pop-pop-pop, faster and faster, like machine gun fire. I'm struggling just to keep up with even processing the bizarre torrent of information that I'm being force fed. There's just no way to comment intelligently.

She keeps circling back to how I'm crippled by my own damn cowardice and how I'll never amount to anything unless I stop being such a fucking chickenshit. Sadly, no matter how crazy this lady may seem, the bottom line is that when it comes to the chickenshit observation, I know she's on point. Everything I do, even acts of apparent bravery, I do out of fear.

Now she's diving into a breakdown of an arms-for-grain deal she brokered with some African revolutionaries and before I can make any response she pauses, looks at me as if her heart is about to crack in half then takes my hands and informs me there's hope for me—I have potential, if only I'll trust her—truly trust her, like with my life. She can help me become who I actually am. "But first," she informs me, "you'll need shave your head and get an eagle tattooed on the base of your skull directly over your cerebellum." She's got a tattoo artist in mind who can handle the job.

Ralph is regularly invoked in word but thankfully never appears in person. Still her passing comments of how I'll be killed by him if he finds us here are increasingly unnerving and suddenly I find myself resolutely convinced that this lady speaks a language of hyper-truth and she's actually done all or most of this shit she's ranting on and on about, ergo Ralph is real.

Suddenly I want to get the fuck out of there but it's too late, she's read me too well and sees it in my eyes and blurts out exactly what I'm thinking then begs me to stay, not for her but for myself, because I have potential. Her plea makes me furious first and foremost because I know she's right; I'm a chickenshit and what good ever proceeded from living life on your heels instead of your toes?

So I stay. I get to studying her hands at one point, trying to see if they actually look like hand model material. Boom, she instantly intuits my motivation and starts yelling at me, saying not to look at them, that she's ashamed she ever made money with them. Then back into the intrigue: a string of scary international dealings with a shady network of underworld characters, Ralph at the center of it all.

By now it's clear that Cheri's monologue will never, ever, ever end. I glance at my watch and—goddamn, it's almost three am. The cab's due back at the fleet in twenty or so minutes. It's a $25 an hour fine if I'm late. Cheri sees my startled expression and, realizing she's lost control of me, recoils. In the pause I tell her I have to leave, the cab is due back.

Without missing a beat she lights into me hard, doing the chickenshit routine, mocking me for being governed by such insignificant limitations as schedules and fiduciary deadlines.

I'm done. I've heard what I need to hear, and plenty more. Apparently I can't help her with Ralph and the abuse she's suffering so I tell her I'm leaving. She stares at me cooly, then says, "Oh yeah. Well guess what? I don't have any money. Not a penny. I owe you seventy-five dollars for three hours, right? And what about the food we ordered? Who's gonna pay for that?"

Jesus. I study her for a long beat, her mirrored sunglasses meeting my eye, bouncing a creepy reflection of myself back at me like that busted mirror back in Amsterdam did, veiling this tormented human being who's just, in her own inimitable fashion, laid her horribly contorted soul bare to a complete stranger, a fucking cab driver, a nobody. "Cheri, I don't care about the money." I tell her, "Just keep the cash. I'll cover the food."

She puts he head in her hands, convulses momentarily, then says, "Argh! You—have—learned nothing!! CHICKENSHIT! It's your money but you're too much of a CHICKENSHIT to claim it! God, why did I waste my time....?" She then goes to furiously digging around in the big shoulder bag she's carrying, yanks out a piece of paper and a pen, scribbles something on the paper then, seething, shoves it at me. "Go to this address! Now! Ring buzzer 3c. A woman will answer the door. Do NOT ask her her name or speak to her in any way! Got it? She's gonna hand you an envelope—bring it back here. Do NOT look inside. Got it?"

Outside the door I feel like my mind has just been gang raped. I stagger toward the cab and turn the key. I know I should just go and not look back, put as much distance between me and Cheri as is humanly possible, but I don't. I do exactly as Cheri says and in the doing am shown just how fundamentally wrong that core intelligence inside of me is. I'm dealing with a maniac, possibly with a maniac with a jealous, homicidal boyfriend. I'm gonna be late returning the cab, but still I rush up in the low teens between A and 1st Avenue.

Sketchy block. Low level drug dealers and such. I double park, run up to the door and ring the buzzer, scanning the periphery for potential threats. A beautiful, groggy, sullen woman wearing a half-closed kimono with not a goddamn thing on underneath it comes staggering down the stairs, cracks the door open and shoves a white envelope at me. No eye contact, not a word spoken. I take the envelope and she slams the door shut.

I do as instructed and hustle back to the Sidewalk Cafe, park the cab and go in, half expecting Cheri to be gone and the envelop to be full of shredded newspaper or cat shit or plutonium dust or who knows what.

But Cheri's not gone. She's there, seated forlornly in the window looking as lost as any human being on earth could ever look. She turns and sees me and for the first time ever smiles. And what a radiant, enchanting smile! Then she bursts into tears as I hand her the envelope. "You came back! You came back! You did it. There's hope for you!"

She rips open the envelope, yanking out five twenty dollar bills. She hands them to me, then says, "Pay the check and keep the rest. That's the money I owe you."

Wow. I'm rendered speechless by this psychological roller coaster ride. I pay the bill. We walk out the door. It's a mere three blocks from where I first picked her up and yet I ask her "Where do you live, Cheri?"

"Ralph's apartment? It's on 7th between B and C."

Yeah. That makes sense. 7th between B & C. I know that block. Everyone does. It's the biggest heroin operation in the city. The whole block is tightly controlled by drug lords. To my utter dismay, I hear myself offering Cheri a ride back to Ralph's apartment.

"You mean like, like we had a date and you're bringing me home?" She asks sarcastically.

"Yeah, but no goodnight kiss, okay?"

She doubles over laughing briefly then, shakes her head and admits. "If Ralph doesn't kill you, you might just make it."

She climbs in the back of the taxi like a proper passenger. I circle around to Avenue

C and come easing up past the corner sentinels of the drug operation, nodding to let them know I see and respect their authority. The closest one shouts code words down to the guy at the main door of the operation, "Gener-al! Gener-al!" He cries, hopefully establishing that we're cool. Maybe he recognizes Cheri, maybe not. I'm just praying he understands we're not cops.

Four doors past the heroin operation she says, "Stop here." We sit in silence for a second, then she says, "You're not scared? To be here…"

"Yeah. I'm scared. But, like you said, I'd be scared anyway. After all, I'm a chickenshit, right?" She doesn't laugh, doesn't acknowledge the self-effacing humor. She stares at me long and hard, then digs in her oversized shoulder bag and, to my utter astonishment, pulls a child's magic wand out of it—a silvery sparkled thing with a glittery star at the end. She hands it to me and says, "You earned that other money. Here's your tip. Good luck."

And out she goes.

I don't wait to see if she gets in safely like I normally do with most women. I hit the gas and get the fuck out of there. I'm a block away, rolling west alone at a good clip when it hits me—that block where Cheri lives, that's where they found Carmello's taxi last winter. The cops found his body on a pile of snow out in Queens, defensive bullet wound in his hand and through his temple. The killer(s) then drove to Manhattan and ditched Carmello's taxi across the street from where I just dropped Cheri, directly across from Ralph's apartment. Which means the killer lives nearby. Ralph?

Jesus.

I roll west, checking my rear view to see if I'm being followed, but who could follow me? I own the grid system in this city, so I zig-zag my way back to the fleet office on 21st between 6th and 7th. Nobody's following me, right?

I gas it up and pay for my shift, then head on foot toward the subway station at 23rd and 6th. For the uninitiated, virtually any New York City subway station at 4am is a terrifying, life threatening proposition, much more so when a theoretical hitman named Ralph is looking for you. The platform's deserted and I'm just standing here scared shitless. I feel like a doomed character in some grim French existential gangster film.

Minutes crawl by and—finally—here comes the F train rumbling into the station. I sit alone in the car, opposite the mid train conductor's booth, knowing it offers at least the illusion of refuge, with that MTA employee who has access to communications a few feet away.

A scattering of passengers come and go, club kids on their way home, blue collar types headed to work, bleary-eyed homeless looking for an empty car to sleep in. Nobody looks quite like a hit man. Okay by me.

In downtown Brooklyn I exit at Jay Street and hustle the eight blocks to the house I'm renting in Boerum Hill, making it home safely. I exhale, then go up to my room and try to figure out how to decompress.

I still have Cheri's magic wand, and for reasons not entirely clear to me I tape that goddamn thing to my bedroom door, like it's a talisman. I then call three friends living in various far away cities, leaving the same message on all three of their answering machines. "If I disappear. Look for a hitman named Ralph on 7th Street between B & C. His girlfriend's name is Cheri."

I try to sleep, but sleep won't come. Too much brain clatter. Did all that really just happen? Do I really need to shave my head and get an eagle tattooed over where my cerebellum is? How do I prove to myself that I'm not a chickenshit? By listening to Cheri? Or by not?

Dawn comes creeping in but sleep remains elusive—no rest for the weary. I give up on repose and gather up my school stuff then head to NYU for my Wednesday morning advanced photo class. Afterward I make a beeline to the photo library and dig up the Lucien Clergue nudes book. It's page after page of gorgeous black and white nude portraiture, but due to all those years I spent in the Pentecostal church, looking at representations of naked women still feels vaguely shameful to me. Flipping through the images I fight the urge to surrender to Calvinist morays—that's chickenshit territory, or so Cheri would likely say.

It's a book of vignettes, with each chapter documenting a different woman, the model's name listed on the title page of every section.

Halfway through the book, there it is; the page with the word Cheri. Just Cheri. I'm terrified to turn the page. Will it be her? I flip to the first image. Despite the fact that Clergue photographed all the other models in full, with faces showing, in every single portrait of this Cheri, her entire head's cropped off, assuring there's no way to identify her. It both pisses me off and makes perfect sense. She's covered her tracks well, I think to myself. I'll never know for sure if that's her. Or will I? Then I look at her hands and I know. It's her.

LOS ANGELES, CALIFORNIA, MARCH 2009

I'm about to embark on the red-eye of all red-eyes, headed to Australia for a series of shows Down Under. Will Nick Cave's drummer be stalking me while I'm there? Maybe so. I've included a stopover in Los Angeles for a few days so I can visit my brilliant sister, who's been fighting cancer. Tough times for her.

The flight's at midnight and I'm running a little late. It's maybe ten-fifteen when I power slide my rental car into the Hertz drop-off lot a few miles from the airport. The check-in takes forever. Once they clear me I set out for the shuttle bus depot, which is roughly fifty yards off. That's a short hike normally, but not when you're lugging a hundred plus pounds of music gear.

The bus idles quietly in a pool of yellow sodium vapor light. The driver's heaving a suitcase into the interior baggage rack for an overweight white woman, the sole passenger on the bus. I'm about twenty yards off now. The lady takes her seat and the driver steps back out onto the sidewalk, presumably checking for other possible passengers. He glances my way and I give him a standard head-nod acknowledgement, letting him know that I'm coming as fast as I can. He studies me briefly, then wheels around and sprints up the aisle, like I was walking towards him with an armload of bloody machetes instead of three guitars and two suitcases.

Although the full-sized bus is empty but for the woman, the doors hiss shut. I shout for him to stop but he lurches away instead. What the fuck!? I curse the driver loudly as the bus veers away and disappears into the darkness. I truly, deeply, profoundly hate bullshit like this. I'm fully pissed, plus now I'm really running late.

I sit down on one of the benches and only then do I notice I'm not alone. A willowy, sophisticated beauty guarding two suitcases and what looks like a keyboard case regards me dispassionately from a nearby bench. He left her too I guess. But why? Maybe he's got a grudge against musicians?

I smile and nod at her which prompts a quick brush off glare in return. She seems uneasy. Is she simply put out with also being left, or with being left alone in the dark dark night with the lunatic who only moments was before shouting obscenities at some random bus driver? Hard to say. Either way, who can blame her?

We sit in silence. Another bus arrives after maybe five minutes. The driver opens the door and greets us warmly, offering the fancy lady assistance lifting her bags. "They're heavy" she coldly informs him, acknowledging his presence only to insure the safe conveyance of her weighty luggage. I give the bus driver a friendly nod and climb on, stowing all my gear in the lower level of the baggage rack. I'm still hot under the collar at that other driver but this guy seems okay. I take a seat in the middle of the bus not far from my gear, in case one of my bags decides to make a break for it in some hairpin turn on the way to the terminal.

Once the driver loads the lady's cases on, she makes her way to the far back of the bus, obviously trying to get as far away from me as possible. I got no problem with that. I'm used to people shying away from me—especially women—and super especially highbrow, sophisticated women. She calls out to the driver, "My husband is dropping the car. Please wait until he gets here."

Great, more delays.

As we sit and wait in the cool dim light she does her best to ignore the jittery, wild-eyed scarecrow, the irate traveling junkman who was shouting foul language a moment earlier. Sensible. A minute or two later an older man in a business suit comes jogging up and boards the bus. It's just us three and the driver. He's got no bags, and immediately starts fussing with the lady's keyboard case, which the driver's placed on one of the upper baggage racks. The lady calls out to him, "It's okay. It's safe up there."

He nods at her, "Yeah? You sure?"

"It's fine." She says, seeming bored.

In profile the guy looks vaguely familiar. He fiddles with the keyboard case a little more then turns and looks me straight in the face and now there's no question—it's him. So as he passes I say, "Hey…Phil? Aren't you Phil?"

Phil's a little startled by this. "What??" he says, stopping in front of me.

So I say, "You're Phil, right? From Ann's Taxi Service…"

"Oh…yeah, that's me." he says, looking slightly confused. "What're you doing here?" he asks.

"Headed to Australia." I say, pointing out my suitcase and gear. "What about you?"

"Taiwan." he replies.

"That's quite a hike." I say.

"Yeah. And I've already been there once this year." He groans. We nod, mutually considering the arduous journeys that lay ahead of us, then he shakes my hand and says, "Okay, have a good trip."

I wish him the same. He eases into the seat next to the sophisticated lady, who remains aloof, even to him. We three ride in silence toward the airport.

A half a mile out from the international terminal Phil's curiosity gets the best of him. He grabs the handrail, works his way over and plops down next to me, leaving the sophisticated lady to fend for herself. "You still at Ann's?" he asks.

"Nope. Not for a long time. I'm a musician now." I tell him, pointing to my gear.

"Yeah," he says, "Me too." nodding toward the keyboard case.

"No more Ann's. No more trip sheets. No more Marty the evil dispatcher." I say.

"Yeah...Marty. I forgot about him..." Phil ruminates, remembering Marty and his poisonous, malevolent disposition.

"Phil," I say, interrupting his reverie, "Is it true that you used to co-own Food Restaurant down in Soho, on Wooster Street?"

Phil cocks his head, puzzled, and studies me for a second. "Yeah....but it wasn't really like I was an owner. It was a collective kind of place."

"Yeah, I know. I worked there right after you left. Right before I started at Ann's."

"Oh?" Phil thinks this over. "Food. Yeah, that was a pretty good place."

"Maybe it was when you were there. You remember Deena? The lady who bought it?"

"No. No. I don't."

"She ran that place into the ground. Skipped out one day with everyone's paycheck never to be seen again." I say.

"Yeah, that happens sometimes, doesn't it?" Phil adds wisely.

We agree that it happens sometimes. The bus pulls up to the international terminal. Phil wishes me a pleasant trip. I wish him the same, ignoring the fashionable lady as she likewise ignores me. I'm off the bus first, hustle-lugging my gear toward the yawning arms of LAX, trying to make that flight.

As I enter the terminal a friendly-looking hipster toting a cello case waves a hearty hello to me. I've worked with a few cello players over the years but have no idea who this joker is. I nod back just the same. Why not? Cello man acknowledges my return gesture with a confused look. It takes me a second to figure it out; he's not waving at me, he's waving at Phil, who's now walking a few feet behind me with the sophisticated lady.

I stop, and even though I'm late and should be running my ass off, all of a sudden I start laughing. And, as so often is the case, I don't have the slightest clue as to why. Then it hits me; it's taken twenty five years, but the mirror's been mended. The mosaic is complete and fragments melded to become a whole. I think of that odd repetitive music carried on fluttering BBC wavelengths, soothing my troubled mind and rejoice at finally finding myself dancing along with Einstein On The Beach.

NEW YORK CITY, DECEMBER 1993

I'm headed to Ann's Service for yet another shift on no sleep again. This insomnia's shredding my mind into tiny, worthless little fragments. It's been weeks since I've slept for more than a few minutes at a stretch.

Going at the cab driving nonstop for the last couple weeks I've been fantasizing increasingly about the tangible relief suicide might offer. Mental health professionals, they call what I'm doing "suicidal ideation"—obsessive thoughts of killing yourself without actually taking action...yet.

But hey, as my old pastor used to say, "If we fail to plan, we plan to fail" and suicide's not a job you want botched, so I spend long stretches of time working the various kinks out of the theoretical death models I come up with.

It's not that I'm fearful or doubtful of the relief death might offer. I'm so lost and in such pain here on this earth and see nothing but an endless supply of misery on the horizon that I'm willing to take my chances. The only factor holding me back is my family, my friends. These people love me. They do. They're good souls who'd endlessly blame themselves forever for not heeding the warning signs. My sister would never recover, nor my mom. I can't bring myself to destroy their lives too, so does that mean I'm stuck here?

Maybe. Maybe not. A couple days back I settled on that plan I'd flirted with during earlier periods of profound depression. I'm a taxi driver, right? And we're in the middle of a crack epidemic, right? So why not go cruising through godforsaken crime-riddled neighborhoods, seeking out hooded, degenerate criminal types hailing cabs, the ones not even the gypsy cabs will pick up? I figure most of these thugs are armed and inclined toward homicide. So I tried my plan out over the course of five, maybe six fares.

Cruising urban war zones like East New York, Hunts Point such individuals were surprised to behold a passing yellow cab, all but stunned when I stopped after they hailed me. In they climbed and off we went, ferrying these men through surreally blighted landscapes where few yellow cabs have ever ventured. Last night mid-trip I was visited by the sickening sweet smell of crack cocaine being smoked right there in the back seat. This was only up in Harlem, at 114th and Park Ave. When we arrived at the project they'd named as their destination I parked and threw the meter. Then when I told them the fare amount there was a long silence.

I was waiting for the sound, the pop-pop-pop, wondering if I'd hear it, or things would just go black. But instead they threw the doors open and simply sprinted away. No homicide. I watched as they darted into the shadows of a nearby building wondering, what does a person have to do to get shot around here?

Hell, one of the thug fares not only paid but threw in a hefty tip. Go figure. The watched pot never boils, I guess. That's how things are shaking out at present. When this kind of mental illness descends upon a soul as poorly equipped to deal with struggle as I presently am, the end result is a psychological paralysis whose logical conclusion can only be death.

This cop I drove out to Queens last year, he said even using a dinky little .22 caliber zip gun the first shot shatters the plexiglass partition, the second passes through the shattered remnants unimpeded like a hot knife through butter. He said that's common knowledge amongst criminals. Plus, the driver's side window isn't even bulletproof so anything fired through it is in play right off.

It's just a matter of time before I hear the pop-pop sound and then I'll be dead. A robbery gone bad. That's an acceptable death, right? That way there'll be no recriminations on my family's part. It's just a tragic incident, rather than some horrific curse I'm casting upon my family.

I'm late for shape-up so I go sailing through the door of the fleet full speed. I'm about to fetch my license from my locker when I notice the long faces all around. Something's wrong but nobody's saying anything. I scan this drab room full of taxi cab lifers and everyone avoids my gaze—I guess they're hoping I already heard the news. I ask Larry what happened. He sighs, then reports, "Clayton. He offed himself."

Clayton. It's no surprise, not really, but still it knocks the wind out of me. I guess this time around he made sure there were no mistakes. The first time he tried to disappear was a few weeks back when he shot up ten dime bags of heroin then called his girlfriend to say goodbye—Clayton and his god damn flair for the dramatic.

She frantically notified the cops, who, when they banged on Clayton's door to investigate, promptly got shot at. Bad idea Clayton. Don't shoot at New York's Finest, even if it's only with a starter pistol and you're just firing blanks in the air from behind a locked door.

The shots sent the cops scattering, shouting oh shit, oh shit, frantically howling for back-ups, reinforcements, the fucking cavalry. A SWAT team was called in and after some strategic observation with mirrors on extension poles, they broke out the ropes and pulleys and shit and, from the apartment above, came rappelling through Clayton's third floor window, crashing in like some souped-up action movie. By then Clayton was out cold and well on his way to the great beyond but somehow they resuscitated him with a hefty dose of Naloxone. When he came to he was en route to the psyche ward at Bellevue.

So apparently yesterday he was released, this after convincing the shrinks there he was no longer a threat to himself—he always had a way with words. He walked up to Times Square, took an elevator to the balcony of the forty-fourth floor there at the luxurious Marriott Marquis Hotel and promptly did a swan dive over the railing. A week before Christmas. The atrium dining area where he landed was jammed with holiday revelers. He was decapitated, but thankfully no one else was hurt. Yep, a real flair for the dramatic.

I'm standing in this room full of heartbroken cab drivers and I guess something snaps inside, like I get a little lost in my mind, because the next thing I know I find myself waking up and realizing I'm staggering down 6th Avenue in a daze, crying. I'm simultaneously heartbroken for Clayton and jealous of him. He was in a world of hurt, just like I am, I know that all too well.

We were close. He told me about it, his childhood, the abuse. His dad was a professor at Harvard. Doctor of Divinity. Meanwhile a family acquaintance, his father's best friend, regularly raped him—this as a seven year old kid. Clayton sought out trouble to equalize his inner pain and guilt. He fell in with hard core criminals, became a professional gambler—a card counter banned from most of the major casinos.

He was a wheel man for some mob figure. He drove like a maniac, like I do. When he had that third wreck in a twelve month period, just a little fender bender but enough to get him fired, he paid the guy he hit a couple hundred bucks to not report it, then found a steel pipe and drove the cab to an abandoned lot over on the West Side. There he pummeled the taxi front to back, broke out the windows, rammed the front end into a wall. Then very theatrically he came limping back to the fleet in the destroyed taxi, telling the dispatchers this tall tale about being ambushed and attacked in the Bronx. He claimed they'd rammed him at a stop light, (a common occurrence at that time) and the hijackers were after the taxi medallion, worth maybe forty grand. But he'd saved it via a daring escape. Management praised his heroism and he kept his job. Fucking Clayton.

I pass a beautiful woman I vaguely know down on 6th Avenue and 10th Street, a secretary who I once had a big crush on. She's strolling along with two tidy, tall, handsome men. They're laughing easily among themselves. She catches sight of me, disheveled, staggering along in tears. She averts her eyes. We pass without a word.

The afternoon stretches and yawns like a fever dream. I walk and walk. I'm briefly in a movie theater, a bar, Penn Station, a novelty store. Mostly I just stagger along aimlessly, thinking what's the use. Eventually I go drifting into a trendy bookstore on St. Marks, Place and find myself staring blankly at an artfully arranged wall of books, none of which I know the slightest fucking thing about. I'm not au currant, not a big reader. The cover of one book at eye level seems strangely appealing, so I open it up. The first line is an embrace,

Dear friend…

Soon thereafter a suicide is described in luminous detail. A drowning—one of the approaches I've been fantasizing about when I think about killing myself. I follow the small markings on the page, those things called words, and find with each word that my eyes consume, a bond is formed between the deepest part of my suffering soul and this unknown book. The words sparkle like brilliant jewels, treasures that've mysteriously appeared at the bottom of my sock drawer in the place where that hidden pistol normally lays, the one I'd intended to use to blow my brains out.

I'm not sure how long I stand there reading. Long time. Eventually the clerk takes me by the elbow and discreetly suggests that I either buy the book or put it back. So I buy the book. It's called Suttree. As I walk home I continue reading. Once inside my tiny studio apartment I continue reading. Fourteen hours later I hit page 471, then immediately start the novel over again.

Dear friend…

The first pass through is all catharsis; the second time the process truly begins to calm my tormented mind. Eventually I drift off into a blessed, dreamless sleep for over two hours—my first real sleep in many days.

I wake up feeling much refreshed and head over to the taxi fleet where I dive into another night shift. As I twist and weave through the urban labyrinth of New York City fragments of the journey Suttree took echo through my mind. His story feels like an amplified, mythic version of my own sad tale.

Later in the night, as the streets empty out, for fleeting moments here and there New York becomes Knoxville, a place both real and imaginary. Each time this sensation descends, I forget my mind sickness, forget about Clayton, about the actress, about everything, and feel momentarily weightless, free.

It's two in the morning. The attractive young hipster woman in the back seat leans forward and says, "Driver, someone has left something back here and I think it's intended for you."

It's an odd remark. At the stoplight I turn and ask her what it is. She hands me five small dime bags of weed. Puzzling. I ask her why she doesn't keep them for herself. She smiles knowingly, saying calmly, "Those aren't intended for me. I'm an addict. Just joined Narcotics Anonymous, in fact, so this feels like a test from God. I intend to pass it. Please, take them." I study the small, concise packets. Since they're not for her should I infer that God sent me this weed? I haven't smoked since I was a teenager.

An hour later I turn the cab in and head home. I open one dime bag and roll a joint, feeling like some filthy degenerate criminal. I smoke it as I read about my new best friend, Suttree. A few minutes later I fall asleep. A deep, dreamless sleep.

I wake up six astonishing hours later. Sleep! The redemption of sleep.

There's the novel, splayed open on my chest. I dive back in. I smoke the weed and read the novel. I sleep again. It's a cycle that repeats itself for several days until all the weed is gone.

In the story, Suttree's world disintegrates and as it does the narrative carries me downward, down, down, down. Fragments disintegrate, then those smaller fragments similarly follow suit, ad infinitum. Eventually it dawns on me that almost every character in the story is simply some mutated echo of Suttree himself. One by one they all die. The first to go was the suicide from the bridge, that suicide being the most symbolic death.

At some wildly liberating point the third or fourth time through the novel I arrive at a state of barometric equipoise, a balancing between my mental state and Suttree's. Then returning to the blessed pages, the narrative arc carries him further and further down, and further, and further. Slowly but surely, by studying this imaginary figure, I no longer feel as though I'm pinned to the bottom of the world, for beneath me lies beautiful Suttree. He took this cross I bear and dove into the pitch black of pure pathos and through this surrogate, through his own sad tale, I'm released from the death throes of suicidal inertia. And with that I begin my ascent.

HAMBURG, GERMANY, JANUARY 1998,

Yesterday me and David Byrne played another big show, this one in Amsterdam. It was beyond surreal to join him in the same venue as where I first saw him spastically dancing on that video screen nearly twenty years prior.

When I left Amsterdam all those years hence I knew without a doubt I was done forever with Holland, with the mixed blessing of foreign city solitude, with the infinite permutations of winter grey so specific to that place. I would never return—I was sure of that, but I was wrong. Good. It's uplifting to be wrong at times.

Before the show last night I traced old pathways around the city, shambling up and down every avenue I haunted all those years now gone, warily eyeing my old apartment next to the Arabs, passing the storefront where I saw the Thalidomide guitarist play, searching for the "Why not" street walker. Where are they now? Probably all dead.

Tonight we're in Hamburg and the weather's gone even more of a dismal, gray. It's spitting rain outside and I've just finished watching my twenty-third David Byrne show in twenty-eight days. You'd think I'd get bored, but every night is different. What a show! This guy on stage is like a man possessed. The dancing! The costume changes! The iconic hits!

Sometimes I ask myself, "How is this possible? Am I a groupie? A roadie? Am I stalking him again?" No, the Unseen Forces intervened and I've been handpicked by David Byrne himself to be his opening act on this grand European tour, nightly playing to crowds numbering in the thousands. I sleep in a bunk on the tour bus just a few feet from him…

Superwhite.

David's just finished his thrilling encore here in Hamburg. As the lights come up I'm checking out the mobs of happy German patrons as they file out, the big room empties and then I notice her, that attractive woman sitting at a table off to the side of the stage. She's clutching a massive teddy bear—so what's up with that? Is that a German thing? After a few minutes a security guard passes by, telling her the show's over and the club's closing.

With that I mosey backstage and begin packing up my gear. Ten minutes pass. I grab my cases and then go walking toward the bus bay when, passing David's dressing room I hear him call out, inviting me in. Is that a hint of desperation in his voice?

It's a typical classy venue dressing room: lengthy formica counter below a rectangular mirror framed with arrays of soft, flattering lights. As usual David's got a guest. He's always being courted by some exotic celebrity—Brian Eno, Adrian Ballou, writers, painters, poets—Superwhite's a magnet for creative excellence types.

But tonight it's not some fellow celebrity: it's that woman with the giant teddy bear.

The vibe in the room is tense. Why is she staring at David that way? So intently, so forlornly, and what is she urgently whispering to him? He introduces me to her then hastily exits the room, moving away at something between a canter and a trot. The woman looks crestfallen. We speak briefly and it's clear that she's a bit touched by the fairies. She explains, pleadingly, that her mission is so very important, she has to give the teddy bear to David. He has to take it from her. From her hands. He just has to.

A moment later several security guards arrive. It takes all three of them to carry her, kicking and screaming, out the door. The last I see of the giant teddy bear it's sitting alone in David's dressing room, as if studying its own profoundly melancholic teddy bear reflection in the mirror. It's such an odd, surreal vision that it jostles something loose in my mind.

It suddenly occurs to me that I can't exactly recall when it was on this tour that I sat David Byrne down and relayed the entire story of Superwhite to him. Was it Salmanca…Paris…San Sebastian?

I do remember how he laughed that shy, implosive laugh of his when I described the spectrum between soulfulness and soullessness, how I was trying to become so exceedingly white that I might accidentally stumble into the realm of cool, just like he did. He appeared to grasp the crackpot physics I was alluding to and I recall being deeply relieved these notions made sense to him.

To his further credit he seemed unperturbed by the revelation that I'd once stalked him, although he had no memory of the incident. After touring with him extensively I now know why, for in every town, in every city in the world, there are incarnations of the slightly off-kilter person who called out Superwhite to him that day long ago… sad, lonely lost souls who believe with all their heart that they're communicating with someone important, someone connected to the center of things, someone who will help them undertake a magical leap from the furthest reaches of Nowhere to the center of Somewhere without ever having to set foot in the soul-crushing middle.

KNOXVILLE, TENNESSEE, APRIL 1998

Walter the ninety-year old unstoppable storytelling machine is on a roll, slowly, incrementally unfurling the bizarre history of downtown Knoxville. Mostly it's variations of hillbilly murders, with a sprinkling of suicides and incest and what have you thrown in for good measure. I been here two full hours now and it's closing in on my sound check time up at the historic Bijou Theater, a grand old palace up on the hill in central Knoxville. Twice now I've politely told Walter I need to get going, but he pays me no mind, just rambles on.

As I watch a shabby bum go trudging past the barber shop's broad picture window on Central Street I'm reminded of the Suttree revelation and the notion starts to hum and ricochet all through my mind again: Suttree was here. He walked past that window, down that street, walked by the Bijou Theater where I'll perform tonight. He was a real person, just like me, just like you. Not imagined at all—like Walter said, you can't cut a man's hair if he ain't real.

He often frequented this very barbershop, a locality I happened upon completely by chance while exploring a random Southern town with Superwhite. And what if I'd let myself be run off with David after Walter accused us of being shifty characters? I'd have never crossed paths with the reality of Suttree. A rhythmic notion comes flying in my mind:

This life's a drunken dance between fate and circumstance…

I should put that in a song. Slipping the notebook out of my coat pocket to jot the idea down I catch a reflection of myself in the barber shop mirror, framed by the crudely carved folk art owl collection. Here I stand scribbling away, jotting down possible future lyrics, words that may one day end up in a song that will be played on Marconi's invention, the radio, and suddenly I feel like I'm Tom Waits and Walter is Hank the toothless bum. And with that I feel redemptive laughter rising up in me and escaping my pursed lips. Walter studies me, puzzled.

What's the joke? Life itself.

I mean, here I am holding my Tom Waits inspired notebook in a barbershop where Suttree got his hair cut on my way to a theater where I'll soon perform to a sold-out house alongside David Byrne. How the fuck did all this magic shit happen? The convergence of far-flung dream worlds and my baseline reality is complete. It's as if my life's morphed into some form of absurdist theater, alternating wildly between hokey artifice and pie in the sky dreams.

But hey, understand this: during all that struggle and tribulation, I was never once deliberately on the prowl for some wild, mystical time. No sir. I was just lost and in a whole lot of pain, forever aiming for higher ground with the broken compass of my heart. I never went beating the bushes trying to flush out paranormal yuks, never held seances to conjure spirits or drank peyote juice with some wild-eyed shaman, never did any of that Ouija Board nonsense with a bunch of pot smoking teenagers or made a secret altar in my closet where I prayed to Baal or Nostradamus or Aleister Crowley or any of those so-called spiritualist anti-heroes.

Nope. Shit just came raining down on me, and there I was slap in the middle of it going what—in—the—fuck—just—happened? Admittedly early on I was bedazzled by the intoxicating feeling of being in the presence of Magic, so I didn't fight it, but quick enough I saw—the fairy tale often turned into a terrifying, slippery plunge into true oblivion. Psychological footholds grew scarce, and with no way to dig in, down I slid, tumbling this way and that, forever at the mercy of whatever psychic undertows might be at play.

Was it a mistake, how I never sought out an overview, never did any research, never got therapy, never studied the topic of synchronicity with the intention of framing my experiences via one tradition or another? Should I have plunged headlong into Jung, Koestler, the Zohar, the Tao de Ching etc? Maybe. Maybe not. The only way I can explain it, it's like when I was a kid riding that giant roller coaster over in Panama City, Florida; if you're getting tossed left and right, willy-nilly like some rag doll, you don't spend a whole lot of time thinking about all the hidden motors and pulleys and chains and mechanical parts making the ride go. You just hold on for dear life. Which is exactly how I came stumbling into Walter's barbershop and shook hands with the person who saved my life, Suttree.

There's a term that took seed in my mind while I was trapped in one of those wildly over-intellectualized cinema study classes I had to take when I was at NYU: simulacrum—the substituting of the signs of the real for the real, the regeneration by models of a real without having any origin in reality. So much art these days feels like simulacrum; references to references of other references, a hollow shell that represents another hollow shell, etc. Standing here in Walter's barber shop talking about Suttree with him, I'm reminded of the power that art can possess when the real is honored, truthfully explored, then magnified.

Again I put my hand on the doorknob and make to leave Walter's barbershop, and again he beckons me back with yet another question. It's a game of some sort—a lonely old man's game. This go-round he asks, "So what line of work are you in, Jim?" Whittle-whittle-whittle.

"I'm a musician, Walter" I say.

This peaks Walter's interest. "A musician? Well, how about that? Now Ike, my former partner here in the barber shop, his boys, they did some music. Oh yes. They sang together real nice. Many a day the two of them, they'd run around here in the shop here just singing to the radio. They had 'em some fine, fine songs of their own too. Sang on the radio themselves when they was growed. Ever hear-tell of them? Called themselves The Everly Brothers…?"

Oh shit. Here we go again. Now I'll never get to sound check.

NEW YORK CITY, JANUARY 1995

It's 3am, and I've just finished my shift—another twelve grueling hours of mind numbingly repetitive Groundhog Day experiences in the fucking yellow crucible.

Twice in the last month I've had guns pulled on me by young gangster types that no self-respecting driver would dare pick up. The second go-round we were parked under the West Side Highway up in Harlem. I heard whisperings in the back seat, then made out the phrase, "Shoot him".

But the hoodlum with the gun, I guess he didn't feel like I was worth wasting a bullet on—bullets are expensive, costing roughly $1 each on the black market. The doors flew open and as they fled on foot I found myself thinking, "Shit, I'm not even worth a fucking one dollar bullet."

My face is slowly morphing into a hollow mask, much like the one Andras Groff wore just before he donned that actual Groucho Marx mask. So what happens when to a person when they become the mask? Is that some physical signifier of reaching the point of no return?

I fight an incessant hunger to just close my eyes, lean forward and plummet into the darkness. The last few months I've run out of psychological tricks, the ones a person uses to benignly accept their fate as an outcast, a failure, a bottom feeding cab driver, a terminally disconnected soul. Having raged against this fate every minute of every day for as long as I can remember, I finally decipher the baseline truth—my raging only serves to hasten the coming darkness.

I pull into the garage and park the cab. The gas men give me a wary nod. I've blown up two engines in the last three months. No one much talks to me at the fleet any more. I climb on my bike and aim for home. The same routine I've followed for six nights a week for years and years and years now.

On 17th Street and 5th Avenue I notice a beautiful young woman walking alone. She's all decked out to party, wearing a provocative mini-skirt and high heels—likely she's been to a nearby club or something. Maybe she's had a few drinks, as she's wobbling a little. This particular stretch of 5th Avenue is desolate this time of night, as it's mostly businesses, storefronts the likes of the one Andras disappeared into.

There's not a soul around and at this hour even sober it's no place for her to be walking alone. So what do I do? Do I become a killer? Would that be a provocative ending to this book? Maybe in fiction. But remember, this ain't fiction.

So instead I just slow down and keep my eye on her. My slowing down coincides with the convoy of blinged-out luxury vehicles that come silently easing up behind her. Although the windows are tinted black, 1 know the score with the occupants of the cars—if you've lived in New York in the late 1980's and early 90's, you know. Inside the cars are groups of filthy rich, utterly amoral young drug dealers from the outlying boroughs; the Bronx, Brooklyn, Queens. And secreted inside the glistening gems of their tricked-out cars, behind secret panels, tucked under seats, hell sometimes even just bulging from their waistbands, are a dazzling array of weapons, lethal little killing machines like Uzis, Mack 10s, Street-sweepers and, of course, lesser threats in the form of knives, baseball bats, golf clubs and chains.

They've come to Manhattan this Saturday night to have a little predatory fun and have spied their ideal target; this petite young woman walking alone. They pull up alongside and slow to her pace. Three shiny vehicles. A malicious caravan. Windows come down and comments are hurled out in her direction. Whoops and guffaws. She's frightened. Terribly frightened. They're trailing her at walking pace, rolling just beside her for a full block, calling out over and over. Presently there's a lull in the downtown traffic. The streets are empty save the cars in the gangster convoy, her and me. I do the math, there's five, six gang members minimum—probably more. Maybe they mean no harm. Maybe they're just having a little fun. Maybe not.

I'm monitoring the situation from across 5th Avenue, keeping pace on my bike, a three speed girl's Schwinn that's stuck in stiffest gear. I found it in a dumpster some months back. It's a chore to pedal it, but it's better than walking.

The young woman picks up her pace. She's hugging herself, looking desperately this way and that for help. She can't see me, the convoy's blocking her view of me as I keep pace. I don't even consider my little garbage can-umbrella-shouting Z words rescue routine—it'd never work with so many of them.

One of the gang member hangs his head out the window and shouts, "Pussy-time!" Another shouts, "It's getting real!"—street slang for an imminent attack. The lead driver gives his car a threatening little burst of gas. "Leave me alone!" the woman cries, as she breaks into a sad, wobbly high-heeled trot. They keep pace with her, jeering. I pedal faster, picking up speed.

The driver of the lead car's a compact musclebound thug. As he lowers his window to shout at the girl, l can make out four occupants in the car. All of them are laughing, dancing, juking in their seats. The driver glances over and notices me shadowing them. Watching too intently. That's all he needs. He banks hard across the four empty lanes. The other cars follow suit. It takes me a second to realize what he's doing. He aims to ram me. I've fucked with his fun. I'm the unwanted witness to their revelry.

I bank almost simultaneously, putting the bike through a hole in the parked cars where a fire hydrant sits, jumping up onto the sidewalk. The line of parked cars shields me from the oncoming vehicle. I hit the pedals hard as I can, as the convoy of thugs pull up alongside me. I'm going as fast as this bike allows and so we're traveling maybe twenty miles an hour. They're idling in first gear, laughing as they keep pace.

One of them hangs out the window and chucks a beer bottle at me. It hits the bike and

I just can't take anymore. I scream obscenities at them, flip them off and that's that. Homeboy driving, he's got strategies. He hits the gas, runs the car twenty yards ahead to the corner and yanks it to a stop. Doors fly open.

He's positioned himself so that I have no way of getting past him. The other cars screech to a stop. More doors fly open. There's a lot of them. I hit the brakes and pivot the bike around, hoping for a flush of traffic coming downtown from the north. I'll use the traffic as a shield to lose them in. When faced with no recourse, you ride mid-lane and weave in-between oncoming cars. It's risky, but no one can chase you on a bike if you're good at it, and years cab driving and free bikes in New York have taught me that I'm good at it.

So I'm digging deep, aiming for the oncoming headlights of the next wave of downtown bound traffic, which are only a few blocks away now and closing fast, but this fucking bike's stuck in third gear, it's stiff to get up to speed from a dead stop. I'm just reaching peak velocity when I hear the footsteps.

I toss a terrified glance over my shoulder and see homeboy sprinting along beside me, laughing. I've never in my life seen a human being run so fast, so effortlessly. He reaches down and latches ahold of the back of my belt. Effortlessly he yanks me up and hurls me into the path of the oncoming traffic, which is now just a few feet away and screaming toward me at forty miles an hour. There's a moment of hushed, suspended animation, where everything goes silent and slow motion-y.

I realize I'm airborne and when I land I'll be hit by the oncoming cab. I can see the look of surprise in the driver's eyes. Somehow, as I fly, I've managed to hang onto the handlebars of the bike just enough so that when the wheels hit the pavement I have a split second to bank right just as the taxi banks the opposite way. Somehow we miss each other. He smacks into the cab next to him. Horns. The sound of breaking glass.

Now homeboy's ready for the real fun. He comes at me, hoping for a clean headshot. I've got the bike in a death grip, holding it at arm's length, which serves to keep him from moving in close enough to hit me. Of course—he's the physical incarnation of that rabid Rottweiler that pursued me down in Florida.

And the chain—this time it's around my neck. See, slung over my shoulder I've got heavy length of chain that I use to lock my bike up. It's case hard steel and a formidable weapon, but if I start swinging it, will someone in one of the cars just shoot me? Is there a code of honor here, and will using the chain break it?

Homeboy, he's wearing a striped tank top. No weapons so far as I can see. Whoosh, his swing just misses my cheek. Compact, expert, well practiced punches come rocketing toward me, but his arms are just shorter than the distance between the bike I'm holding and his swing. He can't quite reach me. At least for now.

Out of the corner of my eye I see two more thugs running toward the scene, one hand each behind their backs. The hidden hand always bears the deadly weapon—common knowledge in the streets. Watch the hidden hand. I know I'm going to have to do something dramatic real quick here or terrible, terrible shit will befall me.

While I'm distracted by the approaching men, homeboy yanks the bike down and slings it to the side. Now there's zero recourse so I grab for the chain. And just as I whip it off and rear back to swing it I hear someone shout, "FREEZE!!".

To my surprise homeboy, he freezes, just like he's been told to—just mid-swing he pulls his punch. I'm standing there with the chain in my hand, thinking, "COPS! Thank-you god, the cops are here!!" But when I look in the direction of the voice, standing on the other side of 5th Avenue I see not a cop, but a regular-Joe. And by regular, I mean way regular. He's wearing those ridiculous topsider boating shoes, a pair of khaki denims and a pastel colored Izod shirt. He's got short-cropped kinky hair and wireframe glasses and looks about as intimidating as someone's half-blind grandma. And yet it's him who shouted "FREEZE!".

Now he strides purposefully into the middle of 5th Avenue and with one bold gesture, a simple outstretched palm, brings the next wave of cars to a screeching halt. Everything's stopped at his command and he's taken complete charge of the scene. He stiff-arm points an imperious index finger at the approaching gang members and shouts, "You two men! Back in the car!"

The thugs pull up short, then give each other sheepish looks. "NOW!" he shouts, and, as if they're willing subjects under hypnosis, they turn tail and saunter back to their cars. Still holding the traffic at bay on 5th, he turns to homeboy who stands before me, jabs a finger in his direction and says, "You! In the striped shirt! Step away from him!" Homeboy gives me a look that says, white boy, your ass has been saved. He steps back.

Regular-Joe commands homeboy to return to his car NOW. He does so. The convoy of cars screeches away.

I'm in shock. And by that I mean, clinically in shock. Among other things, when homeboy chucked me in the path of the taxi, my bowels have evacuated. I'd always heard the phrase, "scared shitless". Now I know it ain't just talk, it's a literal expression.

And, I'm sorry, does that seem a little excessive? That detail? Maybe I should have left that out? I want you to understand something; this is a true story, not a nice fairy tale where the hero is heroic and you're offered some satisfying feeling about life when the reading is done. Maybe you'd like to hear that I fought off the thugs, or that I weaved some magic and we all ended up buddies, or that me and the young woman fell in love and got married. Maybe you'd like to hear that the guy who rescued me was Phillip Glass. Is that what you were hoping for? If so, then you're hungry for fiction. And this ain't fiction.

I've backed my way onto the sidewalk. I'm shaking uncontrollably, head to toe. Regular Joe frees up downtown bound traffic on 5th Avenue then strides over to me. He's the most normal looking human being I've ever laid eyes on. Why did those thugs even listen to him, much less obey his words? I'm wondering if he's some kind of cop—undercover cops sometimes drive decoy cabs—this is well known among criminals. That must be what homeboy and his posse figured.

"Are you okay?" he asks me.

"Are you a cop?" I ask him, shaking violently.

He looks at me like I'm crazy, points to the damaged taxi parked on the far side, the one that nearly hit me and says. "Just a cab driver, man."

He's a taxi driver, just like me.

He smiles, "That was a close call, my friend. Next time you're at the corner of 14th and 5th, you look where you're going, okay?"

He means it as a disarming joke, but do you see? Me holding a bike? A thug? A fight? 14th and 5th? Andras' empty storefront just a stone's throw away, in plain sight. Narrative threads have pulled tight, only this story isn't some product of my overactive imagination—it's real.

My heart's pounding, but behind the pulmonary hammering I hear a secondary beat as if huge nails are being driven into the ancient beams at the center of my soul. Some massive enigmatic structure is being erected. But what is to be made of it?

Maybe with every true beat of your heart another nail is driven homeward and when your heart pulses that last time, then construction of your true self is complete.

Maybe those who suffer in this life, those whose hearts race in desperation, like poor Andras Groff, by virtue of their suffering on this earth discover they've erected grand exotic palaces in the next, constructed by Unseen Forces impelled by the furious winds of fate, time and circumstance.

For some reason as I ride away, heading north into the traffic just in case the convoy doubles back, I start thinking about a story I read when I was a kid. It was called "An Occurrence at the Owl Creek Bridge".

My memory of it's foggy—I recall the basic premise involves a criminal who's being executed. The hangman's noose dangles from a bridge. His captors thread his head through the noose, then push him from the bridge. He falls, but the rope breaks and he escapes, plunging into the raging river. Against all odds he makes his way home but just as he reaches his wife and family he feels a sharp pain in his neck.

His daring escape, the rope breaking, everything turns out it's all just a dream that transpired in the split second as he fell toward the water before the slack rope snapped taut. In reality his neck is snapped by the hangman's noose and he dies.

Maybe the writer wanted to express some simple irony about the relationship between dream worlds and real ones. And how the real world has the final say in such relationships. But to me the point of the story is that time can be compressed, transformed by the power of the mind. Many events can happen simultaneously, or at least appear to. Herein lies the basis of that Heaven that I waited for Jesus to rapture me away to all those years in the Pentecostal church, a place where the crippling rules of this sad causal realm no longer apply. Axiomatically speaking, if a person can dream that a minute is an hour, a day, then who's to say in a second one can't dream an eternity?

I head home and fall into a restless sleep. I dream and in that dream space I find myself somewhere bitterly cold—it's so very cold. And I'm not me, I'm Andras Groff, only as a small child. I hear footsteps in the dark room where I lay. I'm lifted up and feel a strong, masculine embrace. I understand that I'm cradled in the loving arms of my long-lost father Nicolae Ceausescu. He sings to me, a haunting Romanian folk song. Now we're seated at a huge banquet table, surrounded by fat actors. We're swapping jokes with Jerry Lewis and Woody Allen, even Groucho Marx. Samuel Beckett is there, wearing the world's ugliest shirt. A copy of the New Yorker sits on the table, Andras's poem contained in the pages within. At last the Chinese newspaper makes sense.

ATLANTA, GEORGIA, SEPTEMBER 2004

It's just after dawn. I'm hunkered down in that friend's apartment checking out the first reports coming out of my home town. The news reports convey image after image of destruction that is flat-out catastrophic. As predicted, Hurricane Ivan made landfall around 2am just west of Pensacola, the eastern eye wall scoring a direct hit on my neighborhood, spawning a massive storm surge and hundreds of ancillary tornados across lower Alabama and the Panhandle of Florida. I go scrolling through an array of photographs of Ivan's devastation, coming to rest on one image featuring that massive bay bridge I nearly got blown off of as I evacuated late yesterday.

Huge slabs of the roadway are now completely fucking gone. Mid-bridge, perched on a ragged precipice sits the trailer end of an eighteen wheeler, teetering precariously over the edge, the cab conspicuously absent, the driver, apparently dead in the bay waters below. Shit.

There's no power, no potable water anywhere in the area, nor will there be for weeks to come. All roads leading in and out, save one, are under several feet of floodwater. I head to Fed Ex and send out that Hear Music song, then put my head down and aim for that one open road leading back home.

Forty miles into the ride it hits me—I'm headed somewhere where there are now zero basic necessities available, so I bank off the interstate and hit a Super Walmart just south of Atlanta. I'll stock up on necessary shit like water, batteries, cereal, gas cans, canned goods, etc.

Despite it being nearly three hundred miles north of the Gulf Coast, this cathedral of discount commerce is packed with storm refugees. Scores of RVs bearing Florida tags are scattered across the parking lot, joined by clusters of passenger cars overloaded with supplies, sleeping gear, bored, sweaty kids and more. As I'm weaving my way down the produce aisle I bump into childhood friend Randy King, who's guiding two wildly overloaded shopping carts toward the check-out zone.

I ask what he's heard. He's grim-faced. He's from Gulf Breeze, a low lying isthmus situated between Pensacola proper and the beach. It's directly across Escambia Bay from my house and apparently has borne the brunt of the storm. The surge washed over large sections of that finger of high ground, carrying away numerous houses, badly damaging most of the ones left standing.

Out on the beach that cottage where me and Dopey Don took refuge, along with everything else on that block, is just flat-out gone. The beach itself is inaccessible except by boat, that smaller bridge connecting it to Gulf Breeze also having been severely damaged. As Randy conveys the magnitude of what he's heard I flash on Jezebel the pig, how she was trapped in that shed during such a hellacious storm, and I understand my prime directive once I get home—if I can even get through to Pensacola.

Heading south on I-65 out of Montgomery the approaching landscape looks increasingly like a war zone: billboards folded over, roofs ripped off houses, massive trees snapped and uprooted everywhere. I forge on, surrounded by convoys of national guardsmen, tree surgeons and utility trucks, all, like me, making a beeline for the ground zero of my home town.

Closing in on Evergreen, Alabama the war zone vibe gives way to more of a nuclear bomb detonation site type feel. As far as the eye can see entire forests of planted pines lie snapped mid-trunk, like an endless army of giant, broken toothpicks lining the highway.

To my utter amazement, Highway 21 running through dinky little Atmore, Alabama appears to be open. It's slow going, as road crews are still clearing dozens of fallen trees all along the route, but it's moving.

As I hit the northern finges of Pensacola proper the damage is just this side of surreal. A good third of the houses have lost their roofs. As far as the eye can see willy-nilly rows of majestic two hundred year old live oaks lay on their sides, root balls standing twenty or more feet in the air. Massive mounds of debris lay scattered as far as the eye can see and well beyond.

I make my way to my house and find my psycho neighbor John patrolling his front yard in a bathrobe, a military issue Colt .45 in hand. He nods solemnly, then relays the story of the raggedy looking truck that came creeping up to my house at dawn. John stepped out his front door, approached the truck brandishing his pistol, racked the slide and sighted up the driver, whereupon the looters promptly fled. Thank you, crazy neighbor.

I check out my place. I've lost most of my south facing shingles and all my privacy fencing, but other than that the little bungalo held its ground just fine. No flood surge, no major roof leaks to flood the interior, as is the case with many of my neighbors. Hell, almost a foot of rain fell by the time Ivan had departed.

I make my way over to Crazy Maker Acres. Two houses in the cul-de-sac where her gate is located took direct hits from falling live oaks and are totalled. Her long, meandering dirt driveway is hopelessly blocked by a half-dozen or more massive fallen oaks, plus another fifteen or so lesser trees, rendering the house utterly inaccessible by car. I grab a crow bar, an insurance policy in case I cross paths with any hostile crackhead looters, and wade in.

It's a chore, but after ten minutes I'm at her front door. The roof appears intact but for a few strafing blows incurred by falling trees, massive water oaks which now lay on their sides, perfectly framing the front of Crazy Maker's place—she got lucky. The cinderblock shed likewise remains upright. I bang on the shed door and lo and behold, my old nemesis Jezebel sounds off, grunting wildly. She wants out, but that ain't gonna happen just yet.

I hustle her up a tub of water and some more Cheerios, slipping her provisions through a crack in the door, then go scrambling through my neighborhood rounding up a couple volunteers, a ladder and an oversized dog crate.

We return and, using the ladder and dog crate as a sort of improvised litter, we ferry the crated pig over the daisy chain of downed trees and out of the imminent peril of Crazy Maker Acres.

Back at my house I release her in the relatively safe confines of my side driveway, which I've blocked off with sections of privacy fence knocked down in the storm. Jezebel seems fine with being done with that blighted property, and surely won't lose any sleep about the upgrade to my place. Pigs are smart, after all.

It's a few days later now. An insurance adjuster just pulled up outside my house. He asks about the pig in the driveway but I just shrug, telling him it's long story. I comment that I did okay in the storm, losing only that privacy fencing and parts of my roof. Over the roof areas missing shingles I've gone ahead and tacked down several large blue tarps, ones I thankfully picked up at that Walmart south of Atlanta. Presently in Pensacola, if a body could actually locate a tarp for sale, it would go for a king's ransom.

The adjuster's a disaster specialist and is not local. From his accent and demeanor I'm figuring him to be midwestern. He grabs his clipboard and jumps right in with the appraisal, presently studying that tarp configuration on my roof with a somewhat skeptical expression. I ask him does he need me to get up there and pull off the tarp so he can see that the damage is real. He regards me as if vexed by some surreal conundrum, then kindly replies, "Friend, if I can't take your word for it, then what kind of world is this?"

You could knock me over with a feather.

I thank him, grateful for the blessing of this stranger's trust. He walks the property, clip board in hand, checking boxes that detail damage, authorizing full replacement for both garage and house roofs, then throwing in additional compensation for a bunch of ticky-tack crap that's fairly minor, but apparently fits his magnanimous agenda—small trees knocked over, downed fencing, lumber damaged, etc. Once finished, he shakes my hand and wishes me well, telling me a check will be mailed out in a week or so. Thank you, kind, enlightened insurance adjustor!

As he heads back to his truck I notice on the back there's a bumper sticker that says, "Have a Blessed Day" I smile, considering the immense complexities invoked by that quotidian imperative.

Yeah, blessings are always a welcome addition to this business of being, particularly during such times of acute duress. But at this point I won't make the mistake of taking anything for granted here—I've learned better.

If this life of stranger truths has taught me anything it's this indisputable truth: blessings can masquerade as curses, and curses can masquerade as blessings, so there ain't a bit of sense in getting cocky and playing the know-it-all, saying you can tell one from the other.

As I'm studying the tarp on my roof a memory springs to mind that underscores this axiomatic truth. It happened to a friend a few years back. He came home from his landscaping job one fine day to discover a brand spanking new roof on his house. He hadn't ordered one, but there it was.

The roofers were just finishing up, so he asked them what the hell they were doing. Only then did the foreman realize that he'd read the address for the job wrong. It was already a done deal, so my buddy was the recipient of a free $4,000.00 roof.

Quite the blessing, right? Well, a few days later he was out drinking with some friends, celebrating his good fortune, and stumbled into the path of a passing semi-truck. It killed him stone-dead. He was but thirty-seven years old.

At his funeral the pastor was trying make sense of the tragedy, like pastors tend to do. He read us that verse from Corinthians where it says, "For now we see through a glass darkly; but then face to face. Now I know in part, but then shall I know, even as I am known." The "then" they're talking about is death. The inference is that life won't make any real sense until we move on past it and shake hands with the dark messenger. Then we'll know.

And that notion pretty much aligns with what I've worked out so far. I mean, if you were to ask me what certainty a person can claim to know in this life, like a baseline truth, I wouldn't have a clue how to answer that question. I just wouldn't. It's only in death that the truth is finally revealed. But what good is knowing to the dead?

INCIDENTAL CONTACT LINEAR CHRONOLOGY

1980

Born-again surfer phase ends.

1981

European fashion model phase commences.

1983

Provocative incidents occur in Amsterdam, 1st Superwhite encounter.

1984

Fashion industry phase ends, industrial hand injury, relocation to New York City, desperate job search, restaurant worker phase commences, 1st refugee encounter, 2nd Superwhite encounter.

1985

Stolen car episode, 2nd refugee encounter, poignant incident with Tom Waits.

1986

Restaurant worker phase ends, taxi driver phase begins, 3rd refugee encounter.

1987

Drug lord Molock encounter, world's ugliest shirt encounter.

1988

Downward spiral of refugee.

1990

The last days of refugee.

1992

Major celebrity cab driving synchronicity.

1993

Actress encounter, professional psychic encounter, heartbreaking street combat, personal mental health spiral, suicidal ideation.

1994

Dire sickness, crippled in Florida beach house, providential visit from friend, uncanny plumber healing, strategic retreat to NYC, miraculous Superwhite meeting.

1995

Bike fight synchronicity.

1997

Debut album released, touring with Superwhite.

1998

Estranged from Crazy Maker, music box incident, Home Fries song placement, psychic antenna theory, Christmas Day context, touring with Superwhite.

2001

2nd album released, Nick Cave saga, Walter the Knoxville barber encounter.

2003

Fence building lessons.

2004

3rd album released, Hurricane Ivan catastrophe, negotiations with Crazy Maker,

2007

Edinburgh Ophelia synchronicity.

2009

Elegant Glass closure.

Jim White is a Georgia based musician, artist and author. His debut album Wrong-Eyed Jesus, is considered a minor classic in the Americana genre and was the basis for the award winning BBC documentary Searching for the Wrong-Eyed Jesus.

Championed by The New York Times, NPR, Mojo Magazine, Uncut, Breaking Bad's Vince Gilligan, and countless more, White's a noted oddball, releasing ten critically acclaimed albums over a twenty year span. His essays and short fiction have been widely published, with his short story "Superwhite" winning a Pushcart Prize in 2015.